PREY THE SNIPER

A VIET NAM WAR NOVEL

DAVID ALLIN

Text copyright © 2019 David L Allin

All Rights Reserved

PREY FOR THE SNIPER is a work of fiction. Names, characters, and incidents are either the product of the author's imagination or are used fictitiously. Any resemblance to actual persons, other than historical public figures, living or dead, is entirely coincidental.

Table of Contents

ONE 1
TWO 10
THREE 21
FOUR 34
Five 43
SIX 57
SEVEN 70
EIGHT 83
NINE 95
TEN 116
ELEVEN 127
TWELVE 140
THIRTEEN 143
FOURTEEN 158
FIFTEEN 166
SIXTEEN 178
SEVENTEEN 192
EIGHTEEN 203
NINETEEN 216
TWENTY 232
TWENTY-ONE 256
TWENTY-TWO 260

ONE

At first Captain Ward Womack didn't realize he had just been shot. His initial analysis of the blow to his chest was that the engine of the jeep he was driving had thrown a rod, and he had been struck by a piece of the engine block that had pierced the floorboards. Almost instinctively he hit the clutch and the brake to disengage the transmission and slow the vehicle down, putting it in neutral and steering the vehicle over to the side of the wide dirt road. Only then did he take a hand off the wheel and explore the front of his shirt. It felt wet, and when he held his hand up to his face, he saw it was dripping crimson. His confusion was compounded when he realized that the engine of the jeep was still running.

The jeep continued rolling, slowly, and he tried to press harder on the brake, but found he was unable to do so. He was overcome with weakness, an immense fatigue, and his boots slipped off the pedals and lay limply on the floor. A wheel dropped into the ditch that lined the road and the vehicle jerked to a stop. Womack still gripped the steering wheel with one hand, but was amazed that he couldn't actually feel it. His hand was numb. Staring blankly over the hood of the jeep, he tried to mentally reconstruct the events of the last few seconds, with only moderate success. He had been driving the jeep from Cu Chi to his post at Truong Mit, just cruising down Viet Nam's Highway One, when something had slammed into his chest, and he had heard a distant crack. Ah, that was it. The noise he had heard wasn't the engine self-destructing, but the report of a rifle shot. His satisfaction at solving the puzzle was immediately overcome by the dull throb of pain that now enveloped his torso. He saw his hand fall away from the steering wheel and flop down to his side.

Now I'm in trouble, he thought. He had been driving the jeep himself, and he was alone, things that were against policy for advisors assigned to Military Assistance Command Viet Nam—

MACV. But Staff Sergeant Randall had been on duty all the previous night, and needed to get some sleep, and besides, Womack enjoyed driving the jeep and being alone for a while. The reports needed to be delivered to headquarters in Cu Chi, and he had wanted to go to the PX there to pick up a few cartons of cigarettes. He could have returned along with one of the supply convoys, which had MP escorts, but hated to eat their dust. Now he was paying for his hubris. And worse, he wasn't wearing his helmet, which sat on the passenger seat beside him. Not that it would have saved him from the bullet that had pierced his chest, but that was another policy that he had been violating.

He reached over to pick up the helmet and put it on, but discovered his arm wasn't responding to the commands his brain was sending. His entire body was as limp as a dishrag, and his eyes were filled with sunlight as his head tilted backwards. He could feel the heat of the sun, and the slight breeze on his skin, but he had to close his eyes against the glare. He kept expecting the medics to show up and help him. He hoped they would give him some morphine, because the pain in his chest was growing more intense with every moment. *Did I radio for help?* He couldn't remember. *Am I dying?* He didn't want to think about that.

A hand touched the top of his head, the fingers combing into his hair and grasping it roughly. *At last! Help has arrived!* Tugging at his hair, the hand pulled his head forward and turned it toward the side. Womack managed to open his eyes just a slit, blinking to clear them from the spots caused by the sun. Someone was standing next to the jeep, holding his head upright. The person was dressed all in black, and the shade of the conical straw hat on the person's head left the facial features in blurry darkness. In the person's other hand was a strange rifle, unlike any he had ever seen. It had a large telescopic sight mounted on it, and the stock had a big square hole in it.

The person said something to him, but he couldn't understand it. He tried to respond, but instead of speaking, he only coughed up a mouthful of coppery-tasting liquid. The other person spoke again, in a tone of apparent satisfaction, and continued to hold his head up so the person could observe his face. Womack noted that it was getting darker, and decided he must have been out here longer than he had thought. In his final moments, however, Womack suddenly understood what was really happening. His last thought was, *Oh, shit!*

*****

Nguyen Thi Thanh brushed nervously at imaginary lint on the sleeve of her uniform. She was sitting at attention in an anteroom of the Presidential Palace in Hanoi, ignoring the curious glances of clerks and junior officers who hustled back and forth in front of her, performing their mysterious duties in this building that reeked of importance. She wished she had a mirror so she could check her hair and her collar, to ensure she was looking her sharpest and most military. She didn't know why she had been summoned here, and feared it was for some unknown infraction of the rules. Perhaps she was suspected of harboring capitalist tendencies, of not being a good communist. Seven years ago, when she was only ten years old, she had spoken to an Australian man that had been visiting her village with an anti-war group. Had that been discovered, and considered a violation of party principles? All she had done was talk to the young man to practice her English. Or maybe it was because her mother was a devout Catholic, although she tried to keep that hidden. She had attempted to interest Thanh in the tenets of the religion, but Thanh's school teachers had insisted that religion was not compatible with Communist ideals, and Thanh had internalized that belief. Did the authorities perhaps suspect Thanh of being religious?

On the other hand, Thanh remembered the praise she had received following the big parade during the Tet celebrations five weeks ago. Her platoon leader had noted how sharp her uniform was and how smartly she had marched. Maybe she was here to receive an award, although doing well in a parade would surely not warrant a trip to the Presidential Palace. And here it was already the month of March, long past that event. She shook her head, again worrying she had committed some grievous violation of regulations without knowing it.

A man came into the room, saw her, and approached. In his twenties, he wore slacks and a white short-sleeve shirt, with round glasses perched on his nose. "Co Nguyen?" he asked politely.

"Yes," Thanh responded, jumping to her feet, her hat in her hands.

"If you will follow me, please?"

Without waiting for an answer, the young man turned and briskly walked away. Thanh had to hurry to catch up with him. They passed down a wide hallway with doors that opened to busy offices, and then entered a room that was far more imposing than the others. It was paneled in wood, with red velvet curtains framing the huge windows and thick brown carpet covering the floor. The room had some heavy brocade chairs and a small table at one side, forming what appeared to be a waiting area, and a large oak desk behind which sat a stern looking older woman. On the desk were an intercom console and a single telephone, but nothing else. The young man Thanh had been following nodded at the woman, and she nodded back without smiling. The young man stepped past the desk and knocked gently on the massive door at the back of the room. Thanh didn't hear a response, but the man opened the door and then stood back, gesturing for Thanh to enter. She feared her knees would give out as she marched into the giant room, one which was even more luxurious that the outer office she had just walked through.

This room was three times as large, but it, too, had paneled walls, velvet curtains, and carpet. She wasn't used to walking on carpet, and nearly stumbled before she learned to lift her feet a fraction higher as she walked. Despite its size, the room was sparsely furnished. Facing her at the back was a long, ornately carved table, behind which sat three men. She immediately recognized them from photos she had seen in the newspaper. On her left was Pham Van Dong, the prime minister of the Democratic Republic of Viet Nam, who smiled at her. On the right was Ton Duc Thang, the President, whose face was unreadable. In the middle was Le Duan, the General Secretary of the party, reportedly the most powerful man in the country. After Chairman Ho, of course. Le

Duan was scowling. He pointed to the single straight-backed chair that faced the table. "Sit," he commanded Thanh.

She scurried forward and took a seat, grateful that she no longer had to stand on her shaking legs. She straightened her back, held her hat primly in her lap, and directed her gaze over Le Duan's head at the portrait of Ho Chi Minh that dominated the room. She had trouble breathing, for she had never been in such exalted company before, and had no idea what to expect.

"You are Nguyen Thi Thanh?" Le Duan asked curtly, clearly expecting an affirmative answer.

"Yes," Than squeaked, then cleared her throat and repeated it with more conviction, adding a "sir."

"And how old are you?" Pam Van Dong asked gently.

"Seventeen," Thanh responded.

"Your father was Colonel Nguyen Van Phuoc," Le Duan said, glaring at her as if daring her to deny it.

"Yes, sir," she said, trying to quell the trembling in her stomach.

"A hero of Dien Bien Phu," Ton Duc Thang added without emotion.

Thanh's father had died in that great battle of liberation from the French, and she was accustomed to people praising him. That was why she was in the Army, because that was what had been expected of the daughter of the great man.

"How do you like being a solider, Co Nguyen?" Prime Minister Pham asked conversationally.

"It is a great honor," Thanh replied dutifully.

"Yes, of course," Le Duan remarked dismissively. "But are you ready to give your life for your country, if it becomes necessary?"

Thanh was taken aback by this blunt question, and took a few seconds to formulate an appropriate answer. "Certainly, General Secretary," she finally stated as firmly as she could manage.

"Good," President Ton said, his eyes wandering around the room.

"And how is your mother?" Pham Van Dong asked, but was immediately interrupted by Le Duan before Thanh could answer.

"Because of your father," Le Duan said gruffly, "you have been selected to volunteer for a special mission. You will begin training for it immediately. The nature of your mission cannot be revealed to anyone, not even your mother. This mission could bring an end to this war and ensure our nation its inevitable victory. Do you understand?"

"Yes." Thanh understood that her volunteering was a foregone conclusion, and in fact she had no choice in the matter. Nonetheless, she was proud that she had been chosen, and was filled with patriotic emotion about the role she was destined to play.

"Prime Minister Pham will give you the details," Le Duan continued, tilting his head toward Pham, "and introduce you to Chairman Ho. You may wait outside."

Thanh knew she was being dismissed, and jumped to her feet, throwing the best salute she could manage. Le Duan made a vague gesture in return, and then looked down at the papers in front of him. Thanh made a sharp left face, took two steps, made another left face, and marched out of the room, gently closing the door behind her. She took a deep breath and let it out slowly. Did he say she would be meeting Uncle Ho? That would be a dream come true. She saw that the woman behind the desk was staring at her with barely concealed contempt.

"I am to wait out here," Thanh told the woman, feeling more assertive now that she knew why she had been called here to Hanoi. The woman pointed to the chairs in the corner. Thanh marched over and took a seat, letting a small satisfied smile flit across her face. A secret mission!

Ten minutes later the friendly prime minister, Pham Van Dong, had come out of the inner office and beckoned her to follow him to his private office. There, without many details, he had explained that her mission involved intensive training just outside of Hanoi, and then she would be infiltrated down what the Americans called the Ho Chi Minh trail to South Viet Nam, where she would meet up with a People's Liberation Army representative. She would take on the identity of a student, reside in her father's birthplace, Truong Mit, and await the orders to carry out the most important part of her mission. For security reasons, she was told, the actual goal of her mission would not be revealed to her until the last minute. He told her it might be several months before she was notified it was time to act. Then, with a broad smile, Mr. Pham asked her if she would like to meet Uncle Ho.

"Is that possible?" Thanh squealed with delight.

"Of course," Pham told her, and led her out into the hall and through a series of doors to the back of the building. They went outside into a beautiful garden, and down the path Thanh saw the fabled wooden stilt house hidden away behind the Presidential Palace. All school children had been told the story about how Uncle Ho disdained the trappings of power and refused to live in the sumptuous palace. Instead he had built the wooden house on stilts, much like the one in which he had grown up, to show he was still a man of the people. Thanh was suffused with pride and excitement as Pham escorted her down the path to the unpretentious building and led her up the stairs to the main floor.

Like the outside, the inside was humble and sparsely furnished. A simple platform bed was in the center of the room, and Thanh gasped when she saw her nation's famous leader on the bed, propped up by numerous pillows. His white hair was sparse beyond his receding hairline, and his wispy beard reached almost to his chest. His eyes were deep-set, but they burned brightly. He smiled at her, revealing yellow teeth with several gaps. Thanh was taken aback by how sickly the old man looked. He was emaciated, his wrinkled skin sagging around his jowls, and his complexion had taken on an odd color. She had heard he was not doing well, and she knew he was 79 years old, but she had not been prepared for the reality. She had revered the great leader all of her life, and to see him so feeble was terrifying.

"How are you, Miss Nguyen?" Ho said, and Thanh was surprised because he said it in English. She knew he spoke many languages, but still had not expected him to use the language of their enemy.

"I am well," she replied in the same language. "And how are you, sir?"

Ho chuckled. "Not so good anymore. But that is the way of life. You speak English well, my dear."

"Thank you, Chairman Ho."

"Call me Uncle Ho," the old man suggested gently. "Everyone else does."

"Yes, Uncle Ho."

Ho looked at her a moment, smiling benignly. "I knew your father," he finally said. "I can see the family resemblance. He was a great man, and I am sure you will follow in his footsteps."

"That is my desire, Uncle Ho." Thanh stepped closer, to hear him better. She barely noticed as Prime Minister Pham backed away and sat down on a bench near the door. Perhaps, she thought, Pham doesn't speak English, and cannot follow the conversation. She felt sorry for him. Thanh had found learning other languages a fascinating endeavor, one in which she excelled.

As if reading her mind, Ho said, in Russian, "I understand you speak Russian as well."

She responded in the same language. "That is correct, Uncle Ho. I also speak French and a little Chinese." She beamed with pride.

"Very good. You will need the Russian. The person who will be training you is from the Soviet Union, and his Vietnamese is very poor. As I am sure Dong has told you, you must not reveal to anyone that your trainer is from that country. For political reasons, the assistance we get from our friends up north must remain our little secret."

"I understand," Thanh assured him. "What kind of training will I be receiving?"

Ho coughed once, and then coughed again. Shaking his head back and forth, he tried to speak, only to begin coughing continuously. A nurse ran into the room and knelt by the bed, putting her hand on Ho's forehead, gently pushing him into a reclining position.

"You must go," the nurse commanded, without turning to face Thanh.

Thanh was panicked. Was she seeing the death of the great leader right in front of her? Then Ho's coughing stopped, and he began to breathe normally, albeit with a noticeable rasp. He opened his eyes and saw Thanh still standing there. He winked at her, and then lay back with his eyes closed while the nurse fussed with his bedding.

"Come," Pham said. "We must go now."

With one last affectionate look at the old man, Thanh turned and followed Pham back to the main building. She had actually met Ho Chi Minh! As far as she was concerned, this was the pinnacle of her existence, the high point of her young life. To be assigned a secret mission by Uncle Ho himself was the greatest honor she could imagine. She was determined to make him proud of her.

TWO

Clutching the canvas seat of the bouncing jeep with one hand and holding onto his straw fedora with the other, Franklin Goode couldn't decide whether to be totally terrified or simply resigned to his fate. The driver in front of him, a young Vietnamese man whose name he hadn't been told, jerked the steering wheel back and forth as he tried to avoid the bigger potholes and ruts in the dirt road down which they were driving far faster than Franklin would have preferred. In the front passenger seat Major Tran Van Do appeared totally unconcerned, gazing out at the passing countryside with bored familiarity.

Major Tran, the local Regional Forces commander, spoke a little English, but the engine and wind noise in the open jeep made conversation virtually impossible. Goode just tried to hold on and not think about the danger. Or dangers, he should say. Not only did he fear a Viet Cong ambush or an exploding mine, he had to worry about this stupid jeep crashing or flipping over just from the driver's wild abandon. And then there were the bugs and diseases. Goode wondered again whether he should have turned down the opportunity to work as a civilian contractor in Viet Nam. While the money had certainly looked good back in Tennessee, the reality of this war-torn country had convinced him it wasn't really enough. He had been in country only a week, and he was already anxious to go home. Unfortunately, however, he had signed a contract, and much of the money was sitting in his bank account back home, so he was committed for at least six months. Six *long* months. It was now April, so he would not be returning to the States until at least late September or early October. That seemed a lifetime away.

The jeep jerked to a halt to let a young girl herd three water buffalo across the road in front of them. Goode took the opportunity to take off his hat and wipe his forehead with his sleeve, while brushing some of the dust off his pants legs. He was dressed in khaki slacks, a blue long-sleeve shirt, a tan vest with lots of pockets, and desert boots. He had been assured this was the appropriate attire, but he felt like he was wearing a costume for some low-budget jungle movie. Around his waist he wore a military web belt with a canteen. He had declined the offer of a pistol; he didn't want to give any VC an excuse to shoot him. If they even needed excuses.

"How much farther?" he asked Major Tran, as the last of the water buffalo halted in the middle of the road and swung his huge head around to glare at the jeep. Tran seemed very haughty, especially for someone in the Regional Forces and Popular Forces, the militias that the Americans dismissed as the ruff-puffs.

"Not far," Tran told him without turning his head. The little girl in the typical white blouse and black silk pants ran back and began swinging a long thin stick at the animal's hindquarters and yelling at him. With a final snort the buffalo ambled after the others, and the jeep driver took off with a sudden popping of the clutch, throwing Goode back against the narrow seat. This is like Mr. Toad's wild ride, Goode thought, clamping his hat back on.

Goode gazed at the passing scenery, admitting to himself that the bucolic countryside had a certain exotic charm. Rice paddies full of water, groves of verdant trees, farm houses built of bamboo and corrugated tin, it looked peaceful and pleasant, as long as you ignored the oppressive heat, smothering humidity, and ever-present stench. Eventually they came to an area with few trees or farms, just a wide swath of tall yellow grass. The road carved through the grassland, and Goode was trying to decide whether the grass would make good fodder for animals when once again the jeep skidding to a halt, throwing up a cloud of dust that made Goode cough and cover his nose. It had rained heavily only two days before, and yet the road was already dried out and dusty. It made no sense.

Tran climbed out of the jeep, stretched laconically, and said, "Here."

Goode clambered over the side of the jeep, glad to be able to stand again, and brushed the dirt from his clothes. He looked around, and saw the water running across the road about fifty yards ahead of the jeep. Tran strolled down to the stream, and Goode hurried to catch up. The jeep driver stayed in his seat and drew a small transistor radio from his shirt pocket. As Goode and Tran looked at what Goode would call a creek, the discordant tones of Vietnamese music drifted through the still hot air.

The dirt road ran directly into the stream, and reappeared on the other side, so obviously local traffic was forced to ford the stream, which held an appreciable amount of water. During the dry season, Goode figured, this would be acceptable, but with the recent arrival of the rainy season, taking a vehicle across would be a dangerous proposition.

"So this is where you want the bridge?" he asked. Tran nodded. Tran was wearing a pressed uniform, a tailored version of the older U.S. Army fatigues, and had a boonie hat that had been starched and molded into the shape of a cowboy hat like the one worn by James Garner in the "Maverick" TV show. Tran had so far been unenthused about the idea of a bridge out here, and Goode guessed that the major had been ordered to work with Goode by his superiors or his American advisors. Goode shrugged. He was paid to build a bridge, so he would build a bridge, even if it didn't actually make much sense. He let his engineering background take over.

Goode walked down to the edge of the stream, and then stomped up and down stream, testing the soil and looking for relative elevations. The stream bed wasn't really much lower than the surrounding countryside, so he would have to make the bridge fairly long to span the creek at flood level. He took out a small notebook and began making notes. Mosquitoes and gnats began swarming around his face, and he kept swatting at them with little effect. The wailing from the jeep driver's radio ended and was replaced by rapid fire speech that sounded like a news report. Goode glanced over at Tran, who stood serenely watching the water flow by, apparently unaffected by the bugs or the heat.

Goode snapped the notebook shut and walked back to join Tran, waving his arms to deflect the flying insects. He was only a few feet away when Tran turned to look at Goode, just before his head exploded in a spray of white and red matter, his cowboy hat flying off with a piece of skull still inside it. Like a tree felled by a logger, his body slowly topped over into the grass. Goode was so shocked that he stood there transfixed, his mind slowly registering the sound of a gunshot that had occurred just a microsecond after Tran's head had disintegrated.

"Uh, uh," Goode mumbled, and then finally processed what had just happened. He dropped to the ground and covered his head with his hands, knocking his hat aside. The driver's radio was turned off, and the jeep's engine was started. Goode looked up to see the jeep being turned around in a flurry of dust and driven off at high speed. Goode was now alone with Tran's body, unarmed, lost somewhere in Viet Nam, a perfect target for the sniper who had just killed the major. He was terrified. He lay there in the grass and whimpered.

When the MACV soldiers found him, Goode was virtually catatonic, his pants wet and the dust on his cheeks muddy with tears. He was taken to the Cu Chi hospital, and a week later flown back to the States. The company he worked for allowed him to keep the initial payment he had received, and allowed him to keep his company-paid health insurance for one year, but terminated his employment. He later became a school bus driver in a suburb of Nashville.

*****

The old truck hit a bigger bump than usual, and Thanh bounced six inches off the crate she had been sitting on, crashing back down with a force that jarred her teeth. It was pitch black in the back of the canvas-covered cargo area of the truck, and all she could see out the open back was the occasional flicker of the black-out lights mounted on the truck following hers. She wondered if they had yet reached Cambodia. Although it had only been a week, it felt like she had been traveling for a month in this supply convoy destined for the area around Saigon. Of course, the trucks wouldn't go that far. At some point in Cambodia all the cargo and soldiers would be unloaded and they could continue their journey on foot.

"Are you all right, young one?" Bao asked, putting a hand on her upper thigh. Thanh quickly shifted her position to move her leg out from under his grip. Ostensibly Bao was her personal escort and guard, to protect and assist her on her journey to the south, but he was becoming more and more possessive. He kept putting his hands on her and making thinly veiled suggestions about their sleeping arrangements, despite Thanh's polite but firm rejection. So far Lieutenant Dang, Bao's superior, had managed to keep Bao from being too assertive, but Dang would be going back with the trucks when Thanh and Bao continued on foot.

The convoy always traveled at night, to avoid the American aircraft that patrolled the skies during the day. Two days ago the convoy had passed the wreckage of a convoy that had been caught out in the open during the day, and Thanh had been appalled at the carnage. She had heard that the Americans sometimes even flew at night, using night-vision devices of some sort to seek out the convoys and destroy them. Whenever she thought she detected the sound of distant jet engines over the rumbling of the truck, she felt a twinge of fear shoot through her body. During the day wasn't much better. Even though the convoy halted and camouflaged itself, she knew the Americans had radar and other electronic aides that could find them, and it was almost impossible to sleep when there was a constant drone of aircraft overhead. She was terrified one of those planes would detect their hidden encampment and envelop them in the flaming napalm the Americans used so effectively. The thought of being burned alive was even worse than being blown up by a bomb.

The truck lurched to a stop, and Thanh heard men shouting orders. Lieutenant Dang appeared at the back and said, "We have reached the drop-off point, Miss Nguyen. Please gather your things. There are soldiers waiting to guide you to your next destination."

"This is it," Bao said happily. "Now we will be on our own."

"There will be other soldiers with us," she reminded Bao tartly as she redid the straps on the canvas pack containing the smaller metal case.

"Yes," Bao admitted, "But not Lieutenant Dang." Bao grabbed one strap of the larger pack and jerked it upright.

Thanh lowered her pack over the tailgate and set it gently on the ground, leaning forward and bending down to do so. Bao took advantage of her position and brushed his hand over her posterior, pretending it was inadvertent as he reached to help her. She set the heavy load down on the ground and then reached back to swat Bao's hand away. "I have it!" she told him angrily. "You carry yours, and I will carry mine." She scrambled over the tailgate and dropped to the ground beside her pack. Bao lowered his own pack roughly and jumped out beside her.

"Careful!" she admonished him. Bao's case contained the two rocket launchers, while Thanh's case had the two batteries and a grip stock and trigger assembly that would be attached to the launch tubes when it was time to use them. Thanh's case also held something else, hidden under the foam padding. Bao's pack was over a meter and a half long, and when he shouldered it, the top of it rose far above his head. Bao was very tall and strong for a Vietnamese man, which was why he had been chosen to help her, but even he was dwarfed by the giant pack. She wished she had been able to carry everything herself, but the weight and bulk would have been too much for her young girl's body. Bao had been assigned to accompany her until she reached Truong Mit, carrying part of her load and, apparently, planning on taking advantage of their forced togetherness. The Russians had provided sturdy but lightweight aluminum cases for the launchers and the other parts, and special canvas packs had been sewn to conceal those cases and make them easier to carry. Nonetheless, these were big heavy cases, and Thanh was not looking forward to the long march ahead to transport them deep into enemy territory.

"Why must I be careful, young one?" Bao asked, picking up his pack and slinging it over his shoulders. In the interest of security, he had not been told the contents of these packs, only that they were very valuable and important.

"Because I said so," Thanh shot back. "Pretend they have atomic bombs in them, and you will be all right."

Bao scoffed. "Atomic bombs. Ha. More likely they have Russian vodka for our little friends in the PLA." The PLA was the People's Liberation Army, referred to by the Americans as the Viet Cong, and the North Vietnamese soldiers generally regarded them with disdain.

His remark gave Thanh a start. How did he make a connection to the Russians? He must have at least opened the canvas pack and looked at the metal cases, and perhaps saw some Russian writing on them. He had been told not to open the pack, but she was not surprised that he could not be trusted. At least he could not open the cases themselves, because they were padlocked shut and only Thanh had the key, which she kept on a string around her neck. More importantly, Thanh's case had always been in her personal possession, so she was sure he hadn't touched it. She suspected that if he knew everything that was in her case, he would be even more difficult.

A soldier she did not know appeared out of the darkness and asked if they were ready. When she assured him they were, he led them past the line of trucks and onto a narrow trail through the forest. The straps of the heavy pack cut into her shoulders, but Thanh strode behind the soldier with determination. She was on a secret mission for Uncle Ho, and nothing would deter her.

She just hoped she would be up to the task. The training in and around Hanoi had been rigorous. Her Russian instructor had been condescending at first, obviously unhappy at being required to work with a young girl. He had been surprised at her fluent command of the complex Russian language, however, and pleased by her dedication to acquiring the necessary skills. This weapon, he had explained, was the latest advance in Soviet military science, and they called it the Strela, which she knew was the Russian word for "arrow." It was their first shoulder-launched anti-aircraft guided missile, and they were providing some of the early production versions to the Hanoi government both to help the North Vietnamese fight back against the daily air raids and to test the system under real-world conditions.

Thanh had listened to long boring hours of instruction on the theory and science of the weapon, wishing they would quickly get to the important part—how to use the weapon. When the instructor finally moved on to the actual assembly and firing, she paid close attention, repeating the process numerous times until she felt she could do it in her sleep. Of course, during her training she couldn't actually fire the weapon, but each time she pulled the trigger on the dummy rocket, she imagined the burst of flame and smoke as the rocket arced up into the sky and destroyed one of the hated American jets.

Finally, when the Russian admitted she was as skilled as any Soviet soldier in the care, maintenance, and operation of the system, she was handed a live rocket and driven to an area just southwest of Hanoi to await an actual air raid. She was there two days before they told her that American Navy jets were inbound to bomb Hanoi, and her heart fluttered with anticipation. Carefully she attached the blocky grip stock and trigger assembly to the launch tube, plugged in the big cylindrical battery to the front of the grip stock, and removed the covers off each end of the tube. The launcher tube came pre-loaded with a missile, but could be reused after being reloaded at a depot. She stood there with the heavy launcher on her shoulder, staring up at the sky, hoping one of the jets would fly right overhead where she could knock it down.

As she waited, her instructor standing nearby, she went over the procedures again in her mind. The Arrow had two modes—manual and automatic. For manual mode, she would pull the trigger halfway back while following the target through the flip-up iron sight and wait for a signal. If the rocket's infra-red seeker detected the target, she would get a buzz and a red light, meaning it had locked on. She would then immediately move the sight to slightly above and in front of the target, leading it, and pull the trigger the rest of the way, at which point the rocket would launch and streak after the target. In automatic mode, used when the target was moving too quickly to allow the slower manual mode, she would simply pull the trigger all the way back, while leading the target, and if the seeker could lock on, the rocket would launch on its own. Because today's targets were jets, she had been instructed to use automatic mode.

She and her instructor stood in the middle of a dry rice paddy with good line of sight in all directions. A couple hundred meters away some Army officers stood next to a staff car in the shade of a small tree to observe her performance. She hadn't recognized any of them, but suspected they had been sent by Le Duan. Thanh proudly wore her dark green uniform with the red tabs on the collars, and her pith helmet, hoping she looked as military as she felt. The sun beat down on her shoulders, and the weight of the launcher was starting to make her right shoulder ache. Then she heard the distant roar.

"Here they come," her instructor told her unnecessarily.

As the roar swelled in intensity, her eyes scanned the sky for the first appearance of the fast-approaching jets, which were coming in at a low altitude. There! She saw them, zooming through the sky, on a line of attack that would pass over to Thanh's left. Swinging her body around, she moved the ring of the launcher's sight until it circled one of the jets, which she now recognized as an American Navy A-4 Skyhawk, a stubby delta-wing fighter-bomber painted gray with colorful markings. It was all happening so quickly. She pulled the trigger all the way back and led the jet slightly, maneuvering the launcher in a gentle arc to keep it on target.

A buzz and a red light! The seeker had locked on, and less than a second later the rocket fired, zooming out of the launcher at high speed and leaving a trail of smoke as it flew toward the aircraft that was already receding into the distance. Thanh watched, fascinated, as the rocket corkscrewed through the air, gaining on the target and zeroing in on the jet's hot exhaust. With a final turn the rocket hit the back of the jet and exploded, and Thanh was filled with joy at her success. She had done it! She had shot down an enemy plane!

Her exuberance faded quickly when she saw the jet continue flying, leaving only a thin trail of smoke behind it. Then it dropped its bombs on empty fields and left the formation, circling back to the right, out of range of a second rocket, if she had had one. With dissatisfaction she watched the jet head back to the aircraft carrier sailing somewhere off the coast, slightly damaged, perhaps, but not destroyed.

The Russian instructor put his hand on her left shoulder as he lifted the launcher away from her right. "Excellent work, Miss Nguyen," he praised her sincerely. "A hit on your first try. You should be proud."

"But I didn't destroy him," she replied disconsolately.

"No," he agreed, inspecting the empty launcher. "But the American jets are hard to shoot down with such a small warhead. It works much better with propeller-driven airplanes and helicopters, and I have been told that such an aircraft will be your objective on your mission."

That was more than she had been told. Thanh watched the Russian disassemble the battery and grip stock from the launcher and pack them away in the metal case. The launcher tube, she knew, would be returned to an armory where a new rocket would be installed. She had mixed emotions. She was proud that she had successfully fired the weapon and had hit her target, but disappointed in the results. She took some small satisfaction that she had at least forced the American to abort his mission, this time.

It was only two days later that she had left on this journey to the south. Her mother had cried when she left, crossing herself and handing Thanh a small package as she begged her to be safe. Only later had Thanh opened the package, finding in it a small gold cross on a chain. She shook her head and wrapped it back up, stuffing it deep in the pack below the metal case. A good communist did not believe in good luck charms such as this.

She was still thinking about that tearful goodbye when the soldier she was following slowed down and stepped to one side. "Here is where you will rest," he said, sweeping his arm to indicate a small clearing in the forest. She was surprised that she could now see it, for the sky above the trees was lightening with the approach of dawn.

As she wearily pulled the pack off her back and lowered it to the ground, the soldier said, "You two will remain here. Some of our little brothers will meet you here this evening to continue your journey. I must return to my unit. Be safe, comrades." With that the soldier took off, back up the path they had been following. Now she was alone with Bao, somewhere deep in the forest, until the "little brothers" of the PLA came to fetch them. She knew this was going to be a long, difficult day. Bao was already leering at her.

When the two PLA soldiers found her just after sunset, Thanh was ready to go. Oddly, they did not question why she was there alone, with two heavy backpacks that were clearly more than she could carry by herself. And since they didn't ask, she didn't see any need to tell them. One of the men pulled the larger pack onto his back, and together they set out for the next stage of the journey.

THREE

"Wake up, little girl." The voice was coarse and not very friendly. Thanh's eyelids fluttered as she blinked at the morning light streaming in through the open door. She did not want to wake up, for she had been having a wonderful dream about feeding the chickens at her mother's house. She squeezed her eyes shut and try to recapture the good feeling of the dream, but it was hopeless. Finally she opened her eyes and sat up on the hard wooden bed, seeing the interior of the small house in the daylight for the first time. It was sparsely furnished, with just two beds, a table, two bamboo chairs, and a small stamped metal wardrobe. Along one wall was a long shelf used as a kitchen counter, with some dishes and a big metal bowl that served as a sink. Next to it was a small cast-iron oven and a hibachi stove with a tea kettle on it. In a corner was a two-wheeled cart with a large box mounted between the bicycle wheels, now tilted and supported by the thin bamboo poles that allowed someone to push or pull it. In the opposite corner was a bicycle with a large wooden box mounted over the front wheels. The woman she had met last night slid a metal sheet with thin cylinders of dough into the oven and turned to look at Thanh.

"Do you wish to bathe?" the woman asked. Thanh struggled to remember her name. Nhu. Le Duc Nhu. She was older than Thanh, in her thirties at least, with a stocky body and masculine features, her hair done up in a bun. All Thanh knew about her was that she was People's Liberation Army, and she was her designated contact here in Truong Mit. A series of guerillas had assisted her reaching the village, handing her off to Nhu last night in a small grove of trees not far away. When they had reached Nhu's hut, Nhu had lifted up a trap door in the floor so they could hide Thanh's metal cases in the hole beneath, a hole that already contained a large rifle and boxes of ammunition. Thanh looked over at that section of the dirt floor, and could not detect the movable panel at all. The trap door had been constructed sturdily of wood, with a layer of hard-packed dirt on top of it. When it was lowered into place, a few flicks of a broom made the panel disappear, and it would be unnoticeable even if someone were to walk on it. Thanh admired the cleverness and quality of the hiding place.

"Yes," Thanh replied to Nhu's question. "Is there a shower or bath nearby?"

"I will fetch a bucket of water from the well," Nhu told her. "You can bathe in here." The older woman picked up a bucket and went out the door, leaving it partially open. Thanh could see that the house was on the edge of the village, with some chickens pecking in the dirt and a small pen with a pig at a neighbor's house. She felt a little lost. Her orders had only included the trip down from Hanoi and her initial contact with Nhu. She had been told that further orders would come to her through Nhu, and she should do whatever Nhu told her. So far, however, Nhu had told her nothing of her mission here in South Viet Nam. She was already a little homesick, and fretted because she had just missed the big May Day parade in Hanoi. She had hoped to march in that parade and participate in the other festivities, but instead had been on the long trek to this small village north of Cu Chi.

Nhu returned, carrying the full bucket in one hand like it weighed very little, and set it down next to a thick rattan mat on the floor. Next she went to the wardrobe and retrieved a bar of soap, a wash rag, and a dark green towel. Laying them on the table, Nhu took a seat and waited for Thanh to begin, watching her with a bland face. "I have new clothes for you after you bathe," Nhu said, nodding at the wardrobe. Feeling embarrassed, Thanh removed her uniform shirt and pants and stepped onto the mat, leaving her canvas boots nearby. She kept her bra and panties on. She couldn't help but notice the way Nhu watched her, the older woman's gaze traveling up and down her slender young body with a curiosity that didn't seem quite normal. Thanh hoped that the woman was merely judging her strength for the new mission. Nonetheless, she repositioned the bucket so she could turn her back to Nhu, and dipped the rag into the water. After washing her arms and face, Thanh unhooked her bra but kept a strap around one forearm as she hastily washed her breasts, and then immediately pulled the bra back on and hooked it. Next she lowered her panties to mid-thigh and used the soapy wet rag to wash herself down there, wincing a little because she was still sore.

"You have bruises," Nhu remarked.

"Yes," Thanh replied, not looking back. "There were problems on the way here." Images of Bao's empty eyes flashed through her mind, and she hoped Nhu would not pursue the issue. She felt both shame and remorse for what had happened back in those woods, but Bao had learned the hard way that she was not a girl to be trifled with. She quickly pulled her panties up and began washing her legs and feet. When she was done she turned around and picked up the towel to dry herself. Nhu, with one last look at Thanh, got up and retrieved some folded clothes from the wardrobe. Nhu shook them out and handed Thanh the black silk pants first, watching closely as Thanh stepped into them and pulled them tight at her waist. Next as a light blue blouse that hung over her pants. It was very nice, and Thanh was grateful to again be fully dressed. A pair of rubber flip-flops completed the ensemble.

"My turn," Nhu said abruptly, and went over to the mat as she pulled off her own blouse. Thanh looked away, but not before she saw that Nhu wore no bra, although she needed one. Her breasts were large and flaccid, hanging down almost to her stomach. But what caught Thanh's attention were the scars that covered Nhu's back. Her skin was mottled pink and white, puckered and stretched in every direction. Thanh glanced back at Nhu, who was now completely nude, and saw that the scars reached from her neck down across her buttocks and the back of her thighs, ending just above her knees.

Nhu saw Thanh's shocked expression, and turned to face her, causing Thanh to look down at the table top rather than gaze at the naked woman in front of her. "Napalm," Nhu explained in an angry voice. "The Americans, three years ago. I was taken to Hanoi for treatment, where our wonderful doctors saved my life. Now I am here again, to get my revenge."

"I am very sorry," Thanh squeaked. What else could she say?

"Today you will begin your new career," Nhu said sarcastically as she washed herself. "You will be what the Americans call a 'Coke kid.' You will ride that bicycle, and the box will be filled with sodas and ice. I will take the cart, which will have trinkets and sandwich ingredients. We will find some American soldiers and sell things to them. You will talk to them and find out things about their operations. That will help us decide where to strike next."

"Strike?" Thanh asked, a little confused. She had thought she would be a student here, and she had been led to believe that the missiles she had brought were for a specific, pre-determined target.

"I have a rifle," Nhu told her, unselfconsciously drying herself off with the towel between her legs. "You will assist me until we are told the target for whatever is in your metal boxes. The Americans will never suspect that a pretty girl like you and a 'sandwich mama-san' like me are the ones killing their leaders."

Nhu got dressed again, for which Thanh was glad. Nhu took the bucket outside and heaved the water out onto the ground, and then returned and stood before Thanh. "Later you will show me what is in those boxes. Now, however, we must get to work." Nhu checked the oven, and with a rag as a hot pad she pulled the tray out with the baked loaves of bread. "Next we go to the ice house," she announced.

Riding a bicycle with such a heavy load on the front of it turned out to be far more difficult than Thanh had imagined. She wobbled all over the road, and frequently had to put her feet down and stop to prevent the bike from tipping over and spilling the ice and cans of soda from the wooden box. Nhu, behind her, had no trouble keeping up with her, despite the fact that Nhu was walking while she pushed the cart with the sandwich supplies and souvenirs. At the ice house they had joined a couple young boys who also had cold sodas to sell, and the small group was proceeding slowly down the road, only about six hundred meters behind the American mechanized infantry platoon that was providing security for the engineers with their mine detectors. Nhu had explained that the men on the big lumbering armored personnel carriers would eventually pull off the road and set up a temporary camp beside it, at which time they could sell the men cold sodas and sandwiches.

Up ahead the American soldiers had stopped while the men with the mine detectors investigated something suspicious. Nhu came up beside Thanh to watch. "Maybe they found a mine," Nhu remarked. She smiled. "And maybe it will blow up and kill some Americans."

Thanh gave a little shudder. She did not want to see anyone blown up. Yes, she hated the Americans for what they were doing to her homeland, and wanted to shoot down one of their aircraft, but she didn't want to see someone die close up.

"Would we still be able to sell them food and sodas if that happened?" Thanh asked innocently, already knowing the answer.

Nhu scoffed. "Of course not. Are you stupid?"

Thanh had decided to let Nhu think she was an empty-headed young girl. She wasn't sure why she had taken that course, but had a feeling it would help them get along. For now.

Apparently nothing was found by the American engineers, and soon the patrol was moving again. An hour later the engineers packed up their equipment and got on a truck that had blown by Thanh and the others, showering them with dust. The infantrymen arranged their four boxy vehicles in a diamond formation, each one facing out, and settled in for the day.

"Try to get as close to them as you can," Nhu advised as they approached. "They are not supposed to allow us near, but sometimes they do."

This group was not as lax as others, apparently, for when the Vietnamese came within fifty meters, a short sandy-haired sergeant shooed them away, waving them to the opposite side of the road.

"Don't worry," Nhu said, "they will come over to buy things eventually. You must talk to them and flirt with them. You are very pretty, and they will like that you can speak English. Don't ask a lot of questions. They will tell you interesting things just to impress you."

Thanh nodded. She was tense and nervous, for she had never before actually met an American face to face. She had been taught for years that they were the enemy, that they were evil beings determined to kill all Vietnamese who disagreed with them. How could she pretend to be nice to such wicked creatures? She forced a smile as she looked across the road at the men who jumped down from their vehicles and removed some of their helmets and gear. She noted that on each APC one man remained behind the machine gun on top, and the sergeant directed others to set up guard posts away from the formation. The remainder of the men got comfortable, some taking off their shirts and laying their rifles down on top of the boxes strapped to the top of the vehicles.

As Nhu had predicted, eventually one of the young men strolled across the road and approached the group. He was a black man, although his skin color was only slightly darker than a typical Vietnamese. He still carried his rifle, and still had on his shirt, but he had left his helmet and pistol belt behind. His uniform was fairly new, and relatively clean. Thanh studied the name tape sewn to his shirt, sounding it out in her mind. Rancy. A strange name. Thanh took a deep breath and smiled. "Hello, Mr. Rancy. You want a Coke?"

The young man looked at her curiously, perhaps surprised that she spoke English, or, hopefully, he was taken by her appearance. He nodded at her and held out one of the American Military Payment Certificates, which the Americans used instead of American dollars or South Vietnamese Dong. Nhu had told her about this play money, and assured her it could be traded on the black market. "D'you have root beer?" the young man asked. "Root beer," he repeated slowly, in case she hadn't understood him.

Thanh took the small bill and checked it to see what denomination it was. It was one dollar, and the price for sodas was only fifty cents. "I have no change yet," she apologized, smiling warmly at the boy.

Rancy shrugged. "Okay. Give me a Pepsi, too." Thanh pawed around in the crushed ice until she found the requested sodas and handed them to him. "Thanks," he said, and immediately turned and headed back to the other Americans.

"You did not flirt with him enough," Nhu scolded.

"I am just learning," Thanh replied meekly.

"You must do better. Here comes another one." Nhu waved at the young man, and shouted in English, "Sandwich! You buy sandwich! One dollah." Thanh suspected that was about all the English Nhu knew. Hatless and shirtless, the young man was thin, with almost no hair on his chest, but he had thick blond hair cut short on his head. Around his neck was a small wooden cross on a leather thong. He gave Nhu a bill, but his eyes kept straying to Thanh. Nhu opened the lid to her tray and took out a short section of the bread she had baked that morning, slicing it long ways. Quickly she put together the sandwich, adding sliced Spam, sliced American cheese, onions, and tomato. "*Nuoc mam*?" she asked, holding up the small brown bottle. The boy nodded, and Nhu sprinkled some of the fermented fish sauce on the sandwich and closed it up.

When she handed it to him, he quickly turned to face Thanh and asked, "You have Coke?" He was smiling back at her, and holding out another MPC bill. Thanh could see that it was a fifty-cent bill.

"Yes, sir," Thanh replied brightly, taking the bill and digging around in the ice until she pulled the dripping red can out and handed it to him.

"I'm not an officer," the boy said. "You don't have to call me 'sir'."

"What do I call you then?" Thanh asked.

"Robert," he answered. "You speak English pretty well."

"Thank you, Robert," Thanh replied, trying to catch his eyes, which were wandering up and down her body. "My name is Thanh."

"Thanh," he repeated experimentally. "That is a nice name."

"Where are you from?" Thanh asked. Out of Robert's line of sight, Thanh saw Nhu grinning and nodding encouragingly.

"California. Have you heard of California?"

"Sure," Thanh said. "Beach Boys. Surfing."

"You got it!" Robert said, his mouth wide with pleasure. He still held the unopened Coke in one hand and the sandwich in the other, his gaze never leaving Thanh.

"Do you surf?" she asked.

Robert looked down at the ground. "Naw," he said, "I live in Lodi, miles from the ocean. But I'd like to."

"Me, too," Thanh told him. "Do you have an automobile?"

"Yeah," Robert said, his face lighting up. "A Corvair."

"A Corvette? That is a very nice automobile. A Stingray?"

Robert looked a little crestfallen. "Not a Corvette. A Corvair. It's a compact car."

Thanh shrugged. "I do not know this automobile." She tried to think of something else to say, to keep the conversation going, but before she could there was a shout from across the road.

"Crosby!" It was the bandy rooster sergeant. "Get your ass back over here! Let someone else have a turn."

"Okay, Sarge," Robert called back. He nodded at Thanh before turning to jog back to his platoon. But as he went, he kept glancing back at Thanh, and it made her feel good inside. And that made her feel a little guilty, because he was the enemy.

Before she could really analyze her feelings, however, a small Honda motorcycle halted just in front of them. The driver was a young Vietnamese man wearing a black cowboy hat, mirrored sunglasses, a flamboyant red silk shirt, tight black slacks, and pointy-toed boots. Behind him sat a young girl with too much makeup and a purple blouse over white silk pants. Even though this was her first full day in South Vietnamese society, Thanh quickly recognized that this was a pimp and his prostitute. She immediately disliked the young man, and felt a mixture of disdain and compassion for the girl, whose facial expression was one of resignation. Thanh wondered why the young man wasn't in the military.

The pimp looked across the road at the American soldiers for a moment, and then shook his head. "No money here," he remarked. "There's another group about two kilometers farther down. I think I'll try there." He revved up the tiny motor and buzzed away. The two Coke boys who had been with them since the ice house had a quick discussion between themselves, and then they, too, rode away after the motorbike, leaving Thanh and Nhu alone.

"Here comes another one," Nhu said, tilting her head toward the other side of the road. Thanh saw a heavy-set soldier hand his rifle to another and trudge across the road toward them. He had no shirt on, so she could see his well-defined muscles; she also thought his skin looked a little darker than most of the men, but not as dark as the Negroes. The man bought a sandwich—with no *nuoc mam*—and a grape soda, but said little and quickly rejoined the others. Thanh could see that it might be a long boring day here, although she was already learning a lot. She looked across the road and saw Robert sitting on top of one of the armored personnel carriers eating his sandwich. He was looking right back at her. She smiled.

Three hours later the Americans all mounted their mechanical beasts and roared away. Robert wiggled his fingers at her as they left, which pleased Thanh more than she expected.

*****

"Merrill, Pratt, you just volunteered. Set up an LP in the woods over there." Staff Sergeant Aaron Samples stood up on the APC and pointed to a small clump of trees about fifty meters from the road. The two men nodded their reluctant acquiescence and jumped down from their respective tracks. The platoon had just finished yet another road sweep with the engineers, and had set up an outpost position beside the road to wait for the daily supply convoy to come through.

"I gotta get some C's first," Merrill announced, going to the rear of his track to open the personnel door in the ramp.

"Get me some peaches if we have any," Pratt called to him. While Merrill climbed in to root around in the open case of C-rations, Pratt pulled his canteen out of its holster and took a drink.

"Come on, guys, move it," Samples urged. Meanwhile many of the men were now climbing down from the tracks, taking off their dusty shirts and replacing their helmets with their boonie hats. Samples remained on his seat, an ammo can strapped to the top of the one-one track, and took out the small spiral notebook and ballpoint pen he kept in his breast pocket. Pratt and Merrill ambled off to the wood line and disappeared inside the grove, while the four track drivers climbed out of their cramped compartments and stretched. A couple guys started reading paperback novels, and Doc Allman on the one-three was reading an old copy of *The Stars and Stripes* newspaper. One man was left in each of the four machine gun turrets, the .50-caliber barrels aimed at the four points of the compass. The sun beat down like a low-grade flamethrower, but Samples was used to it.

Art Jamison, the one-one's squad leader, had jumped down and gone over to talk to Rich Reedy, the one-two's squad leader, so Samples put his feet on the open driver's hatch cover where Jamison normally sat and used his knees as a table. With painstaking care and neat penmanship Samples began listing the men of the platoon with their full names and ranks, which squad they belonged to, and what weapons they were assigned. Captain Raymond, the company commander, had warned Samples last night that he would soon be assigned a new lieutenant as platoon leader. For the last couple months Samples had been the acting platoon leader, and had enjoyed the absence of any officer oversight. The battalion had been short of officers, and as the most experienced of the NCO's, it had been decided that he could manage without one for a while. That, however, was coming to an end. And Samples wasn't very happy about it.

Due to a bad experience back in the States, Samples had developed a deep and strong antipathy toward lieutenants, and was certain that the new one would be a problem. As a good NCO, however, he did his duty and knew his place, much as it grated on him. Therefore he was preparing this information to give the new lieutenant, to bring him up to speed on the status of the platoon. *I just hope he can read,* Samples thought sourly. His last lieutenant had been a doofus from Florida who had managed to get a college degree without learning anything useful. After the guy had led the platoon into a swamp and gotten all four tracks stuck in the mud overnight, he had been transferred to Headquarters Company to be the mess officer, a job with no real responsibility.

"Can I go get a Coke, Sarge?" One of the new guys, Crosby, was looking up at him hopefully.

Samples looked around, and saw that a small group of Coke kids and a sandwich mama-san had already arrived and gathered across the road in the shade of a single tree at the edge of a rice paddy. The sergeant scanned the road and the sky for the approach of any vehicles or helicopters, and seeing nothing, nodded. "Go ahead. But make it quick."

"Thanks, Sarge," Crosby said with a broad smile, and scurried off. Samples watched him as he ran across the road and stopped in front of a Coke girl in a light blue top. She was a cute girl, and Samples recognized her from earlier encounters. She had recently become one of the regulars, and he noted that Crosby was becoming very friendly with her. The young PFC had been very shy since he joined the platoon, and Samples felt almost fatherly about him, wanting him to come out of his shell and act more mature. Maybe this girl would help with that.

"Hey, Crosby," he yelled. Crosby turned and looked at him. "Get me a gook sandwich. I'll pay you back."

Crosby, who had been looking worried at being yelled at by the sergeant, broke into a grin and nodded. Turning to the mama-san, he gave her the order. *"Nuoc mam?"* he hollered back at Samples.

"Shit, no!" Samples told him, shuddering. The sauce smelled like long-dead fish, and he didn't want anything to do with it. He hadn't tasted it, because he couldn't get past the smell, and didn't want to try. He went back to filling in his notebook.

"Here you go," Crosby said, standing beside the track and lifting the sandwich up to Samples. He had his M-79 grenade launcher in the other.

"Hold on, I'll come down," Samples told him, and put the notebook in his pocket before jumping down beside the young man. Samples pulled out his wallet and extracted some MPC.

"That's okay, my treat," Crosby offered, but Samples stuffed the bills in Crosby's shirt pocket. He couldn't let the men think they could buy him off, even if that wasn't what they were thinking.

He took the sandwich, and Crosby reached into his bulging pants cargo pocket and pulled out a dripping can of Coke. "I got you a Coke, too."

"Thanks. Hey, sit down a minute." Crosby pulled another Coke out of his other cargo pocket and joined Samples as they sat down on the ground by the road wheels, where there was just enough shade for their upper bodies, but their legs were in the bright sunlight. Samples took a bite of the sandwich, appreciating the taste of fresh bread and vegetables, something they didn't get otherwise. C-rations and warm soupy meals from Mermite cans got old really fast.

Crosby opened both their Cokes with a church key, took a sip, and looked at Samples expectantly.

"What's that girl's name?" Samples asked him, taking a drink himself.

"Thanh," Crosby answered immediately. "She speaks English. And French." The boy's face lit up and he glanced back across the road to look at her.

"English and French. Hmm. You kind of like her, huh?"

"Well, yeah," Crosby admitted. "She's a nice girl. Cute, too."

"Not a boom-boom girl?"

Crosby looked offended. "No, Sarge, she's not. She's a nice girl. Went to Catholic school. She's not like that."

"Okay, okay, just asking." Samples took another bite of sandwich. "You're not thinking of marrying her or anything, are you?"

"Me?" Crosby squeaked. "Uh, uh, no." But Samples could tell from Crosby's expression that the thought had indeed crossed his mind.

"Trust me, don't. I knew a guy that wanted to marry a Vietnamese girl. It was a ton of paperwork, and he had to stay in Nam an extra three months to get it processed. I think they do that on purpose, to discourage guys from marrying one. And you can't really get to know her like this, meeting while we outpost. For all you know, she might be a Viet Cong spy or something."

"I don't think so," Crosby insisted, shaking his head. "And I think she likes me, too."

"Well, take it easy, anyway. You've still got a long time to go here. Another, uh, eleven months, right?"

"Don't remind me," Crosby said glumly. "Three hundred and twenty-seven days. Not that I'm counting or anything."

Samples chuckled. "Right. After you finish that Coke, why don't you go and relieve Pratt or Merrill so they can get something."

"Sure, Sarge," Crosby said, and drained his Coke. He grabbed his weapon and stood up, looking for someplace to put his empty can.

"I'll take it," Samples told him, reaching out for it. There was a trash bag inside the track.

"Thanks." Crosby jogged off toward the trees. Samples looked across the road at the Coke kids, and saw the girl Thanh watching Crosby's back as he moved away. Her expression was hard to read at this distance, but to Samples it looked distinctly affectionate. He shook his head and finished the sandwich.

FOUR

Sergeant Ignacio "Nash" Jaramillo shivered as the cool night breeze caressed his wet uniform. The rank odor of water buffalo shit—and probably human shit—filled his nostrils, but he had gotten used to that in the months since he arrived in country. What he worried most about was the possible presence of small insects or dangerous microbes swimming in the flooded rice paddy that might somehow get inside his pants and invade his body. He was lying prone in the muddy water, his sniper rifle and forearms propped on the paddy dike to keep them dry, while he observed the raised roadway fifty meters away, stretching left and right into the night. On his left was Nguyen Van Quan, his ex-Viet Cong team mate, alert and apparently indifferent to the discomfort. On his right lay Harv Albertson, his spotter, who had rolled onto his back, his head cradled in his helmet to keep it out of the water, snoring quietly.

Nash reached over and shook Harv's shoulder. "Harv!" he hissed. "You're snoring again."

Harv snorted as he woke up. "Sorry," he whispered. "Can't help it."

"Sleep on stomach," Quan suggested innocently.

"With my face in the water?"

"You no snore then," Quan pointed out reasonably.

"Shh!" Nash hushed them. "I think there's movement."

Jaramillo and his sniper team had been lying in the rice paddy since an hour after sunset, waiting for the Viet Cong. They had studied the pattern of land mines planted in the main road to Tay

Ninh over the last few months, and they had concluded that this stretch of the wide dirt road was the most likely place for the next ones. As a former Viet Cong himself, Quan knew how guerillas planned such attacks, and Nash had studied the maps thoroughly, looking for windows of opportunity. Quan's experience and Nash's inherent analytical ability gave them a powerful edge over the enemy.

If Nash were the brains of the outfit, Specialist Fourth Class Harvey Albertson was the brawn. A gentle giant, he had played on the line in high school football, but not well enough in college to keep from flunking out and getting drafted. Nash valued Harv's strength, endurance, and dependability, and he really liked the young man as a personal friend as well. More significantly, the three of them now shared a secret, one that could possibly put them in jail if it were discovered. That secret bonded them like nothing else could.

Pressing his eye to the starlight scope to uncover the grainy green image, Nash slowly swept the focus up and down the road. Just to his right Harv did the same. Nash's scope was attached to his XM-21 sniper rifle, an accurized version of the M-14 that fired powerful 7.62 mm bullets through the attached noise and flash suppressor. Harv used his own starlight like a telescope, separate from his M-16 rifle which lay on the grassy dike, allowing him greater freedom of movement. To Nash's left Quan brought his Korean War-vintage M-2 carbine to his shoulder, depending on his excellent natural night vision to guide his aim. The starlight scope amplified ambient light electronically, but the resulting bright green image was like an old black-and-white television with bad reception, resulting in "snow" that blurred the picture slightly. Nash could easily see the sparkling pinpoints of light that represented the stars, but the seemingly endless checkered plain of rice paddies was nothing more than dark irregular shapes against a gray-green background of sky.

The Army had tried building elevated firing platforms along the road and stationing snipers in them at night to deter the laying of mines by the VC, but the enemy had quickly learned to simply avoid the areas within sight of the sniper nests, and in one case had somehow booby-trapped the structure during the day, resulting in the death of one of the American snipers when he came to occupy it in the evening. Nash's first assignment as a sniper had been on one of those towers, where his partner had accidentally killed an old farmer carrying a fishing pole. Nash had concluded that the towers were pretty much useless, since they were essentially a giant billboard advertising the presence of snipers. Instead he had chosen to set up in an area surrounded by rice paddies, the least likely place for a sniper to hide, hoping that would be the place most likely for the Viet Cong to lay mines.

Another hot August night, Nash thought. He still had six months to go before he could return to the World. Back home in the New Mexico mountains it didn't get this hot, even in August, and it never stank like this. He couldn't wait to go home and breathe that fresh, cool air.

"There they are!" Harv whispered. "Across the road."

Nash swung his rifle to the right silently, sweeping the focus of the scope down the raised roadway. There! He saw the two lumps of darkness on the opposite side of the road, about three hundred and fifty meters away. The shapes were moving, which helped him distinguish them from the grainy background. As he studied the scene, his eye adjusted to better interpret what he was seeing, and the images reconciled themselves into two figures carrying something between them supported by poles. Nash allowed himself to feel relief that the two people were moving in his direction; although his rifle with the daytime scope was accurate out to much greater distances, the starlight scope's lack of adjustability limited night shots to about two hundred meters. He tracked the figures with his scope, mentally begging them to keep moving. But all for naught.

"Shit!" Harv muttered. The two men had stopped about 250 meters away, setting down their load and stretching. Nash hoped they were just taking a break, but then he saw one of them bend down to the stretcher and rise up holding a small shovel. The other man unslung an AK-47 from his shoulder and scanned the surrounding area with the rifle at the ready. He stood guard as the other man walked to the middle of the road and began digging. It was an extremely quiet night, and Nash could hear the chunk of the shovel as it bit into the hard-packed dirt of the roadway.

The dike behind which the sniper team hid ran parallel to the road, and with the targets so far to the right, Nash was in an awkward position trying to line up with them. His left elbow was on the dike, but his right arm hung down over the water, giving him no support. Moving extremely slowly, he twisted his body around to get better aligned, but he had to avoid splashing, the sound of which could easily carry to the Viet Cong. No matter how he tried, however, he could not find a comfortable firing position that would allow him to accurately sight in on the targets. He was thinking he might not be able to shoot at all when Harv began moving beside him.

"Here," Harv whispered, and moved in closer. He had sensed Nash's predicament, and had found a solution. He oozed closer and closer to Nash, until he was lying directly alongside him, and his shoulder was in just the right position for Nash to prop his right elbow on it. Nash was grateful, but said nothing; he would thank Harv later. He made small twisting body movements and minor arm adjustments until he felt stable, and then took aim again through the starlight scope. The guy with the shovel had set it aside and was carrying a heavy object over to the hole. Nash couldn't tell if it was an anti-tank mine or an artillery shell rigged with a pressure-sensitive trigger, but it didn't matter. Either one would blow the wheel off a big truck or damage the treads of a tracked vehicle. Nash began controlling his breathing, taking deep breaths and letting them out slowly.

Which man should he shoot first? That was an easy decision. The man with the AK was standing and alert, while the other man was now squatting down, lowering the explosive device into the hole in the road. He clicked off the safety. Nash brought the cross-hairs to center mass on the standing target, then made a wild-assed guess about range and lifted the rifle just enough that the reticle was centered above the man's head about six inches. Mentally checking his hold on the fore stock, his cheek weld, the feel of the butt against his shoulder, and the position of his finger on the trigger, he took one last deep breath, let it out halfway, and then held it. With a gentle pull he dragged the trigger back until it released the firing pin, and the rifle bucked slightly in his hands. There was a loud pop from the end of the suppressor, and he both felt and heard the bolt mechanism operate, sending the empty casing out the side as it cycled and fed another round into the chamber.

Through the scope Nash saw the standing man jerk and then crumple to the ground. Nash quickly but smoothly swung the rifle a degree to the right and found the other man, who had done just the wrong thing. Instead of immediately going prone, he had jumped to his feet and was wildly looking around, clearly confused by what had happened to his partner. Nash wasted no time, and fired a second shot, aiming just as he did the first time, and saw the man spin around and fall. He saw some jerky movement, but the man didn't seem to be crawling away. Nash took his eye from the starlight scope and blinked, trying to restore his night vision in that eye, while he relaxed his body.

"You got 'em?" Harv asked quietly, his voice muffled because his face was buried in the grass that covered the side of the paddy dike.

"Yep," Nash said. As always, he had mixed feeling about what he had just done. He was pleased and gratified with his success at hitting the targets, but conflicted because he knew he had just killed two men he had never met. It was his job to do that, but it still bothered him. He had grown up with the Ten Commandments pounded into his head by the priest, and the semi-official exception to the "Thou shalt not kill" commandment that said it didn't count in a war was something Nash had trouble accepting. Killing was killing, in his mind, and from an intellectual standpoint he felt that war didn't really excuse it. On the other hand, however, he was a little disturbed that at an emotional level he felt no real remorse about his actions. But that was simply another conundrum of the Viet Nam war, a war that seemed to have no real purpose.

Harv moved away and picked up his starlight scope to survey the kill zone. "Looks like they're both down," he remarked quietly. "Want to go check 'em out?"

"Let's wait a minute, see if there's anyone else around." Nash put his eye back to the scope and moved it in small increments around to his left, searching for any movement or shapes that shouldn't be there. He knew Harv was doing the same to the right.

"What do you think, Quan?" Nash asked the little man beside him. With his background on the other side, Quan has a sixth sense about what the VC were doing.

"They alone," Quan decided in a normal voice. "We go."

"Okay," Nash agreed, and stood up, water dripping from his uniform. Harv and Quan rose as well, and Harv handed Nash his backpack, which had been lying in the water on the other side of Harv next to Harv's pack. Nash slipped his left arm through one of the pack straps and climbed up on the dike to look around from this higher angle. He did a slow spin, concentrating on what his peripheral vision showed. Behind them, a few miles away, the bulk of Nui Ba Den mountain rose above the plain, lights twinkling at the top. After the disaster in 1968, the defenses of the American base at the peak of the mountain had been reinforced, and lights had been set up around the perimeter. Other than that, the countryside was dark and silent.

The three men walked along the dike to the next intersection of berms, then took a sharp left along a dike that led them to the elevated road. They spread out across the road and approached the two bodies cautiously. When they reached them, Harv moved left, kneeled down next to the man with the AK, and shook his shoulder. "He's dead," Harv pronounced, picking up the AK. Quan scooted past Nash on the right, and squatted by the second man, feeling the man's neck.

"Still alive," Quan said. "Shoot him?"

"Negative," Nash said calmly. The sniper teams normally did not take prisoners, but in this case he saw no reason to commit what was essentially a war crime. "Harv, call it in. Tell them we'll wait here for the engineers." Nash had no desire to mess with the mine, which might already be armed. They would just wait here and guard the site until dawn, and let the engineers disarm the thing and haul it away. If the wounded VC didn't die before then, they could haul him away as well. Nash and his team could then hitch a ride back to Cu Chi, avoiding a long walk. Another mission completed successfully, if you judged success by the body count, which the politicians and generals had chosen to do.

*****

With no farewell to the woman inside the small isolated house, Tran Van Tung stepped outside and took a deep breath. The sun hung low over the distant wood line, throwing long shadows across the empty fields. Tung was feeling very satisfied with himself; he was a National Policeman, with a fine black and white uniform and a shiny new Honda 50 motorcycle, and he had just had very good sex with the woman inside, whose name he couldn't remember right now. All he had had to do was threaten her with arrest on some trumped-up charges, and she had quickly acquiesced to his demands. This was the third time he had visited her in the last week, and he idly wondered if he should find out her name. No, he decided, that wasn't important, not for a lieutenant in the National Police. Besides, if he knew her name, he might accidentally use it with his wife, and have to listen to her scream at him for half an hour.

After making sure his pistol was secure in its holster, Tung climbed on his motorbike, retracted the kickstand, and kick-started the motor into life, with its usual ring-ding-ding-ding sound. He blipped the throttle a couple times, relishing the roar and vibration that made him feel even more powerful and manly. Grinning, he made sure his hat was on securely and put the bike into gear. Before he could release the clutch, however, he felt a thump on his back, and looked down to see a spray of blood on the speedometer and handlebars. He was still trying to understand what had happened when the world went black and the bike lurched out from beneath him to wobble crazily across the farmyard and fall over on its side.

*****

The bike's motor was still running, the rear wheel spinning in the air, when Thanh and Nhu arrived. Nhu carried her rifle, which Thanh had learned was a Soviet-made Dragunov sniper rifle, while Thanh carried a shoulder bag with extra ammunition for it. Thanh watched warily as Nhu walked over to the fallen policeman, pointing her rifle at his head, and nudged him with her sandal-clad foot. Convinced that he was dead, she spit on him and then roughly poked him with the end of the rifle. "Capitalist scum!" Nhu muttered. Then she turned to Thanh, an evil smile splitting her face, and said, "See what we can do! We will rid our land of these puppets and their foreign masters."

    Thanh understood the logic, but the reality was making her a little sick. She had seen death before, after bombings in her homeland, and on the trail down to here, but this was somehow different. It had been done in cold blood, and Nhu seemed to get more than just satisfaction out of it. Killing the enemy was part of war, Thanh knew, but she didn't think one was supposed to actually enjoy it. An image of Bao flashed through her mind, but she quickly suppressed it.

    To get away from the body, Thanh walked over to the motorbike, squatted down, and after a minute studying the controls, figured out how to turn off the engine. In the ensuing quiet she stood back up and noticed the woman peering out of the doorway of the house. Her hair was tousled, and she was clutching a dark blue blanket around her body. She showed no emotion when she saw the policeman's body in the dirt, his white shirt red with blood, but when she looked up at Nhu, her fear was obvious. "Who are you?" the woman asked.

    "I am Thanh," Thanh said gently, "and this is Nhu. What is your name?" Nhu shot Thanh an angry look and shook her head. She squatted down, laid her rifle across the body, and jerked the dead man's pistol from its holster. It was a chrome-plated revolver with white plastic hand grips. The woman in the doorway said nothing, watching Nhu with wide eyes.

Standing back up, Nhu turned the gun over in her hands as she examined it. "Why did you sleep with this pig?" she asked the woman in a conversational tone.

"He made me," the woman answered, straightening her back a little. "I did not like him."

"But you let him do what he wanted." Nhu's voice was calm, but Thanh detected the hint of disgust in the way she said it.

"He made me," the woman repeated, this time more assertively. "Now he is dead, and they will blame me for it."

"Perhaps," Nhu said, then raised the pistol and shot the woman in the chest. The woman's expression was one of total surprise as she let the blanket drop around her, revealing her nakedness. It also revealed the hole in left breast, blood just starting to trickle down from it. The woman looked down at the hole, moaned, and collapsed in a heap. From the awkward angle of the woman's limbs, Thanh knew she was already dead.

"Why?" Thanh stammered. She was utterly shocked by the sudden and unexpected murder.

"You told her our names," Nhu said without rancor. "And she was a government sympathizer." Nhu then fired a bullet into the policeman's body, her mouth tilting up at the corners at she did so. Next she walked over to the woman's body and leaned down to feel one of her arms, to ensure she was dead. She picked up the woman's limp right hand and wrapped it around the handle of the pistol, and then let both drop into the dirt. "Let's go home," Nhu said, retrieving her rifle.

FIVE

The sun was low in the western sky, suffusing the village of Truong Mit with a golden glow that made Thanh think of her days here as a small child. She could barely remember those times, and she suspected that most of her memories were actually imaginary, created by the stories her mother used to tell. She had left here at the age of two, after he father had been killed and the country divided.

Standing in the doorway of Nhu's small house, she watched a chicken scratching in the dirt and heard the stuttering whine of a motorbike out on the highway. The village was actually bustling, as everyone tried to finish up their chores before the evening curfew. In theory she was back home, but she wasn't sure if she felt that way or not.

The village was very different from what her mother had described, and even more different than the village she had grown up in, far to the north. Although they were the same country, according to Uncle Ho, South Viet Nam and North Viet Nam were almost exact opposites when you considered the lifestyle of the people, the attitudes, and the general tone of society. In the north everything was very organized, even regimented, with no one concerned about money or luxuries, and everyone working for the common good. Or so she had been taught. Here in the south, despite the war, people were all trying to succeed, to get rich, and to have lots of nice things. At first she had despised such materialism, but now she often caught herself coveting the possessions of others, wishing she could have a new blouse or even a transistor radio. And people seemed happier here, she had to admit.

Back home the war was limited to bombing raids by anonymous American jets, but here the war was more personal, with Vietnamese killing each other, and Americans killing and being killed by Vietnamese. She had hated and feared the American airplanes, but now that she had met some Americans, she realized they were not all the devils that the government in the north insisted they were. Especially Robert. She smiled as she thought of the young man, touching the cross that now hung around her neck.

After seeing Robert wear his cross, she had dug the one her mother had given her out of the bottom of her pack and began wearing it, telling Nhu it would help her earn the trust of the Americans. She had even told Robert she had attended Catholic school, although that was technically a fib. She had always attended good communist-run schools, but her mother had insisted on teaching her the tenets of the Catholic religion in the evenings. At the time Thanh had merely tolerated the lessons to honor her mother, but now she could use that knowledge to impress Robert. He was so nice and good-looking, like the photos she had seen of California surfers. Even though he was a soldier, she knew that he had been drafted, and didn't really want to fight the Vietnamese. She didn't really want to kill anyone either, but she had been sent on a mission by Uncle Ho, and she had to complete it. It was her duty. But she couldn't help thinking about how wonderful it would be if she could spend more time with Robert, and maybe even visit him in California.

"What are you thinking about, girl?" Nhu's question seemed more of an accusation than idle curiosity. The homely woman was sitting on her bed, cleaning her rifle, while Thanh was supposed to be a lookout, in case someone came around. The rifle, Thanh had been told, was an SVD Dragunov, a special sniper rifle the Soviet Union had provided to Hanoi in limited numbers. Thanh had never seen one when she was in the Army up north, but had heard of them. One of them had made its way south with Nhu, who had demonstrated unusual skill with it.

"I was thinking about how different things are here in the south," Thanh said truthfully, if not fully.

"Yes, but things will be better when we have won," Nhu assured her, making metallic clicks as she reassembled the rifle. "We will eliminate the corrupt officials of the puppet government and make our country into the socialist paradise the Great Teacher has promised."

"I hope so," Thanh said with a sigh. She meant the socialist paradise part, not the elimination part. Nhu was already working on that, and had been for several months. She was using her shooting skills to kill the people she believed were corrupt officials, or people who supported such despicable men. Thanh had understood the logic, but she had been disturbed when she discovered how much apparent pleasure Nhu took in these murders. Thanh also felt a little guilty, because she was aiding and abetting these killings. She helped Nhu find the best locations to shoot from and acted as a lookout to ensure no one saw them. Their roles as a Coke girl and a sandwich mama-san gave them an excuse to be all over the area, talking to people, including Americans, without raising any suspicion. It also gave them money to live on. Thanh was supposed to give all the money she earned to Nhu, "for safekeeping," but when she was paid in Dong, the South Vietnamese currency, instead of MPCs, she would sometimes hide the money in her bra and not tell Nhu about it. Thanh wasn't sure why she did this, but rationalized that it was necessary in case Nhu was no longer around for some reason.

Nhu completed the reassembly of her rifle and slid it into the hidden compartment under the sandwich ingredients tray of her cart. She walked forward and put her hand on Thanh's shoulder. Thanh resisted the urge to pull away, for Nhu was officially her superior, not to mention a cold-blooded killer. Nonetheless, Thanh hated the older woman's touch, and knew that Nhu wanted more than just a touch from Thanh. She had made the mistake early on of telling Nhu some of what had happened with Bao on the trip down from Hanoi, and Nhu had used that knowledge to imply, and sometimes state outright, that men were not to be trusted. "We women must band together," Nhu had told her, "to be compatriots in the struggle who are equal to the men, not slaves to them."

No longer needed as a lookout, Thanh turned away from Nhu and walked back to the small table, where she had left an incomplete drawing of Chinese characters. To keep her mind occupied, she had been teaching herself calligraphy, using a thin brush and black ink to draw the complex symbols on cheap paper. She had found the process relaxing, but lately it had become more of a retreat from Nhu than anything else.

"Tomorrow," Nhu announced behind her, "we will begin the training."

"Training?" Thanh asked innocently, not turning around.

"On the missile."

Thanh grimaced, knowing Nhu couldn't see her face. When she had first arrived in Truong Mit, Thanh had been bursting with patriotic fervor, and had happily told Nhu about the missiles she brought and the training she had received. Ever since then, however, Nhu had demanded that Thanh train her on how to use the missiles, "just in case." Thanh had resisted, for several reasons. First and foremost, she had personally been sent on this mission by Uncle Ho, and she was the one responsible for completing it. Secondly, she had quickly learned to dislike Nhu, and to distrust her as well. She felt sure that given the chance, Nhu would take over and claim all the glory. And, from a practical standpoint, Thanh worried that removing the missile launcher from its case and handling it might accidentally damage it. Nhu had her fancy rifle, and all Thanh had was the missile launcher. She didn't want to give up her slight advantage.

"But we must go out and sell our wares tomorrow," Thanh protested weakly.

"We will," Nhu agreed. "But afterward we will have time. We must do it soon, for I have received a message."

"A message? From whom?" Thanh turned to face Nhu.

"My source in the puppet government." Nhu reached into her pants pocket and pulled out a crumpled slip of paper. She unfolded and straightened it before handing it to Thanh.

In hastily written pencil the note said: "Two weeks. Nui Ba Den. 10,000."

"What does it mean?"

"It means our mission will be revealed to us very soon, and it will have something to do with the mountain."

"And the ten thousand?"

Nhu sniffed. "That is the amount the man wants in return for his treason. In dollars"

"Ten thousand dollars? Do you have that much?" Thanh was shaking her head in wonder, looking at the floor.

"No, but you do." Thanh looked up to see Nhu grinning at her and holding a small key dangling from a string. It was the key to the metal cases containing the missile launcher and accessories. Thanh had hidden the key in the end of a bamboo pole that supported her bed, but obviously Nhu had discovered it. And at some point she had opened the cases, without Thanh knowing, and discovered the cache of money the smaller case contained. Thanh had not told Nhu, or anyone else, about the stacks of American hundred-dollar bills, which had been given to her with strict instructions for their use.

"That is my key!" Thanh barked at her angrily. "You had no right to take it!"

Nhu sneered. "I am in charge here, little girl, not you. Remember, in a socialist society all property belongs to the state, and I represent the state."

"That money was given to me by Uncle Ho," Thanh insisted, fighting back tears. "I was given strict instructions for its use."

"And what were those instructions?" Nhu's question was tinged with both disinterest and curiosity.

"It is to be used if I decide we need something to complete the mission, or if we need to bribe puppet government officials."

"And so it will be used," Nhu countered. "We will bribe this man to tell us what we need to know. A target for the missiles has been selected. All we need to know now is the time and precise location of this target. This corrupt official will provide us that information, but only for a price."

"What is the target?" Thanh demanded, only partially mollified.

"A helicopter that is carrying someone of importance. That is all I know so far."

"Someone important? Who?"

Nhu shook her head. "I have not been told, for security reasons. But I have been assured that his death will greatly affect the outcome of the war. It will cause the Americans to end their occupation of our country and support for the puppet government, so our land can again be united. The Americans have lost their resolve, and they are rioting in the streets in Washington. We need only one more push to drive them out."

Thanh knew she was supposed to feel inspired by the political rhetoric, but in the last few months she had become somewhat disillusioned by the means in which the restoration of a united Viet Nam was being achieved. As soon as she thought that, though, she mentally chastised herself for her momentary loss of faith. "How will he give us that information, and when?"

"He will come to us while we are selling to the Americans. He will pretend to buy from us as well. I do not know exactly which day."

"How will we recognize him? Have you met him?"

"No," Nhu admitted with a wry grin, "but I have seen him through my telescopic sight. I wanted to shoot him, but for now he is a useful tool."

Thanh suppressed a shudder. She understood that this was a war of liberation, and enemy deaths were a necessary part of the war, but she still found Nhu's approach to the task a little disturbing. The older woman seemed to take far too much pleasure in the process. Thanh, on the other hand, was finding the almost daily killing more and more distressing and reprehensible. This was far more personal than shooting down screaming jet airplanes that were laying waste to her homeland. In some ways Thanh was relieved that Nhu wanted to learn how to fire the missiles, because Thanh was no longer sure she wanted to contribute to the constantly growing death toll. She still wanted to help her nation, but was no longer convinced that committing murder was the way she wanted to do it.

They heard the sound of a motorbike approaching, and Thanh, as always, felt the tightening in her chest, fearing it was the approach of a policeman. Nhu, however, simply sighed and went to the door. Cowering inside, Thanh saw a young man skid to a stop in the yard and hand a cardboard box to Nhu. "Here is your Spam," he said, chortling. "It will make a good sandwich." And with that he sped off again. Nhu brought the box in and set it on the table to open it, pushing aside Thanh's papers. Inside were the oddly shaped cans of Spam, of course, but also another note.

"The missile training may have to wait," Nhu said after reading the note. "We have a mission tomorrow."

*****

Nash pulled his arms from the backpack straps and threw the bulky pack on his cot; next he unhooked his pistol belt and let it drop, the canteen hitting the floor with a heavy thunk. Harv Albertson just flopped face down on his cot next to Nash's without taking anything off, letting his M-16 clatter to the floor and the backpack radio antenna whip in the air above his head. As tired as he was, Nash couldn't ignore the needs of his XM-21 sniper rifle, so he sat on his cot, took a rag from his pocket, and wiped it down. A full cleaning would have to wait. At the cot behind him Quan laid his M-2 carbine down and shrugged out of his backpack, whistling tunelessly. Quan showed no sign of the weariness that beset Nash and Harv, and Nash found himself resenting that a little.

They had just returned from a five-day-long patrol, had been awake for nearly twenty-four hours, and it had all been a major waste of time. They hadn't seen anything or done anything worth noting. They had returned to the Cu Chi base camp just after dawn, made their way across the sprawling complex of wooden buildings, checked in, and headed for the barracks to finally rest up. Nash planned to sleep the rest of the day, with a possible break for lunch. And maybe a trip to the PX, to see if they had gotten in anything good. Propping his rifle against the wall, he leaned forward so he could unlace his boots, but before he could do so a new guy whose name Nash had already forgotten poked his head in the door and called to him.

"Sergeant Jaramillo, Captain Banning wants to see you and your team ASAP." Then the young man was gone.

"Shit!" Nash cursed. "What now?"

"Tell him I died," Harv moaned, his voice muffled by his pillow.

"Me, too?" Quan asked brightly. He began brushing the dust from his uniform with his hands. Somewhere, and Nash never asked where, Quan had acquired one of the tiger-striped camouflage uniforms normally reserved for the Special Forces, and he had had it tailored to fit his slender body almost like a glove. He was proud of the uniform, which he had accessorized with a dark green bandana around his neck.

"Come on," Nash told them both, his voice heavy with resignation. "Let's get this over with."

Harv struggled to stand up and took off his radio, backpack, and pistol belt, dropping them all on his cot. "I feel ten pounds lighter," he remarked facetiously.

"More like fifty, I would guess," Nash told him. Harv was the biggest and strongest member of the team, having played football in high school, and thus had been selected to carry the heavy PRC-25 radio in addition to his other gear. Although he was a big man, with brown hair and eyes, and a year or two older than Nash, he had the personality of a first grade school teacher. Always pleasant, Harv rarely cursed, and seldom complained. Yet he was always ready to do whatever task was assigned to him, and do it well.

Leaving their boonie hats behind, all three men picked up their rifles and trailed out the door into the bright morning sun, squinting against the glare.

When they entered Banning's office, the captain was talking to a tall gangly man with glasses; Nash's heart nearly stopped when he saw the pins on that man's collars. Instead of rank, he simply had "U.S." pins, and the only soldiers Nash knew of who wore those were members of the Military Police Criminal Investigation Division. *Oh, shit!* he thought, *they've caught us.* A few weeks earlier his team had recovered a huge cache of money being brought down from North Vietnam to fund Viet Cong operations in the area. While they had turned in most of the money, they had secretly kept some for themselves, sending home tens of thousands of dollars hidden inside things they had bought at the PX. Nash had always felt guilty about the money, even though he knew he was only repurposing money that had belonged to the enemy. Now it looked like the chickens had come home to roost.

As they filed into the room and gathered around Banning's desk, Nash shot worried glances at Harv and Quan. Harv was biting his lower lip and staring at the tall man, whose name tape read Atkinson. Quan, who probably wasn't aware of the significance of the missing rank pins, was smiling at the man.

"Gentlemen," Banning announced, "this is Mr. Atkinson, an intelligence liaison to the South Vietnamese." Nash let out the breath he had been holding without realizing it. So the guy wasn't an MP! Banning continued. "Mr. Atkinson, this is Sergeant Jaramillo, Specialist Albertson, and Nguyen Van Quan, the best sniper team in the Division." Everyone nodded at each other in greeting. Nash wasn't sure if he was supposed to salute or shake the guy's hands, and Atkinson seemed equally uncertain about the proper protocol, so they all let the nods suffice.

"Mr. Atkinson works at the DIOCC in Bao Donh," Banning said, and started to continue but was interrupted by Nash.

"Dee-yock?" he asked, puzzled by the unfamiliar acronym.

Atkinson explained: "District Intelligence and Operations Command Center. It's a South Vietnamese setup, with American advisors."

"Okay," Nash said vaguely, still not sure he understood.

"Anyway," Banning said sharply, apparently a little perturbed by the interruption, "they've been receiving reports that there is a Viet Cong sniper operating in the area between here and Tay Ninh, and yesterday their District Chief was killed by this sniper."

Atkinson broke in. "He was inspecting a location where they plan to build a new ruff-puff compound. It was just him, a sergeant, and his driver. Just a single shot, from quite a distance. The sergeant and the driver claim they returned fire, but they didn't really know where the shot came from."

Banning took over. "There's been several KIA over the last few months in that area, but until now no one had noticed a pattern. Mr. Atkinson coordinated with other districts and did some analysis, and the brigade commander is convinced that what we have is a trained sniper who is selectively taking out senior personnel, both American and Vietnamese."

"What's the connection?" Nash asked Atkinson. Banning looked a little pissed that Nash had gone to the source.

"One thing is the target profile," Atkinson told them. "All of them have been senior people traveling alone or with just one or two others, far from any possible quick response by armed units. There's been a MACV captain driving a jeep, a ruff-puff major escorting an American civilian contractor planning a bridge, and now the District Chief. There were some others that might have been shot by the sniper as well, including a National Police lieutenant and his mistress. All were shot at long rage with surprising accuracy. The MACV captain's jeep was actually moving when he was shot, we're pretty sure."

Nash nodded. It did sound like there was a sniper, and not just random killings. "Do you know anything about the sniper or his weapon?" he asked.

Atkinson shook his head. "None of our sources seem to know anything, or will admit to it, anyway. The sniper seems to just disappear after each shooting. One of the MACV guys suggested the rifle might be a Dragunov, but that's just a guess." Nash had heard of the Dragunov, a Soviet-made sniper rifle that fired 7.62mm rounds similar to those used in the SKS and AK-47. Reportedly it was very accurate at long ranges, so it was possible that was the weapon being utilized.

Banning swept his hands across a map on his desk to smooth it. "Here's where the District Chief was killed," he said, pointing. Nash leaned over to study the map, which had a red dot placed in an open area not far from a village. Nash saw other red dots, which he assumed were other locations where the sniper had supposedly struck, and noted that they all were near Highway One, the main road from Cu Chi to Tay Ninh. Quan leaned forward to take a look, and then mumbled something in Vietnamese.

"And no one saw anything?" Nash asked.

Atkinson shook his head. "The incidents have all occurred away from populated areas. Never when there are troops close by, and the survivors, if any, don't have radios. So by the time we find out about the killing, the sniper is long gone."

"That's smart," Harv commented. "He knows what he's doing."

"That's why we brought you in," Banning said to Nash. "Kind of a 'to catch a thief' theory."

Nash felt a little trill in his chest from the "thief" remark, but realized it was unrelated to their secret.

Atkinson expanded on Banning's remark. "We're hoping that your skills and knowledge as a sniper team will give you some insights on how this VC sniper works, and maybe allow you to predict where he'll strike next."

"I don't know," Nash said doubtfully. "That's kind of like trying to predict where lightning will strike. But, you know, we could go check out the sites of previous shootings, look around, and find where the sniper took his shot from. That might give us an idea of what type of locations he prefers."

"That would certainly help," Atkinson said. "Then maybe we could stake out such locations, set a trap."

Nash made doubtful face. "Since he knows where his targets are going to be ahead of time, I don't think you can set a trap he wouldn't find out about. He's obviously got local sources of information." Nash was politely stating what they all knew: you couldn't fully trust anyone in the South Vietnamese government or military, nor, in fact, any of the civilians. Virtually anyone could be a communist spy, or at least a sympathizer.

"We do it," Quan said out of the blue. Nash looked at him, raising one eyebrow. "You, me, Harv," Quan explained. "We be trap. We tell nobody."

"Hmm," Banning said speculatively.

"Yeah," Harv enthused. "We wouldn't tell anyone where we were, and stay out of sight."

Nash considered the idea, and saw the merits. "That might work," he admitted. "All the shootings have been in daylight, right?"

"That's correct," Atkinson replied.

"So we could move at night, set up just before dawn, and wait for the sniper to show up. Assuming we were at the right location."

"I think that's a great idea," Atkinson said, nodding. He turned to Banning. "Captain, can you spare these guys for a few days to try this out?"

"Probably be several weeks," Nash cautioned.

Banning frowned as he thought about it. "I'll have to clear it with the BC," he finally said, meaning the brigade commander, "but I think we can manage it. What will you need, Sergeant?"

Nash rubbed his forehead as he thought about it. "First we'll need to scout out all the possible locations. I'm thinking we go up and down Highway 1 from, say, Trang Bang to Tay Ninh. But we need to do it surreptitiously, so the locals don't know what we're doing. Maybe go along with any American sweeps in the area and pretend we're part of that particular unit. But first I want to check out the previous shooting sites."

"Of course," Atkinson said. "How do you want to do that?"

"Good question," Nash said. "Don't want the locals to suspect anything."

"We could pretend to be reporters," Harv offered. "You know, with notebooks and cameras, doing a story on the sniper."

"That might work," Banning agreed. "With Quan as your interpreter. That also might be a good cover when you make the sweeps with the infantry units. That way some GI wouldn't accidentally tell the wrong person what you were doing."

"We'd have to look like reporters," Nash said. "Press credentials, or whatever."

"I can arrange that," Banning said. "Have you got a camera?"

"All I've got is a little Instamatic," Nash said. Quan shook his head.

"I'll buy one," Harv said. "I've been saving my money to buy a good camera anyway."

"It would have to look professional," Atkinson warned.

"I know," Harv said. "A good Nikon thirty-five millimeter, with maybe some extra lenses. I wonder where I can get one of those cool vests with all the pockets."

"How about an M-79 ammo vest?" Nash suggested.

Harv made a face. "That'd work, but would a real pro photographer use one?"

"I'll check around, see what I can find," Banning assured him. "But can you afford all that?"

Nash and Harv exchanged glances. Harv had plenty of money, but he had sent most of it home, and hidden the rest. It was a lot more than a Spec 4 could realistically have accumulated in a few months.

"Payday is tomorrow," Harv noted.

"And I can help him out," Nash jumped in. "Maybe Quan can find a used camera for sale somewhere, maybe in Saigon. A used camera would be even better."

"True," Harv agreed, although he appeared a little disappointed that he wouldn't be getting one that was brand new. "And maybe he can find a photographer's vest."

"Saigon?" Banning asked. "How would he get there?"

"Uh, hitch a ride maybe?" Nash looked questioningly at Quan. He knew that Quan owned a new Honda 50 motorcycle that he stored with a cousin off post, but that wasn't something they wanted to reveal.

"Yes," Quan said, "or take taxi." That meant he would pay to ride on one of the little three-wheeled Lambretta scooters that putt-putted all over South Vietnam, packed with cargo and passengers.

"You'd need a pass," Banning commented. "I'll have one made." Since Quan was a Chieu Hoi, a former Viet Cong, he couldn't travel freely without proper paperwork. "Anything else?"

"We'll have to leave our weapons behind, if we're pretending to be reporters," Nash noted. "I'm not sure I like that."

"When you're with the sweeps, everyone else will be armed," Banning said. "I don't think the sniper would want to take out a reporter, anyway. Bad publicity."

"Let's hope," Nash said. "Okay, we need to get started. Sir, can I take this map?

Banning folded up the map and gave it to him. "I'll get that pass for Quan, and press credentials. How soon do you think you'll be ready?"

"Give us a couple days to get the camera and make ourselves look like reporters."

Atkinson said, "If you've got time right now, I'll brief you on the shootings we know about." Nash really wanted to go back to the barracks and get some sleep, but he needed the information from Atkinson. Reluctantly he nodded.

"Good enough," Banning said, speaking for Nash and the others. Nash was already having doubts about this plan, but didn't see any alternative. He definitely did not like going out in the countryside without his rifle.

SIX

"Stay alert!" Lieutenant Stephen Carr yelled to his men, knowing such a warning was unnecessary. The dismounted men of the platoon were spread out on either side of the narrow dirt road, wading through the tall grass. The tracks had stayed on the road, in a herringbone formation, their engines idling. This close to the river, Carr feared one of them might hit a soft spot and get stuck in the mud, since the rainy season was already upon them. Carr himself was walking on the slightly raised dirt road, the muddy surface of which did not appear to have been used lately, his eyes sweeping across the fields of grass and fixing on the distant clumps of trees that bordered the nearby stream. The road itself ran right down into the river, where apparently the locals could ford it in the dry season. Right now it needed a bridge. Off to his right, at the far end of the sweep, Carr could see his platoon sergeant, Aaron Samples, cautiously approaching a small grove of bushes and trees to check it out.

"I think this is it," a voice said behind him. The speaker was Sergeant Jaramillo, an Army sniper Carr had worked with in the Michelin rubber plantation a few weeks back. Except now Jaramillo was dressed like a news correspondent, carrying a map and a notebook instead of a rifle. With him was his spotter, Albertson, who was randomly pointing a large camera in every direction, and his Vietnamese Kit Carson scout, dressed like a civilian in white shirt and black slacks.

Carr turned to face the young man, who was pointing at the side of the road. "Looks like several vehicles turned around here," Jaramillo said. Carr looked closer, and was almost able to envision the tire tracks and crushed grass that the sniper apparently could clearly make out. If the signs hadn't been pointed out to him, he would never have noticed them. Jaramillo studied his notes, glancing from them to the road, then from them to the distant trees in several directions. "I think Sergeant Samples is on the right track," he said finally.

They had been looking for the spot where a Vietnamese RF/PF major had been shot by a sniper several months earlier while escorting an American contractor. Any remaining marks would mostly have been obliterated by the weather and the passage of time, but somehow Jaramillo had found it. Carr wasn't entirely sure he understood the subterfuge of having the sniper team pose as combat correspondents, but he had gone along with it anyway. Unlike the other platoons the snipers had worked with lately, Carr's entire platoon already knew their true identity from the firefight in the Michelin, so the lieutenant had sworn his men to secrecy about their subterfuge. He was confident the men had complied.

Earlier Jaramillo had explained it to him in general terms: "I need to go to each of the locations where the VC sniper has operated in order to study his methods and perspectives. Once I know how he plans his kills, I can better judge where he might strike next."

While Albertson adjusted his camera and took a photo, Carr and Jaramillo watched Samples duck into the thicket. He reemerged a few yards from where he had entered, shaking his head. "Sir," Jaramillo said, "could you stay here? I'm going to go take a look. Quan, Harv, come on." The three men plunged into the high grass and hurried over to where Samples waited. Carr watched them have a brief discussion and then all four disappeared into the darkness of the grove. Occasionally he would see one of their faces peer out through the bushes, and once he saw Quan's white shirt high in one of the trees. It occurred to Carr that they were checking out possible sniper nests, and that he was a stand-in for the dead Vietnamese major. Suddenly Carr felt very vulnerable, and to take his mind off his fear he turned his attention to the other men of the platoon.

"Just go to the river and come back," he shouted at them, feeling immediately foolish after he said it. What else could they do? They weren't going to swim across, that was for sure.

"Sir!" Eberhart, the platoon radio-telephone operator, said with a touch of urgency. He was standing a couple yards away with the radio on his back, and he had the handset pressed to his ear. "Something's happening."

Carr hurried over to Eberhart and gave him a questioning look. The RTO lifted his index finger from the handset to signal to Carr to wait one minute while he answered a call. "Good copy, out," Eberhart finally said and looked at Carr. "Change of mission," he said. "A civilian was killed just north of Bao Donh. They think it's the sniper. We're supposed to go hunt for him."

Carr took a deep breath and hollered, "Mount up! Everybody back on the tracks. Hustle!"

There was a mad rush as the men ran through the grass and headed for the parked APCs. Samples and the sniper team were the last to arrive, questioning looks on their faces.

"The sniper hit again south of us," Carr told them as the rushed to the waiting vehicles. "They think he's still in the area." No further explanation was necessary, for they all knew what they had to do. The sniper team joined Carr in climbing up on the one-three track, while Samples ran down the road to mount the one-one track. As soon as everyone was on board, Carr grabbed the track's microphone and gave the order to head back to the highway. Each of the drivers locked the laterals and slewed the big boxy machines around, one set of treads not moving, and the other clawing the dirt to swing the vehicle around in a one-eighty so they could head back the way they had come. Samples, who had arrived on the last vehicle in line, now led the platoon away from the river location. As they bounced over the rough road, Carr pulled out his map of the area and looked to Eberhart, who was writing down coordinates as he received them. He passed the slip of paper to Carr, who quickly plotted them. The location was only three miles from where they were, but Carr worried that the sniper would still have plenty of time to get away.

*****

As the line of tracked vehicles roared away from the river lowlands, the road became drier and rougher, and the treads began throwing up a cloud of reddish-brown dust that enveloped the last track, the one Nash was riding on. Squinting his eyes to keep out the dirt, he pondered what the sniper's team should do. They had their weapons and equipment stored down below, but he wasn't quite ready to relinquish their pretense as correspondents. In fact, he felt somewhat powerless, for they were simply being carried along by events, constrained by circumstances to accompany this platoon wherever it went.

"Do we get our weapons?" Harv asked him. Harv was sitting directly behind Nash on the top of the track, and had leaned forward and placed his hand on Nash's arm to get his attention over the road and engine noise. Harv's question pushed Nash into making a final decision. He shook his head and half turned to look at Harv over his shoulder.

"Not yet. We'll let these guys handle it for now." Nash had a feeling that the location of the shooting would soon devolve into a giant cluster-fuck, with soldiers running around in all directions following contradictory orders issued by too many officers on the scene. Their best option was to continue to act like reporters, while quietly advising Carr and Samples on where to look for the sniper. It was their specialized knowledge that was needed, not their minimal firepower.

When the platoon made the right turn onto the main highway, the ride got smoother, but the clouds of dust got even thicker with the increased speed. In only a couple minutes they slowed and veered off the road onto the narrow verge separating the road from rice paddies. Up ahead two jeeps were parked at angles on the road, and between them a red motorcycle lay on its side next to a man's body sprawled awkwardly in the dirt. Beyond the jeeps Nash saw another mechanized platoon arriving from the south, this one stopping on the road with the lead track only a few meters from the growing crowd of soldiers around the body.

"Come on," Nash said, nodding to Harv and Quan, "let's go get the story." The three of them jumped down from the track, Harv cradling his camera to keep it from being damaged, and began walking swiftly toward the jeeps. Lieutenant Carr joined them, followed by Eberhart.

As they passed the one-one track Carr looked up at Samples and said, "Get the men ready for a sweep, but keep them mounted for now." Samples nodded.

There were already six men milling around the body when Nash and the others arrived. Nash saw that one of the men had the gold oak leaf of a major and a MACV patch on his shoulder, but he seemed a little flustered. Nash stayed close behind Carr as the lieutenant approached the major.

"Lieutenant Carr," he introduced himself, "Alpha Company. What would you like us to do, sir?"

The major, whose name tape read Krolick, seemed to take heart in the arrival of a seasoned combat officer. A lieutenant from the other platoon rushed up and joined the group. Nash had recently met the man, who looked too young to be a first lieutenant, and remembered that his name was Masters. "Uh, I guess," Major Krolick stammered, "you need to search for the sniper." He looked at Nash, who had crowded in. "And you are?"

"War correspondent," Carr answered for him. "They're working on a story about the sniper."

"Oh. Of course."

Carr turned to Masters and said, "Harry, why don't you take the east side of the road, and I'll take the west. Better leave the tracks on the road. Don't want to get stuck in these paddies."

"Roger," Masters said. "What are we looking for?"

Major Krolick shrugged. "A sniper."

"Do we know how it happened?" Carr asked.

Krolick shrugged again, and tilted his head toward the body. "He's the mayor of Trang Bang, or was, anyway. Riding his motorcycle up to Tay Ninh for something, I guess. All alone, I presume. I was on my way back to Bao Donh when I found him in the road, just like that."

"Any idea how long he's been here?" Nash asked, pretending to scribble in his notebook.

Krolick frowned in concentration. "Not long, I imagine. This road gets a lot of traffic. The blood looked pretty fresh." He shuddered a little.

"And when did you get here?" Carr asked.

Krolick looked at his watch. He exhaled loudly. "Maybe fifteen minutes ago? Twenty?" Suddenly he looked around nervously. "He could still be out there, right? Waiting to pick us off?"

"Doubtful," Carr told him. "Snipers tend to shoot and run. With all these troops, he wouldn't stand a chance in a firefight."

Nash nodded, but didn't say anything. He didn't want to reveal his knowledge of sniper tactics and possibly blow his cover as a reporter. Carr was correct, however. It would be suicidal for a sniper to hang around after a kill, and with a twenty-minute head start, their chances of finding him were virtually nil. He looked up as a helicopter roared overhead and began to circle. It was a loach, an egg-shaped light observation helicopter, normally used by battalion and brigade commanders.

"It's Brigade, sir," Eberhart yelled over the noise. "They want to know why we're not searching for the sniper yet."

"We just got here," Carr grumbled through clenched teeth. "Okay, Harry, time to go play hide and seek. And we're 'it'." Carr and Masters, followed by their RTOs, ran back to their platoons and began deploying the troops. Nash stayed with the major, hoping for more information, while Harv began taking pictures. Quan wandered over and stared down at the body for a minute, before squatting down by the motorcycle to inspect it.

"The mayor of Trang Bang," Nash said to the major. "That's quite a ways from here."

"Yes," Krolick agreed absently.

"Do you know why he was going to Tay Ninh, or why he was alone?"

"No. No idea. It's a free country, I guess."

Nash was a little puzzled by that remark, but excused it due to the major's apparent distress over the incident. Pretending it was only idle curiosity, he stepped over to the body and studied it. The mayor had been an older man, with a few long hairs on his chin and wrinkled cheeks. He lay on his back, his arms outstretched, and one leg tucked under his butt. He wore the typical white shirt and black slacks, like Quan, but the front of his shirt had a fist-sized hole and was soaked in red. He had been shot in the back by a high-powered rifle, apparently as he was moving away from the shooter. Nash raised his head and looked to the south, searching for a possible hide that would have given the sniper the right angle. There were a couple places that qualified.

Leaving the bewildered major, Nash walked over to where Lieutenant Carr was simultaneously waving directions to his men and talking on the radio, and waited for a chance to speak to him. The platoon's men were moving out in an ever-expanding semi-circle, mostly staying on the paddy dikes, and probing any bushes or reeds. Carr finally finished reporting and handed the handset back to Eberhart. "Waste of time," he commented to Nash.

"Definitely," Nash agreed. "I'm pretty sure the sniper was somewhere down there," nodding toward the south. "We're going to go down there and check it out, see if we can find the actual spot. Not that it matters much now."

"Okay," Carr said. "Want an armed escort?"

Nash scoffed. "The sniper's probably back in Tay Ninh or wherever by now. And look at that." A group of civilians was arriving on bicycles and on foot down near the suspected sniper hide. It was the usual gaggle of Coke kids, boom-boom girls, and sandwich mama-sans. Nash and Carr exchanged looks. Both knew that the presence of the civilians meant that the sniper, or any other Viet Cong, was nowhere near. It was an article of faith among the GIs that when the Coke kids were around, the enemy wasn't, and when the Coke kids disappeared, that was the time to be worried.

Nash headed in their direction, gathering up Harv and Quan along the way. "Harv," he said as they strolled down the road, "I want pictures of the hide when I find it, and pictures of the Coke kids, too. Quan, talk to the Coke kids and see if anybody saw anything suspicious."

It didn't take long for Nash to find where the shot had come from. There was a small stand of trees surrounded by bushes just east of the highway, roughly oblong in shape, with a small open area in the center. It was like an off-shore island from a larger stretch of forest that expanded farther east. The leaves and seedlings in that area were recently crushed, and when Nash crowded into it, he could easily see the stretch of road where the mayor had been traveling. He could imagine using such a spot himself. He probed around the area, but found no empty shell casing. Not that he had expected to. This sniper was too professional to leave a tell-tale cartridge behind. He had Harv take a picture of him in the hide, and then one with it empty. Nash was getting a clear impression now of how the sniper operated, and how he chose his hides.

When he and Harv returned to the highway, they found Quan flirting with one of the Coke kids while he sipped from a can of Coke he had obviously purchased from her. Harv, who was always hungry, wandered over to a hard-looking sandwich mama-san with a two-wheeled cart and ordered a sandwich.

"This is Thanh," Quan said when Nash joined them. "She talk English and French."

"You want a Coke?" she asked Nash brightly.

"Sure," Nash answered, and dug out his wallet.

She pushed the ice around in the wooden box mounted on the front of her bicycle and pulled out a dripping can. She had a can opener on a string tied to her handle bars, and she quickly opened the can and handed it to him, taking the fifty-piaster note he held out.

Nash took a long sip of the cold beverage. "Anyone see anything?" he asked Quan.

Quan shook his head. "Thanh see farmer back there," he said, pointing to the south.

Thanh nodded. "He was old man," she told Nash. "I do not think he is Viet Cong."

"Was he carrying anything?"

"A rake, maybe. He was far away."

Nash considered it, but decided it was unlikely the sniper would have allowed himself to be seen. He took another drink. Harv wandered over, munching on his gook sandwich. Harv had obviously requested the *nuoc mam* sauce be added, the dead fish smell assaulting Nash's nose. "Jeez, Harv, how can you eat that?"

"What? It's good, once you get past the smell."

"I'll take you word for it."

"You want a Coke?" Thanh asked Harv.

The sandwich mama-san, with no other customers approaching, let her cart down on its poles and ambled over to join them.

"You got any orange?" Harv responded.

"Oh, yes, certainly," Thanh said, searching through the crushed ice. "Here," she said, unearthing a brightly colored can. While she opened the can and took Harv's money, Thanh asked, "Who was killed?"

"The mayor of Trang Bang," Harv answered as he took the soda from her.

"Oh, that is very sad," she replied, frowning. Nash was a little surprised by the sincerity of her remark. She seemed truly upset by the man's death.

"Did you know him?" Nash asked.

Thanh shook her head. "No, but there is too much killing all the time."

"You can say that again," Harv commented.

Thanh wrinkled her forehead in confusion, and then said, "There is too much killing all the time." Nash decided she had never heard Harv's expression before, and he found her response a little amusing. She was a cute girl, he had to admit, and he could see why Quan was flirting with her. He just hoped he hadn't given away anything to her.

Harv finished gobbling down his sandwich, drank some of his soda, and then lifted the camera hanging from the strap around his neck. "Can I take your picture?" he asked Thanh. She quickly covered her face with her hands.

"Oh, no!" she said in a scared voice, but then forced a giggle. "I am very shy. Please, no pictures."

Harv turned toward the sandwich lady, but before he could even ask she gave him a scowl that would stop a train. Harv let the camera down to the end of the strap, looking very sheepish. Nash wondered what that was all about. Vietnamese civilians normally enjoyed having their pictures taken by the GIs.

One of Lieutenant Carr's soldiers ran up, breathlessly saying, "Hi, Thanh," with a warm smile. Nash recognized the young man, whose name was Crosby. He carried an M-79 grenade launcher, which hung loosely from his left hand, and a newspaper in his right.

"Hello, Robert," Thanh responded with equal warmth. Nash saw the looks that passed between them, and also noted the jealous look on Quan's face, and the angry look on the sandwich mama-san's face. He understood Quan's expression, but the older woman's attitude didn't make sense. Surely this older woman with the squat body wasn't involved with any of the men.

"I thought you might like to have this," Crosby said shyly to Thanh, holding out a recent copy of *The Stars and Stripes*, the military newspaper. "To practice your English," he added.

"Yes, thank you," Thanh responded warmly as she took it.

From across the road came an angry shout from Sergeant Samples. "Crosby, get your sorry ass back here."

"Okay, Sarge," Crosby answered, but turned to Thanh one last time. "I'll see you later," he told her. She smiled and nodded.

Nash smiled at the innocence of the two young people, especially here in the middle of the war, but then sighed at the futility of it all.

*****

"It is good that you did not let that man take your picture," Nhu praised her mildly. Thanh and Nhu were returning to Truong Mit, with Nhu pushing her car and Thanh walking her bicycle alongside.

"I was worried that the picture might appear in the newspapers," Thanh explained. "I would not want my mother to see what I am doing here."

"Nor our leaders back in Hanoi," Nhu told her. "We are on a secret mission, and if our pictures are seen, someone might recognize us and report us to the authorities. You must always be careful around the Americans." Nhu suddenly looked at Thanh suspiciously. "You have not let Robert take your picture, have you?"

Thanh felt a twinge of guilt. She wondered if she should lie to Nhu, but feared the woman would see right through her. Looking down with shame, she murmured, "Yes, but it was a Polaroid. It cannot be used in the newspapers. It was only for him."

Nhu growled in disgust. "You are such an empty-headed girl! I do not understand why Uncle Ho chose you for such an important mission. Just because your father was supposedly a hero does not mean that you are."

"You may not talk about my father!" Thanh retorted angrily. "And do not worry; I will carry out my mission, with or without your help."

Nhu grimaced at Thanh in what was apparently supposed to be a smile. "That is better. You must show the fire of the revolution. No more swooning over an American now. The time for our mission is coming soon, and we must be fully prepared. I am doing my part, and soon you will do yours."

Nhu had just reminded Thanh of what had happened earlier that day. The two had stopped beside the road and rested in the shade of a tree that was the point of a triangular grove that stretched away from the highway. When no one else was visible, Nhu had slid her rifle out of the hidden compartment and told Thanh to wait there. While Thanh kept an eye out for anyone approaching, Nhu slipped into the forest and disappeared. Thanh was thankful that anything Nhu did would not involve Thanh directly. She did not want to be there when Nhu assassinated someone and gloated over the death.

Traffic on the highway was very thin that day, and Thanh had seen only a few of the Lambretta mini-buses and a couple American truck convoys. An hour had passed since Nhu had left, and Thanh was wondering if she should try to find her, when a motorcycle approached. It was an older red Honda, driven by a frail man in a white shirt, a man who looked to be at least fifty years old, which was ancient from Thanh's perspective. As he drove by he glanced over at Thanh, and she gave him a polite wave. He went past her, but then stopped and turned around. He drove back and pulled up beside her bicycle.

"Ciao, co," he greeted her. "Are you having a problem?" He nodded at the sandwich cart and raised his eyebrows.

"No," Thanh hastily improvised. "My friend is having bowel problems. She is in the woods."

"Ah," he said knowingly. "I have such problems myself some times. More now than when I was younger."

"Are you thirsty?" Thanh asked, sweeping her hand toward the box of ice-covered sodas.

The old man shook his head. "I do not drink those American sodas. They give me gas. But I would be grateful if you could give me some ice to suck on."

"Certainly," Thanh answered, and picked up a handful of ice, picking out the rice hulls that had been used to insulate it at the ice house.

He took the ice and popped the chunks into his mouth. He smiled at her as he sucked on them. As the last one melted, he announced, "Well, I must continue my journey. I hope your friend is feeling better soon." He popped the clutch of the motorbike and zoomed away.

About twenty minutes later Nhu returned, her ugly face glowing with pride and pleasure. She quickly stored the gun in the cart and picked up the handles. "Come, girl, we must hurry. The Americans will arrive soon." And with that she had led Thanh back onto the road and headed in the same direction as the old man on the motorbike. They had gone only a short distance when four of the big American armored personnel carriers had roared past them, leaving them in the dust. It was only when they caught up with the vehicles, which had joined many more, that Thanh saw the inert form next to the fallen motorbike, and realized what had happened.

Now, walking along with Nhu to their house, Thanh felt even more detached from the older woman than before. She knew that Nhu killed people from afar, and had even helped her find the spot to shoot from and then later get away, but until today she had not actually met any of the victims when they were still alive, other than that woman who Nhu had killed with the policeman's pistol. The old man had seemed very nice, and did not appear to be an enemy of the people, yet Nhu had gunned him down without a thought. Yes, he was the mayor of Trang Bang, and therefore a member of the puppet government, but Thanh had a hard time believing he was a danger to anyone. Worse, in Thanh's mind, was the apparent joy Nhu derived from the killing. She shuddered at the thought.

After they reached their house, Thanh stayed outside and washed her bicycle while Nhu went inside and cleaned the rifle. Thanh wanted to spend as little time as possible with Nhu, and dreaded the inevitable closeness of the evening. Nhu would once again demand to be trained on the missile launcher, and Thanh would have to comply. She had gone over the procedures with the woman several times already, but for some reason Nhu just did not understand it fully. That did not bother Thanh all that much, however, for that meant Nhu would have to defer to Thanh when the time came to actually use it. Or so she hoped.

SEVEN

Nash tried not to think about what kind of bug might be crawling up his pants leg. He could feel something, that was certain. He just hoped it wasn't something poisonous. It was all he could do to resist the urge to jump up and swat at whatever it was. The mosquito buzzing around his ears didn't help either. Sweat rolled down his neck and his nose was filled with the stench of rotting vegetation. And it annoyed him that Harv and Quan, on either side of him, didn't seem to be suffering like he was.

They had been under this bush since midnight, and now it was approaching noon. Nearly twelve hours of lying motionless in a forest, and so far nothing to show for it. After visiting all the previous locations the VC sniper had used, Nash felt that he had a good handle on how the sniper chose his hides, and had scouted out possible new locations the sniper might use. His plan was to set up at these locations himself, and catch the sniper arriving. Yesterday's attempt had been a bust, so today they were trying a new possibility.

From studying the nests the sniper had used, the timing of the shootings, and traffic patterns, Nash had determined, to his own satisfaction at least, that the sniper somehow moved into position in the mornings, took his shot, and then immediately disappeared. He still had not figured out, however, how the sniper did this without being observed. Almost certainly the locals had guesses, or hints, about who the sniper was and how he operated, but so far no one had passed on these rumors to the authorities. Nash's working theory was that the sniper was one of the old farmers in the area, and he was burying his weapon the night before a shooting, retrieving it for the kill, and then immediately reburying it so he could return to the fields and innocently tend the rice plants.

A Lambretta three-wheeled mini-bus puttered by, with people hanging off the sides of the overloaded little vehicle.

"How much do you reckon he charges per person?" Harv whispered. Nash glanced over to his right, where Harv lay with his binoculars pressed to his eyes, following the departing scooter.

"One hundred piaster," Quan answered quietly, using the GI word for South Vietnamese money.

"A dollar a person, huh?" Harv mused. "I guess that could be profitable."

"Sh!" Nash admonished them. They were supposed to stay quiet, although it was unlikely anyone could hear them. They were at the edge of a finger of thick forest that came within fifty meters of the roadway. Across the road were fields and paddies. Between the forest and the road was an area that had been cleared with bulldozers, and now was covered with thick grass and small bushes and seedlings. It was a perfect place for a sniper to set up, which was why Nash had chosen it, but so far it had been a bust. Nash was beginning to think that maybe his analytical skills were not what he had thought. Or maybe the sniper had simply chosen a different location. It had been three days since the sniper had shot the mayor of Trang Bang, and he was due for another attack.

"Harv," Nash whispered, "when was the last radio check?"

Albertson glanced at his watch. "Twenty minutes ago," he answered. "Want me to do another one?"

"Yeah," Nash decided. "See if there's been anything." Harv reached back and switched on the radio, and then began murmuring into the handset. Nash wanted to know if the sniper had already struck somewhere else; if so, there was no point in lying around here.

"Nope, nothing," Harv said after a minute, switching the radio off again.

"Shit!" Nash had been sure the sniper would be active today, most likely here, but almost certainly somewhere. So far, though, it had been another quiet day, other than at the ammo cache. One of the mechanized infantry platoons had been sweeping through the forest east of there and had stumbled across a big bunker hidden in the trees. Harv had listened to the radio traffic and passed it along to

Nash and Quan. The bunker contained a bunch of ammunition of all types, including rifle and machine gun rounds, mortar rounds, RPG rounds, Bangalore torpedoes, and hand grenades. As far as Nash knew, they were still in the process of retrieving the ordnance and hauling it back to the base camp. Maybe, he thought, all that activity had dissuaded the sniper from doing anything today. Nash looked at his watch again. Maybe it was time to pack up and go home.

"Somebody's coming," Harv warned in a harsh whisper.

"Where?" Nash followed the line of Harv's binoculars, and saw two distant figures far to their right, walking down the road toward them. He could barely make them out, but he could tell they had bicycles or something, and looked to be female.

"It's a Coke kid and a sandwich mama-san," Harv said dismissively. "I think it's the same ones we saw the other day."

Nash sighed. If there were Coke kids in the area, that meant there was no sniper. Now he knew they were wasting their time. "As soon as they're gone," he announced quietly, "we'll pack up and get the fuck out of here. Harv, call in and have them send out the jeep for us."

"Roger that," Harv said with enthusiasm, and switched on the radio.

Nash continued watching the two women, and as they got closer he could see that it indeed was the two they had talked to near the place where the mayor had been killed. He briefly wondered why they were here, but realized that with the GIs tied up recovering the ammo cache, their customers were not available, so they were probably on their way home. The older woman with the scary face was pushing the sandwich cart with little effort. *She must be a strong woman,* Nash thought. The younger woman, a girl, really, was walking her bicycle, balancing the heavy box of iced sodas over the front wheel. Nash tried to remember her name.

"Yes," Quan murmured beside him. "That is Thanh. Maybe we talk to her again?"

"No," Nash reprimanded him. "She thinks we are reporters. If she sees us with guns, she'll know the truth."

The two were now nearly abreast of their location, and Nash felt a tinge of alarm when they angled across the road and onto the cleared area beside it, headed almost directly toward the sniper team. Nash looked around, seeing if they had time to back out of their position and go deeper into the woods without being seen. It didn't look promising. He couldn't let them discover the team, but he couldn't think of any way to head them off without revealing who they were. The pair was only a few meters away when Nash heard the sound of heavy vehicles approaching from the south. The older woman frowned and looked down the road, then said something to the younger one. The both turned and headed back toward the road, pushing the bicycle and cart over the rough field until they were again on the road.

They were just in time to greet a line of four armored personnel carriers, and from their shiny and clean condition, Nash knew they were ARVNs, not Americans. The lead vehicle stopped right next to the women, and the others pulled up close behind. A Vietnamese soldier wearing a starched boonie hat and pressed fatigues jumped down from the first track and swaggered over to the women.

"Is that. . .?" Harv whispered, training his binoculars on the group.

"Yes," Quan affirmed with snarl. "That is Captain Nguyen. He number TEN!"

Although Nash sometimes had trouble distinguishing individual Vietnamese soldiers, he recognized Nguyen right away by his body language, if nothing else. They had run into this nasty egomaniac in the Michelin, and Nguyen had tried to have them killed so he could take the money they had found. They hadn't been able to prove his avaricious treachery at the time, but they had managed to keep him from getting the money, something that had made him livid with anger. Nash had heard that Nguyen had been transferred, at American insistence, but didn't know where he had gone. Now he knew.

While his men sat stoically on their tracks, the diesel engines idling, Nguyen bought a sandwich and a soda. Nash was a little surprised to see that Nguyen actually paid the women. Nguyen had seemed like the kind of asshole who would simply take the food with threats. Instead he smiled at them, took the food, and ambled back to his APC. Handing the sandwich and Coke up to a sergeant to hold for him while he climbed aboard, he took his seat, took back the Coke and opened it, accepted the sandwich, and ordered the unit to move out while he had his lunch. The two women watched the APCs roar off, ignoring the plumes of dust that wafted over them, and then turned and resumed their journey to the south.

"Whoo," Harv breathed. "That was close."

"No shit," Quan said, using a favorite American expression he had picked up.

Nash relaxed. "Is the jeep coming?" he asked.

"Half an hour," Harv answered. "Where they dropped us off."

"All right," Nash said, pushing himself up. "Let's get there."

*****

Specialist Robert Crosby was in a foul mood. It had started this morning, when Sergeant Samples had noticed how dirty his uniform was.

"What the fuck, Crosby? You look like shit. Put on a clean uniform."

"This is the only one I have, Sarge. I'll wash it later."

"The only one you have? You were issued five sets when you got here."

Crosby shrugged. "The others got lost in the laundry." Once a week the men in the field would bundle up their dirty clothes and send them in to the base camp to be washed and folded by Vietnamese civilians. The clothes were tagged, but sometimes things didn't come back.

Samples rolled his eyes. "Then go to Supply and get some new ones." They had come into the Tay Ninh base camp, the new home for their battalion headquarters, yesterday evening, and the platoon was supposed to spend the entire day there doing track maintenance, with a chance to go to the EM club for a beer later. It was a welcome break from the daily grind of patrolling, outposting, and sleeping in a night laager or the fire support base.

It had taken Crosby nearly half an hour to even find the new Supply building, and when he finally did, it was still in pretty much of a mess from the move. There was a warrant officer named Gloster checking things off on a clipboard, and a Spec 4 named Donelson sorting and stacking items on the rows of shelving. Crosby went to the desk and waited for the warrant officer to notice him. After Crosby cleared his throat a couple times, Mr. Gloster looked up from his clipboard, scowled, and growled, "What do you want?"

"I need some new uniforms," Crosby told him politely. "Mine were all lost in the laundry."

The man sighed and shook his head slowly. "You're only authorized five sets. To get new ones, you have to turn in the old ones."

"But I don't have the old ones," Crosby pointed out. "They got lost. In the laundry."

"I can't help you," Gloster said unsympathetically. "Those are the rules."

Donelson, who was behind Gloster, caught Crosby's eye and made a face at Gloster's back.

"So what am I supposed to do, sir?" Crosby was getting mad, but he was talking to an officer, so he had to keep it military.

"Not my problem," Gloster said, turning away. Crosby glared at the man's back, unsure what to do next.

"You could try over at the hospital," Donelson offered. "Sometimes they have old uniforms they took off guys who were wounded."

Gloster turned sharply toward Donelson. "Those have to be turned in to Division Supply and accounted for," he scolded. "They are not for the use of soldiers who can't maintain the Army property they signed for."

"Yes, sir," Donelson replied with false contrition. When Gloster turned away again, Donelson winked at Crosby and jerked his head toward the door. Crosby nodded and left.

Stomping back to the company area, Crosby was surprised to see that his platoon was no longer there. The area around the company headquarters building was bare of anything but churned up mud. Crosby rushed into the building, where he found a buck sergeant he didn't know sitting at a desk reading a comic book. In the back room he could see the XO and the first sergeant going over some paperwork. "Where's First Platoon?" Crosby asked the sergeant, feeling a little panicky.

"Urgent mission," the sergeant said. According to the tape above his shirt pocket, his name was Kelley. "You Crosby? Samples said for you to wait here."

"Oh, heck," Crosby said, and sat down on an empty chair. "They even have my weapon."

"An M-79? I got it right here." Kelley reached around the desk and brought out the bloop gun, handing it across to Crosby, along with his ammo vest. Crosby felt a little better, because his training had made the weapon a part of him, and he felt naked without it. "So where were you?"

"Supply, but it was a waste of time." He explained his problem to the sergeant, and asked where the hospital was.

"You don't need to do that," Kelley told him. "I'm going to Long Binh tomorrow to out-process, then Oakland to ETS. You can have my old uniforms. I won't be needing them." ETS stood for Estimated Termination of Service, the day a soldier was scheduled to be discharged.

"You sure?"

"Why not? They'll just make me turn them in at Long Binh anyway."

"Well, thanks!" Crosby was truly grateful.

When Crosby returned to the Supply building, he had the four uniforms, which looked suitably worn and used. He and Kelley had removed all the sewn-on sergeant stripes and name tapes, and randomly ripped the shirts and pants to make them unusable. As a final touch, Crosby had dropped them in the mud outside and jumped on them until they were filthy. Mr. Gloster was leaning his elbows on the counter reading a paper while Donelson neatly stacked some poncho liners on a shelf.

"Here's four uniforms to exchange," Crosby told Gloster, with just a hint of defiance. Gloster picked each item up and inspected it closely before dropping it on the floor behind the counter. He shot Crosby a dirty look, and then turned to Donelson.

"Okay, give him four new sets. And be sure you fill out the paperwork. I'm going to the mess hall." Gloster kicked some of the old uniforms out of the way, came around the counter, and strode out the front door.

"What a douche bag!" Donelson grumbled as soon as Gloster was out of earshot. "What size do you need?

Crosby told him, and Donelson went down a row of shelves poked around. He finally brought out a stack shirts and a stack of pants. "Try these on," he said. Crosby took a shirt and a pair of pants over into a corner of the building and turned his back to Donelson while he undressed. He wasn't wearing underwear, and wanted at least the semblance of privacy. When he put the new uniform on, he was surprised at how well it fit. It was an old joke that in the Army everything came in only one size—too big, but this uniform fit like it had been tailored for him.

"These are perfect!" Crosby marveled.

"Give me the one you were wearing, and I'll exchange it too." While Donelson went to the back to get another set, Crosby removed all his stuff from the pockets of his old uniform, and the rank pins from the collar. He had recently been promoted to Specialist Fourth Class, and was proud of his new rank pins. He'd have to go over to the PX tailor to have new name tapes made and sewn on, along with Combat Infantryman Badges and division patches. But having five brand new uniforms, and ones that were exactly the right size, was worth the expense. He handed the old uniform to Donelson, who tossed it on the floor with the others.

"What else do you need?" Donelson asked. "With the move, the inventory will be all fucked up anyway, and he'll never notice. How about a new poncho?"

"Sure," Crosby told him. "Mine's got a rip in it."

Donelson retrieved a neatly folded poncho still wrapped in clear plastic and put it on top of the folded uniforms. "We're running a special on helmets," he joked, reaching under the counter and coming up with helmet, complete with camouflage cover and elastic band. "It's even got a chin strap," Donelson pointed out, lifting the helmet up with one hand while he flicked the canvas straps with the other. Chin straps were virtually unheard of among the infantry in Viet Nam; the environment made them quickly rot and fall apart.

Crosby took it and set it on his head. The inside headband was already the correct size, so he snapped the chin strap and wiggled his head. "Nice," Crosby said appreciatively.

"It's yours," Donelson said. "You need it more than he does."

Crosby hastily took off the helmet and looked closely at the front of it to see if it had a rank insignia there.

"No," Donelson said, "it's not the one he wears. But he thinks everything in here is his. I'll make sure the books balance. Don't worry about it."

"Wow," Crosby said, admiring his new helmet. "Say, do you have any of those two-quart bladder canteens?" He had seen one carried by a regular foot-slogging infantryman, and liked the idea of carrying more water than the one-quart hard plastic canteen he had been issued.

"I wish," Donelson said. "I've been trying to get some, but they all go to the leg units. Sorry."

"No sweat. This stuff will do me fine anyway." Crosby put the helmet back on, picked up the stack of uniforms with the new poncho, and said, "Thanks again."

"I used to be in the field myself," Donelson told him. "I know what it's like. But they stuck me here with Mr. Asshole. You better be gone before he gets back, though. Don't worry about the paperwork, I'll sign it for you. Go ahead, take off."

Grinning, Crosby left the building and made his way back to the company area. He might have missed the platoon's departure, but he had made a haul of good stuff. He decided he would add one of his new black Spec 4 pins to the front of his new helmet, like officers did with their rank pins. Now he just had to figure out how to get back to the platoon. Maybe he could hitch a ride with someone. Just as he reached the company headquarters building, the first few raindrops began hitting his shoulder. It looked like he would be using his new poncho even sooner than he had thought.

*****

The rain drummed on the tin roof, or what was left of it, and water dripped everywhere. Thanh had her conical straw hat on, which deflected most of the drops, but her sandal-clad feet were getting soaked. She huddled in the driest corner, tired and dispirited, while Nhu stood in the doorway watching the road, with her rifle, wrapped in a sheet of plastic, lying on a wobbly old table next to her. The bicycle and the sandwich cart were parked in the back of the room, water glistening on every surface. They had been in this abandoned farmhouse for over two hours, and Thanh was ready to go home, even if it meant walking in the downpour.

They had gone out this morning for their usual day of selling to American soldiers, and Thanh had been hoping they would meet up with Robert again, but that hadn't happened. In fact, around midmorning, all the soldiers they saw had dropped what they were doing and sped off somewhere to the east. Later she had heard distant gunfire. She guessed that fellow soldiers of the North Vietnamese Army had ambushed an American convoy or something. She hoped that no one she knew, on either side, would be killed. She and Nhu had wandered up and down the road, but had found no customers, and when the rain came they had taken shelter in this old house just off the road.

When the rain showed no signs of letting up, Nhu had pulled her rifle out of the cart's secret compartment and loaded a magazine. "Perhaps we will have a target here," she said with an evil smile. "I was not planning to kill any of the devils today, but perhaps now I will."

Thanh hoped no suitable victim would appear today. The killing of the National Policeman and his mistress had sickened her, and she desperately wanted to avoid being in the presence of such violent death again. She was aware of the contradiction: she was a soldier, just like Nhu, who was sworn to kill her enemy, but she no longer had the heart for it. She was still prepared to carry out her mission, because it promised to end the war completely, but she hated the thought of these individual assassinations that just prolonged the conflict.

Traffic was light on this rainy afternoon, and Thanh had seen no civilians at all. Whenever there was major combat occurring in the area, the people knew to stay home, to avoid being caught up in the violence. The only military traffic they had seen had been large trucks and occasional armored vehicles, none of which were suitable targets for Nhu's Dragunov.

"Wait here," Nhu commanded Thanh, and darted out the door into the sheets of rain. Thanh moved to the doorway to watch what the older woman was doing. Nhu found a section of corrugated tin with pieces of wooden roof beam still attached, and lifted it experimentally. The wreckage was about three meters long, but Nhu was able to lift it with little effort. She took one end and dragged it across the farmyard and out onto the road. Looking up and down the road first, she moved the debris around to get the maximum blockage, and then hurried back to the farmhouse, pushing Thanh back in.

"That should do it," she said with satisfaction.

Thanh heard the sound of an engine approaching. It sounded like a jeep or a small truck of some sort. Nhu heard it, too, and quickly unwrapped her rifle. Moving to the only window on that side of the house, she crouched down and rested the barrel of the rifle on the sill. At Nhu's insistence, Thanh pressed her back against the wall just inside the doorway, peering around the frame to see what was going to happen. The rain blurred the air and made it hard to see any distance, but at last she picked out the shape of a jeep approaching from the north. When the driver saw the makeshift barricade across the road, he immediately skidded to a halt.

The jeep had its windshield up and had a canvas roof erected. The windshield wipers slowly swept back and forth, and Thanh could just make out that there were two people in the jeep, and they seemed to be discussing what they should do next. Other than the mud it had picked up driving on the highway, the jeep was clean and well maintained, indicating to Thanh that it probably belonged to a high-ranking officer. And that meant that the passenger would be an attractive target for Nhu. She heard Nhu chortle under her breath, confirming her suspicion.

After a short discussion, the passenger of the jeep got out and looked around. He was wearing a helmet and a poncho, both of which looked brand new, confirming to Thanh that he must be a senior officer. She could just make out a black rank pin on the front of the helmet, and she knew that meant he was a colonel of some sort. The man stuck his head into the jeep and spoke to the driver again, and then began walking toward the pile of wood and tin. He had only taken a few steps when Thanh's ears were assaulted by the explosive report of Nhu's rifle, the bang reverberating inside the brick walls of the house. Thanh saw the man's helmet fly backwards and his hands go up, and then he fell backwards on stiff legs and plopped onto the muddy roadway. The jeep driver shouted something to the fallen man, and when he got no response, he put the vehicle into gear and spun the steering wheel, throwing up a spray of mud as he turned the jeep in a tight circle and roared away back the direction he had come.

Thanh stood staring in shock at the still body in the road. While she had seen people killed before, something about this particular death gripped her stomach in a knot. The man had been unarmed, and the deliberateness of Nhu's shot seemed unfair and unwarranted. Suppressing a sob, she turned to look despairingly at the woman, who was picking up the empty shell casing.

Nhu bit her lip as if making a difficult decision. "I want to go look at him, and see who he is," she explained to Thanh, voicing the decision process, "but the driver got away, and will quickly bring others back here. So we must move quickly. Get your bicycle." Anxious to escape from the horrible scene, Thanh did as directed. She pushed her bicycle out into the rain and across the yard to the road, not waiting for Nhu. She was fifty meters down the road before Nhu could catch up with her, running as she pushed the cart ahead of her.

When Nhu finally came abreast of Thanh, she matched Thanh's pace and took a few deep breaths. "That was good," she said with satisfaction. "A perfect head shot. Did you see that?"

Thanh shuddered, but could only nod.

"That was a colonel, I am sure," Nhu said. "Only colonels get such nice jeeps with tops and windshields. I wonder which one he was?"

Thanh, unable to speak, just shook her head. She didn't want to be reminded of the image that was burned into her brain of the man's head exploding in a bloody spray. Her stomach churned, and she knew that if she had eaten anything lately, it would be coming back up right now. As much as possible, she drew away from Nhu, who was chuckling with self-satisfaction. Thanh had never liked Nhu, but now she totally despised the woman. The only saving grace was that her mission was supposed to end in the next few days, and then she could return to her mother up north.

EIGHT

First Lieutenant Stephen Carr held his helmet on as he jumped down from the top of the armored personnel carrier. With no chin strap, he had to keep one hand on it, to keep it from flying off in mid-air and cracking him on the head when he landed. After landing with a jarring thud, he readjusted his pistol belt, Claymore bag full of magazines, and his rifle, before striding out a ways from the line of tracked vehicles that stretched down the road. All around him other soldiers were dismounting and gathering together in loose gaggles waiting for someone to give them orders. And that someone, Carr acknowledged, was himself.

"All right!" he hollered, "spread out, get on line." Casually, but quickly, the men followed his orders, chattering among themselves and repositioning their gear. The entire company was here, stretching down the narrow dirt road, with all the tracks facing toward the right side of the road. Behind the vehicles stretched an almost endless checkerboard of rice paddies, flooded and green with new shoots. In front, however, was a plain of high amber grasses spotted with small groves of trees and low thickets. Over his head helicopters circled and swooped. And in the near distance loomed the conical dark shape of Nui Ba Den, the Black Virgin. The mountain was the only elevation in the area, rising above the surrounding flat terrain like a new volcanic island in the middle of the Pacific. Although it was miles away, it dominated the area, not only because of its size and shape, but also because of its military significance. While the Americans controlled, mostly, the surrounding flatlands, and had a permanent radio-relay camp on the peak, the slopes of the mountain were entirely controlled by the communists. The steep rocky and shrub-covered flanks hid a vast network of caves and man-made bunkers infested with Viet Cong and North Vietnamese regulars who had easily repelled all American attempts to dislodge them. Fortunately, Carr thought, their mission today did not involve the mountain.

Carr looked down the line to his left and saw Sergeant First Class Samples, his platoon sergeant, anchoring the far end of the platoon. After an initial rocky start when Carr arrived in April, he and the feisty sergeant become close friends who worked extremely well together. Samples caught his eye and signaled they were all ready. A glance to his right revealed the rest of the company stretching for a couple hundred yards. Third platoon was next to his, and he nodded at Lieutenant Masters, their new platoon leader. Beyond Masters was the headquarters platoon, with Captain Gordon, the temporary company commander, and at the far end of the line was second platoon, whose new leader was Lieutenant Zee. Captain Raymond, their official company commander, was on R&R in Hawaii, and the battalion commander had tasked Gordon to replace him for the time being. Carr didn't really know Gordon, but so far had not been terribly impressed with the man. Gordon was very average looking, with short brown hair and a slight build. He spoke with a southern accent, when he spoke at all, and had seemed a little indecisive. Carr realized the young man was new in country and unexpectedly placed in a command position, so he gave him the benefit of the doubt. He wondered, however, how Gordon had made captain at such a young age without any previous combat experience. Carr guessed that Gordon was related to some general or politician.

Gordon gave a big wave of his left arm and then pointed forward, signaling that the sweep should begin. Raggedly the long line of men surged forward, pushing their way through the high grass with their weapons at the ready, but clearly not expecting any real danger. Carr watched his men move out, noting that they didn't look too bad and were mostly staying on line. He saw Samples admonish one of the newer members of the platoon for not keeping up, and the young man quickly complied. Specialist Eberhart, the platoon's radio-telephone operator, was just to his left, pressing the black plastic handset to his ear as he monitored all the company radio traffic. "Second platoon ran into a ditch," Eberhart informed him. "CO told them to catch up."

Carr nodded. His own platoon was wading through the waist-high grass heading toward a small clump of low trees. The company's APCs were slowly following the dismounted men, about twenty meters behind. The men would have to be careful when they reached the trees, since it would be a good place for the VC to be hiding. That is, if there were any VC around here. The company had been sent to this location because of some intelligence reports that a VC sniper had been spotted in the area. The battalion's Area of Operations—AO—had been unusually quiet the last couple weeks, and any indication of enemy activity, no matter how dubious, generated a massive over-reaction. Thus they had a company-wide sweep, at least three helicopters, and reportedly an ARVN company approaching from the southeast in a pincer movement. Carr hoped someone was keeping a close eye on the ARVNs. The Army of the Republic of Viet Nam was not highly regarded by most of the American soldiers, and had a reputation for firing wildly at the slightest excuse. Carr worried that the two allied forces might meet up unexpectedly and end up shooting at each other.

Meanwhile they slogged on across the countryside, looking for something more interesting than an abandoned hut and an occasional snake. Behind them the tracks trailed at a snail's pace, ready to back them up if they did indeed make contact. The sun beat down, the gnats swirled around their heads, and the day dragged on. At noon they broke for lunch, the men taking turns to go back to the tracks and rummage through the open case of C-rations to find their favorite meal, or at least the one they found the least distasteful.

Carr opened a can of ham slices with his P-38 can opener, draining off the excess juices. Then he opened a can of the round crackers and made small sandwiches, eating them without really tasting them, which, he had found, was the best way to do it. He squatted next to a large bush, trying to get at least a minimal amount of shade. Eberhart, walking back from the track gnawing on a non-melting chocolate bar, said, "Choppers are leaving."

Carr had not really noticed the diminished sound from the sky, but now he did. "Are they coming back?" he asked.

Eberhart shrugged. "Don't think so. Sounded like they didn't want to waste any more fuel looking for a ghost."

"I can understand that," Carr said, standing up. "What about us?" Eberhart, with his ear to all the radio traffic, knew or inferred everything that was going on in the company, and usually knew more than the company commander.

"I'm guessing another couple hours," Eberhart ventured. "There's nothing else for us to do. And like my drill sergeant always said, it's *gooooood* training."

Carr nodded. That sounded about right. They would continue sweeping the vacant countryside, knowing that if there actually had been a sniper out here, he would be long gone by now. Then, when everyone was really tired and bored, they would let the company return to the fire support base, just in time to miss the evening meal at the mess tent. And then they would probably have to send out an ambush patrol. It was times like these when Carr wished they would actually make contact with the enemy, just to relieve the boredom.

Samples walked up and took off his helmet to wipe his forehead. His short sandy hair was matted down by sweat. "I'm putting Kirk back on the track," he informed Carr. "Stupid shit's got a blister on his right foot." Samples shook his head in disgust.

"Dirty socks?" Carr asked, knowing the answer.

"Hasn't changed them for a week. What's this world coming to?"

"Daily sock inspections?" Carr suggested lightly.

"I guess so," Samples answered morosely. "How much longer we gonna be out here?"

"Eberhart thinks about two more hours."

"Makes sense. When you're totally wasting your time, you might as well waste as much as possible."

Carr noticed Samples gaze shift, and turned to see Harry Masters approaching. The young lieutenant had saved Carr's and Samples' butts a few weeks earlier in the Boi Loi Woods, and they were both very grateful.

"How's it going?" Masters asked, smiling.

"Same-same as always," Carr replied. "Great day for a stroll in the weeds."

"Exactly." Masters tilted his head toward the distant figure of Captain Gordon. "What do you think about our fearless leader?"

"I've seen worse," Carr said without conviction.

"I had to explain map coordinates to him this morning," Masters griped. "How did he get to be a captain anyway?"

"It's who you know or who you blow," Samples offered.

Masters scoffed. "I think I know which one it was in his case."

"Now, now, Harry," Carr chided him. "If you can't say something nice. . ."

"Right. Okay." Masters pretended to ponder the issue, with one finger touching his chin. "Well he does put his boots on the correct feet most of the time."

"See," Carr joked, "that wasn't so hard." All three laughed.

"So when will Captain Raymond be back?" Masters asked.

"Four more days," Samples responded. "Not that anyone is counting."

Eberhart interrupted. "Sir? We're moving out now."

"Talk to you later," Masters said and hurried away to join his own platoon.

"Get 'em moving," Carr told Samples, tossing his last, uneaten sandwich into the bushes.

An hour later the word came down that the ARVNs to their southeast had made contact. Carr hadn't heard any shots, and wondered just how much contact they had encountered. Regardless, the company was told to mount up and prepare to move out quickly. Carr climbed up on his track and did a visual headcount of the men on the other personnel carriers of his platoon. Satisfied that everyone was accounted for, he listened for the command from

Captain Gordon to blare out on the track's big radio mounted inside, just below him. Eberhart, sitting on the other side of the track, still had the handset clamped to the side of his face, where he could hear it better over the noise of the engine and track blocks. Sergeant Montoya, the squad leader for the one-three, sat directly in front of him wearing a CVC helmet which contained headphones and a small microphone, allowing him to communicate with Aiello, the driver, by intercom while simultaneously monitoring the radio traffic. Behind him sat Doc Allman, the platoon medic, and behind the 50-cal machine gun sat PFC Merrill. The new guy, Handleman, sat behind Eberhart. As was normal practice in Viet Nam, everyone but the driver rode on top of the vehicle, using strapped-down ammo crates and cans as seats. Not only was it too hot to ride inside, but the danger was greater should the vehicle be hit by an RPG or landmine, which would pepper the interior with molten metal. In such cases, the driver was pretty much SOL, which was why most drivers cranked up their seats so that they drove with much of their upper body exposed.

He saw Captain Gordon's track lurch forward and heard the command to move out, but that was followed by a garbled instruction about the azimuth. Carr looked over at Eberhart with a puzzled expression.

"He said move out on a one-seventy degree azimuth," Eberhart elucidated. "Platoons on line, but squads in column."

It took Carr a second to figure out what Gordon meant. Each platoon would form up in a column, the four tracks one behind the other, and the lead track of each platoon would be travelling parallel to the commander. It wasn't the standard formation for this sort of operation, but not unreasonable. He picked up the porkchop mike hanging off the side of the machine gun turret and waited for a break in the jumble of commands that filled the company frequency. When it came, he quickly told the other three tracks the march order, and then tapped Montoya on the shoulder to let him know Aiello could start moving out. As the one-three plunged forward into the grass, the other three tracks fell into line behind it. Soon there were four relatively neat columns of APCs sailing through the sea of yellow grass, occasionally curving around larger clumps of bushes or trees, and all heading in a generally southern direction.

They had gone less than a kilometer when the radio whined as it spun up and Gordon's voice barked out a new order, one which Carr, again, didn't understand. "Now we're shifting to a ninety-five azimuth," Eberhart explained with a raised eyebrow. That meant a shift to almost directly east. The four columns of vehicles swung to the left and raggedly got back on line, Carr's first platoon slowing way down to let the other platoons catch up. Carr decided Gordon must have gotten corrected coordinates from Battalion. Now they were headed directly toward Nui Ba Den. It was still a couple miles away, but Carr began to worry they might end up there.

After about ten minutes, the radio crackled again, and this time Carr heard the command clearly. Gordon told them to now move out on a 230 degree azimuth, which was virtually the opposite direction of their current heading. This led to mass confusion, as no one was sure if they should do a massive wheeling movement to one side or the other, or should each platoon simply do a J-turn and resume the formation on the opposite side of the commander from before. Gordon himself didn't seem certain how he wanted them to achieve this course correction, so Carr stepped in before things got totally out of hand.

"Each platoon, to the rear march," he ordered over the radio, providing the simple directions the drivers needed to complete the unusual maneuver. Now knowing what was required of them, the drivers of the lead track in each platoon did a sharp turn to the left until they were headed roughly west and passed down the line of the other tracks in the platoon, each of which followed suit. In two minutes the entire company was headed in the new direction, back on line and running smoothly. Again, Carr gave Gordon the benefit of the doubt, since the man had never been in command of a mechanized company before. The new course, however, left Carr very confused. Had the ARVNs broken contact and no longer needed their support? Was the company heading back to the road and eventually to the fire support base or base camp? Gordon had not uttered a single word since pronouncing the new azimuth. Carr wondered if the man felt ashamed that he had to have a platoon leader give the proper orders, or perhaps he was in deep discussion with Battalion on the other frequency.

At least they were heading away from the mountain, Carr thought. Presumably they were headed to the FSB, although technically the camp was directly south of them. The quickest route, however, might be to head west until they intersected a road that would lead them eventually to the protection of the concertina, berm, and bunkers. Twenty minutes later his supposition was contradicted by a new order.

"Zero one five" Gordon ordered succinctly, with no explanation. Carr looked across at Eberhart, who surprised expression probably mirrored Carr's own. "Zero one five?" Eberhart mouthed. That was just east of due north. Now Carr was totally confused.

The company wheeled around, with first platoon acting as the pivot point, and assumed the new heading. Montoya turned around and gave Carr a questioning look. All Carr could do was shrug. They pushed on across the plain, and Carr began to worry as the number of trees and bushes increased, forcing them to detour around them more often and temporarily lose sight of the rest of the company. A good way to get ambushed, he thought, except for the fact that the enemy had no way of knowing where they were headed. Hell, no one seemed to know where they were headed.

Finally the company rolled into a broad area of low grass surrounded by trees, and Gordon called a halt. "Fifteen minute break in place," came the order over the radio. Everyone began climbing down to stretch their legs and get a drink of water. Sergeant Samples sent a few men out to the tree line in their sector to guard the approaches, and the other platoon sergeants did the same. Sergeant Montoya, having left his CVC helmet on top, walked around to the opposite side of the track and squatted down to take advantage of what little shade it provided. Aiello climbed out of the driver's compartment without his helmet and immediately removed his shirt, revealing the nice even tan he had on his thin upper body.

Doc Allman came over and stood next to Carr, looking across the grass at the command track. "What the fuck, over?" Allman said quietly. Captain Gordon had disappeared inside his track and was nowhere to be seen. Carr didn't answer, because he didn't know either. He kept expecting the commander to call for the platoon leaders to confer, but so far he had not.

Carr looked over at Eberhart, who was leaning against the side of the track with a bemused expression, the handset, as always, pressed to his ear. When Eberhart saw Carr's questioning look, he just shook his head. Carr took a swig of water from his canteen and pondered the ways of the Army. It was an old maxim that there are three ways of doing things: the right way, the wrong way, and the Army way. Carr had no idea what they were doing, or why, and Captain Gordon didn't seem inclined to share his thoughts. As commander, that was certainly his prerogative, but Carr didn't approve.

After exactly fifteen minutes the order came over the radio, "Mount up!" Gordon rose up through the cargo hatch of his track and climbed onto his seat. The rest of the company took their places and the idling engines of the tracks were blipped a couple times as if clearing their throats. "The new heading is one hundred twenty degrees," Gordon intoned over the radio. Carr looked to the sky for a moment and sighed. East south-east. Back toward Nui Ba Den. He checked his watch. They only had a couple more hours of daylight. The company pivoted around first platoon again and left the clearing, dodging around the thickets as if they actually knew where they were going. After only five minutes, Carr was surprised to hear a familiar voice on the radio—the battalion commander.

"Seven-seven Tango, this is Papa Seven-seven, over." The colonel was calling on the company frequency, and not on the battalion freq to which the command track kept tuned on a second radio. That in itself was unusual. It also meant the entire company could hear what he had to say, and he didn't sound happy.

There was a long pause before Gordon answered. "This is Seven-seven Tango Charlie, over."

"Where the fuck are you?" Carr was surprised at the bluntness of the question.

There was another long pause as Gordon apparently told his driver to stop. Using hand signals, the captain's RTO told the rest of the company to halt as well. "This is Seven-seven Tango. I believe we are at Chevrolet plus two right. Over."

Carr winced. They had stopped using the automobile checkpoint system three weeks ago. It had been replaced by a beer-name system that everyone was supposed to have used to update their maps. Apparently Gordon hadn't gotten the memo.

"Bullshit," the colonel said. "Give me your exact coordinates. To hell with security."

"Wait one," Gordon replied meekly. Carr stared at the surrounding countryside, keeping his face bland so he didn't reveal to the men under him how worried he was getting. Finally the radio squawked again. Gordon read of a series of numbers and letters. There was a long pause before the colonel came back on the radio.

"Say again, over," the battalion commander ordered, his anger evident. Gordon repeated the coordinates.

"Do you see any buildings or other landmarks?" the colonel asked.

"Uh, no, sir," Gordon answered.

"Well, that's fucking strange, because the coordinates you gave me are for downtown Dau Tieng. Jesus H. Christ, Gordon. Where are you really? Never mind, I'll find you. Just stay put. Out."

A minute later Gordon came on the radio and addressed the entire company: "Men, uh, hold fast at your current location. Out." As if the command wasn't redundant.

"Better put out some O.P.s," Carr added on the radio. Gordon didn't answer, but each platoon leader, knowing that was standard procedure, sent pairs of men out into the brush to watch and listen for the approach of any enemy forces.

Like many of the other men, Carr stood up to stretch and look around. To his left the other three columns of armored personnel carriers sat idling, the men obviously bored but used to the usual

Army "hurry up and wait." Carr turned to the rear and surveyed his own platoon lined up behind him. Some of the men took advantage of the break to drink from their canteens or smoke a cigarette, and on the last track Samples stood up scanning the countryside, alert to any unusual sights or sounds. Carr couldn't help but notice how long were the shadows cast by the boxy tracked vehicles. It was getting late, and he didn't want to have to find their way home in the dark.

Carr saw Sergeant Samples' head jerk to the south as he turned and looked up at the sky. Then Carr heard it, too. A helicopter was approaching. In moments the loach—light observation helicopter—was circling overhead. As promised, Colonel Duran had located the company. He didn't land, as Carr had expected, but made two wide circles, and then a hand reached out the side and dropped a small canister. Before it even hit the ground, the device started spewing thick yellow smoke, bouncing before it settled in the grass directly to the west of the formation. The chopper then flew a several hundred yards further to the west and dropped a second smoke bomb, this one purple in color. Instantly Carr understood the colonel's intent—he was marking a trail for Gordon to follow out of the wilderness. Carr unsuccessfully tried to stifle a smirk.

"Wheel left, follow me," came the order from Gordon over the radio. In response to shouts the guards ran back in from their outposts and jumped on board, and then the formation swung to the left, with Carr's platoon on the outside of the wheel this time. With a line of smoke plumes to guide them, the drivers had no problem maintaining the right direction, and the four columns of tracks rolled across the plain at relatively high speed, now that they knew just where they were going. He heard Allman snickering behind him, and he could see the grin on Eberhart's face, but as the leader Carr had to maintain decorum and pretend this was a normal procedure. And it was, sort of. It was the perfect illustration of the old acronym SNAFU—situation normal: all fucked up.

Within thirty minutes the company reached a dirt road, and the colonel, finally convinced Gordon knew where to go now, zoomed off in the chopper back to the fire support base. With little instruction the many tracks formed a line on the road and headed south. Carr wasn't happy that his platoon was tail-end Charlie, eating the dust of the rest of the company, but at least they were on their way home for the night. He wondered what the colonel would be saying to Gordon in the privacy of the command bunker, but his imagination failed him. Carr would be very surprised if Gordon retained his command for even the few days left until Captain Raymond returned.

NINE

    A single red light bulb hung from a roof beam, its dim crimson illumination suffusing the interior of the barracks building just enough to make out the crowd of figures jostling around between the bunks. Nash tugged at Harv's radio and backpack straps to ensure they were secure, while Quan did the same for his. Then Harv checked Quan's pack, as Nash mentally went over his checklist: weapons, ammo, water, C-rations, binoculars, maps, compass, starlight scope, ponchos, and spare batteries. There was probably something he was forgetting, but they would just have to manage without it. He felt a little out of place, because he didn't know the other men in the room, who were also loading up and checking their packs. Those men were exchanging gripes and jokes, laughing and playfully shoving each other, because they were all in the same platoon and knew each other well. Nash had only been introduced to their platoon sergeant, an E-7 named Nixon, but that was all Nash really needed to know. His sniper team would be going out with this ambush patrol, but only until they were well away from the populated areas of Tay Ninh.

    Once they were all in the countryside, Nash and his two buddies would peel off quietly and march independently to the site where Nash suspected the sniper would strike next. He sat down on one of the cots and pulled a map from his pants cargo pocket, spreading it across his knees. The red light made it hard to read, changing the colors and blurring the fine lines, but Nash had studied it enough in the daylight to remember what it should look like. They would leave the main gate of the base camp and then veer southeast, avoiding the shops and houses of Tay Ninh City, until they were out into farm country. With the curfew, they should see no one, except possibly some Viet Cong, for civilians were forbidden to travel at night. When Nash had discussed the route with Sergeant Nixon, they had settled on a small patch of woods as the place where they would diverge. From there the ambush patrol would continue on south to a larger forest area, while Nash and his team would veer east toward Highway One. Nash traced the route with his finger, but before he could point to their ultimate destination the red light was extinguished, and Nixon's voice boomed out into the room.

"Okay, drop your cocks and grab your socks. It's time to earn your pay, such as it is. Skip, you're on point, and I'll be right behind you. Clark, you're behind me. The rest of you stay in line and don't get lost. You sniper guys, you'll be last. Any questions?"

"Where we goin', Sarge?" someone asked.

"The boonies. Where'd you think?" A couple guys chuckled appreciatively.

"Please, Mr. Custer, I don't want to go," another voice sang off-key. From the lack of reaction, Nash guessed that the song had been sung many times before.

"All right, let's move out. Maintain your interval."

With only some quiet muttering the men shuffled toward the door. Nash, Harv, and Quan waited until all the other men were outside until they followed. Nash squirmed a little to get his pack settled on his shoulders as he hurried to catch up to the last man of the AP. He glanced back and saw the dim dark shapes of Harv and Quan right behind him, then nodded in satisfaction. They had a long night of walking ahead of them, but he was optimistic about their chances this time. For reasons he couldn't define, he was convinced that he would catch the sniper tomorrow.

The building they had met in was near the main gate, and it took the line of men only a few minutes to reach the opening in the berm line. The gate guards pulled open the barbed wire and watched silently as the ambush patrol filed through. "Is that it?" one of the guards whispered as Nash's team passed.

"Yep," Harv answered. The guard nodded and began pulling the concertina wire back across the road. There was a three-quarter moon rising, and visibility was fairly good, especially for the rainy season. Clouds might move in later, but for now it was easy for Nash to keep up with the patrol and simultaneously watch where he was putting his feet. The line of heavily laden soldiers walked down the middle of the road for a couple hundred yards before turning sharply across a vacant field and heading south. Nash could see scattered buildings, some of which had flickering lights behind closed curtains, but they were all far enough away that they posed no immediate danger.

Silently the men trudged through an area of high grass and low bushes, around stands of bamboo and occasional trees, and soon left the houses far behind. Surrounded by the dark, Nash was alone with his thoughts, wondering again what he was doing here. A year ago he had been a recent high school graduate in northern New Mexico, cruising with his friends, sneaking beers, and enjoying life. Now he was a soldier in a foreign land, traipsing through the dark on a mission to try and kill the enemy. He felt like he was the same carefree youth he had been a year ago, but knew that he had to have changed. Yes, he had gone hunting in the mountains with his dad, but that wasn't the same. The deer and elk hadn't been shooting back, and they weren't actual humans. Now he was killing people, and his Catholic upbringing told him he should feel extremely guilty about it. Yet somehow he didn't, and that worried him.

As they slogged through the mud of an abandoned rice paddy, Nash tried to analyze his feelings, but only got more confused, so he pushed those thoughts aside. Marching a long distance at night, carrying a heavy pack and a rifle, through the residual heat and humidity of the typical Vietnamese day, was not a pleasant experience by any means. It was drudgery and discomfort, with mosquitoes and disgusting odors adding their own torments, but deep in his chest Nash felt a tingle of excitement. Despite the annoyances and exertion, it was also an adventure. It was like actually living a scene from a movie. He wasn't just a drifting aimless teenager anymore; he was a man with a mission, a real man who did real and significant things. And what gave him the most satisfaction was that he no longer felt constant fear. While he was sometime temporarily scared, it quickly went away, and fright did not affect his actions. He wasn't a coward, and knowing that gave him great contentment.

After an hour they reached the grove of trees he and Sergeant Nixon had agreed upon, where Nash and his team took a short break in the woods while Nixon's men continued on south without them. When the ambush patrol had faded away into the night, Nash led Harv and Quan out to the east.

Skirting around farmhouses far enough to avoid setting off any dogs barking, and walking along paddy dikes to keep from splashing water, Nash steered his team across the quiet countryside, the pale moonlight providing enough silver illumination to make the going fairly easy. By midnight they had reached Highway One southeast of Tay Ninh. To their north, a halo of vapor lights circled the peak of the dark hulking mountain, Nui Ba Den. Nash knelt by the side of the road to get his bearings. They had scouted this section of the highway a week ago, but that had been in the daytime, and everything looked different at night.

"Is this it?" Harv asked softly.

"Not sure," Nash answered. "Quan, what do you think?"

Quan moved up and squatted down beside Nash. Nash saw the young Vietnamese man's head swiveling back and forth. Then he shook his head sharply. "Not here," he said. "Down there." He pointed to the south. Nash trusted the scout's opinion, especially at night. Quan's night vision was far superior to his and Harv's.

"How far?" he asked.

"Half click, maybe," Quan said. "Big trees, that side."

"Okay," Nash said, standing up. He turned and headed away from the road before turning south, confident that the other two would follow him. Walking down the middle of the road would be faster, but it would leave them too exposed. He didn't think the sniper positioned himself at night, but he couldn't be sure, and there might be other VC out as well, setting up an ambush. Paralleling the road, the three men cautiously travelled through paddies, pastures, and bamboo thickets. As they crossed an open area, Nash heard a snort and immediately froze. He slowly lowered himself into a kneeling position and raised his rifle to his shoulder. Behind him Harv and Quan did the same. The sound had come from their right, so Nash moved his head and eyes in short steps from left to right, concentrating on his peripheral vision, which was better at night than his direct sight. On the far side of the field, in the shadow of a tree, he saw a black menacing shape that seemed to be swaying slightly, although there was no breeze.

Quan snickered. "Buffalo," he said. And then the shape resolved itself in Nash's eyes, and he saw the broad horns. He exhaled and slowly rose to a standing position. It wasn't the enemy, but they still had to be careful. Water buffalo, for some reason, did not like Americans. While they could easily be bullied by small Vietnamese children with a stick, they would charge American soldiers at the slightest provocation. Nash certainly didn't need such a confrontation right now. Keeping an eye on the hopefully sleeping animal, they continued their trek, and Nash didn't feel safe until they had passed through a thicket and were out of sight of the dangerous creature.

"Here," Quan announced a few minutes later. They stopped while Nash looked around. The dark ribbon of the highway was a couple hundred meters away, with a tree line barely visible on the other side. On this side there were mostly open fields, except for a small thicket of bamboo and bushes alongside a ditch that had at one time channeled water to rice paddies that were long abandoned. It all clicked in Nash's mind. He remembered this spot well. While posing as reporters, Nash and his team had accompanied a mechanized platoon as it guarded engineers clearing the road with mine detectors. While the engineers swept their devices back and forth inches above the roadway, the infantrymen had spread out on either side to provide security and look for any indications of an ambush. He had jotted down the location in his "reporter's notebook."

On the far side of the road the forest only came within a couple hundred meters of the thoroughfare; in between the land had been cleared to provide a buffer area. Nash had noted that when the platoon had swept through this section, they penetrated several yards into the forest, looking for signs of an ambush, but had mostly ignored the thicket on this side of the road. Bamboo had long leaves with very sharp edges, and the thicket was on the opposite side of the ditch. To thoroughly check the thicket the soldiers would have had to wade through the muddy channel, climb the slippery bank, and risk deep paper-cuts to probe the stand of bamboo. The small size of the thicket, and vast open terrain around it, made it an unlikely place for the enemy to hide. For Nash, however, this made it perfect.

He felt sure that the sniper would avoid the thicket for many of the same reasons a larger enemy force would. For the sniper, in particular, the lack of an exit route would be the biggest problem. While the sniper had, in the past, always chosen targets that were unaccompanied, in locations far from any reaction force, he could not depend on that always being the case. He needed to be able to make his shot and then quickly disappear without anyone seeing him. The other side of the road, however, offered a much better opportunity. That stretch of woods, Nash knew from maps and recon, went back nearly a mile, with one arm that curved around back toward the road farther south. The sniper could approach through the woods, set up somewhere in the tree line, take a shot at someone on the highway, and disappear back through the woods without ever being seen. It was a perfect location, and Nash was a little surprised the sniper hadn't already used it. Perhaps, he thought, this would be the day.

"This way," Nash told the other two, and led them to an area south of the thicket, where he remembered seeing an easier way to cross the ditch. Here the banks had partially collapsed, damming up the old aqueduct but providing a muddy saddle over which they could cross. Helping each other with their free hands, they scrambled across the ditch and regrouped on the solid ground just beyond. Nash rubbed his boots in the tall grass to remove some of the mud that had accumulated on his feet and then led the team back north to the thicket. If he remembered correctly, there was an opening in the clump of bushes and bamboo on the side opposite from the ditch, and thus not facing the road either. He found it with the help of the bright moonlight.

Pushing his way through the branches of a large bush, he probed forward in the dark almost entirely by feel. He found the first bamboo plant, it's smooth tubular stalk almost two inches thick, and immediately after brushed against one of the leaves. A sharp intake of breath was all he allowed himself as he felt the leaf slice into the side of his little finger. They should be wearing gloves, he thought, but those were a rare commodity in tropical Viet Nam. Moving more slowly now, he sidled sideways farther into the stand, until he finally found an opening in the center. As Harv and Quan crowded in behind him, Nash pushed his rifle between two stalks and gently spread them apart. The road and the tree line beyond it were easily visible. This would work.

There were some muttered curses as the three men jostled around in the confined space, pulling off their packs and trying to get comfortable. They pulled up some bamboo shoots and small bushes and trampled down others until there was a relatively level clear space big enough for all three to lie prone. Nash was in the center, with Harv to his left and Quan to his right. Nash used Harv's bayonet to remove some of the leaves and grass in the screen of bamboo stalks through which his rifle rested, and squirmed around on the ground until he felt he had a decent firing position.

"I'll take first watch," he told the other two. "Quan, you'll be second, and Harv last. Harv, be sure to wake me up just as it starts to get light." Nash squinted at the barely legible glowing dial of his watch. "Two hours each. Get some sleep." Harv made a final adjustment in his position and laid his head down on his pack, then raised his head again to check the radio to be sure it was turned off. Satisfied, he put his head down again and almost immediately began softly snoring. Quan pulled out his canteen and took a drink, then put it away and curled up on his side. Without disturbing his two teammates, Nash pushed himself up into a kneeling position prior to sitting down with his legs drawn up, the stock of his rifle clamped between his ankles. He was tired, and feared that if he lay down to stand watch, he might fall asleep. This position was just uncomfortable enough to keep him awake.

The thick bamboo stalks gave him only a limited view of the road, but since nothing was moving out there, that wasn't really a problem. In the pale moonlight he assessed this position and wondered if he had chosen correctly. The opening in the stand was smaller than he had thought, and if the team got in a firefight, they would be getting in each other's way. The range to the tree line across the road was more than he would like, especially since he would be firing from such a low angle. And if the GIs who swept the road in the morning wandered farther out than usual and actually inspected this thicket, how would Nash and his team deal with that without getting shot by accident? He also pondered the possibility that some Viet Cong might come along in the next couple hours, perhaps looking for a place to plant mines. What should he do in that case? Take them out, and reveal his location, or let them go and hope that the engineers would find the mines and disarm them?

Beset by doubt, Nash forced himself to think of other, more positive things, but his mind kept roiling. What if someone found out about the money he had sent home? What if he didn't make it home? Other unfortunate possibilities kept occurring to him, such as a helicopter flying overhead spotting them and raking the thicket with machine gun fire, or a heavy rainstorm rolling in and flooding this area. Worst of all, the sniper might not show up here at all, and they would have wasted an entire day. Then he thought about the cute Coke girl that Quan had been flirting with the other day, and her image finally chased the bad thoughts away. She wasn't a boom-boom girl, so out of respect he avoided fantasizing about a sexual encounter with her, but he tried to imagine what it would be like if he could take her home to New Mexico to meet his family and enjoy the tranquility of the mountains. She was attractive, refined, and exotic, and Nash could just see himself showing her off around town and being envied by his friends. In the winter she could see her first snow as it blanketed the slopes. Of course he knew that was never going to happen, but it was nice to think about.

After two hours he touched Quan's shoulder, and the young man was instantly awake. "Time for your watch," Nash told him, to keep him from thinking there was someone approaching and getting alarmed. Quan nodded and scrambled up into a squatting position.

"Starlight?" Quan asked quietly.

"Don't need it," Nash whispered back. The moonlight was bright enough to spot anyone approaching their isolated position, and their view from inside the bamboo was limited anyway. The heavy and bulky starlight scope would just get in their way, since Nash had no intention of shooting at night.

"Okay," Quan agreed. "You sleep now."

Nash stretched out on his back, his head on his pack, and stared up at the stars visible through the bamboo leaves. It was a nice night for doing this, he mused. There was no rain, no immediate threat of contact, and a cozy hide. Now if he just had a soft bed and clean sheets...

Nash awoke with a start when Harv jabbed him in the side with a finger. "Wakey, wakey, Nash," Harv sing-songed softly. "Time to catch a big fish."

Nash rubbed his eyes and sat up. He was pleasantly surprised that he had dropped off to sleep so quickly and slept so soundly. He actually felt refreshed. He looked up and saw the sky had turned a bluish-gray and very few stars were still visible. The moon was now low in the western sky, and the eastern horizon was starting to glow. He took a couple deep breaths, and noticed the pain in his bladder.

"I need to take a piss," he said.

"Better do it now, before it gets too light," Harv suggested. "I took one about an hour ago. Went out and down into the ditch a few yards away."

"Yeah," Nash said, acknowledging the merit of the idea. He stood up and pushed his way out of the thicket, smiling as a cool breeze caressed his body. After first checking to make sure there was no one in sight, he walked over to the ditch and headed south along it, looking for a good place to descend. When he found a place where the bank had partially collapsed, he scrambled down it until just his head was above ground level, and then unbuttoned his pants. He aimed the stream at the standing water in the bottom of the ditch, and the relief of the pressure was truly wonderful. He hoped that the stagnant water in the ditch would disguise the smell of his urine, for he had frequently been warned that the Viet Cong could easily differentiate the odor of American piss from Vietnamese. After he finished and buttoned up his pants, he just stood there enjoying the cool breeze and watching the eastern sky gradually lighten. It was simple pleasures like this, he thought, that made serving in Viet Nam almost tolerable.

"I feel much better now," he told Harv when he returned to the hide, sitting down behind his rifle. "You want to go back to sleep?"

"No, I'm good." Harv pulled his pack around and dug into it. "But I'm hungry. I think I've got a cinnamon nut roll in here somewhere." He pulled out a small C-ration can and tried to read the label. When that proved impossible in the dark, he shook the can and listened to it. Sighing, he pulled his dog-tag chain out from under his shirt and unfolded the tiny P-38 can opener. With rapid experienced fingers he jiggled the opener around the top until he could lift it free. "Shit!" he muttered. "Pork slices."

"Pretend it's breakfast sausage," Nash joked.

"Eat shit and die," Harv responded, and then added "Sergeant," with a tone of mocking respect.

Nash chuckled.

"Quiet!" Quan muttered without moving from his fetal position on the ground. "I sleep!"

"So you're talking in your sleep?" Nash asked him curiously.

Quan growled.

"You want some pork slices, Quan?" Harv asked. "They're nice and cold and greasy."

Quan hissed. "You guys number ten!"

"Aw, that's not nice," Nash admonished him with a laugh. "What would you do without us?"

"Sleep!" Quan answered with feigned anger, still lying on his side with his eyes squeezed shut.

"Go ahead," Harv said, "we're not stopping you."

Quan snorted and sat up. He pulled a pair of chopsticks from the pen pocket of his uniform shirt and stabbed one of the pork slices from the can Harv was holding. Keeping the dripping round slice away from his clothing, he bent forward and nibbled around the edges. "How you eat this shit?" he asked with a grimace.

"Ain't easy," Nash agreed.

Maintaining a look of disgust, Quan finished off the meat, and then took a drink from his canteen.

"Better than dried octopus," Harv said, digging out the last slice with his plastic spoon.

"Anything is better than dried octopus," Nash agreed. "That's like chewing rubber bands."

Quan rolled his eyes and tried to stretch, which was difficult in the limited space available. Quan had once bought some dried octopus from a shop in Trang Bang and offered some to his friends. Nash and Harv had been ragging him about it ever since.

Nash searched through his own back pack and found a can of cheese and crackers. He opened the can and dumped out the hard round crackers onto his lap, then used his P-38 to open the small flat can packed within the larger can. The smaller disk-shaped can contained a yellow cheese-like substance. Using his plastic spoon, he spread some of the cheese on one of the crackers and took a bite. "Yum! This is delicious." He put on a happy face, like he was in a TV commercial.

"Yeah, right," Harv scoffed. He changed the subject. "So what's the plan, Stan?"

Nash shrugged. "We wait. If the sniper's coming, he'll set up in those woods over there. Hopefully we'll see him before he takes a shot. I figure we don't have to worry until there's very little traffic on the road, and someone important comes by."

"How do we know who's important?"

"That's Quan's job. Right, Quan? You can tell if someone is important just by looking at them?"

"Maybe," Quan said semi-confidently.

"See?" Nash told them. "Simple. Quan picks out the target, Harv, you spot the sniper, and I'll shoot him. No sweat."

Harv scowled. "And if he shoots somebody and you don't get him, it will all be my fault, right?"

"Of course," Nash answered blandly. "That's only fair."

"Fair, my ass," Harv grumbled, trying to suppress a grin. The three young men enjoyed giving each other a hard time, knowing that the others would always be there when they were needed. Harv pulled the radio over closer to him and switched it on. "Time to call in a sitrep."

While Harv spoke quietly into the handset, Nash stretched out behind his XM-21 sniper rifle and took the lens covers off his ART scope. The XM-21 was a highly modified and perfected M-14, machined to minute tolerances to provide extreme accuracy. It didn't look much different than a standard M-14, the rifle used by the US Army throughout the world, but it worked much better. The ART—adjustable ranging telescope—sight was mounted on top, and minimized the need for accurate range estimation and elevation calculations. All Nash had to do was rotate the bezel to focus the sight on the target, and the cross hairs would automatically raise or lower so that the rifle was properly aimed for that distance. He still had to allow for windage, but the scope did everything else. He had not mounted the noise suppressor, deeming it unnecessary for this operation, especially since it could possibly affect the ballistics.

He put his brow to the eyepiece, but it was still a little too dark for the scope to be effective. Once the sun came up, however, he would be able to focus in on any target with little effort. Nash rolled over onto his side and relaxed.

"Nothing new," Harv reported, switching off the radio.

"Good." No news was good news, Nash thought. He looked up through the leaves and saw the sky had turned indigo. Sunrise was only about thirty minutes away, and then the local Vietnamese would be out on the road again, along with the military traffic. "Quan, Harv, you can probably go back to sleep if you want. There won't be anything happening for a while."

Harv let out a theatrical sigh. "I'm awake now," he complained.

"I gotta piss," Quan announced.

Nash told Quan where he and Harv had gone, and told him to hurry before it got light enough for him to be seen. When he returned, Nash had him find a place that allowed him to look down the road to the south, while Harv got out his binoculars and pushed them through the bamboo until he could observe the road to the north. Nash got back down behind the rifle and prepared to study the tree line through his ART scope. He took a deep breath and let it out slowly. He didn't expect the sniper to show up until sometime after noon. It was going to be long day.

It was around nine hundred hours when Nash first heard the distant growl of diesel engines at low rpm. Up until then the only traffic they had seen were occasional motorbikes and Lambretta mini-buses. The sound was coming from the south, but Nash was unable to see far in that direction, his line of sight being blocked by the thick yellow bamboo poles and their blade-like leaves. He looked over at Quan, who had found a hole in the foliage that gave him a view in that direction.

"Road sweep," Quan announced in a matter-of-fact voice.

Nash nodded. It was a little later than he had expected, but he had known it was coming. Fifteen minutes later the first soldiers came into his field of view. Spread out perpendicular to the road, the men walked slowly, checking out the area. Wearing helmets, web gear, and ammo bags, each carried an M-16 or an M-79 grenade launcher. Although they looked bored, they were doing a good job of providing security to the small group of engineers who walked down the road sweeping their mine detectors back and forth. The detectors were flat rounded rectangle plates mounted at an angle at the end of long poles, and the engineers, bareheaded or wearing boonie hats instead of helmets, had headphones connected by wires to the poles. Waving the plate a few inches over the ground, the engineers listened for any signal that might indicate something metallic was buried under the surface.

Behind the soldiers and engineers four armored personnel carriers followed at low speed, starting and stopping to keep pace with the dismounts. There were two of the vehicles on either side of the road, in single file, ready to react with the firepower of their fifty-caliber machine guns if necessary. Nash could see that the soldiers on the ground were paying particular attention to the wooded area across the road, while those on this side were obviously less concerned.

"One guy check ditch," Quan said quietly. Nash assumed that meant that one of the soldiers on their side of the road had come over and sighted down the drainage ditch to make sure no one was hiding there. With the vacant fields on this side of the road, the ditch was about the only place a major ambush could hide. Nash hoped that the soldiers didn't decide to check out this small stand of bamboo, which would inevitably give away their position. Nash pulled his rifle back very cautiously and pressed himself into the earth. One of the soldiers was wandering over toward them, looking like he might want to inspect the thicket.

"Hold up!" someone shouted, and everyone froze in place. Nash peeked out and saw that all the dismounts were now watching the engineers on the road, all of whom had stopped what they were doing. One of the engineers pulled off his headphones, carefully laid down his detector behind him, and withdrew a bayonet from a scabbard on his belt. Kneeling down, he gently probed the surface of the dirt road, poking and sweeping the blade through the muddy gravel. While his buddies watched from a distance, the man gingerly shoveled the dirt away in one spot with the blade of his bayonet, and then laid the knife down and began feeling around with his bare fingers. A moment later he extracted something from the dirt, inspected it closely, and then tossed it into the weeds that lined the road.

"Lug nut," he announced loudly as he grabbed his detector and stood back up, returning the bayonet to its scabbard with his other hand.

"Hey," one of the track drivers shouted, "that might be mine." The engineers laughed.

"Has it got your initials on it?" one of them asked jokingly.

"Come on, guys," the officer in charge insisted. "Time's a-wastin'." Nash thought the voice sounded familiar. He was pretty sure it was Lieutenant Masters, one of the platoon leaders he had gone out with when pretending to be a reporter. With relief Nash noted that the soldiers continued their sweep, and the guy who had been eyeing the thicket moved on to keep up. Within minutes the entire formation had moved past them, continuing on their mission to clear the road of mines before the first truck convoys came through.

Nash wasn't surprised that trailing the road sweep was a gaggle of civilians: Coke kids, a sandwich mama-san, and some young boys who would be begging for candy.

"Thanh," Quan said. Nash wondered at the way his Vietnamese friend said that single name. It was almost affectionate. He hoped not, because he didn't want Quan being distracted. Nash slowly pushed his rifle back out through the opening and studied the civilians through his scope. Sure enough, one of the Coke kids pushing their bicycles with the boxes of iced sodas was the cute girl called Thanh. As always, she wore a light blue blouse and black silk pants. Behind her, pushing the two-wheeled cart, was the sandwich mama-san he had seen with Thanh the last time. As before the stocky older woman wore the typical black pajama-like outfit common among the farmers. Both she and Thanh had the usual conical straw hats, although Thanh's was hanging down her back from a leather thong around her neck.

"A sandwich and a soda would taste good right now," Harv said wistfully.

The slow-moving entourage passed by and eventually disappeared around a bend in the road. It would be another hour or so before military traffic would be allowed to travel on the road, and because of the road-clearing sweep, civilian traffic to and from Tay Ninh was prohibited. Taking advantage of the break in the action, what little there was, Nash sat up and had an early lunch—a can of cold, gummy spaghetti and meatballs. He finished it off with one of the bars of bittersweet chocolate that came in the SP packs, candy so hard it was like eating brown chalk, but made that way so it wouldn't melt in the Southeast Asian heat.

"Here they come again," Harv announced laconically. Peering through a gap in the bamboo, Nash saw the four armored personnel carriers approaching, all the men now sitting on top. This time they were in line on the road and traveling at about thirty miles an hour.

They had finished their sweep and were now heading for whatever location had been chosen for them to set up their outpost. The tracks roared by, leaving a cloud of dust slowly settling in the air behind them. A minute later the civilians followed, the young boys pedaling their bikes hard to catch the Americans, and Thanh and the sandwich mama-san hustling on foot. Thanh walked her bike and the older woman pushed her cart. Nash resumed his position behind his rifle and watched the procession go by. He had to admit that Thanh was a very attractive young lady.

It was late morning when the convoys starting coming through, the line of large olive-drab trucks roaring past in choking clouds of dust, escorted by a couple jeeps at each end. Closely studying the woods across the road, Nash watched for any sign that the sniper had moved in over there and was taking aim at anyone on the road. The dust obscured his vision considerably, but he was hoping that the sniper's scope would cause a noticeable light reflection that would give the sniper's position away. The woods, however, remained dark and silent.

After the dust had settled from the last of the convoys to Tay Ninh, civilian traffic appeared going both directions. Knowing that the sniper had often targeted South Vietnamese officials and even civilians, Nash and his team became hyper vigilant, identifying as best they could the type of people on the road to determine their likelihood as a target, while watching the distant trees and brush for any sign of movement. Most of the travelers were clearly ordinary people taking their goods to market or doing other business, riding small motorbikes or crowded onto the Lambretta mini-buses. All three men tensed up when they saw a motorbike carrying two people stop at the side of the road. A man was driving, with a woman on the seat behind him. When he pulled over the woman jumped off the bike and ran into the woods.

Nash trained his scope on the woman as she entered the tree line, focusing it to ensure the crosshairs were accurately aligned. She was clearly not carrying a rifle, but he thought she might be meeting the sniper to give him information about a potential victim. Instead, through the leaves of the bushes that lined the edge of the forest, he saw her squat for a minute, then stand up and adjust her pants before running back out to the motorbike.

"Piss break," Nash told the others. The woman climbed back on the motorcycle and it whined off.

"I could use one of those," Harv moaned softly.

"I told you to go before we left home," Nash chided in a motherly tone.

"Not here!" Quan warned. "You stink."

"Can I borrow your canteen, Quan?" Harv asked with feigned innocence.

Quan scoffed. "I give you string," he suggested. "Or you tie dick in knot."

"Ouch!" Nash laughed.

"It is long enough," Harv mused thoughtfully. "What do you think—square knot, or bow line?"

"Dream on, Harv," Nash chuckled. "I doubt you could manage a double-overhand."

"What? What does that mean?"

"You figure it out, cowboy."

"Jeep!" Quan warned suddenly. All three went back to watching the road. A jeep zoomed by at high speed, carrying the driver and three passengers. The vehicle had no top or windshield, and was covered in dried mud. All the men riding in it were in full combat gear. It clearly was not assigned to anyone of high rank or importance. After it had disappeared up the road, the team went silent for a while, staring out through the stalks and waiting for something—anything—to happen.

Halfway through the afternoon the truck convoys, now mostly empty, rolled by heading south back to Cu Chi. Harv turned on the radio to call in a sitrep and check for any news.

"No sniper attacks today," he reported. "They want to know if we're done here."

Nash mulled it over. "Let's give it another hour," he finally said. "He's struck in the late afternoon before."

Harv relayed the message, listened for the response, and finished the transmission. "The jeep will be here to pick us up at sixteen-thirty."

Nash checked his watch. Not quite an hour away, but close enough for Army work. Out on the road the civilian traffic had picked up a little. Now that the military convoys were done for the day, presumably the Vietnamese felt more comfortable traveling their own roads. If the sniper was looking for a civilian target, there were plenty now.

"Hey!" Harv said sharply. He had his binoculars to his face, trained on the wood line across the highway. "I think I saw something."

"What? Where?" Nash shifted his body around so he could aim his scope in the same general direction as Harv was looking.

"See that big tree with a bush right below it?"

"I see a lot of trees, Harv. Can you be more specific?"

Albertson sniffed. "Uh, okay, see that Coke can on the side of the road?"

"Wait. Yeah, now I see it."

"Straight in from there, and then right about twenty yards. Big tree with a fork that juts out over the cleared area."

Nash followed Harv's directions and finally focused on what he thought his friend was describing. "Okay, got it."

"I saw some movement right behind the tree. Don't see anything now, though."

Nash held the rifle rock steady, concentrating on the round picture in the scope. With minute adjustments he rotated the bezel until the trunk of the tree was in sharp focus before he began sweeping the scope back and forth to take in the entire area. All he could see were trees and bushes and leaves. With the sun lower in the western sky, the interior of the wood line was more illuminated than earlier, but the sharp contrast between sunlight and shade made it even harder to make out details. Breathing shallowly to avoid shaking the scope, Nash would stare at one area for three or four seconds, then shift his view a few feet and pause to study another area, alert to the tiniest of movements in the foliage.

He moved the rifle so it pointed back at the tree Harv had originally identified, then scanned up and down the trunk. A sunbeam lit up part of the lower trunk like a spotlight, making the bark look almost white by comparison to the shaded greyish-brown of the upper levels. Nash started to move the rifle again when he noticed the tiniest of flickers just below the bright patch of the trunk. There was a bush near the base of the tree, and the leaves partially obscured the trunk in that area, but he was sure something had moved there. He checked his other senses, and determined there was no breeze right now, nothing that would cause the leaves to move on their own.

He stared at the shadows and light near the base of the tree, trying to differentiate between individual leaves and the darkness behind them. It was like one of those optical illusions he had seen in a book—was it a white vase on a black background, or two black silhouettes of faces? Nash let his mind go blank and see the scene from a different point of view. Suddenly it all came into focus. He could see a part of a face, and the distinctive shape of a rifle with a telescopic sight mounted on it, buried deep in the branches of the bush.

"I've got him!" Nash whispered excitedly.

"Me, too!" Harv echoed.

"Car!" Quan barked.

"What kind?" Nash demanded. Regular cars were unusual out here.

"Citroen," Quan answered. "New one."

That had to be the sniper's target, Nash thought. Only a senior official would be in a car like that.

"How far out?"

"Half minute."

Nash took a couple deep breaths and let them out slowly, calming his body. He checked the positions of his hands and his cheek's spot weld on the stock. Flicking off the safety, he lightly touched the pad of his right index finger to the trigger. He had to take the shot quickly, before the car arrived. He centered the cross hairs of the sight on where he thought body mass would be. He could only see the sniper's rifle and part of his face, but Nash was sure the sniper was in a kneeling position, using the tree trunk for additional support. Another deep breath, and let it halfway out, as he slowly increased the pressure on the trigger. In the back of his mind he noted that the rifle was now pointed almost directly at him, but he dismissed that as a coincidence. The sniper was probably planning on shooting at the car just as it came abreast of him.

A flash followed by a distant pop made Nash jerk the trigger, and his own rifle fired before he was really ready. The sniper had fired first! Right at Nash! He had no idea where his own round had gone. He refocused in preparation to firing again, but the face had disappeared.

"I'm hit!" Albertson exclaimed. Nash ignored the problem for the moment, searching through the scope for any sight of the sniper. There! He saw a running figure vanish into the shadows, and he fired a shot that he knew was wasted. The sniper was gone.

Nash rolled onto his right side to look at Albertson. "How bad?" he asked. Harv had his right hand pressed against left shoulder, close to his neck, blood seeping between his fingers.

"I don't know," Harv said with remarkable calm. "How bad does it look?" He removed his hand, marveling at the blood on it. Nash could see the blood welling up in the curve of Harv's neck, but he noted with relief that it wasn't spurting.

"Let me see your back," Nash told him. Harv rolled onto his stomach. There was no exit wound that Nash could see, which was very troubling. "Any trouble breathing?"

"No," Harv replied, rolling over onto his back. "But it's starting to hurt."

Quan crawled over Nash's legs and pressed a field dressing to Harv's shoulder, the gauze strips hanging down loosely. "Take off shirt," Quan told Harv. With Nash's help Harv unbuttoned the shirt and sat up so Nash could pull it off. Nash took the opportunity to again look for an exit wound, and saw none. That really worried him. The bullet was still inside Harv, perhaps stuck in a vital organ. Quan used the gauze straps to tie the dressing in place, but it was already getting soaked with blood.

Nash grabbed his pistol belt and got up on his knees so he could buckle it around his waist. "Call for a dust-off," he ordered, looking at both Quan and Harv. "I'm going after the bastard."

"By yourself?" Harv asked with a worried look. Nash detected a shakiness in Harv's voice, but he didn't let it deter him.

"I might not get another chance," he told them, picking up his rifle and standing up. "Quan, take care of him." Pushing his way through the back of the thicket, Nash rushed down to the crossing and scrambled across the ditch. The sniper had just made it personal.

TEN

When he dashed across the highway, Nash nearly collided with a motorbike carrying a family of four. The bike swerved to miss him and wobbled down the road until the driver regained control of the overloaded vehicle. Nash ignored them. The Citroen was already gone, apparently unaware of the exchange of gunfire. Nash was completely focused on the opening in the tree line where he had last seen the sniper, heedless of the possibility that the sniper was still there and at that very second taking aim at him. Hurdling an old log and plowing through some low shrubs, he rushed to the woods and stopped at the tree where he had last seen his enemy. Panting a little from the burst of activity after laying low for so long, he scoured the area for signs.

Broken stems and ruffled dead leaves showed where the sniper had been, and a yellow glint led him to the expended cartridge that had been left behind. Nash jerked his head around, searching the surrounding forest for clues about which direction the man had gone. The woods were quiet and appeared undisturbed for many years, but Nash knew that was just an illusion. He paused to consider his next move.

Peering out to the west, shielding his eyes from the sun with his hand, he saw Quan helping a stumbling Harv out of the bamboo thicket and sitting him down a few yards out to await the medevac helicopter. At least they were safe now. He could not say the same for himself, though. Chasing after the sniper alone was foolish and extremely dangerous, but he didn't care. The sniper that Nash had been chasing for weeks had just wounded his friend, and spoiled Nash's attempt to shoot back. His pride was at stake, and the desire for revenge welled up within him like a flood. With one last look at Quan and Harv, Nash turned and plunged deeper into the woods.

Logically the sniper would have initially headed directly east, to put as much distance between himself and Nash as he could, before then turning in some other direction, so Nash did the same. The light was dimmer here in the woods, making it harder for Nash to pick out the miniscule indications that someone has passed there moments before, but he thought he could still do so. Broken limbs, depressions in the carpet of fallen leaves, and maybe even a vague scent of human sweat—he hoped these were real signs, and not just things he imagined that he had detected. He almost missed the small drop of moisture on the ground, having passed it before it registered in his mind. He jerked to a halt and stepped back to find it. Kneeling down he touched his index finger to the spot and then inspected his finger tip. It was red and slightly sticky, definitely blood. His chest swelled as he took a deep breath. He had hit the sniper after all, and that was extremely gratifying. And if the man was wounded, he would be moving more slowly, leaving a blood trail, and thus would be easier to catch. Or so Nash hoped.

Checking his rifle to make sure it was locked and loaded, Nash sprang up and sprinted through the trees, anxious to catch up, disregarding the danger of his being ambushed. After a few yards, however, he realized that such a pace would only make it harder to follow the trail, in addition to the chance he would stumble upon the sniper just waiting to shoot him first. He slowed to a jog, convincing himself there wasn't that much of a hurry, since the man was wounded. It was simply a matter of tracking him methodically and finishing him off when he was found. He saw another drop of blood, and continued his pursuit at a fast walk, his XM-21 held at port arms, ready to aim and fire. The blood trail was very intermittent, and the size of the droplets was small, making Nash reconsider his estimate of the seriousness of the wound. If the man was not terribly hurt, he would be even more dangerous. Nash kept shifting his gaze from the ground to the surrounding forest and back, following the trail but mindful of the peril.

Sensing a change in the ambient light, Nash slowed down and took stock. Ahead the forest seemed to be thinning, and it was getting brighter. Another drop of blood, glistening with its freshness, told him he was gaining on the sniper, but as he continued he saw the woods ending, and some sort of open area beckoned.

Almost unconsciously Nash lowered himself into a crouch and crept forward, ready to go prone if necessary. The woods ended abruptly, and Nash found himself staring out over a jumble of old fallen tree trunks. It was a Rome Plow area, where the Army's giant bulldozers had come through and leveled the forest in an effort to hinder the movement of large enemy units and their supply trains. The area was about a hundred yards wide, and stretched far into the distance to Nash's left and right. It was like a huge random obstacle course, with tree limbs jutting up from the fallen trunks, and root balls like a nest of wooden snakes blocking the way.

Across the field of broken logs another tree line waited, dark and foreboding. Crossing the open area would require climbing over and under and around, exposing him to the sniper at every turn. Looking at the sky to judge how much daylight was left, Nash saw the bulk of Nui Ba Den peeking over the far tree line. The mountain was closer than he expected, and directly in front of him, which meant he had lost his sense of direction. He had thought he was facing southeast, but now knew he was headed north. How had he gotten so turned around? Nash wondered if he should just turn around and head back to the highway, but hated to give up when he was so close. There must be a couple hours of daylight left, which gave him plenty of time to catch the sniper and finish him off. He stared out at the Rome Plow area and tried to plot a route through the clutter that might let him cross safely. He had been through Rome Plows before and was well aware of the potential dangers. He had about decided to give up and go back when he saw a flicker of movement out of the corner of his eye.

There, about halfway across the strip of broken trees, he saw a black-clad figure slide over a trunk and vanish behind it. Nash raised his rifle to his shoulder and scanned the place where the man had been through his scope. As he watched the log, he saw a stick or something poke up, followed by a dark rounded shape. It was the sniper, and he was taking aim at Nash! Dropping to the ground, Nash heard the snap of a bullet overhead immediately followed by the clap of the shot from the open area. Scrambling forward on his hands and knees, Nash found a fallen tree whose main limb jutted skyward, using the fork as a place to rest his rifle as he peeked around the base of the limb. Another shot rang out, and Nash felt the bullet bury itself in the thick limb right by his head. Angrily he rose up and fired back without really taking aim, just to show the sniper he was alive and serious.

After waiting a few seconds to see if the sniper would try again, Nash kept low as he alternately crawled and ran in a crouch around and between the trunks, trying to close the gap to the sniper. He slid on his stomach under one trunk that angled up from its base, and vaulted over another that blocked his way, slamming into the ground on his shoulder and feeling the pain as a broken tree limb jabbed him in the back. Poking his head up, he saw the sniper scrambling over a log, closer this time, and brought his rifle up to fire. It was too late, the sniper was hidden again. Nash waited almost a minute, hoping the sniper would reappear, but no such luck. So he continued the slow-motion chase through the tangle, the lowering sun off to his left, the wood line beckoning to the north, and beyond it the forested slopes of Nui Ba Den. That had to be where the sniper was headed, Nash realized. He was seeking the protection of the sides of the mountain that were totally controlled by the Viet Cong and NVA.

And if the sniper was going to the mountain, Nash didn't have to actually follow the man, he could perhaps get ahead of him and catch him unawares. Having made the decision, Nash angled away from the last place he had seen the sniper and sought the fastest route through the Rome Plow to the woods on the other side, west of where the sniper would enter the tree line. If he hurried, and the sniper kept watching directly south for pursuit, it was possible he would get into the woods sooner, where he could travel faster.

Crossing the last log, Nash ducked into the wood, hoping he hadn't been seen. There had been no further shots from the sniper, but that didn't mean anything. Free of the tangle of fallen logs, Nash could now move swiftly through the forest, and he set out on what he hoped was a wide circling movement that would bring him to a point just ahead of the other man. The trees were farther apart in this section of woods, and Nash could feel the ground rising beneath his feet, meaning he was getting close to the mountain. The relative openness of the woods here allowed him to cautiously jog double-time, watching to his right through the ever-changing gaps in the trees for any sign of his adversary.

Two minutes later Nash came to a clearing in the forest, a roughly oval space where no trees or bushes grew, carpeted only by some tall grass. It was nearly a hundred meters wide, and he skirted the clearing on the left until he found a small patch of bushes on the north edge of the open space, next to a small tree with low branches. Inserting himself between two of the bushes, Nash knelt down and brought the rifle up to his shoulder, peering over the top of the scope at the woods on the far side of the clearing. He took rapid shallow breaths, catching his wind after the run through the forest, while he searched the darkening forest for any tell-tale movement. When he could, he held his breath for a few moments so he could listen for any unusual sounds. He just had to be ahead of the sniper, and he was sure this was the way the sniper would come. But in his mind he knew that was an iffy prospect. He told himself that if the sniper didn't show up in five minutes, he would give up the chase and return to the highway, where he hoped he could find some Americans to give him a ride.

Nash was about to abandon his wait when he saw some branches move in the woods on the far side of the clearing. A tree limb over there blocked part of his view, as did some low bushes, but he could just make out the torso of a person standing next to a thick tree trunk. The black pajamas and the flashing glimpse of a long rifle with a scope told him it was the sniper. The person obviously expected Nash to be coming from behind, and wearily leaned against the north side of the wide trunk. Leaning the rifle against the tree, the sniper lifted the bottom of the black shirt to shoulder height, revealing two large sagging breasts, one of which was covered in blood.

Nash had been preparing to shoot, but the sight of the woman's breasts caught him completely off guard. Fascinated, he watched as she explored her wounded right breast, gingerly poking and lifting it with a gasp Nash could hear even at this distance. He couldn't see her face, because of the intervening tree limb, but she was clearly an older woman with a stocky build. She lowered her shirt and picked up the rifle, causing Nash to remember why he was there. Doing a quick check of his firing position, he put his finger on the trigger, regardless of the sniper's gender. And then he heard the voices.

Talking in Vietnamese and laughing, five men entered the clearing from the east, all dressed in black pajamas and conical straw hats. All five carried AK-47s and had ammo vests with extra magazines. One of the men was older and walked with a slight limp, and he seemed to be in charge. Their relaxed approach changed when they heard the voice of the sniper call out to them, and they all crouched and brought their weapons up. The leader called out something, and the sniper answered. Her words apparently calmed them, as they all stood up and lowered their rifles, looking over at the south edge of the clearing where the sniper was. The five men walked over and began talking to the woman, whose answers were short and apparently painful. Nash still couldn't see the woman's face, but her body language betrayed extreme fatigue. She told them something that caused the four younger men to spread out and raise their weapons as they scanned the forest to the south. Looking for me, Nash thought.

He lowered his rifle and tried to melt into the foliage, slowly sagging into a prone position. Six against one—the odds were terrible. He had only his sniper rifle, and they had five automatic weapons. He wouldn't stand a chance. From ground level he couldn't really see the group well, but caught enough glimpses to figure out what they were doing. The older man picked up the sniper rifle, while two of the younger men took the sniper's arms to assist her in walking. They all began crossing the clearing, heading right for Nash. He tensed up, putting his head in the musty dead leaves and wondering how visible he actually was, afraid to move a single muscle. The voices got closer and closer, and then they were almost beside him, pushing into the forest from the clearing and chattering away. Then the voices and footsteps moved away from him, fading into the forest behind him as they took the sniper toward the mountain.

Unmoving, Nash waited for a full ten minutes, opening his ears to all the sounds of the forest, before he became convinced that no one had stayed behind. He slowly relaxed and lifted his head to look around. The woods were silent with a deepening gloom. No sunlight reached the clearing, and Nash wasn't sure if that was due to the sun setting, or perhaps some clouds moving in. Either way, it was time to leave. He didn't want to be out here in the woods at night.

By the time he reached the Rome Plow, Nash could see that indeed the clouds had moved in, and those to the west were tinted dark orange by the setting sun. Also to the west he heard the stuttering rumble of a helicopter, and tried to spot it against the crimson clouds. It was moving slowly along the Rome Plow, and coming in his direction. He hustled out into the middle of the strip and climbed up on a fallen log to wave his arms. As it got closer Nash could see the red cross on the nose and tell it was a Huey. Apparently they saw him as well, as the tone of the rotors changed and it headed directly for him. Nash looked around for a place the chopper could land, but there was no space clear enough. With its blades stirring up clouds of dust, the aircraft went into a hover directly over Nash, and then slowly lowered itself to just a couple feet over his head. Two hands reached out the side for him, and he let them grab his upper arms and pull him in until he collapsed on the aluminum floor. He looked up at his rescuers. One was a crewman with a visored helmet, but the other one was Quan.

"You late," Quan chided him with a smile.

"Sorry," Nash said, sitting up. "I've been busy." His stomach lurched as the chopper rapidly gained altitude and swerved as it changed direction and zoomed off toward Cu Chi.

*****

"Where were you?" Thanh demanded as she rose from her bed. Nhu had just slipped through the door and was setting her rifle on the small table where she normally cleaned it. Ignoring Thanh's question, Nhu shut the door and switched on the small light hanging over the center of the room. Thanh blinked her eyes against the sudden glare, noticing that Nhu was dripping water all over the floor, and her hair was plastered to her skull. Only then did Thanh notice the drumming of the rain on the roof, which had become so common she mentally filtered it out. Nhu made sure all the window shutters were closed, and then plopped down in the room's only chair, letting her arms hang down by her side.

"I was worried," Thanh told her. "I had to tie your cart to my bicycle and pull it back here by myself."

Nhu looked up at her with a weary expression, but still said nothing. She was breathing heavily, and as her eyes adjusted to the light, Thanh noticed that the front of Nhu's black blouse had a large red stain on it. With jerky motions the older woman clutched at the bottom of her shirt and lifted it up over her head, struggling to pull her arms out of the sleeves. She finally let the shirt fall to the floor, one sleeve still bunched around her wrist as her arm hung limply by her side. Thanh gasped as she saw that Nhu's right breast was swathed in brown cloth that wrapped around her chest and shoulders, and blood had soaked through to turn most of the bandage a deep maroon.

"What happened?" Thanh whispered. All sorts of scenarios raced through her mind, most of them involving sexual assault.

Nhu shook her head slowly from side to side. "Shot," she finally said. "Need clean bandage."

"Of course," Thanh gulped, and went to the sink. There were two clean towels there, and she grabbed both of them and took them over to Nhu. Then she just stood there, unsure what to do next. Nhu's head had fallen forward, and at first Thanh feared the woman had died, until she saw her chest heave and she looked up again.

"What are you waiting for?" Nhu growled impatiently. "Take this off and put a clean one on."

"Uh, uh," Thanh stuttered, but came closer. She laid the towels on the table next to the rifle and searched for a way to remove the old bandage without further hurting Nhu. She found a knot and plucked at it with her fingers until it came undone. There were two more knots, pulled so tight and then soaked with blood and rainwater that they were rock hard. When Thanh finally untangled them, the bandage fell in Nhu's lap, and Nhu angrily swept it off and onto the floor. Nhu had larger breasts than most Vietnamese women, but they had sagged badly over the years, looking like two tan socks each holding a rice ball. Her right breast had two small holes in it, one on each side of her brown nipple. The holes had been crudely sewn up with ordinary thread. Both holes were slowly leaking blood that ran down the curve of her breast and dripped onto her stomach. Thanh stared at it, both fascinated and repelled. "Does it hurt?" she asked wonderingly.

"Of course it hurts, you stupid girl," Nhu snapped at her. "Bandage it up!"

Thanh picked up the top towel, a thin cotton kitchen towel, and using her teeth to start it, she ripped it in half lengthwise. Hesitantly she approached Nhu, not really wanting to touch the woman's breasts, even under these circumstances. Overcoming her revulsion, Thanh lifted the wounded breast and wrapped the narrow strip of cloth around it vertically, making it stand out like it might have when Nhu was younger. Thanh tucked the end of the cloth in to hold it in place, then folded the other half and placed it over the woman's nipple. "Hold this," she told Nhu, who winced as she complied.

Thanh picked up the second towel and shook it out, but realized it was not going to work, even torn into strips and tied end to end. Instead she went to her clothes box and found a clean pair of her silk slacks. "Raise your right arm," she ordered, and Nhu did so, with a grimace of pain. Thanh put the waistband of the pants over the wounded breast, allowing Nhu to withdraw her left hand that had been holding the compress in place. One leg of the pants went under Nhu's right arm and the other over her left shoulder. Thanh had Nhu lean forward so she could tie the legs together at the back. When she was done, Nhu sagged back on the chair and let out a breathy groan.

"In the morning," Nhu said hoarsely, "you must go to the store and get antiseptic and bandages."

"Yes," Thanh agreed, coming around to face Nhu. "And something for the pain."

Nhu shook her head. "Just antiseptic and bandages. Help me over to my bed."

Thanh grasped Nhu's left bicep and hoisted her to her feet, then guided her over to the bed and let her collapse gently onto the thin mattress. Nhu lay down on her back, but grunted with discomfort due to the knot of the make-shift bandage, and rolled over onto her left side. Her face was pale, and her breathing rapid. Even though she didn't like Nhu, Thanh felt compassion for the woman's pain. At least until the older woman finally spoke again.

"You will have to clean the Dragunov," she ordered. "Now!"

"I do not know how," Thanh protested.

"It is like any other rifle, you idiot. You are supposed to be a great warrior up north, and you do not know how to clean a rifle? Just do what I tell you."

Sighing with resignation, Thanh found the cleaning supplies, moved the chair over, and sat down at the table. With Nhu giving instructions, she disassembled the rifle and began cleaning it.

"How did it happen?" Thanh asked as she ran a cleaning rod through the barrel.

"A sniper. An American, with his spotter. They were hidden across the highway. I think they were waiting for me. We both fired at the same time. I believe I hit his spotter, and he hit me. He chased me all the way to the mountain. Fortunately our comrades found me before he did, and they treated my wound and helped me back here."

"How did he know you were going to be there?" Thanh put a clean patch on the end of the cleaning rod and ran it through the barrel again.

"I do not know. Did you tell someone?" Nhu's face flared in anger as the suspicion came to her.

"No!" Thanh denied vehemently. "I told no one. How can you think that?"

Nhu winced with pain, and then relaxed a little. "I am sorry. The pain makes me angry. Besides, he must have been there all day, and I did not decide to go there until this morning. Somehow he knew what I would do before I did."

Thanh began wiping down the bolt mechanism with an oily rag. "That makes no sense," she commented.

"Maybe it was just bad luck," Nhu said, her voice weaker now. "I need to sleep. Be sure that rifle is clean." Nhu closed her eyes and began breathing more slowly and deeply.

Thanh finished cleaning the rifle and reassembled it, before hiding it under the floor with the two metal cases. Then she checked Nhu one last time, switched off the light, and returned to her own bed. Things were not going well, and she was worried about what might happen if Nhu died. To distract herself from her worries, Thanh thought about Robert, and wondered what life would be like in California. While she had waited for Nhu this evening, she had reread the newspaper he had given her, learning new phrases and trying to understand the humor of the cartoons. Somehow the paper made her feel closer to Robert, and she wondered if he had chosen that particular issue to give her for some special reason. She kept the newspaper hidden under her thin mattress, for she knew its presence would anger Nhu, but the optimism of the articles in the paper lifted her spirits. With a slight smile on her face, she finally fell asleep.

ELEVEN

The table was at least twelve feet long, and made of highly polished hardwood that gleamed in the bright fluorescent lights. It was surrounded by heavy chairs upholstered in black cloth and mounted on swivel bases that rolled on castors. Quan kept running his hands across the smooth tabletop, marveling at its sheen. Nash leaned back in his chair and felt the seat tilt back on a hidden spring. It all seemed incredibly luxurious, especially in a war zone. He was used to folding metal chairs and tables cobbled together out of rough one-by-sixes and two-by-fours. "Rank does have its privileges," he commented softly.

"What?" Quan asked absently. Nash shook his head to dismiss the question, which Quan probably didn't care about anyway. They were in a conference room at Division headquarters, waiting to study all that was known about Nui Ba Den. There were maps and diagrams mounted on the walls of the room, but all had been covered with sheets of black cloth, pinned down by thumb tacks around all the edges to ensure Nash and Quan didn't peek beneath. The room itself had been a compromise. The men at G2, Division Intelligence, had refused to allow Quan anywhere near their offices, and Nash suspected they didn't want Nash himself in there either. They were obsessed with security, and Nash didn't have the necessary clearances. Quan, of course, was a former Viet Cong, which made him doubly suspect. Captain Banning and Nash had pressed the issue with various staff people, and finally the Deputy Commander had ordered the G2 to provide at least some of the intel to Nash and Quan, and had cleared them to use the division commander's conference room, after it had been suitably "sanitized."

Nash's stomach growled, and he felt the growing hunger pangs as it neared lunchtime, but he wasn't about to abandon this room until he had what he needed. He was certain that if they left to get something to eat, the room would be barred to them when they got back. They had to take what they could get, when they could get it.

They were behind schedule as it was. Quan and he had gone to the hospital first thing this morning to check on Harv Albertson, only to find that he had already been transported to the airfield. An orderly told them Harv was going to be flown to Japan for surgery to remove the bullet lodged in his chest. The orderly didn't know anything else about Harv's condition, and all the doctors and nurses were busy dealing with an influx of new patients from a firefight in the Parrot's Beak. By the time Nash and Quan had run to the air strip, Harv had already been loaded on a C-130 that was taxiing for takeoff. Nash figured they would take him to Tan Son Nhut and then put him on a jet to Japan. Whether Harv would ever be back was an open question, but Nash thought the odds were very low.

The door to the conference room burst open and a thin young man with glasses pushed in, his arms loaded with cardboard tubes and three-ring binders. He kicked the door shut behind him and dumped his load on the table. Nash saw that the guy's name was Carotto and he was an E-7 Sergeant First Class. His wavy brown hair was neatly trimmed, and his uniform was sharply pressed. Nash thought he looked awfully young to be an E-7, but figured maybe rank came quicker in Military Intelligence.

"Here's what we have, Sergeant Jaramillo," Carotto said. Nash involuntarily smiled when the other man pronounced his name correctly.

"Call me Nash," he told him. "This is my scout, Quan."

"Quan," Carotto acknowledged with a nod. He lowered his voice conspiratorially. "Actually, we have more, but this is all I'm allowed to show you."

"I understand," Nash assured him. "Anything will be helpful."

Carotto pushed the binders off to one side, along with two of the cardboard tubes. He pulled a map from the third tube, unrolled it, and slid it in front of Nash. When the map tried to roll back up, Quan pressed down on the side with his hand, and Carotto held the other side down, leaning over the table. The map was about two feet square, and was a large scale representation of the mountain, which took up most of the multicolored sheet. "Here's the radio-relay camp at the top," Carotto said, circling the peak with a finger. Nash could see the cleared area and the black outlines of buildings. "The rest of the area is pretty much VC," Carotto said, sweeping his hand over the rest of the map. "I guess you know that, though."

Nash nodded. "I've heard there's a bunch of caves and bunkers on the sides of the mountain. Is that true?"

Carotto stood up straight, and Nash quickly moved his hand to keep the map from curling back up. "Yeah, that's what we think. We can't go in and verify, but from old records and recent interrogations, we've identified several caves and possible bunkers. There's probably a lot more, but. . ." Carotto shrugged.

"Are they shown on this map?" Nash asked, leaning forward to peer closely at the sheet.

"No," Carotto admitted, looking over at the door. He stepped over and turned the center of the doorknob, and then twisted the knob to be sure it was locked. Coming back to the table, he picked up one of the other cardboard tubes and slid a roll of acetate out of one end. He unrolled the clear sheet of plastic, flipped it to get it oriented, and quickly laid it down over the map. "You've never seen this overlay," he instructed Nash and Quan. "Understood?"

"Roger that," Nash replied with a wry grin. The overlay had a narrow cross drawn on it at the lower corner, which Nash adjusted until it matched the corner of the colored section of the map. The overlay had red circles and squares scattered across it, each with a letter and map coordinates printed in black next to it.

"The circles are caves," Carotto explained, "and the squares are bunkers. We think most of the bunkers were built over existing caves, using a combination of rocks and sandbags."

"Yes," Quan confirmed, speaking for the first time to Carotto, who raised his eyebrows.

"You've been there?" he asked in surprise.

"One time," Quan said. He pointed to the north side of the mountain. "Here, maybe."

"What are they like?" Carotto asked, his voice rising with curiosity and professional interest.

"VC?" Quan asked, confused.

"No, the caves and bunkers. How deep are they? How many men in them? What weapons do they have?"

Quan shook his head. "I there only one time. At night. Cave not very deep, only hold maybe ten men."

Carotto opened his shirt pocket and withdrew a small notebook and a pen. Opening the notebook to the next blank page, he sat down at the table and began taking notes. "Is the cave on that map?" he asked.

Quan stood up to lean forward over the map, still holding down one curling edge with his left hand while he pressed the overlay down with his right index finger. "This one, maybe," he said. Carotto took down the letter and map coordinates. "I remember it not very high up. I see this other part over here." Quan pointed to the ridge that ran northwest from the mountain.

"Just that one cave?" Carotto asked. "Ten men?"

"Yes."

"What weapons did they have?"

"AK-47. Maybe SKS. I no see all weapon."

"Any machine guns or RPGs?"

Quan sat back and closed his eyes for a moment. "Don't know. Very dark."

"Okay, thanks. That really helps." Carotto kept scribbling in his notebook.

Nash pointed to the south slope of the mountain. "Actually, I'm more concerned about this area. That's where the sniper was headed." He tilted his head down closer to the map. He could see two caves and a bunker on that side of the mountain that might have been the sniper's destination. "Can I have this map and overlay?" he asked.

"Not the overlay," Carotto hastened to say. "You can have the map, but you can't write anything on it."

Nash reached into his shirt pocket and brought out his own notebook and pen. He opened it and began writing down the coordinates of the three locations. Carotto took a deep breath and acted like he was going to object, glancing worriedly at the door.

"Officially I can't let you do that," the intelligence specialist said, but made no move to stop Nash.

"And officially I didn't," Nash replied airily. He finished taking down the numbers and then snapped the notebook closed and put it back in his pocket. "What else can you tell us?"

"Okay," Carotto said, frowning as he made a decision. Pulling one of the binders closer, he opened it to the first page, which was a neatly typed title page. "This is a report I did last month on our best intel regarding the forces on the mountain. It's classified Confidential, but I think you can see it." He passed the binder to Nash. "I'm going to go get something to drink. You want a coffee or Coke or something?" He looked at Nash with a forced blank expression.

"A Coke would be good for me," Nash told him. "Quan?"

"Coke, yes. Or grape."

"I'll see what we have," Carotto told them. "It might take me a couple minutes." He left the room, leaving it unlocked.

As soon as the earnest young man was gone, Nash reached for the remaining cardboard tube and slid out another overlay. This one was similar to the first, but had more information on it, including unit designators and approximate number of troops. Spreading it out over the first overlay, Nash got out his notebook again and hurriedly copied over the information that he thought might be relevant. Quan studied the diagrams and looked doubtful, but didn't say anything. Quickly Nash rolled the overlay back up and slid it into the tube, while Quan did the same with the first overlay.

Nash opened the second binder, and found it contained a detailed report on the battle that had occurred on the top of the mountain more than a year earlier. He scanned the report, noting that the camp had been poorly defended and had suffered tremendous casualties. The attack had occurred at night, and clouds and rain had prevented any relief or reinforcement by helicopter, the only method available since there were no roads to the peak. Although the camp defenses had been improved since then, support and supply could still only be done by helicopter, leaving the camp vulnerable. The camp, however, was not Nash's concern, so he closed the binder and pushed it back. He went back to the report Carotto had prepared and began reading it.

When Carotto returned with three cans of soda dripping with condensation, Nash was immersed in the report, and Quan was studying the map. Carotto sat the cans down, noted the overlay had been put away, and nodded approvingly. He passed Nash a church key with which to open his soda and sat down beside him. After Quan had opened his can, which Nash noticed was indeed a grape soda, and both had taken a long drink of the sweet carbonation, Carotto opened his own Coke.

"Is that helping?" he asked, nodding toward the open binder.

"Definitely," Nash said.

"So tell me, what exactly are you looking for?"

Nash took another drink. "Yesterday a female sniper shot my spotter. I wounded her, and then chased her to Nui Ba Den, but she met up with a squad of VC and I had to let her go. My guess is that she's still there, and that's probably her base of operations."

"And you're going to try and find her?" Carotto sounded very dubious.

"If I can."

"There's a lot of VC on the side of that mountain," Carotto warned him. "Are you just going to go there by yourself and hope you run across her?"

"Quan will be with me," Nash said, as if that made it better. When Carotto had put it that way, Nash realized how improbable and dangerous his quest really was, but he couldn't quit now. He had been given the mission to find and neutralize the sniper, and that woman had shot Harv, so now he was committed. His original plan to wait in likely locations had worked, sort of, but he couldn't count on it working again. She would probably figure out what he had been doing and would change her methods. At least now he had a lead on her, and knew where she was recently. An active pursuit was better than passively waiting for the next attack. Nonetheless, he needed to think more about how he could continue. He went back to reading the report, hoping something there would trigger a new approach.

*****

Sergeant Samples walked up the lowered rear ramp of the one-three, ducked his head down, and sat down on the narrow bench inside, laying his rifle and helmet down beside him. Across from him was Lieutenant Carr, holding the porkchop mike to the track radio, listening to the crackling message blaring out of the tinny speaker. Samples thought about the days just before Carr had been assigned to the platoon, and how he had dreaded that arrival. In the months since, however, the two men had developed a strong friendship based on mutual respect, especially after the days they had spent together escaping the enemy in the Crescent.

"Roger, out," Carr said into the mike, and then clipped it on the radio's pull-out handle.

"So what's the word?" Samples asked, running his hand through his short sandy hair. They were alone in the track, as the driver, Spec 4 Fred Aiello, was out front checking the engine. The rest of the crew, including Eberhart, the lieutenant's RTO, were either standing guard or relaxing in the shade. Sergeant Montoya, the squad leader, was sitting behind the 50-cal machine gun on top, listening to a transistor radio.

"Same shit as always," Carr replied, leaning back and stretching his legs out. "Looks like we'll be here a while. One of the convoy's had a breakdown, so they're running late."

"Well," Samples said dryly, "it's not like we have anything better to do, like win the war or something."

"At the captain's briefing this morning, Gordon said there's a chance we'll be doing a sweep tomorrow or the next day, and probably set up a night laager."

"Speaking of tomorrow," Samples said, "we've got to choose somebody for the Bob Hope show." The comedian was doing his annual tour of Army bases, and was scheduled to perform in Cu Chi the next day. Each platoon was allowed to send one man to the show, and Carr and Samples had been debating on who it should be. It was a hard decision, because almost everyone deserved the reward, and those who weren't chosen would be justifiably disappointed.

"Jamison has been here the longest," Carr proposed.

Samples shook his head. "Can't be one of the sergeants. Wouldn't look right."

"Not one of the new guys, either," Carr said. "Otherwise I'd pick Handleman."

"Mr. Baseball," Samples chuckled. During a bad firefight in the Boi Loi Woods, the skinny little New Yorker had snagged a live grenade out of the air and tossed it back toward the gooks, saving a lot of American lives.

"I think it has to be Sweet," Carr said with a bit of reluctance.

Samples nodded. "Yeah, I'm afraid so." Sweet was a problem child sometimes, doing things he shouldn't just to make the other guys laugh. When they made contact, however, he was an excellent soldier, and had never done anything that was actually against regulations. He had been in the unit for nine months, and all the other soldiers liked him. When he returned from the show, he would inevitably act out the entire experience for the rest of the platoon, allowing them to share in the event even if they couldn't actually attend. "You want me to tell him?"

Carr shook his head. "No, I'll do it. Where is he?"

"Out on LP right now. Want me to get him?"

"No, I need to get out and move around anyway. I'll find him." Carr put on his helmet and picked up his rifle, but before he could step out, PFC Kirk came running up.

"Coke kids are here," Kirk said breathlessly, with a worried look on his face.

"So?" Samples asked. "They're always around."

"That girl that Crosby liked is out there, and she's asking about him. I didn't want to say anything."

Samples closed his eyes and cursed under his breath. Crosby's chaste attraction for the girl had been a topic of conversation for weeks in the platoon, resulting in a lot of ribbing for the young man. Now, however, Crosby was dead, killed by a sniper while hitching a ride in a colonel's jeep the other day. Apparently the girl hadn't gotten the word yet, which meant Samples would have to tell her.

"What's her name again?" Samples asked Kirk.

"Thanh."

"You want me to tell her?" Carr offered, stepping out of the track so he could stand erect.

"Nah, I'll do it," Samples said. "You go give Sweet the good news, and I'll go tell this girl the bad news. I just hope she was only pretending to like him so he'd buy more Cokes."

While Carr went into the woods to find Sweet, Samples took a deep breath, put on his helmet, and strolled out to the road, taking his time as he tried to compose a suitable way to break the news. There were five bicycles on the far side of the road, four with young boys, and one with a girl in a light blue blouse. As Samples approached, they all began shouting their sales pitches. He held up his hand to quiet them.

"Where's the sandwich mama-san?" he asked as a delay tactic, to postpone when he would have to tell Thanh what had happened.

"She is sick today," Thanh said, narrowing her eyes slightly. Samples wondered what that was about. The two had always been seen together in the past, and he had assumed they were related.

"Docker pecker," one of the boys offered, holding up the dripping purple can. Samples shook his head at the boy and moved closer to Thanh. He looked at her, but couldn't bring himself to say anything.

"Where is Robert today?" Thanh asked. Samples could see the worry in her eyes.

"Uh, the other day, there was an incident."

"Incident?" Thanh's face fell as the import of Samples' words sunk in.

"A sniper," Samples told her. "He was riding in a colonel's jeep. I guess the sniper thought he was a colonel or something."

"He was wounded?" Thanh asked almost hopefully, her voice cracking.

Samples shook his head. "He didn't make it. I'm sorry."

Thanh looked totally stricken, stunned by the news, unable to talk. As she finally accepted it, she dropped her bicycle and began shaking and sobbing, tears running down her cheeks. The box of ice and sodas spilled out on the ground, but no one moved to clean up the mess. Samples reached out to touch her shoulder, and she responded by pounding his chest with her fists, and then collapsing against him, her face buried in the front of his shirt and her hands clutching at the fabric. Overwhelmed by uncertainty and compassion, Samples tentatively patted her shoulder, and then put his hand on her back and pulled her close. He still had his rifle in his hand, and felt awkward, but wanted to give her what comfort he could. The other Coke kids moved a few feet away and stared. From across the road one of his men gave out a wolf-whistle, but was quickly silenced by someone else. Samples had never felt so helpless and unsure of himself.

Suddenly Thanh pulled away from Samples and wiped her face with her hands. Her expression changed to one of fury, and she spat some imprecation or threat in Vietnamese. Samples stepped back, wondering what he had done, but then he saw she wasn't directing her anger at him. She jerked her bicycle back up, ignoring the ice and sodas that had spilled out on the ground, and mounted it.

She took a deep breath and looked at Samples in despair. "Thank you," she said bitterly, and then pedaled off, pumping at the pedals with all her strength.

Samples looked down at the wet spots on the front of his shirt, looked around at the Coke kids who were still there, and trudged back across the road. He decided he would rather make contact with the enemy, or run into a tree full of red ants, than go through something like that again.

*****

"You bitch! You whore!" Thanh was screaming almost hysterically, her hands balled into fists, as she stood over Nhu, who was struggling to rise up from her bed. Thanh had never cursed at anyone before, and wasn't even sure how to do it. "You killed Robert!"

"What?" Nhu had been asleep when Thanh burst into the house, and she was blinking her eyes and trying to sit up.

"You shot Robert! Why did you do that?"

Nhu winced with pain as she swung her feet off the bed and raised her face toward Thanh. "Calm down, girl," she commanded. "I did not shoot Robert. I have been here all day."

"Not today," Thanh barked at her impatiently. She could feel the hot tears running down her cheeks. "Three days ago."

Nhu narrowed her eyes. "The man in the jeep? That was a colonel."

"No, it was Robert. And you killed him!" Thanh's legs gave out from under her and she collapsed on the dirt floor, crying uncontrollably.

"Are you sure?" Nhu asked, not entirely unsympathetic.

Thanh nodded and choked back her sobs enough to say, "His sergeant told me."

Nhu reluctantly reached out a hand to comfort Thanh, but Thanh brushed it away. She pulled herself up to sit cross-legged. She continued to whimper and sniff, wiping her eyes on her sleeve.

"I am sorry," Nhu said in a matter-of-fact tone.

"Are you sorry because you killed my friend," Thanh challenged her, "or because he was not a colonel?"

"Both," Nhu admitted with a nod.

"You are a terrible person! I hate you! I am leaving."

"No, you are not." Nhu looked at her sternly. "We have a mission. Uncle Ho sent you here to me, and I will make sure we complete our task. After we are done, then you may leave, but only then."

Thanh glared back at Nhu, but recognized that Nhu was right. She could not let Uncle Ho down. But after they fired those missiles, she was done. She would go back home to her mother and become a farmer. She would no longer fight the Americans. Let others do that. People like Nhu.

Nhu gently probed her swollen breast and grimaced. "I must change my bandage. When you have come to your senses, you have a letter over on the table. A comrade delivered it this morning after you left."

Biting her lower lip, Thanh forced herself to stopping sobbing and breathe more normally. Finally she was able to stand up and go over to the table, where a simple white envelope lay. She picked it up and stared at it. The outside had only her name, and no return address. For a split second she hoped that it was from Robert, but immediately realized that was impossible, and her name had clearly been written by a Vietnamese, not an American. Nhu had gathered up the medical supplies and dumped them on the table in preparation, and was now taking off her shirt. Nhu took the envelope over to her bed and sat down. For a minute she just looked at the envelope and wondered who had sent it. It wasn't her mother's handwriting; that she knew for sure. It looked more like a man's writing.

Finally she opened the envelope and pulled out the single sheet of paper with only a short paragraph on it. She first read the signature, and recognized the name of the village chief for the area where her mother lived. With a deep sense of foreboding, Thanh read the letter. She was stunned by the words. "Oh!" she sobbed. "Oh! Oh! Oh!"

"What is it now?" Nhu asked, swabbing her wounded breast with antiseptic.

"My mother!" Thanh squealed in torment.

"What about your mother?"

"She is dead!" Tears again began to flow from her eyes, and her chest heaved. The letter indicated she had been accidentally hit by an Army truck on her way to the market. The local official who had written the note offered his condolences but little more in the way of information.

"That is truly a shame," Nhu remarked as she began putting on a clean bandage. "Was she killed in a bombing?"

"No," Thanh said shaking her head, which sent tears flying. "It was an accident."

"You must feel terrible," Nhu said with only minimal sincerity. "Tomorrow we will both rest. The day after tomorrow we will meet with my source and learn the target."

Outside the first large drops of rain began falling, plopping on the tin roof. Thanh stumbled over to her bed and flopped down on it, still sobbing. How could things be going so wrong for her?

TWELVE

Outside there was a slow but steady rain, the large drops smacking on the tin roof of the barracks hooch with a monotonous dull roar. Inside Nash and Quan sat at the small field table next to the end of Nash's bunk, studying the map of Nui Ba Den. Despite the rain, or perhaps because of it, the barracks was like a steam bath, and Nash was bare-chested. On his lap was an olive drab scarf that he frequently used to wipe the sweat from his face and forearms, trying to keep the map dry. Quan, more accustomed to the heat, still wore his tiger-striped uniform, and wasn't sweating at all.

"It's got to be one of these three," Nash said, not for the first time. With one finger he circled the three spots marked on the map with pencil: two caves and a bunker, the coordinates of which he had copied down when they were at G2 the day before. Quan nodded. "But which one?" Nash asked rhetorically. Another pencil mark on the margin of the map indicated the approximate location where the sniper had met with the other VC. Nash traced the route from there to each of the possible hideouts on the slopes of the mountain, trying to guess which one was the most likely destination. Nothing jumped out at him.

Quan pointed to the westernmost cave. "Near," he said, sweeping his finger from the cave to the X on the margin. Then he pointed to the eastern cave and said, "Big." Then he touched the mark for the bunker in between the two caves, shook his head, and said, "Small." Nash had to agree. The bunker, based on the limited information in Carotto's report, would only hold two or three people, and the sniper had met up with five men. Unless they had split up, they wouldn't have taken her to the bunker. So the question was, would it be the cave that was closer, or the one that was bigger? According to the report, both caves were sufficiently large to accommodate the entire group, but Nash suspected the larger one would be more likely to contain medical supplies. But even if they had taken her there, that didn't mean she would stay there after treatment.

"Where we go?" Quan asked, and Nash realized that was the more important question. They had to find spot where they could hide and wait for the sniper to reappear, regardless of which cave or bunker she was using as her base of operations. Plus, there was a niggle at the back of his brain that maybe she wasn't based on the mountain at all, and she had just gone there for temporary refuge. Even if that were the case, he thought, she might still be there recovering from her wound. At any rate, it was the last known location for her, and he had no other place to search.

"Let's look at the pictures again." Nash reached over to the bunk and retrieved the manila folder lying on the wool Army blanket. He opened it and withdrew the two eight-by-ten glossies with the red CONFIDENTIAL stamp across one corner of each. They were black and white aerial photographs of the southern lower slopes of Nui Ba Den that Nash had found in the back of one of Carotto's binders. While the intel sergeant was gone for sodas, Nash had slipped them under his shirt. They had gotten a little sweat-stained, but they were still otherwise clear and detailed. Nash wished he had a magnifying glass; he had gone to the PX earlier, but, of course, they didn't have any.

Laying the photos on top of the map, Nash leaned over and peered at the tiny details. Quan, who had never seen aerial photos before, nearly bumped heads with Nash as he too bent down. The photos had been taken in the afternoon, which meant there were distinct shadows that helped give Nash a sense of perspective on the size and shape of the rocks and trees. Somebody, probably Carotto, had drawn red arrows on the print to indicate the location of the two caves and the bunker, although Nash had a hard time actually making them out. After about fifteen minutes his eyes, or his mind, adjusted to the way the pictures depicted the terrain, and the photos started to make sense to him.

He could make out the rocky paths leading to the three sites, and dark areas that were the entrances. Expanding his search, Nash looked for outcroppings or bushes that might possibly be a suitable sniper nest for him and Quan. The first two places he found, although they looked ideal in the photos, were dismissed when he studied the lines of elevation on the map, which showed those locations did not have line of sight to the entrances.

"Here?" Quan suggested, pointing to an outcropping at the upper edge of the photo. Nash initially considered it too far away to be useful, but after taking measurements on the map using the scale grid in the margin, he changed his mind. He studied the photos, trying to imagine what the semi-circle of rocks would look like at ground level, and what kind of view he would have from there. The more he looked at it, the more he liked it. It was almost two hundred meters higher on the mountain that the target sites, roughly half way between the western smaller cave and the bunker. From what he could tell, he would have a good view of all three entrances, or at least of anyone exiting them. The range was more than he would like, and he would have to allow for the downward slope when firing, but it seemed workable. There were no obvious signs that anyone frequented that area, and some low trees that grew around it would provide cover from higher up. Now all he had to do was figure out how to get there, and, more importantly, how to get away.

THIRTEEN

"Take down the RPG screen, Sarge?" PFC Kirk called from the front of the track. Lieutenant Carr suppressed a smile while Sergeant Samples rolled his eyes.

"Yes, Kirk, we're taking the RPG screen." Samples leaned down to look inside the one-one, where Sergeant Jamison, the squad leader, was stowing some gear. "Art, look after your boy there."

"Right," Jamison grumbled, finishing what he was doing and stomping outside. "Can't take him anywhere," he muttered as he went around to the front with a pair of pliers.

Carr looked at his watch. It was eight-thirty, which meant they had half an hour until roll out, which should be plenty of time. He and Samples were sitting on top of the one-one track discussing the plans for the day and avoiding the mud that last night's rain had caused.

"Nice sleeping in for a change," Samples commented, having noticed Carr's glance at his wrist.

Carr nodded. Today they weren't doing a road sweep, so the colonel had let them take it a little easier this morning. The men had all gotten a nice hot breakfast at the mess tent, and had time to shave and clean up without rushing. The down side was that tonight they would set up a night laager out in the field somewhere, and would have to take all their gear with them. Lately they had been spending the nights here in the fire support base, and leaving some of their equipment there during the day with a stay-behind guard. The RPG screens had been erected on the berm in front of each APC, but they would need them tonight. The screens were simply large pieces of chain-link fencing held up with angle-iron stakes in a semi-circle around the nose of the tracks. In theory, any RPGs fired at the tracks would hit the fencing and either explode there, or get caught in the mesh, leaving the vehicle safe. Today they would roll up the screens and pull up the stakes, stowing them on top of the trim vane at the front of the track, just below the driver's hatch.

Carr watched the men load up, strapping the RPG screens up front and loading the inside of the tracks with their cots, full water cans, waterproof bags of clothing, and the platoon's single blue-and-white ice chest, currently containing no ice and only a few warm sodas. Fourth squad was behind the others in the process, their new squad leader bouncing around alternately trying to help and getting in the way.

"What do you think?" Samples asked, nodding toward the group at the end of the row.

"Baker?" Carr asked. The new squad leader was a shake-and-bake named Roger Baker, a lanky Wyoming boy who was the same age as his crew, but with less experience. He had been selected from Advanced Individual Training at Ft. Polk to attend the NCO development course at Ft. Benning, and had arrived in Viet Nam as a buck sergeant. Carr's experience with these "instant NCO's" had been mixed. Some quickly accepted the mantle of authority and learned how to lead men in combat, but others found themselves lost at sea. Baker had been with them only a few days, so Carr had not yet determined which type he would be.

"Yeah," Samples said. "Think he'll make it?"

"Let's hope so. He hasn't really screwed up so far."

"Unlike our glorious leader," Samples remarked gloomily. Captain Gordon's performance on that company sweep had not impressed anyone, and Samples was particularly critical.

"Everybody makes mistakes," Carr told him, and tried to be as forgiving as his words were. The fact of the matter was that nothing Gordon had done in his few days in command had given Carr a warm fuzzy feeling. He seemed out of his depth, and struggling to maintain. It was unfortunate that the man had reached the rank of captain with virtually no command experience, and had been thrust into a job that was perhaps the most demanding in the Army: an infantry company commander in combat. In a way Carr felt sorry for him, but not as much as he felt sorry for himself and his men, who could possibly become victims of Gordon's inexperience.

Samples made a face, but said nothing more about it.

Carr watched approvingly as Sergeant Baker finally got his track loaded and then had his men line up so he could give them a cursory inspection. He made sure they had full canteens on their web belts, and took a quick look at their weapons, but did it in an informal way that wouldn't piss anybody off. If Baker had made them stand at attention and present their rifles for a white-glove inspection, he would have lost them forever.

"Not bad," Samples noted, nodding.

"It's a learning experience," Carr said, hoping Samples understood he was addressing both Baker and Gordon. The two of them climbed down from the track and moved into the center of the perimeter road to avoid getting in the way of the loading.

Both turned as Sweet walked up, looking unusually sharp in a clean uniform and boots with most of the mud wiped off. "I'm ready, sir. Where do I go?" Since he had been selected to attend the Bob Hope show, Sweet wouldn't be going out on the sweep with them.

"Report to the battalion headquarters for now," Carr told him. "Later a deuce-and-a half will take you and the other guys down to Cu Chi. Try not to get into trouble."

"Me, sir?" Sweet asked, pretending to be shocked at the implication.

"Yeah, you," Samples growled at him. "And take your weapon."

"No sweat, Sarge. And thanks for letting me go to the show."

"Go on, get out of here," Samples told him. Carr smiled and wished him luck.

As he watched Sweet walk away, Carr saw the sniper and his Vietnamese scout approaching from the center of the FSB. Both were loaded up with backpacks, and the scout had a PRC-25 radio as well. Carr noticed that the scout seemed to be handling the extra weight pretty well. The scout, whose name Carr had forgotten, carried a Korean-war vintage M2 carbine, while Sergeant Jaramillo had his modified M-14. The two men approached Carr and Samples with grim smiles.

"Sir," Sergeant Jaramillo said in greeting. "Where do you want us?"

"Why don't you ride with Sergeant Baker on the one-four? He's got the most room."

"Good enough," Jaramillo replied, turning toward the track and signaling the Vietnamese to follow him.

"Aaron," Carr said to Samples, "you better go with them and explain things to Baker."

"Roger that," Samples said, and hurried to catch up with the other two.

Carr scratched his ear. They had done this before. They would make a RIF—reconnaissance in force—and drop the sniper team off somewhere. This time it would be a company RIF, and not just his platoon. Carr hoped Gordon wouldn't get them lost again, and embarrass the company in front of these outsiders.

*****

With one hand Thanh adjusted her straw hat, ostensibly to better shield her face from the sun, but in reality to block her sight of Nhu. She had come to truly despise the woman, and was glad that soon she would be rid of her. This morning's argument had been exhausting, and Thanh hadn't spoken to Nhu since. They had gone to the ice house silently to fill their boxes, and then joined the other Coke kids and sandwich mama-sans on the long trek down the highway, following the Americans who were sweeping the road and providing security. It was a different group of soldiers today; their armored personnel carriers had extra machine guns, and there were tanks as well. Nhu had informed her that it was an armored cavalry unit, but Thanh had ignored her. She didn't want to give Nhu even the satisfaction of acknowledging her remarks, and she truly didn't care what kind of unit it was. If Robert wasn't there, nothing else mattered. The news of her mother's death had been the last straw, and she was drifting in a cloud of depression.

The group of soldiers Thanh and Nhu had been following met with another unit coming the other way. After a brief exchange of greetings, the two groups separated again and went to their assigned locations for outposting. Thanh and Nhu, along with two boys, followed one group, while the other Coke kids and older women split off and went in the direction of the other group. This group of Americans, which had two of the heavily armed APCs and one tank, found a cleared area and set up their outpost, while Nhu, Thanh, and the two boys parked across the highway and waved at the soldiers to encourage them to come buy things.

"That is a Sheridan tank," Nhu said, proud of her military knowledge. As if Thanh cared. Thanh rolled her eyes and faked a smile at the men across the dirt road. Actually, she hoped some of them would come over and want to talk, as that would take her mind off other things. Her emotions were roiling inside of her, a bizarre mixture of anger, sadness, excitement, concern, anticipation, and confusion. Much of her mind was focused on the package in Nhu's cart, the one hidden where she usually kept her Dragunov sniper rifle. That package had been the source of their quarrel this morning. It contained two stacks of money, which was more than Thanh wanted to bring, but less than Nhu had insisted upon.

The money was to pay Nhu's source, the venal and untrustworthy ARVN Captain Nguyen. When Nguyen had stopped to buy a sandwich and soda the day Nhu was wounded, he had told them he wanted the entire payment when he provided the final targeting information. Since the amount he wanted was less than Thanh had brought down from Hanoi, Nhu was ready to load up the cart with the four stacks of bills and give them to him when he showed up today. Thanh, not trusting the treacherous little captain, wanted to give him only one fourth of the money, with a promise of the rest upon a successful completion of the mission. They had argued bitterly, but quietly, for over half an hour this morning, because Nhu was sure Nguyen would refuse to tell them anything if they did not give him all he was asking for. Although she didn't say so, Thanh wasn't even sure she wanted the information. She had lost her enthusiasm for the mission, and frankly did not care if she ever fired the missiles at anyone. In the end they had compromised at half the agreed-upon sum now, and the rest afterward.

One of the crewmen from the tank jumped down from the behemoth and strolled casually across the road toward them. He was a black man, his hair closely cropped and a holstered pistol on his hip. Nhu smiled warmly at him as he came up and pulled a can of Coke from the ice in her bicycle's box. She held it out to him, saying, "Only fifty cents, sir."

"Looks good, girl," he responded with a grin. He pulled a small bill from his pocket and examined it. Thanh could see that it was a one dollar Military Payment Certificate. He handed it to her, saying, "Why don't you give me two of them things. I am really thirsty."

"Yes, sir," Thanh replied happily, digging in the ice for another one.

"You don't have to call me sir, girl," the man said. "I'm a sergeant, I work for a livin'."

Thanh laughed as she handed him the second Coke, even though she had heard that same line countless times. The man seemed nice, and she wanted to keep him there as long as possible, just so she wouldn't have to listen to Nhu. She took the can opener on the end of a string attached to the handlebars and reached out to open one of the Cokes, holding his hand in hers to steady it while she punched a triangular hole in the lid.

"Sandwich?" Nhu asked him encouragingly.

He glanced over at her and shook his head. "No, thanks, ma'am. I got to get back." He seemed a little disappointed when Thanh withdrew her hand, but didn't turn away yet. "What's your name, girl?" he asked Thanh. She told him. "Thanh, huh? That's pretty, just like you." He smiled at her with a twinkle in his eye.

"Hey, Rip, get your ass back here!" someone called from across the road. "Give someone else a turn."

The black man made a face and then winked at Thanh. "See you later, Thanh," he told her, and then turned and strolled back across the road, purposely taking his time.

After that a steady stream of men came over to guy sodas and sandwiches, but the nice man called Rip didn't return. When they heard the sound of an approaching helicopter all the soldiers quickly put on their helmets and tried to look busy. The helicopter, one of those small egg-shaped ones, circled once over the group of vehicles and then continued down the road. A few minutes later there were shouted orders and all the men loaded up on their vehicles, the engines cranked to life, and the platoon moved out onto the road and roared away.

As the dust settled, the two young boys that had been there with them mounted their bicycles and pedaled away, leaving Thanh and Nhu alone beside the road. Thanh wondered what they should do now, but didn't want to ask Nhu. Nhu, however, seemed oblivious to Thanh's growing dislike of her and spoke in a friendly manner.

"We will wait here until Captain Nguyen arrives. Perhaps we can sell something to our own people."

With the departure of the American soldiers, civilian traffic increased on the road, and Nhu began calling out to passers-by offering her sandwiches and Thanh's sodas at a much lower price than they charged the Americans. Even at the equivalent of ten cents, they had few takers, but they remained at that spot for over two hours, the sun burning down on their straw hats and melting the ice in their boxes. Finally a jeep appeared to their right and came to a halt on the side of the road across from them. Telling the driver to stay there, Captain Nguyen jumped out of the passenger seat, walked around the back of the jeep, and swaggered across the road to them.

"Good afternoon," he greeted them with a false smile. "I believe you have something for me."

"Yes," Nhu answered subserviently, and opened the hidden door on the bottom of her cart's wooden box.

"Wait," Thanh warned Nhu, surprised at her own temerity. "What is your information?" she demanded of Nguyen. Nhu stopped, her hand inside the box, and looked at Thanh with a puzzled frown.

"When I get my money, you will get the information," Nguyen said smugly.

Thanh stood tall, pulling her shoulders back, but was momentarily disconcerted when Nguyen's eyes immediately went to her breasts, which now thrust forward. She resisted shrinking back, and took a deep breath. Maybe she could use his distraction to their advantage. "When we have your information, we will give you the money. Some of it."

That last part caused Nguyen to look up at Thanh's face, his eyes narrowing.

"Some of it?"

"Yes. We will pay you half of the money now, if your information seems adequate, and the rest after we complete our mission."

Nguyen scoffed. "What if you die completing your mission? What then?"

Thanh stared at him defiantly. "If we die, then it will be because you did not give us good information."

"I do not need this," Nguyen snarled at her, and started to leave. But Nhu had drawn out one of the cloth-wrapped bundles and set it on top of her cart, letting one corner of the rag fall away to reveal the stack of bills inside. Nguyen's gaze locked onto the money, and he stopped dead in his tracks. He reached out toward the money, but Thanh grabbed his forearm and stopped him.

"Not yet," she warned. Reluctantly he withdrew his hand.

"How will I get the second payment?" he asked sullenly. Thanh was emboldened by his capitulation.

"The day after our mission is completed, you will come to Nhu's house. We will pay you then." She paused and looked into his eyes. "If your information is very good, and our mission is a great success, we will pay you a bonus as well."

"And if you do not succeed, or you are killed?"

"We will leave a note telling you where the money is."

"Including the bonus?" he asked greedily.

"Perhaps. Now what is your information?"

Nguyen looked over at the package Nhu was covering with one hand, but said nothing.

"Give him that stack," Thanh ordered Nhu. Thanh was feeling very confident now, and secretly amazed at how she had taken charge, and that Nhu had allowed her to do so. Nhu slide the package forward. Nguyen snatched it up, peeked inside the cloth, and then stuffed it inside his shirt. Nhu reached down and withdrew the other packet of cash and put it on top of the cart box, but kept it close to her, out of Nguyen's reach.

Nguyen looked hungrily at the packet, and then turned to Thanh. "Tomorrow there will be a helicopter going to Nui Ba Den."

"There are always helicopters there," Nhu spoke up disparagingly.

"Yes," Nguyen agreed, nodding, "but this one will be special. It will be carrying Bob Hope, the American entertainer."

Thanh looked at Nguyen blankly. She had never heard of this man. "Why is he important?" she asked.

Nguyen looked exasperated. "He is their greatest entertainer. He is loved by all the Americans. If he is killed, it will be such a tragedy that the American people will demand an end to the war."

"An entertainer?" Nhu marveled. "Does he sing, or dance?"

"He tells jokes. He will have singers and dancers with him."

"I do not understand," Thanh said. "Why would a man who tells jokes be so important? I thought the mission would involve a general or a politician."

Nguyen shrugged. "Who knows about Americans? All I know is that this decision came from Hanoi. Perhaps they know more than we do."

"Who in Hanoi made this decision?" Thanh asked, unsure if Nguyen would even know.

"Le Duan himself," Nguyen boasted.

"Does Uncle Ho agree?" Thanh asked.

Nguyen's face darkened. "Have you not heard? Ho Chi Minh is dead."

"What?" both Thanh and Nhu exclaimed.

"It has not been publicly announced yet, but I have been assured that it is true. He was very old, you know."

Thanh's shoulders slumped as the enormity of the news sank in. She had seen how frail he was when she met him, but somehow she had hoped he would continue to lead her country forever. She wasn't surprised by his death, but she was definitely disheartened. Her mood turned black, and she allowed Nhu to take over the negotiations.

"How will we know which helicopter?" Nhu asked.

"Bob Hope is doing a show in Cu Chi today for thousands of American troops. Tomorrow morning he will fly to Nui Ba Den to do a small show for the Americans up there. The Nui Ba Den show is a big secret, and not even the men up there know about it. A man I know in the Air Force found out about it when the Americans arranged for the air space to be cleared. The flight is scheduled to arrive at the mountain at nine in the morning, and leave about an hour later, so you will have two chances at it. He will be in one of those big helicopters with two rotors, the one the Americans call the Chinook. It will be escorted by gunships, I am sure."

"Nui Ba Den," Nhu mused. "That will make it easier. Do you not think so, Thanh?"

Thanh nodded. The helicopter would have to come in low enough to land on the peak, and they could fire the missiles from the side of the mountain. The target would be moving slowly, and the

Chinook had two jet engines that put out a large heat signature that the missile could easily home in on. All her training came back to her, and drove away the darkness that Ho's death had brought her.

"It would be better to strike as the helicopter is leaving," she said thoughtfully. She started to explain why, but stopped when she realized that Captain Nguyen probably did not know about the Arrow missiles. Perhaps he thought they were going to use an RPG or a small cannon of some sort. She did not want him to know more, for he might double cross them and turn them in to the Americans for a big reward.

"If you say so," Nguyen remarked with little interest. He again focused on the packet of money. "Give me the money now. I must go before my driver gets suspicious."

Thanh nodded at Nhu, who handed the package over. Nguyen stuffed it inside his shirt, saying, "Day after tomorrow, at your house. The money better be there." Grabbing a Pepsi out of Thanh's ice box, he marched away to his jeep.

As they watched the jeep make a U-turn and speed away, Nhu shook her head. "An entertainer. A comedian. This makes no sense."

"Apparently he is a very popular man with the Americans," Thanh said. "He comes here to entertain the soldiers, so he must be very patriotic. Le Duan would not have given us this assignment if it was not important."

"I guess," Nhu said, packing up her cart.

Suddenly the man's name rang bells in Thanh's mind. His first name was Bob, which she knew was a nickname for Robert, and that reminded her of the young man Nhu had killed. His last name was Hope, and she just realized that it was a word with significant meaning in English.

"His name, Hope," Thanh explained excitedly to Nhu. "That is the English word for *hy vong*. If he is killed that will symbolically end the hope of the Americans for winning this war. That must be why he is so important."

"Yes," Nhu blurted, "that must be it. We must hurry home and get ready. We will have to travel to the mountain tonight."

Thanh nodded as she lowered her bike to the ground and let the ice water in the box pour out while she held the remaining cans of soda in place. She felt a growing anticipation of culmination of her training, and the thrill of doing something important, while suppressing the worry about the danger and what could happen to her, especially if they failed. The excitement of the mission pushed her dark thoughts of death to the back of her mind. Nhu was already on the road pushing her cart quickly, and Thanh hurried after her.

*****

"At least we're not lost," Lieutenant Harry Masters said as he walked up. Lieutenant Carr and Sergeant Jaramillo were standing at the front of the one-four track looking at the map that Carr had spread out over the sloping trim vane.

"Yet," Carr responded cynically, and then mentally chastised himself for saying that in front of the young sniper next to him. Jaramillo, or "Nash" as he preferred to be addressed, wasn't part of Alpha Company, and wasn't aware of the recent incident involving Captain Gordon. Carr would rather Nash didn't find out about it either; there was no use in airing their dirty laundry. So he hastened to add, "We're right on schedule, in fact. I was just talking to Nash here about where the night laager will be, and how he wants to go from there."

The company had stopped for an afternoon break in a small grove of trees just southeast of Nui Ba Den. The area around the shady stand was mostly high grass, with other, smaller groves and thickets of brush scattered in the distance.

Masters was the new platoon leader for Third Platoon, a thin recent college graduate with curly dark hair. He had originally been assigned to Bravo Company, but had displeased a jerk lieutenant colonel from Division and been transferred to Alpha Company, where he had shown great leadership in the recent firefight in the Boi

Loi Woods. "So you're really going up the mountain?" Masters asked Nash with undisguised questioning of his sanity.

"Got to, sir" Nash replied with a shrug. "That's where the VC sniper is, I'm almost positive."

Masters slowly shook his head from side to side. "Wouldn't catch me doing that. The mountain is crawling with gooks. There's a reason we haven't gone in and cleaned them out."

"Well, he's not trying to take the hill," Carr pointed out. "He's just going to sneak up there, find the sniper, and take her out."

"Her?" Masters asked with a puzzled look.

"Didn't you hear? The sniper is a woman. Nash wounded her a couple days ago."

"That's how she's been getting away with it," Nash added. "Nobody was looking for a woman."

"Still," Masters said, "playing hide and seek on the side of a mountain doesn't sound like much fun."

"She shot my spotter," Nash remarked bitterly. "I can't let that go."

"Okay," Masters conceded. "So where do you think she is?"

Nash circled the south slope of the mountain on the map. The brown lines of elevation were very close together there, indicating the slope was very steep. "Somewhere in here," he said. "The gooks have a couple caves and a bunker there, and I figure she's hiding out in one of them."

"So," Carr asked doubtfully, "are you going to actually go into those caves?"

"No, no," Nash replied. "I'm going to set up above them, and wait for her to come out. She's got to take a leak sometime."

"Then what?" Masters asked. "Won't the other gooks come after you?"

Nash nodded. "Probably. You guys might have to come get me." Nash smiled at Masters.

"Up the mountainside with tracks? I don't think so."

"Oh, well, then maybe I'll call a cab. Don't worry, I have an exit strategy."

"Damn well better," Carr told him. "You'll be stirring up a hornets nest. I don't know how many gooks there are on the mountain, but I've heard there's more than a couple."

"Don't mean nothin'," Nash replied insouciantly, and then changed the subject. "So where are you guys going to camp out tonight?"

"We prefer to call it a night laager," Carr said mildly, knowing Nash was joking with them. "Right around here somewhere," he continued, pointing to an area on the map just southeast of the base of the mountain.

"That'll work," Nash said, bending over to study the map more closely. "Me and Quan will sneak out after dark and curve around here to this area. We'll find a good spot, set up, and wait."

"Better you than me," Masters said. "I wouldn't do that on a bet."

Carr looked at Masters and grinned. "You're full of shit, Harry. You'd do it in a New York minute. I know you."

Masters faked a crestfallen look. "Okay, maybe. But not today."

PFC Knox, the track's driver, popped his head out of the driver's hatch and said, "Sir, the CO says we're moving out."

"Roger," Carr replied, folding the map up quickly. Masters took off to rejoin his platoon, and Nash started climbing up the side of the track to take his seat on top. Carr stuffed the map in his pants cargo pocket and strolled over to the one-three track. He didn't hurry. They weren't leaving without him.

By the time he got there all the company's APCs had fired up their engines, black diesel smoke rising into the canopy of leaves, the roar of the engines echoing among the tree trunks. Climbing up the side of the track, Carr took a seat on the metal ammo can behind Sergeant Montoya, who sat on a folded up bench cushion stuffed in the concave cover of the open driver's hatch, his boots on either side of the hatch where Aiello's head poked out. Both Montoya and Aiello had their CVC helmets on, so they could hear the radio and could talk to each other on the intercom. Carr tapped Montoya on the shoulder, and when he turned around, Carr raised one eyebrow at him.

"Same as before," Montoya yelled over the noise. "We're on the left flank."

Carr nodded his understanding. The company had been operating in a fairly standard way all day. They would proceed mounted, with the company on line, through the wide grassy areas, but the men would dismount to proceed through the occasional forested areas. First Platoon was on the left, with Second Platoon between them and Headquarters Platoon, and Third Platoon was on the far right. Along with Headquarters Platoon were two Zippos—M-113 APCs fitted out with flame throwers. The Zippos were temporarily op-conned (operationally controlled) to A Company from Battalion. Carr wondered if the Zippos were spending the night with them, and decided they would have to. They couldn't head back to the base camp on their own. Carr, like almost everyone else in the unit, had a healthy respect for the Zippo crewmen. Those tracks had interiors filled with tanks carrying the napalm and propellant. Carr could just imagine what would happen if one of them was hit by an RPG. The danger was such that the Zippos had to use up all their fuel before they would be allowed back in the fire support base. Having them in the night laager, with its much closer spacing of men and vehicles, presented an even greater hazard.

FOURTEEN

With his XM-21 rifle across his lap, Nash swayed back and forth with the gentle motion of the armored personnel carrier, the ride of which was surprisingly smooth for such a heavy metal machine of war. It was kind of like riding a horse at a walk, and Nash never felt the need to hold onto the shield of the machine gun turret next to him. He glanced back at Quan, who was sitting on the cargo hatch cover, and saw the scout's eyelids drooping as he fought to stay awake. Nash sympathized. It had been a long day, with not much happening. The sweep had changed directions several times, but Lieutenant Carr had assured him that was intentional, to prevent the enemy from guessing where they were headed. Even though Nash had never expressed any concern about their route of advance, Carr had seemed anxious to reassure him that it was all planned. Now they were headed directly toward Nui Ba Den, which loomed over them with a subtle menace. Wisps of clouds trailed from the peak. The west side was brightly lit by the afternoon sun, but the eastern slopes were already in shadow, and the southern part facing Nash was a study in contrasts, with bright areas mixed with deep shade in an irregular pattern.

The company's tracks all gradually came to a halt, and the men began climbing down. "Are we there?" Nash asked the 50-cal gunner, a soul brother named Johnson.

"Naw, somebody saw something. Looks like a trail, maybe."

Nash and Quan joined the others on the ground. Most of them, at the direction of the squad leaders, spread out and searched the surrounding grassland. This area had a lot of small bushes and larger thickets, but no clumps of trees nearby. Nash and Quan, since they weren't part of a squad and thus exempt from the deployment, wandered over to where several of the company's leaders were gathered in front of Second Platoon. In addition to Lieutenants Carr and Masters, there was another lieutenant Nash didn't know, presumably the leader of Second Platoon, and the temporary company commander, Captain Gordon. There were a couple sergeants Nash had seen but didn't know, and a radioman who stood a few feet away, monitoring the traffic on his backpack radio. Nash and Quan didn't join the group at first, circling them instead while they inspected the ground.

The yellowed grass was about knee high, but there was a noticeable path cutting though it at an angle to their advance, roughly from the northwest to the southeast. Quan and Nash both knelt down to examine the strip of bare dirt between the low walls of weeds. Some foot prints were barely visible, and it looked to Nash like a mixture of bare feet, the tennis shoe-like boots of the NVA, and the tire tracks of Ho Chi Minh sandals. "Many soldiers," Quan commented. "Last night." The tracks were well defined because yesterday's rain had softened the earth.

They stood up, and while Quan walked slowly down the path, examining it and the grass nearby, Nash turned to face the officers who had wandered over to see what he had discovered.

"Did you find something, Sergeant?" Captain Gordon asked. Gordon was shorter than Nash, and his uniform was sharply pressed and clean. Nash noted that Gordon's boots were highly polished, which was unusual for field soldiers.

"It's a VC-NVA trail," Nash told them. "Lots of traffic, some as recently as last night. Good march discipline—everyone kept to the trail to keep it from getting wider and more noticeable."

"So it might be part of the Ho Chi Minh Trail?" Gordon asked, his voice rising a little.

Nash shrugged. "In a way. The Ho Chi Minh Trail is actually a vast network of trails, especially here in South Viet Nam. This might be one branch of it. Or not. Regardless, the trail seems to be used frequently."

Behind him Nash heard Quan grunt and turned to see him holding a rifle magazine up in the air. It was an AK-47 banana clip, and brass cartridges glinted in the sun at the open end. "Soldier in big trouble," Quan said with a grin.

"Yep," Lieutenant Masters chuckled, "loss of government property. That'll come out of his pay, I'll bet."

"And they don't make all that much," Carr added.

"Probably just spank his winkie," one of the sergeants suggested, and some of the others laughed. Captain Gordon didn't, and frowned at the joke.

"Perhaps this would be a good place for our night laager," he intoned.

"I don't know, sir," Carr said respectfully, "I think we're supposed to be closer to the mountain."

"Yes, Lieutenant, but here we might catch them unawares and capture a supply column or something."

Nash made a point of looking all around them before speaking. "They'll know you're here and take some other trail. It's too open."

Carr agreed. "I think he's right, sir. We should set up a klick or two away, act like we didn't see this trail, and then send out an ambush patrol."

Gordon scowled a little and was silent as he considered the suggestion. Nash got the feeling the captain was annoyed that his idea had been overruled. Everyone waited for Gordon to reach a decision. Finally he took a deep breath. "All right, here's what we'll do. We'll mount up and RIF to the west, find a good location, and go into the laager. As soon as it's dark, we'll send out a platoon-sized AP to come back here and watch the trail." Without waiting for any comments or objections, Gordon ordered, "Let's move out."

*****

Less than an hour later Captain Gordon found a location he deemed suitable, and Sergeant Samples was the first to jump down from his track and began guiding the platoon into place. The captain had chosen a wide area with only short grass and stunted bushes, and Samples had to admit it was not a bad place for a laager. There were a couple small groves of trees nearby, one about fifty meters to the west, and one maybe seventy meters to the southeast; otherwise there were just small thickets of bushes around, none of which were very close to the laager site. The base of Nui Ba Den, which rose up abruptly from the plain, was only a couple klicks away, its conical shape blotting out most of the northern sky.

The laager was the normal configuration, for the most part. The three line platoons formed a large circle, facing outwards, while headquarters platoon, which included the two mortar tracks, the mechanics track, and the commo track, along with the CO's track, formed up in the center. Initially Gordon had proposed placing the two flamethrower tracks in the center as well, but at Samples' insistence Lieutenant Carr had convinced him there was a better way. Gordon's concern had been to protect the Zippos from incoming RPGs, but Carr and Samples had pointed out they would be unable to use their flamethrowers from there, rendering them useless in a firefight. Instead the two Zippos had been placed with one on the southeast side, between Third Platoon and First Platoon, and the other on the northwest side in the middle of Second Platoon.

Once everyone was in place, Samples began giving orders to the men who had all dismounted. "Get the RPG screens up, and start digging fighting positions," he yelled. His orders were mostly unnecessary, he knew, for the men all knew the drill, and the squad leaders were fully capable of ensuring things were done right, but Samples wanted to remind everyone who was in charge. Since Sergeant Baker was the newest guy in the platoon, and certainly the least experienced leader, Samples went over to help the young squad leader.

While Samples had intended to offer his assistance, he was pleased to see that wouldn't really be necessary. The sniper and his Vietnamese scout had both pitched in, and the squad was operating fairly smoothly, so Samples just stood back and watched. Knox, the driver, had crawled out of his hatch and crouched on the front of the track, undoing the straps that held the rolled-up chain-link fencing and the angle-iron stakes that comprised the RPG screen. Once the straps were free, the screen rolled down the sloping front and bounced on the ground, while the stakes followed. Two of the men, Johnson and Rancy, picked up the stakes and walked out a few feet from the track, measuring the distance with their eyes, then jammed one of the stakes in the ground. Delaney came around from the back of the track, where Knox had already dropped the ramp, carrying the sledgehammer. Since he was taller and stronger, Johnson took the sledgehammer and raised it above his head, holding it horizontally. Rancy held the six-foot stake upright while Johnson awkwardly pounded the stake into the ground. Meanwhile Delaney picked up another stake and jammed the pointed end into the ground a few feet away.

On the right side of the track the sniper, his scout, and PFC Wilson had a pick and a shovel, and were digging the fighting position. The scout, Quan, held open sand bags so Jaramillo could fill them with the dirt he was digging up after Wilson broke through the surface with the pick. Just beyond this group was one of the Zippos, and its crew of two was struggling to get their own RPG screen erected. Seeing where he was needed, Samples went over and picked up their sledgehammer. Mimicking Johnson, Samples lifted the sledge over his head and began tapping the top of a stake while the Zippo driver held it in place.

Once all four stakes were pounded in, arrayed in a rough semi-circle in front of the track, the three men unrolled the fencing in front of the stakes and then lifted it up to a vertical position against them. While the two crewmen held it in place, Samples used baling wire to secure the chain-link to the stakes. When he was finished, Samples stepped back to admire his own handiwork. Curving around to either side of the track, the screen would protect it from most RPG rounds. The rocket-propelled grenades had shaped charge warheads with contact fuses that ignited the round as soon as it hit something. The shaped charge was effective against armor only when it exploded right against the metal, punching a hole by sending a super-hot stream of molten metal through the mild armor of an

APC. If it hit in the right spot, it would shower the inside of the vehicle with slag and fragments that were devastatingly destructive. If the RPG hit the screen, however, the concentrated explosion would effectively dissipate in mid-air and cause only minor damage to the vehicle behind the screen.

He was about to offer to help the Zippo crew dig a fighting position, when he realized they didn't have a use for one. With a crew of only two men, both of whom were needed to operate the flamethrower, the track was the only fighting position they would need. "You guys need anything else?" he asked.

The buck sergeant who was the TC—track commander— chewed his lip while he thought about it. He was a short muscular black man, and his driver was a tall skinny white guy. "Hey, Dickie," the sergeant said to the driver, "you need anything?"

"A ticket home?" Dickie suggested quickly.

"No, dipshit, something for tonight."

"Oh, well, I could use a cold soda."

"They'll probably chopper in ice and sodas later," Samples told them. "I'll make sure you get some."

"Thanks, Sarge." The sergeant, whose name Samples didn't know because he wasn't wearing his uniform shirt, just a sleeveless olive drab T-shirt with sergeant's chevrons drawn on it with a pen, then turned to the driver and said, "Come on Dickie, time to set up our deluxe accommodations."

Samples followed them around to the rear of the track, where the ramp was still up, but the personnel door was open. Through the open hatch he could see the giant apple-green tanks that contained the napalm and propellant that fed the oblong nozzle protruding from the front of the squat turret on top of the track. Samples had observed that there was a machine gun barrel sticking out of the turret as well.

"Is that a 30-cal in the turret?" he asked. This was the first time he had inspected a Zippo close up.

"Yeah," the sergeant said, "for all the good it does." He stepped back as Dickie, who had climbed inside the crowded interior, began tossing out cots and bedrolls. "Fucker jams a lot, and it's hard to get ammo for it. That's why Dickie's got that M-60." He nodded toward the front of the track, where an M-60 7.62mm light machine gun had been mounted on a pintle directly in front of the driver's hatch.

"I noticed the other Zippo has a 50-cal," Samples said. That gun was mounted on a standard tripod that had been strapped down on top of the track to the right side of the turret.

"Wish we did," the sergeant said, unfolding a cot. "But we ain't got anyone to operate it, anyway. They've got a full crew of three, but we're shorthanded, as always."

"We've got you covered," Samples assured him, tilting his head at the A Company tracks on either side.

"Why?" the man asked, looking at Samples with a touch of worry in his eyes. "You think we'll get hit tonight?" Dickie climbed out of the track and stood beside the sergeant, waiting for the answer.

"Probably not," Samples said. "But you never can tell."

"So why are we here, Sarge?" Dickie asked, voicing the existential question that all infantrymen constantly asked.

"Some officer thought it was a good idea," Samples told them. "Actually, we're also delivering a sniper team that's going up on the mountain, but don't tell anybody."

"Yeah, right," the sergeant said sarcastically. "Like I was about to call my buddy in the VC and tell him all about it. The sniper's going up on Nui Ba Den? Man, that's crazy."

"Bet that," Samples agreed. "And we're going to send out an AP back to that trail we found this afternoon, see if we can zap a few gooks hauling goodies."

"Well, you boys keep 'em busy," the sergeant said with a grin. "Me and Dickie'll stay here and get our beauty sleep, if that's all right with you."

"Long as you sleep with one eye open," Samples replied with a wry grin of his own.

FIFTEEN

The sun had just slipped below the horizon, but it was still too light outside for them to leave yet. Nhu had been in a quandary, pacing back and forth across the room, wondering aloud if she should take her Dragunov rifle or not. They had brought out the two canvas-covered hard cases with the Arrow missiles and accessories, adjusting the carrying straps so they would fit on their backs and trying them on. Nhu had found the long case heavier than she had expected, especially since she was still recovering from her wound. Positioning the shoulder strap so it wouldn't rub against her breast had required some modifications, and even now she said it was uncomfortable at best.

"You will not need the rifle," Thanh pointed out impatiently. "We will be on the mountain, and only firing at aircraft."

Nhu finally conceded. "You are right. But we need protection." She went over to the still open hole in the floor where the missiles had been hidden and knelt so she could reach inside. Sitting up, she brushed the dirt from a small cloth-wrapped bundle and pulled the folds aside. Inside was a gleaming black pistol, a squarish automatic like Thanh had seen officers carry in North Vietnam, one she knew was called a Makarov. With it were three slender magazines of bullets. Holding the cloth like a sling, Nhu got to her feet and went over to lay the items on the small table.

"How will you carry it?" Thanh asked, always the practical one.

Nhu pursed her lips and looked around while she patted her body. "Ah!" she said after a minute, and went over to the cabinet where they kept their clothes. She reached inside and pulled out a green canvas bag with a shoulder strap. Thanh recognized it as a Claymore mine bag, an item most of the American infantrymen used to carry their extra rifle magazines. "I gave a soldier a sandwich for this," she explained. "I knew it would be useful someday." Back at the table she put the pistol and magazines inside the bag, and then slipped the shoulder strap over her head so that it hung down on her left hip. "See, that will work."

"What about the missiles?" Thanh asked, thinking about the modified straps.

Nhu picked up the long pack and struggled to put her arms through the carrying straps. Once it was on, she stood erect and wiggled her shoulders to test the fit. The Claymore bag bounced against her hip, and when she tried to reach down to access the pistol, the strap for the missile case started sliding down her arm. That, in turn, shifted the other strap against her wounded breast, causing Nhu to yelp in pain. She quickly squatted and let the pack slide off her arms and drop to the floor.

"You must carry the pistol," she told Thanh. "Your load is lighter." And that was true. Unlike Nhu's long case with the launchers, hers contained only the batteries and gripstock assembly. Nearly half of the cash it had previously carried had already been handed over to Captain Nguyen, and the rest had been buried out in the garden, making her case reasonably easy to carry. "I am not familiar with that gun," Thanh protested. In fact she had been trained to operate it, and had actually qualified on it, but she didn't want Nhu to know that.

Nhu, wincing, carefully slid the shoulder strap of the green bag off and handed the bag to Thanh, who reluctantly took it. "You will not be firing it," Nhu explained. "You will simply carry it and hand it to me if I need it. Try it on with your case."

Thanh draped the shoulder strap around her neck and then squatted and shrugged into the carrying straps of the launcher case. For her it was slightly uncomfortable, but tolerable. The brown straps of the launcher case and the green strap of the Claymore bag contrasted sharply with the light blue of her blouse.

"You're changing blouses, of course," Nhu ordered. She went to the clothes cabinet and withdrew one of her own black shirts. "Here," she said, passing it to Thanh. Thanh took off the case and the Claymore bag, and then turned her back to Nhu while she replaced her blue blouse with the overly large black one. "Now you look like a true member of the People's Liberation Army," Nhu said proudly. "We should eat before we leave," she added. "It will be a long night."

*****

When Lieutenant Carr returned from the leaders meeting at the CO's track, Sergeant Samples and the squad leaders were waiting for him. Although he struggled to keep his expression bland, Carr could tell that they were reading his face and realizing he wasn't bringing good news. He motioned for them to follow him and led them away from the platoon, close to one of the mortar tracks.

"No hot chow tonight, guys," he told them when they had gathered around him.

"How come?" Sergeant Jamison asked.

"Captain Gordon feels it would give our position away to have a chopper come in, and we're too far from a road for them to bring it in a truck."

"Like the gooks don't already know we're here," Sergeant Montoya noted sardonically.

"Yes," Carr agreed, "I know. But realistically, a chopper coming in this close to the mountain would be a real inviting target."

"So no ice or sodas, either, I guess," Sergeant Baker commented morosely.

"Nope."

"I guess the Zippo guys are SOL, then," Samples said. "I promised them cold sodas tonight. Oh, well."

"I've got some extra C rations," Sergeant Reedy said brightly. "Anybody want some ham and lima beans?"

As if on cue, everyone else made a face and said, "Yuck!"

Carr was just as disappointed as the rest of them. Usually when they set up a night laager, Battalion would send out a truck or chopper with hot food in Mermite cans, blocks of ice, and cases of soda, along with the mail. Tonight they would get none of that. Although he understood Gordon's reasoning, he didn't necessarily agree with it. Montoya was correct: the gooks probably knew they were there already. A company of APCs made a lot of noise that could be heard for a couple miles, and they were in plain view of anyone on Nui Ba Den who had a pair of binoculars. Their location was no secret. The only question was whether the gooks would decide to attack them, or simply ignore them. The battalion commander, as well as his superiors, was undoubtedly hoping for the former. Although it wasn't publicly acknowledged, the role of the mechanized infantry in Viet Nam was to be big rolling targets, to draw enemy fire so that the enemy could be located and destroyed by artillery and air power. In order to win a war of attrition, as this one had become, it was necessary to first find the enemy and draw them out into the open.

"That's not all the good news," Carr told the sergeants. "We're sending out a platoon ambush patrol, and guess which platoon gets to lead it?"

"Shit!" Reedy cursed.

"Fucked again," Jamison remarked with abject resignation.

Nobody liked going out on ambush patrol, but not because of the potential danger. It was the discomfort and lack of sleep that was most distasteful. Lying in the weeds or the woods all night, suffering through bugs and rain and being poked by sticks, while in full uniform, was in no way a pleasant prospect. And then, the next day, the soldiers were expected to carry out some other mission with no time for recovery. Worse, in some ways, was the fact that APs by mech units were rarely productive. The enemy knew they were in the area, and simply avoided the ambushes.

"I'll be leading it," Carr told them. "I'll take Eberhart, two of you squad leaders, and eight men. Sergeant Samples, I'll need you to stay here and take charge of the platoon."

"Why don't you let me take it, and you stay here, sir," Samples protested.

"Negative. I'm the platoon leader."

"We getting any guys from the other platoons?" Montoya asked.

"Not that I know of. I'd rather it just be our guys anyway."

"I'll go," Sergeant Baker volunteered. Carr could see the trepidation in his face, and knew he was volunteering mainly to prove he was part of the platoon. But the young shake-and-bake needed the experience, so Carr nodded.

"Who else?"

"Might as well," Reedy groaned, "can't dance."

"Sergeant Samples, you pick out the eight men. Have them ready to go at twenty-one hundred. Oh, and let Jaramillo know. He and the scout will go out with us, but peel off somewhere."

"Roger that," Samples acknowledged. "I still think I ought to go."

"I wish you could," Carr told him, and meant it. He would feel a whole lot better about the mission if Samples were coming along. The sergeant's tactical expertise and combat proficiency were invaluable. Although this was called a platoon ambush patrol, with only twelve men it barely constituted a squad. The platoon was always shorthanded, and they had to leave enough men behind to man the tracks and guard their section of the perimeter, so the small patrol was the best they could do. Gordon had promised to send some of the mortar guys and mechanics over to fill out the guard roster on the platoon's tracks tonight, which would help. Still, Carr was more concerned about an assault on the night laager than any possible contact with the AP, and worried that their side of the circled vehicles was severely undermanned.

It was long past sunset, but the ghostly light of a half-moon directly overhead illuminated the laager well enough that Carr could see the dark bulk of all the tracks while his patrol shuffled and milled around, awaiting his orders. Reedy and Baker had double-checked each man's equipment, making sure they had plenty of ammo, a full canteen, a helmet, and their poncho in case it rained. Carr had thought about leaving the helmets behind, but Gordon, perhaps reading his mind, had insisted that everyone wear their steel pots. At night the helmets restricted the men's vision and hearing somewhat, and the shape readily identified them as American soldiers, but they did provide some protection from incoming, and formed a suitable headrest when trying to sleep on the ground.

"Dubois, you'll take point," Carr said when everyone settled down. "I'll be right behind you. Sergeant Reedy, you bring up the rear. Initially we'll head north from here, then once we get in the trees we'll turn east, except for Sergeant Jaramillo and Quan. Maintain a three-meter interval; with this moon, you shouldn't have any trouble seeing the guy in front of you. Everybody keep an eye out for that trail we saw this afternoon. That's where we'll set up. Any questions?"

"Can I count cadence?" Rancy asked with feigned enthusiasm. Sweet was the platoon's smartass, but with him gone to Cu Chi, Rancy had felt like he had to fill in.

"Sure, Rancy, as long as no one can hear it."

"Aw, that's no fun." Reedy, who happened to be standing next to Rancy, punched him on the shoulder.

"Anyone else? Okay, let's move out."

Dubois led them out between the one-one track and second platoon's two-four track, with everyone dodging around the fighting position and threading their way past the RPG screen. Three men from Second Platoon fell in behind them, but dropped off a hundred meters out at a small clump of bushes to be a Listening Post. That was another concern of Carr's: there were only two LPs tonight. This one on the north side from Second Platoon, and one on the south side from Third Platoon. Ideally there would be LPs to the east and west, but there simply weren't enough men in the company to do that when a platoon AP was going out.

The patrol moved swiftly through the knee-high grass. The moonlight was bright enough to keep in line and avoid obstacles, and the lights on top of Nui Ba Den gave Carr an unmistakable north star to follow. After the debacle at the peak last year, lights had been erected around the perimeter of the small camp up there, looking like a sparkling halo high in the sky above them. Carr had his compass, but didn't think he would need it very much. With those lights on top of the mountain, he would always know where he was.

*****

When the patrol entered the woods, they paused to regroup. Nash and Quan separated themselves from the others, and the column closed up to fill the gap they had left. After the lieutenant had taken a quick compass bearing, the patrol continued, now heading straight east. Leaning against a tree, Nash pulled out his canteen and took a drink, while Quan squatted down at his feet and rubbed his face. Unlike the mech guys in the patrol, Nash and Quan wore boonie hats instead of helmets, and both had backpacks, although the packs were only half full. Quan didn't ask why they were waiting in the woods, and Nash was glad his buddy had learned the ways Nash thought. He figured that if any VC had been watching or following the patrol, they wouldn't notice that there were two fewer men, and they would continue to track the patrol as it made its way east. After the enemy's attention had shifted away from these woods, Nash and Quan could continue north unseen.

Fifteen minutes later Nash pushed himself away from the tree and whispered to Quan, "Okay, let's go." Quan led off as they quietly slipped through the woods, and soon they emerged back onto the open plain of grass, the dark cone of Nui Ba Den rising up in front of them. Nash could feel the ground rising under his feet as they hurried across the open areas, and the patches of woods began to increase in frequency. From his study of the maps and aerial photographs, Nash knew that as they got closer to the mountain, they would enter a vast forest that climbed up the foothill area and covered the lower slopes. That forest held both promise and danger. In the forest they would not be visible at more than a few yards, but likewise, neither would the enemy. They would have to proceed very cautiously in order to avoid stumbling on a VC encampment or encountering an enemy patrol. Nash would have to depend primarily on the slope of the earth to guide them in the right direction, since his view of the sky would be blocked by the overhead canopy.

It took them nearly two hours to reach the foothill forest, longer than Nash had anticipated. He began to worry about the time element, for they still had to climb nearly halfway up the mountain and search for a good hiding place where they could set up and camouflage themselves, and do that all before dawn. The forest was fairly dense here, and little moonlight filtered down through the leafy branches. Nash touched Quan on the shoulder to signal him to stop, and then pulled out his compass, just to make sure they were still heading in the right direction. He worried that simply going uphill by feel could lead them astray if there were a hidden fold in the earth or ancient ravine that had been disguised by the trees. "Shit!" he muttered, watching the faintly glowing needle on the compass swing wildly back and forth. Apparently the mountain had some magnetic anomalies that were interfering with the compass needle, not surprising since the ancient volcano was directly between them and the North Pole. Nash slipped the compass back into his pocket with a sigh. "Onward and upward," he murmured to Quan, knowing that while the Vietnamese might not understand the actual words, he would grasp the underlying meaning. Together they resumed their stealthy hike through the rising forest.

They had gone only a few hundred meters when Quan abruptly stopped, so quickly that Nash nearly ran into him. They both squatted down, and Nash tried to determine what Quan had detected. Although he could see little inside the gloom of the forest, Nash heard the unmistakable sound of voices to their front right, and they seemed to be getting closer. Quan eased down into a prone position, and Nash did the same, stretching his legs out behind him and edging closer to a large tree trunk. He brought his rifle up to his shoulder, and debated internally about switching on the starlight scope that was mounted on it. He decided against it, because the scope made a noticeable whine when it spooled up, and in such close quarters the scope would be superfluous anyway.

Nash could now hear the sound of boots on the leaves of the forest floor, and the swish of branches against fabric. Momentarily he had considered the possibility that it was Lieutenant Carr's ambush patrol, somehow very lost, but then he heard the voices again, and they had the distinctive cadence of Vietnamese. From the noise they were making, Nash estimated that it must be a very large group of men, and they would be coming very close to where he and Quan were lying. Nash buried his face in the dead leaves, to keep his pale face from giving away his position. He had to depend solely on his hearing now, and that told him the men would pass only a few feet in front of him. He tried to melt into the ground, flattening himself as much as possible while avoiding any movement, hoping he would be no more noticeable than a pile of leaf debris or a low bush.

Gripping his rifle tightly, Nash fought the urge to jump up and start firing wildly. Instead he lay there frozen, using his hearing to paint a mental picture of what was happening only a few feet away. It was a military patrol, Nash was now certain, because he could hear the unmistakable sound of wood and metal banging against canvas, and the men's footsteps were often in time with each other, an unconscious tendency of soldiers who were trained to march in step when in formations. The first man in the group passed only a couple yards to Nash's front, angling across the path he and Quan had been following and proceeding in a southwesterly direction, assuming Nash and Quan had been headed north as they believed. As they passed, Nash counted the sounds that seemed to belong to each individual, which he could now even smell, and determined that the patrol had at least twenty men.

As the last man in the column went by, Nash raised his head slightly and peered from beneath the brim of his boonie hat at the backs of the men fading away in the darkness. He couldn't see much, but he did catch the distinctive shape of a North Vietnamese Army pith helmet.

"NVA," Quan whispered, confirming Nash's impression. They waited until the patrol could no longer be heard, and they were certain there was no straggler catching up, before standing up and brushing themselves off.

"That was close," Nash said, pointing out the obvious.

"Where they go?" Quan asked curiously.

"Good question. Think they're going to attack that laager?"

"Maybe."

"Let me see the radio." Quan turned away so Nash could operate the controls on the PRC-25. The radio had been turned off, and the handset was clipped to the side of it. Nash turned it on and unhooked the handset, but then said, "Shit! I don't remember that company's freq." Their radio had been set to the frequency used by the Division sniper teams, monitored in Tay Ninh. He had asked Eberhart what frequency the mech company was using, and had even written it down, but he had quickly forgotten it, and it would be impossible to read in the dark, even if he remembered where he had put the slip of paper with the numbers on it. And of course, they had not brought a flashlight. Berating himself for his lack of foresight, Nash decided to at least call it in to Division, and tell them to pass the word down to Alpha Company.

Speaking quietly, Nash tried to call, but got no answer. All he got was the whoosh of static when he turned off the squelch. He briefly turned on the dial lights, which were just bright enough to read the settings, and confirmed they were on the right frequency. He repeated the freq mentally a couple times, to be sure he had memorized it, and then began flipping through other frequencies to see what he could pick up. The only voices he heard was a call for artillery fire from somewhere, and a brief snatch of Vietnamese that could have been either ARVN or NVA. Resetting to the correct freq for the sniper teams, he turned everything off and reclipped the handset.

"No go," he told Quan. "Probably the trees." The VHF radios the Army used had a limited range, usually less than thirty miles, and that was under ideal conditions. They were essentially line-of-sight radios, which meant that anything that came between the transmitting radio and the receiving radio could disrupt the signal. Here, deep in the forest, the radio's range was severely compromised by the trees, and there could also conceivably be a ridge stretching out from the base of the mountain between them and Tay Ninh. Regardless, they were unable to make radio contact from where they were now. Once they got up on the mountain he would try again.

This time Nash took point, holding his rifle almost vertically in front of him to ward off the thin branches that threatened to whip his face. Aside from the sound of insects and a slight breeze rattling the leaves, the forest was now silent, and Nash strived to keep from disturbing that quietness. He raised his feet with each step, not quite high-stepping, but careful not to let his feet drag, both to avoid tripping and to keep from making so much noise. Like a couple of avenging ghosts, they glided through the forest, sensing the slight but increasing change in elevation as they neared the mountain.

Nash noticed that he was beginning to breathe deeper, and realized the incline had gotten much steeper without his realizing it. The woods began to thin out, and they were now climbing up a fairly steep grade. Nash stopped and turned around, and found he could see occasional gaps in the canopy that revealed the plain below them bathed in silver moonlight. They were now definitely on the slopes of Nui Ba Den, and that meant they were in enemy territory. They would have to be even more cautious now, for the intelligence reports indicated that the Viet Cong and NVA had essentially fortified the entire mountain, except for the peak. He and Quan could run into bunkers or caves at any time, and the VC in particular were well known for their ability to camouflage their positions.

"Maybe you better go first," Nash told Quan. As a former VC himself, Quan would be more likely to recognize hidden positions or signs of activity. Nash didn't want to stumble onto a gook fighting position in the dark and get shot up by a bunch of AK-47s. That could fuck up his whole day.

As Quan moved past him to take point, he said, "Radio?"

Nash knew he should try again to warn the mech company about the NVA soldiers they had seen, but he suddenly felt very exposed. The woods here were just thick enough keep him from seeing or hearing more than a few feet, which was plenty of space for a gook sentry to be nearby and unaware of their presence. His talking on the radio would undoubtedly be audible to anyone within a hundred meters, due to the hush that prevailed in the forest, and he wasn't willing to take that chance. Besides, he rationalized, the mech guys had a whole company, with mortars, machine guns, and flame throwers. They could easily deal with twenty gooks armed only with AKs and maybe RPGs. He would call his sighting in later, after they had found a good position higher up and were sure there was no one else around.

SIXTEEN

"Do you need to rest?" Thanh asked solicitously. It wasn't that she was really concerned about Nhu, but she herself wanted to stop, and hoped that Nhu's wound was bothering her enough that she, too, would be tired. The long hike across country in the dark, carrying the heavy pack, pistol, and water bottle, was starting to really wear Thanh out. She dodged around a low-hanging branch while she waited for Nhu to respond. The patch of woods they were in was dark and gloomy, but the ground was soft and the trees widely spaced.

They had traveled another few meters before Nhu finally answered, obviously trying to speak without gasping. "No, I do not, but if you do, I suppose we could pause a few minutes here." Nhu walked over to a fallen tree trunk and sat down on it heavily, nearly falling as the heavy pack pulled her backwards. Stifling a groan, she slipped her arms out of the straps on the heavy oblong case and let it tip over and fall to the ground behind her.

"Careful!" Thanh admonished her. "The missiles are in there!"

"Sorry," Nhu said with very little contrition. Free from the weight of the pack, she stretched her legs out in front of her and rubbed her breast. It was too dark for Thanh to make out Nhu's facial features, but she could tell the woman was in pain.

Thanh gingerly lowered her own case to the ground and sat down beside Nhu. Her water bottle was on a strap wrapped around her neck and shoulder, and she pulled it up to unscrew the lid and take a long drink. She did not offer any to Nhu, and not just because the older woman had her own water bottle. "How much farther?" she asked.

Nhu took a deep breath and let it out slowly. "Two or three hours," she said finally. Thanh could detect the weariness in Nhu's voice. She almost wished Nhu would decide the mission was too arduous to continue and decide to return home. Nhu, however, was dedicated to the cause, and would press on regardless. Thanh felt a twinge of guilt because she no longer shared that burning zeal. She no longer cared who won this battle, or this never-ending war. She wasn't entirely sure what she did want, either. Her mother was dead, Uncle Ho was dead, and Robert was dead. She felt totally alone in the world, with no real goal to strive for, and no real friends. Pretending to scratch her chest, Thanh fingered the tiny gold cross through the fabric of her blouse. She had put the necklace on just before they left the house, when Nhu wasn't looking, because she knew how the older woman would scorn her for "atavistic religious beliefs." But the cross was the only thing of her mother's that Thanh had, and it gave her comfort.

"Our comrades have a big cave," Nhu mused wistfully. "It has beds, and food. We will be able to rest there until it is time to fulfill our destiny."

Thanh frowned at this overblown description of their mission. Not only was it too dramatic, it hinted that Nhu suspected they would die in the attempt. Thanh, despite her feelings of despair and loneliness, was not ready to sacrifice her life for a cause she no longer believed in. She would now have to watch Nhu even more carefully, vigilant for signs that the older woman was risking both their lives unnecessarily.

Nhu took another deep breath and pushed herself up to a standing position. "Let us continue. The sooner we get there, the sooner we can rest." She stepped over the log to retrieve the pack and struggled into the straps, grunting with the effort. While Thanh put her arms through the straps of her smaller pack, Nhu bounced on her heels to settle her load, leaning her head back to touch the tall pack, and took a deep breath. With no further conversation, she went back to the path and strode forward with renewed vigor. Thanh sighed and followed.

A few minutes later they emerged from the woods onto a grassy plain, and after the dimness of the woods, the moonlight lit up the fields comparatively brightly. Thanh could see dark clumps that represented small groves and thickets of bushes, but they were all distant across the fuzzy waves of high grass. The conical shape of Nui Ba Den rose up before them, the twinkling lights at its peak giving it an oddly festive look. Traveling across this vast open area, they would be apparent to anyone watching and make easy targets. But, Thanh knew, the Americans rarely ventured out after dark, especially in this area, so close to the mountain. They were following a narrow but well-worn path, and Thanh was sure that the only ones they might run into here were other communist Vietnamese.

The trail veered around a low thicket of bushes that was around thirty meters in diameter, with a single thin tree rising up from the middle like a flagpole. After making a semicircular detour around the thicket, the trail straightened out and continued straight north. After a kilometer and a half it led them into a wide wooded area. Back under the forest canopy, it was so dark Thanh could barely make out the tall case Nhu carried in front of her, but somehow Nhu could see well enough to follow the trail, and they pushed forward without slowing. Thanh wondered what time it was; she knew it must be still a while before midnight, but it felt like she had been lugging this case through the darkness forever. Worse, the case seemed to be getting heavier, but finally she realized the sensation was due to a slight rise in the trail. They were starting to go uphill, which was both good and bad. It meant they were getting closer to their destination, but it also meant more exertion as they climbed. Thanh sighed again.

*****

Lieutenant Carr felt almost naked. The patrol was crossing a wide area of knee-high grass, bathed in silvery moonlight, seemingly visible for miles in every direction. Nui Ba Den rose to his left, blocking out the stars to the north, and closer in, dark irregular mounds represented distant patches of woods or thickets of bushes. Any of those could be hiding an enemy force just waiting to ambush the ambushers. He glanced back at the line of men snaking behind him, concerned at how starkly the dark shapes of the men stood out against the light grey of the grass. They were extremely exposed, but there was no way to avoid that. The occasional stands of trees were too small and too infrequent to provide cover along the route to the trail they had discovered in the afternoon.

PFC Dubois, who was about twenty feet ahead of Carr, threw up his left fist in a signal to halt, and Carr echoed the signal, knowing the men behind would do the same. All of them stopped and knelt down. Carr watched Dubois take a few steps to his left, and then a few more steps to his right, checking out the ground ahead of him. Although Dubois, a slender soul brother from Mississippi, was fairly new to the platoon, he had proved himself capable and unafraid. The young man knelt down and felt the ground with his hand, and then stood up and walked back to Carr, kneeling down to face him.

"That's the trail, sir," he said with his Southern drawl. "Been used lately, too, I reckon."

"How do you know?"

"Felt like fresh footprints. Couldn't tell which ways they was headed, though. Too dark."

Carr was mildly surprised by Dubois's ability to make such a determination. He surmised that Dubois must have been a hunter back home, and learned tracking skills that way. Regardless, he was impressed.

"Good job," Carr told him. He stood up and looked around. This was clearly not the place to set up an ambush; there was neither cover nor concealment in the low grass. He saw a dark mass about fifty meters to their north. "Let's check that out," he told Dubois. "Keep away from the trail." Dubois nodded and stood up, took another look around, and set out to their left. He clearly understood that the patrol should avoid leaving a noticeable trail of their own that might alert any enemy coming by. "Spread out," Carr told the rest of the men in a low voice. "Advance on line." The men all stood up and turned to their left, wading through the grass toward the distant clump of foliage.

As they got closer, Carr could see that it was large patch of low bushes, roughly circular and about thirty meters in diameter, with a single slender tree rising from the middle. He had the men halt and kneel again while Dubois went forward and inspected. The point man walked around the thicket to the left, disappearing behind the bushes for a minute, and then reappearing directly in front of Carr as he popped up out of the foliage.

"Trail curves around over there," he reported, sweeping his arm toward the east side of the thicket. "Bushes is pretty thick, but there's room to hide in there."

"Think it'll work?" Carr asked him.

"Prolly won't find nothin' better, sir."

Carr nodded to himself. The thicket provided concealment, but no cover from flying bullets. In this area, however, they were unlikely to find any convenient ditches or foxholes, and digging in was impractical. Dubois was right; this was probably the best they could do. They needed to get out of sight quickly. With hand gestures and whispers he and the squad leaders moved the men into the bushes from the west side and had them crawl through to take up prone positions along the east side, facing the trail through the edges of the thicket. Carr followed them and took a position in the center, with Eberhart beside him, and pulled out his map. Shielding the beam with his hand, he used his flashlight to quickly look at the map, trying to determine their grid coordinates. With no landmarks other than the mountain, however, he was unable to narrow it down enough to help.

"Call for a marking round," he told Eberhart, "on checkpoint Pabst." While the RTO murmured into his handset, Carr stood up, pushing his head up through the branches, and lifted his compass up to his face. Unfolding the two parts of the sight, he prepared to aim it. It took a couple minutes for the request to go from Captain Gordon to the 105mm howitzer battery at Fire Support Base Wood, but finally a bright white spot exploded in the sky almost a mile to the southwest. Carr quickly aimed the compass at the quickly fading dot of light, and stared through the eyepiece to see where the needle was pointing. The needle wavered back and forth, but he got an approximate reading. Dropping back down into the bushes, he spread the map on the ground and had Eberhart hold the flashlight. While he had been waiting on the marking round, he had shot an azimuth to the peak of Nui Ba Den. Using the compass he drew a back azimuth on the map from the mountain top to the south with a grease pencil, and drew another back azimuth from checkpoint Pabst, which had been marked on the map prior to leaving the night laager. Where the two lines crossed was their approximate current location. The unsteadiness of the compass needle concerned him, but he had no other option. Peering closely at the dimly illuminated map, he determined the grid coordinates and wrote them on the acetate, then handed it to Eberhart so he could call it in. The location was not precise enough to call for artillery, but if they needed arty support, they could call for another marking round close by, and use that to walk HE rounds even closer.

Carr would have liked to have the company's artillery forward observer along on the ambush patrol, but Gordon had insisted the man stay with the rest of the company in the night laager, a not unreasonable decision. The AP had the ability to shoot and move quickly if they made contact, while the tracks of the company were pretty much stuck in place until dawn.

"CO says 'good hunting'," Eberhart whispered to him after a short conversation on the radio. Carr rolled his eyes in the dark. Good hunting! What an asinine thing to say. Frankly, Carr was hoping they wouldn't see anything all night. Just in case, however, he had Johnson and Dubois set up Claymores about ten feet from the trail at the north and south ends of the thicket. The two quickly inserted the blasting caps, screwed down the shipping plugs, and hustled back to the bushes letting the wire play out behind them. Johnson slid down on Carr's left and attached the firing device. He didn't bother using the testing set that one was supposed to employ to verify the circuit. Carr wasn't even sure if anyone had one of the testers. Either the mine worked, or it didn't. Johnson set the firing device, a plastic block with the wire plugged into one end and a lever-type plunger on top, where either he or Carr could reach it. Now they were ready.

"I'll take first watch," he told Eberhart. Before they left the laager he had told the men they would be on 50% guard, which meant the men paired up so one could sleep while the other remained on guard, switching every hour. Eberhart passed the handset over to Carr and then curled up on his side, resting his head in his helmet, the stock of his M-16 between his legs. Carr could hear low shuffling and whispers as the other men did the same. Soon everyone was settled, and the area fell silent except for the clicking of insects and the rumble of very distant artillery fire. Carr took a deep breath and shifted his body into a more comfortable position. It was going to be a long night.

*****

"Anything happening, Sarge?" Specialist Greenberg asked as he climbed into the machine gun turret of the one-one track.

Sergeant Samples, having just vacated the spot, said, "Not much. I heard Vasquez snoring." He stood beside the turret, looking out across the grassy plain, staring at the ring of lights at the top of Nui Ba Den, just to his left front.

"Yeah, he does that." Greenberg settled in, trying to find a comfortable position on the curved inner side of the open hatch cover.

"You get any sleep?" Samples asked.

"Not much," Greenberg replied. They were both talking in low tones, trying to avoid disturbing the other men, and keeping the noise down so they could hear anything outside the laager. "That's why I hate the middle guard shifts. Just about the time I fall asleep, it's time for me to pull guard. And after I pull guard, I'll just get to sleep, and then it's time to get up. This sucks."

"You should have joined the Air Farce," Samples suggested. "Those guys sleep on clean sheets every night."

"I didn't 'join' anything," Greenberg complained. "They drafted my ass."

"Quit your bitchin'. You had your chance." Samples smiled, knowing Greenberg couldn't see it. He enjoyed this kind of conversation with the men. Listening to them gripe not only helped him know if trouble was brewing, it allowed the guys to blow off a little steam and made them feel like Samples actually cared what they thought. Greenberg grunted disgustedly. "I'm gonna go check the rest of the platoon," Samples told Greenberg. "Don't wake up Hicks until exactly midnight. He gets real pissed if he doesn't get his full three hours of beauty sleep. And God knows he needs it."

Samples climbed down the side of the track, avoiding the cot that Sergeant Jamison had set up next to it, and wandered over to the one-two a few yards away. The guard there was sitting on the open driver's hatch instead of in the machine gun turret, rubbing his close-cropped hair. Even in the dark, Samples could easily distinguish the distinctive shape of Specialist Tenkiller's head and broad shoulders. "How's it going, Carl?" he asked quietly. Tenkiller turned and looked down at him.

"Fine, Sarge. Peachy keen. A-OK. Couldn't be better." The words were dripping with sarcasm.

"Good," Samples told him brightly. "I'm always glad to see a man who enjoys his work."

Tenkiller scoffed.

"Why aren't you behind the fifty?" Samples asked out of curiosity.

"If the shit hits the fan, I'm jumping inside and driving the hell out of here," Tenkiller explained. Samples knew he was joking, but went along with it.

"What about the other guys?" he asked. "You gonna leave them all behind?"

"Hey, that's on them. Fuck 'em if they can't take a joke."

"Oh, you young people today," Samples said, trying to sound like an old lady. Then, in a more commanding voice, he told Tenkiller, "Stay awake. I don't like being this close to the mountain."

"Roger that, Sarge."

Samples turned and walked around the back of the track, intending to check on the one-three, when he literally bumped into another man coming the other way.

"Oops," the man said, and Samples recognized the voice of Captain Gordon, their temporary company commander.

"Can I help you, sir?" Samples asked him, annoyed that the man was sneaking around in the First Platoon area.

"Sergeant, uh. . .?"

"Samples, sir."

"Right. Uh, I was just checking to make sure everyone is awake."

"That's what I was doing," Samples told him in a mild rebuke. Samples had a firm opinion on what the duties of officers were as opposed to what sergeants did. It felt like Gordon was infringing on his territory.

"Good. Good. So everything's all right?" Samples heard a tinge of nervousness in the captain's voice. It was understandable; this was the officer's first night laager. Still, Samples couldn't help feeling a little disdain for the man.

"Hunky dory, sir," Samples told him, intentionally using a goofy phrase to see how the man would react.

"That's great. Glad to hear it." Samples shook his head. The man was so worried he didn't know when he was being ridiculed. Samples sighed, resigned to the fact that it was now his job to calm the man down and reassure him. And maybe give him a backbone.

"Yeah, I'll check the Zippo, too," Samples told him. "I gave them an extra man to help out with guard duty. We're looking pretty good."

"Yes, I , uh. . ." Gordon trailed off, and then started a new sentence. "Do you think we'll make contact?"

"You never know," Samples said. "But even we didn't know we would be here tonight, so the gooks aren't likely to pull together an attack at short notice. And with all this open area, we'd see them coming a long way out."

"That's true," Gordon agreed, sounding a little more in control. "And the FO already has predetermined calls for fire." Samples knew Gordon was talking about Sergeant Real, the artillery forward observer who was currently assigned to the company. The fact that Real was with them made Samples feel a lot safer, as well. If they were attacked tonight, they would need the arty support, and Real was an expert at laying down a barrage just where it was needed.

"So we're okay," Samples said. "Good to go. Plus, we've got the two Zippos. I don't think the gooks are going to fuck with us."

"I hope you're right, Sergeant. Oh, and doesn't your platoon have the company starlight scope tonight?"

"Yes, sir. It's over on the one-three. You want to take a look?" Each platoon had a single small starlight scope, with its light-intensifying electronics, but First Platoon's had gone out with the ambush patrol, so Samples had borrowed the seldom-used company scope, which was much larger. While the platoon scopes could be mounted on a rifle or machine gun, the company scope had a special tripod to support its weight. About three feet long, and the size of a mess-hall coffee can at the far end, it was too heavy and bulky to be used in most circumstances. Samples and Sergeant Montoya had retrieved the heavy black metal case from the headquarters track just after sunset and set up the scope on top of the one-three, just to the right of the 50-cal.

"Yes," Gordon said, showing some almost childish enthusiasm. "I've never looked through the big starlight before. We had the small one in training, of course."

Samples led him over to the track, saying, "Well, it's about the same, just bigger and stronger."

Gordon scrambled up the back of the track with more dexterity than Samples had expected, and Samples followed him. Sergeant Montoya was behind the 50-cal, and he looked back as the two men stepped around the ammo cases strapped to the roof.

"Sergeant Montoya," Samples said more formally than usual, "Captain Gordon here would like to take a look through the scope." He said it that way to warn Montoya who was with him, so he wouldn't say or do anything out of line.

"Sure thing, sir. I just checked it a few minutes ago. Nothing happening."

Gordon made his way over and sat down on the wooden ammo crate behind the scope, putting his face to the eyepiece. Samples reached over and turned the scope on, listening to the high-pitched whine as it spooled up, then stepped back and leaned against the back of the machine gun turret. Gordon pressed against the spring-loaded rubber cup with his eyebrow, opening the automatic shutter inside so he could see the bright green image.

"Wow!" Gordon said. "That's amazing."

Samples wasn't sure how to respond to that, so he didn't. Gordon panned the scope to the left and right slowly, scanning all the area to the north and east that the tripod would allow.

"Those woods look a lot closer than I thought," Gordon remarked. "I mean, I know the scope magnifies things, but still."

"Yeah," Samples agreed, "about a hundred meters or so."

"Amazing," Gordon said again. He lifted his head from the scope and stood up to face Samples. "Looks like you've got it all under control, Sergeant Samples. Thank you." Gordon reached out to shake Samples' hand, which totally flummoxed him. One didn't see many handshakes in a combat situation.

After Gordon had climbed down, presumably to return to his own track, Samples turned to Montoya, who had stood up to stretch. "Did that seem strange to you?" he asked.

"He's an officer," Montoya replied, as if that explained everything.

"Yeah. Okay. Well, I'm going to go check on the Zippo."

"Night, Sarge."

*****

    Nash's calves ached. The side of Nui Ba Den was steeper than he had expected, and he was breathing heavily as they climbed. He had hiked the mountains a lot when he was a civilian, back home in New Mexico, but since he had arrived in Nam his walking had always been on level ground, and now he was using muscles that had gone soft. He could hear Quan gasping a little, too, so he didn't feel so bad.

    Zig-zagging up the slope, they had climbed for a couple hours through the thinning forest, moving slowly to make sure they didn't stumble upon some gook cave or position. The large easternmost cave on his map was around here somewhere, and Nash needed to locate it without being detected. First and foremost, he wanted to know where it was so they could make their way around it without disturbing the occupants. Secondly, once he knew where the cave was, he would know exactly where he and Quan were, and thus better find a suitable place to nest.

    When they came to a large rock outcropping, Nash paused to catch his breath. He turned to look out over the surrounding plain, marveling at how far he could see, even in the pale moonlight. There were wide light gray swales of grass interspersed with dark mounds that represented groves of trees or clumps of bushes. To the west, just visible around the shoulder of the mountain, were the twinkling lights of Tay Ninh, and to the east, many miles away, he could see a lighter area of sky above Dau Tieng. Nash took a deep breath through his nose, and had to stifle a cough. The pungent smell of human waste assailed his nostrils, and Nash quickly turned to Quan, thinking his partner was taking a dump right beside him. Instead he saw Quan looking back at him with alarm. Both of them slowly lowered their bodies to a crouch and listened for any unusual sounds. Nash heard a disgusting squirting noise, followed by a low moan. Someone just on the other side of the outcropping was having diarrhea. Trying not to breathe, Nash waited and listened. After a few moments he heard the rustle of clothing and then footsteps going away. He was about to stand up when he heard voices. A man was complaining in Vietnamese, and another was taunting the first man and laughing. A third voice shouted a command, and all the talking stopped.

Nash eased up to a standing position and edged along the wall of stone until he could just peek around it. About forty meters away he could see a flicker of muted orange light through the small trees and low bushes. A figure suddenly appeared out of nowhere, headed right toward him. Nash ducked back and tapped Quan's arm urgently to warn him. The man grunted with disgust, and hurled some sort of imprecation. Grumbling, the man turned and headed downslope a few feet before stopping to urinate. When he was done he headed away again, and Nash leaned forward enough to see the man's back as he reached the area where Nash had seen a glow and then disappeared.

"The cave," Nash whispered to Quan. "This way." He pushed at Quan, indicating they should head away from the cave and upward. Nash followed Quan as they climbed up and to the east until they were way above the level of the cave, and then turned back west, still angling upward. The ground was getting more treacherous here, consisting of a mix of loose rock and soft soil, held together by low brush and occasional stunted trees. He worried that they might step on just the wrong rock and start a small landslide that would alert the gooks in the cave, which was now somewhere just below them. Although his feet slipped sideways a couple times, it was not enough to send a shower of stone down the mountainside, for which he was truly grateful.

If the map overlay Carotto had shown them was accurate, the bunker between the cave they had seen and another cave to the west was slightly higher than either of them. Nash wanted a position that was directly above the bunker, with line of sight to both caves as well as the bunker. He wasn't sure if that was even possible, but that was what he needed. Deciding they were high enough now, he tapped Quan's leg to signal him to stop. He found a rock big enough not to move and placed one foot on it to steady himself, then brought up his rifle and switched on the starlight scope. Beside him Quan squatted down to keep from blocking his view.

Starting behind him, Nash peered through the scope at the jumbled landscape, moving a few degrees at a time as he swept in a full circle, keeping his left foot firmly planted on the rock. He was nearly blinded when he inadvertently pointed the scope at Tay Ninh, whose lights were greatly intensified by the scope. He moved on, scanning the uphill portion of the slope intently, not sure what he was looking for, but knowing he would recognize it when he saw it. With his body twisted uncomfortably, he finished the circular search, and then did it again in reverse. When he finished he took the scope from his eye and squatted down next to Quan, blinking to try and restore night vision to that eye.

"Two places," he murmured to Quan. He pointed down slope from where they were squatting, to a clump of bushes. "Check that one out. I'll look at the other one, up there." He gestured again, this time at a lump jutting out from the slope with three small trees growing on it. It looked somewhat like the spot he had seen in the aerial photograph, but he wasn't sure. Quan stood up and carefully began picking his way down the slope, while Nash began climbing toward the small cluster of trees. In a few minutes he was there, and was very pleased with what he had found. It was a small shelf where soil had accumulated and saplings had taken root, creating a flat area with overhead cover, the perfect size for two men to hide. Nash carefully lay down and pushed his rifle between two of the trees, scooting forward until he could aim it down the side of the mountain. Switching on the scope again, he searched his sight lines, and even caught a little of the glow coming from the big cave they had passed earlier. This would definitely work. Through the scope he saw Quan emerge from the bushes below, shaking his head. Nash gave a low whistle that he hoped sounded like a bird, and saw Quan nod and begin climbing toward him.

As soon as Quan and he had settled in, shedding their packs and making themselves comfortable, Nash called in about their sighting of a small group of NVA headed southwest, as well as letting headquarters know that he and Quan were in place. Quan volunteered to take first watch, so Nash stretched out and closed his eyes, still breathing heavily from the climb. He had just fallen asleep when Quan touched his elbow. "Movement!"

SEVENTEEN

Thanh was exhausted. Ahead of her Nhu kept climbing up the narrow winding trail like a machine, but Thanh felt like she was going to collapse at any minute. "Wait!" she pleaded. "I must rest a minute." She was surprised at her own weakness, for normally she had plenty of stamina. Perhaps her depression and trepidation were affecting her physically.

Nhu paused and turned around. "We are almost there. For a soldier you are terribly weak."

"This case is heavy," Thanh protested.

"Not as heavy as mine, and you do not see me crying."

Thanh gulped in deep breaths of air and sank to her knees on the hard dirt. "Please. Just a minute."

"No," Nhu barked. She grabbed Thanh's wrist and pulled her back up. "We will rest when we arrive. You go first, and I will push you." With the tall canvas pack rising far above her head, Nhu squeezed past Thanh and got up close behind her, pushing on the bottom of Thanh's load. Wearily, her legs feeling like they were made of rubber, Thanh started walking again, actually appreciating the additional support from Nhu. She was a little embarrassed by her feebleness, although she was loathe to let Nhu know that. She stumbled over a root, but managed to stay upright. This journey had become a nightmare.

"Stop!" a voice ahead of them ordered. Thanh could see no one. The trail wound up through widely spaced trees and big rocks, any of which could be hiding someone. Her heart thumped in fear.

"The night bird sings sweetly," Nhu said behind her, and Thanh was caught completely off-guard by the incongruous phrase.

It took her a couple seconds for her fatigued mind to realize that it was a recognition code of some sort.

"Come ahead," the hidden man told them. As they moved forward, a figure appeared out of the darkness. "You are late," the man accused.

"The girl is weak," Nhu answered. "But we still have plenty of time. Take us to the cave."

Without another word the man turned and led the way up the trail, glancing back occasionally to ensure they were keeping up. Knowing that their destination was now close, Thanh felt a renewed energy and plunged ahead, staying right on the man's backside. Within a few minutes they emerged from the trees onto a shelf of rock that jutted a couple meters out from the mountainside. Other people were there, standing or squatting, some smoking cigarettes. It was too dark to make out faces, or even determine the gender of the people, but all were dressed in the black shirts and pants of the PLA, and none wore the green uniforms of the NVA.

As Thanh stopped and tried to catch her breath, she saw the opening to the cave on the far side of the shelf. It was almost perfectly round, and maybe two meters in diameter. A curtain was pushed aside as someone exited the cave, letting a blast of yellow light assault Thanh's eyes for a moment until the curtain dropped back into place.

"Welcome, my sisters," the man who had come out of the cave said. "We have been expecting you. Come inside and remove your loads. We have hot tea for you."

Tea had never sounded so inviting before. Thanh rushed ahead of Nhu to follow the man into the cave, brushing aside the heavy curtain and squinting as the bright light inside almost blinded her. The mouth of the cave was a tube about three meters long, but it then widened out into a giant hall several meters across with a smooth dirt floor that was littered with boxes, equipment, and low beds. Several kerosene lanterns were burning, placed on stacks of boxes, and they threw dark shadows. Only a couple of men were inside the cave; Thanh assumed that most had gone outside to enjoy the cool night air. The man who had spoken to them led them over to where two empty beds lay on the hard-packed earth. It was only then that Thanh noticed the man had a slight limp, wondering if he had been wounded in a battle. The beds were made of bamboo, with short legs that raised them only a few inches from the floor, and each had a single dark green wool blanket.

"You will rest here tonight," the man told them, sweeping his hand toward the beds. Thanh noted that he was very well spoken, as if he had been a school teacher at one time, and he appeared to be in his middle thirties in age. Were it not for the pink and marbled burn that covered part of his face where one eye had been, he would have been a handsome man. "You may call me Tiger. Please do not tell me your names. I will fetch your tea."

Tiger walked over to the far side of the cavern, where a young man squatted by a small stove. Thanh and Nhu removed their packs and set them down near the beds. Thanh dropped her bag with the pistol in it onto the case she had been carrying, while Nhu stretched her arms and unselfconsciously rubbed her wounded breast. Tiger returned with two fine porcelain cups of tea and handed them to the women, and then all three squatted down to talk.

"You have been entrusted with a great mission," Tiger said solemnly. Thanh wondered how the man knew of it. Nhu must have passed the word somehow. Or maybe someone in the north had told him. "What can we do to assist you?"

Nhu spoke firmly and authoritatively. "In the morning, by nine o'clock, we must be in position high on the mountain, just below the American landing place."

Tiger nodded. "Do you need an escort?"

"That would be good," Nhu said. "Is there any danger of an American patrol?"

Tiger shook his head. "The Americans at the top never venture outside the wire of their compound. You will be totally safe. I can only provide you a single soldier to escort you, however. Most of my men will be departing shortly to transport supplies to our northern comrades."

"If there are no American patrols," Nhu told him, "then one soldier will be enough. We only need him as a guide."

"You have everything you need?"

Nhu patted one of the metal cases. "Yes. These cases contain the weapon that will end the war. Correct, Thanh?"

Thanh nodded. She didn't want to think about the weapon, or how it would be used. She was overcome with fatigue and depression, and all she wanted to do was go to sleep, hoping she would be more positive in the morning. She drained the last of the tea and passed the cup back to Tiger with a murmured thanks. She flopped onto the bed with a groan and closed her eyes against the glare of the lanterns. Within seconds she was asleep.

*****

Lieutenant Carr rubbed his eyes and tried to focus. Eberhart handed him back his watch, which he had loaned the RTO so he would know when to wake Carr up. As he strapped it back on his wrist, he could just make out the faintly glowing hands, and saw that Eberhart had let him sleep an extra half hour. He was a little perturbed that his radioman hadn't followed instructions, but grateful for the extra sleep. He didn't bother asking for a sitrep. If anything had happened, he would have been awakened instantly. For now, it was the same as before, the quiet of a field of tall grass glimmering in the moonlight, the spread of stars overhead, and the occasional rumble of distant artillery. Carr wanted to check all the men, to make sure at least half were alert, but there was no way to do that without making a lot of noise. He would just have to trust his men, which he normally did.

Lying on his stomach, propping his shoulders up on his elbows, Carr picked up his helmet and put it on, and then checked his M-16. He had been sleeping on his back with his head cradled in the steel pot, and now his neck ached. He heard someone stifle a cough a few feet to his left, and knew that at least someone else was awake. It was now well after midnight, and he was beginning to think this ambush patrol, like so many others, would be a waste of time. At least, he thought, no one had attacked the night laager, for they would have certainly heard it if they had. Next to him Eberhart tried to find a comfortable position so he could sleep, no easy task with the prick-25 radio strapped to his back.

"Pst!" Someone at the far left end of the ambush hissed, and Carr heard muttered whispers being passed down the line. "Someone's coming," Johnson leaned over and whispered to him. Carr jabbed Eberhart with his elbow and repeated the warning, and Eberhart rolled over on his stomach and passed it on. Carr could hear his men getting ready, and wished they could do so more quietly. "Don't shoot until I do," he whispered to Johnson and Eberhart, and heard them pass the command down the line in either direction. They should know that already, but Carr had learned never to assume in situations like this. They rarely made contact on ambush patrols, and someone might get antsy.

Since the warning had come from the north end of the ambush position, Carr leaned forward and peered through the leaves toward the dark shape of Nui Ba Den. The bushes in which they hid blocked most of his line of sight, but he heard a clink of metal against metal, just barely audible. His senses heightened by the tension, Carr listened for more sounds, and picked out footsteps and a slight grunt of effort as someone shifted the weight they were carrying. Finally, with his peripheral vision, Carr detected some kind of movement. Careful not to stare directly at it, he focused on the leaves instead, and suddenly made out the shape of a man coming down the trail, carrying what looked like an AK-47. Behind him another man appeared, this one with a large bulk on his back.

Within seconds Carr could see the entire party, eleven slightly built men in black pajamas, some with straw hats, and all but the first and last man loaded down with oversized backpacks. Carr held his breath, his left hand clutching the Claymore firing device. He didn't remember picking it up. As the first man came abreast of Carr, he looked to the left to make sure there wasn't another group behind this one. Because of the curve the path made around this clump of bushes, he could see all eleven men clearly in the moonlight. Sergeant Reedy, at the left end of the ambush, had the starlight scope, and presumably he was looking to see if anyone else was coming. Since he hadn't said anything, Carr decided there wasn't.

Carr counted off the men as they passed in front of him, and when the fifth man was directly opposite, Carr squeezed the lever on the Claymore. Nothing happened. Mentally kicking himself, he flipped the safety bail out of the way and squeezed again. This time there was a satisfying explosion, and all hell broke loose. The other Claymore was blown, and rapid rifle fire erupted up and down the line inside the brush, spraying the line of VC with hundreds of rounds of 5.56mm bullets. His night vision temporarily impaired by the flash of the Claymore, Carr joined the others and firing a constant stream of bullets at ground level, to hit anyone left alive who had sought shelter by going prone in the high grass. There was a burst of return fire from the lead end of the column, but the last few rounds of the burst arced up in the air as the man holding the AK fell backwards.

"Cease fire!" Carr yelled, and quickly the firing stopped. Along with the other men, Carr cautiously rose to his feet and shoved his way through the bushes out onto the plain, His rifle held ready. Nothing moved, and the only sign of the gook patrol was some dark lumps rising above the grass, the loads the men had been carrying. Staying on line, Carr's soldiers advance slowly to the trail and surveyed the damage they had caused. "Get a count," Carr quietly ordered Eberhart. "Anyone hit?" he asked loudly enough for all to hear. He got a chorus of "no's". "Pick up any weapons you find. Let's check out what they were carrying."

Carr kept a sharp eye out up and down the trail while his men searched the packs. Doc Allman went from one fallen VC to the next, verifying they were dead. Eberhart, who had run up and down the trail counting bodies, reported back. "Eleven, sir."

"Good." That meant no one had escaped.

"Looks like ammo," Johnson said, pulling a small wooden crate out of one of the packs still attached to a dead man.

"RPG rounds here," Sergeant Baker reported from the far left end of the line.

"Fuckin' Claymores!" Vasquez announced with amazement, kneeling down beside another pack. "How the fuck did they get Claymores?"

"ARVNs," Rancy answered him simply.

"Shit."

"What do you want us to do with it, sir?" Reedy asked from the right end of the line.

Carr thought about it. Ideally they would blow it in place, but they had brought no demolition supplies with them, and C-4 would mostly just scatter the stuff rather than destroy it all. Carr exhaled loudly. "Take it with us," he said grudgingly.

"Aw, hell," Merrill complained. "This shit's heavy."

"We can't leave it for the gooks to use later," Sergeant Baker replied. For a new guy, Carr thought, Baker was catching on quickly.

"And we can always use the Claymores ourselves," Greenberg chimed in.

"I got dibs on one of the AK's," Rancy called out.

"How many are there?" Carr asked.

"The last guy had one, but it got shot up," Baker said.

"The first guy's seems to be okay," Reedy announced, holding it up.

"So we only captured one?" Carr asked innocently. All captured weapons had to be turned in, and soldiers were not allowed to keep any, unless they were the old SKS carbines.

"No, we've. . ." Baker started to object, and then belatedly realized what Carr meant. "Yeah, that's right. Just one."

"Sir," Allman called out, kneeling next to one of the fallen Viet Cong. "This one's still alive."

"Shoot him," Merrill suggested without emotion.

"How bad is he?" Carr asked, walking over to where Allman was.

"Gut shot," Allman said. "Both legs, too."

"We can't take him with us," Carr explained patiently. "Rancy, get his pack."

Allman reached into his aid bag.

"What are you doing, Doc? We'll have to leave him."

While Rancy pulled the heavy pack off the man's limp arms, Carr saw a hypodermic in Allman's hands. "I know," Allman said, "but I can't let him suffer."

"He's going to die anyway," Rancy pointed out as he adjusted the straps on the dying man's pack. "Just leave him."

"Can't do that," Allman said, and jabbed the unconscious man with the needle. "At least he'll die easy."

Carr understood and sympathized with Doc Allman's humanitarian instincts, but they had to get moving. "Come on," he hoarsely called, "load up and move out. Let's get back to the laager." Other gooks in the area would certainly have heard the gunfire, and possibly were coming to see what happened. Groaning under their loads, the men lined up again and headed back west, to the armored security of the company's night laager. Carr was pleased that the ambush had gone off successfully and none of his men had been hurt. But he also felt a little remorse for the Viet Cong who had just died. They were the enemy, and would have killed him if they had the chance, but they were still humans. What a fucked-up war this was.

*****

"There they are," Sergeant Samples announced quietly, his eye glued to the rubber cup of the company's oversized starlight scope. With the combined magnification and light intensification of the scope, he could just make out the lead figure as it came out of a distant grove of trees. They had been expecting the return of the ambush patrol for almost an hour, after Eberhart had called in the results. Everyone had been awake since they had heard the distant firefight, on full alert in case they enemy tried to retaliate in some way. Eberhart had said they were bringing in some captured ammo, but Samples was still surprised by the large packs the men of the AP were now carrying on their backs.

Samples stood up and backed away from the scope, making room for PFC Handleman to replace him. Aiello was behind the 50-cal, and Sergeant Montoya was sitting on the ammo can to the left of the turret. "Come on, George," Samples said, "let's go help them." Both men grabbed their rifles and jumped down from the track. They walked around the RPG screen, dodging the small fighting position between the one-three's screen and the one-two's, and stopped just beyond it, staring out into the darkness.

"I see 'em," Montoya said. Samples saw them too, emerging from the darkness like a giant hump-backed snake crawling through the high grass. Walking out to meet them, Samples called quietly, "Welcome back, oh great and mighty warriors. Heard you had good hunting."

"We made a haul, that's for sure," the first man in line said. Samples recognized his voice; it was Dubois, hunched over from the load on his back, his rifle dangling from one hand. Montoya offered to take his pack, but Dubois waved him off. Behind him Lieutenant Carr stepped out of line and came over to Samples, balancing two AK-47s on his shoulder. Carr put his M-16 between his knees and then brought the AK's down and quickly inspected them. "Rancy wants this one," Carr told Samples, handing him one of the rifles. "I'm turning the other one in."

Samples understood, and took the AK, holding it alongside his M-16 so it was less obvious that he had two weapons. "I'll put this in the track," he told Carr. "Gordon's really excited about your AP. I think he's gonna take credit for it."

"Whatever," Carr replied wearily. "Don't mean nothin'."

They watched the rest of the patrol file by them and enter the night laager.

"Man, that is a bunch of shit," Samples marveled at the heavy loads the men were lugging on their backs.

"Go put that AK away," Carr told him. "We've got to open all of that stuff up and get an inventory. Any problems here while we were gone?

"Nice and quiet here. Gordon got an intel report of some NVA moving in our direction, but we haven't seen anything."

"Well, if they do attack, they won't have much ammo to do it with," Carr noted, and trudged on into the laager. Samples peeled off and went to the rear of the one-four track by himself. He opened the personnel door at the back and tossed the AK in onto the bench seat. "This is Rancy's," he told Knox, who was standing in the TC hatch behind the 50-cal.

"I'll keep an eye on it," Knox promised.

Samples walked over to the middle of the laager, where the men were dumping their captured loads next to the company commander's track. He found Carr standing next to Captain Gordon, detailing what had happened out on the trail.

"Eleven body count!" Gordon marveled. "The colonel will be very pleased with that."

"Yeah, well," Carr said; Samples knew the lieutenant was not a fan of the Army's current method of measuring success. "More importantly, where were they taking all this ammo?"

"Who knows?" Gordon said. "Doesn't really matter, does it? We have it now."

Samples added his two cents. "Probably would have used it to attack a base camp."

"But only one AK-47?" Gordon asked.

"Yeah," Carr said. "I think there was another one, but it was pretty dark out there. We didn't want to hang around and look for it."

Samples admired the way Carr had not really lied about the other one. "Sir," he said to Carr, intentionally changing the subject, "I've got to redo the guard list, now that everyone's back. Any special orders?"

Before Carr could reply, Gordon jumped in officiously. "Make sure everyone stays alert, Sergeant. We received word from G-2 that an NVA patrol was seen in this area."

"Probably the guys we ambushed," Carr remarked.

"I don't think so, Lieutenant. Intel said it was definitely NVA, not VC, and they were armed with AK-47s and RPGs."

"Okay." Samples thought Carr didn't sound convinced; they were used to intel reports that turned out to be wrong. When Carr had nothing further to say, Samples walked back to the platoon line and gathered up the squad leaders for a brief meeting. Dawn was still several hours away, and they would need to make sure no one fell asleep on guard.

EIGHTEEN

Nash shivered a little. He knew the temperature had to be in the seventies, but that was cool for Nam, and a light breeze wafted over his body and rattled the leaves just above his head. Actually, being chilled was a nice change of pace, and he took a deep breath of the brisk air. Up here on the mountain, the air didn't stink of human waste and rotting vegetation. Off to the east he could now almost see the horizon, a blurry dark line above which the sky was a lighter shade of black. "You awake?" he whispered, sensing movement from Quan next to him.

"Yes. Cold, too."

"Enjoy it while you can," Nash told him. He rolled over to his side and reached down for the pack near his feet. He pulled out the cloth case Quan had requested to be fabricated in Cu Chi by a local tailor and went through the process of switching the starlight scope on his rifle for the ART daylight scope. It would soon be light enough to use the more accurate sight, and he wanted to be ready. Although there was no way to be sure, Nash was still convinced that the female VC sniper was somewhere on the mountain, and she would not be expecting him to be waiting for her.

Not long after he and Quan had found this position far above the VC bunker, they had seen movement around the cave down to their left. Even with the starlight scope, it had been hard to determine exactly what was going on. It appeared that two people had arrived at the cave with large boxes on their backs and quickly disappeared inside. Shortly afterwards a larger group of maybe ten or eleven had lined up outside the cave, most of them with bulky loads also strapped to their backs, and had filed down the mountain until they were out of sight. Obviously a supply convoy of some sort, Nash had concluded. He surmised that the group had been waiting for the two loads that had just arrived before adding them and departing.

Things had settled down after that, and Nash had told Quan to get some sleep while he stood guard and kept an eye on the cave. Less than an hour later he was startled by two explosions and a burst of automatic weapons fire far out on the flats, perhaps two miles away. Quan had come instantly alert, asking what was happening. The firefight was over in less than thirty seconds.

"Ambush," Nash suggested. "Maybe our guys spotted that supply convoy."

"Maybe," Quan agreed. The action had been too far away for Nash and Quan to really be concerned about it, and when nothing further was heard, Quan offered to let Nash sleep a while, since he was now wide awake. Later they switched again, and nothing had disturbed the rest of the night.

As the sky slowly brightened in the east, Nash wished he had a cup of hot coffee. And some doughnuts, as long as he was wishing. He briefly considered opening up a can of C-rations, but decided it was too much effort for too little reward. He looked up at the stars, watching them wink out one by one.

"Pst!" Quan hissed, and pointed down at the cave. It was still too dark to use his scope, so Nash peered over his left forearm, squinting to bring things into focus. Three figures emerged from the cave and stood on the small semi-circle of bare dirt that formed a sort of porch. One of them, the tallest, walked with a limp. A slightly shorter person had long hair flowing down her back, obviously a woman. The third figure was the shortest and stockiest of the three. The tall one pointed off to the side, and the young woman hurried away, clutching some paper in her hand. Nash figured she was going to the communal toilet area. The tall one and the short one then discussed something, and the short one lifted her shirt to reveal her drooping breasts, one of which was swathed in bandages. The sniper!

"It's her!" he told Quan excitedly. Swinging his XM-21 rifle around, he put his eye to the scope and tried to center it on the distant figure, but it was still too dark out. All he could see through the scope was blackness. He chastised himself for switching out the starlight scope too soon, even though he knew the starlight would not have been accurate enough at this range. "Shit!" he complained, raising his eye above the scope. The tall guy inspected the sniper's wounded breast in a professional manner, and then let her drop the hem of the shirt. The young woman returned and all three disappeared back in the cave.

At least he now knew for sure where the sniper was. It was only a matter of waiting until she reappeared, and he would be able to take his shot and end her killing spree. He wondered when that would be. The last stars winked out, and the sky turned a pale grey. Nash settled in to wait. He didn't have to wait long. Just as the sun began peeking over the horizon, there was movement again in front of the cave. This time there were four people—the three he had seen earlier, and a fourth man armed with an AK-47. The two women had big packs strapped to their backs, which confused Nash. Why would a sniper need a big pack like that? The one the sniper carried was very long and narrow, reaching from below her butt to more than a foot above her head. The younger woman's pack, although still large, was only a couple feet long. Both packs were very rectangular, and appeared to have considerable weight to them. The younger woman also carried a Claymore bag with something heavy in it.

Nash sighted in on the sniper, but she had her back to him, and that large pack obscured all but her legs. There was no guarantee that a bullet he fired would penetrate whatever was in the pack, so he held off. Opening his left eye and using it to take in the entire scene, Nash observed the tall man with the limp speaking at length to the other three, and then waving as the man with the AK led the other two around the far side of the cave entrance and into the woods. Nash cursed under his breath, because he had never gotten a clear shot at the sniper.

"You look down, I'll look up," Nash told Quan, who nodded. Nash's real worry was that neither direction applied. If the three figures went directly east, they would soon be disappear around the shoulder of the mountain, and Nash would be unable to track them. "Keep looking," he told Quan, "but get ready to move. We may have to chase them." Still searching with his eyes, Nash blindly fumbled with his pack and pulled it onto his back. Next to him he sensed Quan getting to his knees and slipping the radio and his own pack on. The sky beyond the mountain was now noticeably brighter, and the side of the mountain, with its small trees and bushes, was clearly silhouetted.

Out of the corner of his eye Nash detected something, and quickly swung his gaze in that direction. "There they are!" he chirped. He saw three round straw hats moving through the brush, briefly outlined against the grey sky. They were moving up and away from him, and would soon be out of sight completely. "Let's go!" he told Quan, jumping to his feet.

*****

Lieutenant Carr finished shaving and rinsed his razor off in the up-turned steel pot cradled in his lap. He sat on his ammo crate beside the turret of the one-three track, wishing he could have had another few hours of sleep. With a brown towel he wiped the remaining soap off his face and gazed up at Nui Ba Den. The top of the mountain was now lit by the sun, and the demarcation line between the sunlight and the remaining darkness was slowly creeping down the slopes. In a couple minutes the entire night laager would be bathed in the glare of the morning sun, turning the tracks into alloy ovens as the day progressed. Carr dumped the soapy water from the helmet over the side and passed it through the open cargo hatch to Sergeant Montoya, who was waiting below with his own shaving gear and towel.

Carr grabbed his shirt and jumped down from the track before putting it on. As he buttoned it up, Eberhart walked around from the rear of the track and held out a canteen cup to him. "Coffee, sir?"

"Thanks." The aluminum cup was hot, and Carr immediately shifted it around until he could hold it by the folding handle. Then he took a sip, wincing as the hot liquid burned his tongue. The water had been heated up by a small ball of C-4 explosive that had been set alight inside an old coffee can with holes punched in it. The C-4 burned white hot, and quickly heated anything placed above it. Then packets of the instant coffee and powdered creamer from the C-rations had been added, making a brew that was basically terrible, but satisfied the inherent need for caffeine.

"They're bringing breakfast," Eberhart told him. Eberhart seemed to know the scoop on everything before anyone else in the company.

"How about ice and sodas?" Carr asked.

"That, too."

"When?"

Eberhart turned to face the southern sky. "I think that's them now," he said, nodding at a distant speck. Carr had learned not to question how Eberhart knew these things. Seeing Captain Gordon emerge from the commander's track in the center of the laager, Carr reached up to find his M-16 on top of the track and wandered over to where Gordon was standing and looking up at the sky.

"Morning, sir. I hear we're getting a hot breakfast."

"That's right. I insisted on it. After what we accomplished last night, I thought we deserved it."

Carr felt a touch of annoyance at the "we" references, since Gordon hadn't really done anything, but let it pass.

Gordon looked over at Carr. "Can you get a detail together to unload the chopper?"

Carr was about to suggest that perhaps another platoon could do that, since his platoon had done the ambush last night, when Lieutenant Masters came up.

"We'll get it," Masters volunteered, and Carr shot him a grateful look. "Are we gonna load the captured ammo on the chopper?"

"Uh, umm," Gordon stumbled. It was obvious to Carr that Gordon hadn't even considered the possibility before that moment. "Yes, I believe that is the plan. I'd appreciate it if you organized that, Lieutenant Masters."

"Roger that, sir," Masters replied brightly, winking at Carr when Gordon wasn't looking.

By then the Huey was clearly visible and approaching the laager. There was a sling underneath it, and it dropped the canvas wrapped load just outside the laager before settling down a few feet away. The pilot let the turbine wind down as the blades continued to circle lazily. Some Second Platoon men ran out to unload the brown Mermite cans that held the hot breakfast meal, while some other guys went out to the sling, which held a huge block of ice covered in rice husks. The Mermites were brought in to the center of the laager, and Carr saw the mortar sergeant take charge of lining them up and assigning KPs to dish out the contents. Meanwhile several men toting civilian ice chests gathered around the block of ice with ice picks in hand, hurrying to get the chunks of the ice into the coolers before it all melted in the morning heat.

Carr glance back at his platoon line, and was glad to see that all the 50-cals were manned, maintaining a guard while the other men took care of the welcome load on the chopper. When he looked back at the activities around the helicopter, one of the men carrying a Mermite set down his load and sauntered over to Carr. It was Sweet, back from his trip to Cu Chi.

"Top of the morning, sir," Sweet greeted him with exaggerated exuberance.

"Glad you made it back, Sweet. How was it?"

"Oh, man, it was great! Hope had everybody in stitches. And those round-eyed girls really looked good up there."

"Well, you can tell the whole platoon about it later. Right now, why don't you help load up this gook ammo in the chopper."

"Gook ammo?" Sweet looked at the stack of unfamiliar crates and cans.

"Tell you about it later. Hop to it. Here, let me take your weapon."

Sweet handed Carr the M-16 and petulantly went over to the pile and picked up a crate, theatrically moaning like it was too heavy for him. Other men came over to help him, and soon there was a line of men carrying loads back out to the chopper. Carr was left standing there alone, watching the other men work, and sipping coffee from his canteen cup. Masters had left to supervise the unloading and loading, and Gordon had gone back into his track for something. "Another fine day in the Army," Carr said out loud to no one.

*****

"Wait!" Thanh gasped, sinking to her knees. The climb was exhausting, and her sandals kept slipping on the loose rocks. Ahead of her Nhu and the man named Sang stopped and looked back at her. Nhu's face was a mask of scorn, but Sang looked sympathetic.

"We do not have much time, girl," Nhu chastised her. "We must be in position soon, before the helicopter arrives."

Thanh kept gulping in large amounts of air, trying to catch her breath. The side of the mountain was steep here, and the weight of the launcher parts on her back and the pistol in her pouch made the ascent even more arduous. She tilted her head to the right so that her hat would block the searing rays of the sun, which was now rising above the horizon. Up here there were only a few stunted trees and some low brush scattered among the sharp rocks and loose gravel.

"I can carry the pack," Sang offered.

"No!" Nhu answered for her. "She will do it. You must keep a watch for enemy aircraft."

Reaching out with her left hand, Nhu grabbed Thanh roughly by the wrist and jerked her to her feet. "Come on!" she demanded.

Thanh nodded weakly and resumed the hike up the mountain. This was the mission she had trained for in the north, the one she had accepted so enthusiastically from Uncle Ho, but now it no longer seemed glorious. Trekking up this giant mountain with an uncomfortable heavy load on her back, just to try and kill a mere entertainer, seemed ludicrous. This man Hope was here to brighten the day of the American soldiers who had been sent to a foreign land by their government, mostly against their will. He posed no existential threat to the people of Viet Nam, and had killed no one. She failed to fully comprehend why his death would end the war and send the Americans back home, and worried that it might even have a reverse effect, strengthening the American resolve and leading to even more deadly attacks on her homeland in the North.

She had promised Uncle Ho, however, and still had a strong sense of duty. And if she was successful, Thanh herself would be showered with praise. Still, she wondered if this mission was actually Uncle Ho's idea, or something dreamed up by the dislikable Le Duan and pushed on the Great Teacher in his waning days of life. Back home, with the almost daily air raids by the Americans, and the constant "education" of the propaganda ministry, it had been easy to hate the Americans and the puppet government in Saigon, but after a few months here in the south, actually talking to American soldiers and seeing the relative affluence of the Vietnamese here, her attitude had undergone a fundamental shift. The politics of the war seemed far removed from reality, and were somehow irrelevant to the lives of the people.

Would the daily lives of the average South Vietnamese be any different under a communist regime? Would they not continue to grow their rice and raise their families as before? She pondered these heavy questions as she trudged ever upward, wincing as small stones became trapped between her sandals and her feet and she stubbed her already bloody toes on bigger rocks. She had far more questions than answers. For now, however, she was committed, and would carry out the mission. What would happen afterward, she could not even imagine.

Staring at the ground to pick out where her next step would be, Thanh nearly bumped into Nhu, who had stopped suddenly and shushed her. Nhu turned her head to look out over the plain, cupping one hand to her ear. Thanh heard it, too. A helicopter was approaching.

"It is too soon," Thanh said, thinking it was the helicopter carrying the man named Hope. She turned around, and her feet slipped out from under her, dropping her to her butt, the backpack the only thing keeping her upright. The stones had hurt when she sat down, but she appreciated the rest her position afforded her. She held her left hand up beside her face to shield her eyes from the horizontal rays of the morning sun.

"It is a Huey," Sang announced from above her. "Just one."

"It is landing," Nhu observed, calmer now.

Thanh finally found the insect-like object low in the sky, settling down toward the distant fields of grass. Then she saw that it was landing near a circle of armored vehicles. She wondered if it was the unit that her beloved Robert had belonged to. The vehicles and the helicopter were so distant she could not make out any details, but she imagined the aircraft was bringing supplies, or perhaps picking up wounded. Tiger had told her of the short burst of gunfire last night, somewhere out on the plains, and knew there had been a brief firefight of some sort.

"Get up!" Nhu demanded. "They cannot see us. We must hurry." With a deep sigh Thanh rose to her stinging feet and turned to resume the climb. Would they never reach wherever they were going?

*****

"It's going to A Company," Nash said to Quan. They had both stopped at the sound of the distant chopper and watched its approach. He licked a few drops of blood off the palm of his left hand where he had scratched it grabbing a rock outcropping to keep from falling.

"Warm food," Quan noted enviously.

"What, you don't enjoy cold spaghetti from a can?" Nash teased him. They were both hungry, but they were used to that.

"You want dried octopus?" Quan countered, knowing Nash hated the Vietnamese delicacy.

"Fuck that," Nash said. He looked around, holding his hand up to shield his eyes from the rising sun. "Lost them again." They had been trying to follow the sniper and her two companions for over an hour, scuttling up the rocky slope parallel to the path Nash thought the enemy group was taking. He needed to get above them without their seeing him, a difficult task when he didn't really know where they were going. Because the mountain was essentially conical in shape, the other group was always just around the shoulder of rock, just out of sight. If Nash got close enough to see them, he would be close enough for them to hear him as well. It was kind of like tracking a deer in a heavy mountain forest; one couldn't get too close for fear of scaring the deer into flight, but if you stayed too far back, you risked losing the deer entirely.

Nash believed their only hope was to climb faster than the sniper, get above her, and wait for her to come into range. That, however, was easier said than done. Climbing the rocky slope was difficult enough, and the lack of significant vegetation made it almost impossible to do so without being seen. He had no idea how many gooks might be out on the mountain or hidden in unseen caves or bunkers that he and Quan might stumble into. They had to proceed very cautiously, but rapidly as well, a dangerous combination.

While they ascended toward the peak of the mountain, Nash kept glancing to his right, hoping to get a glimpse of the sniper before someone in that group spotted him and Quan. There! He saw a straw hat bouncing along, silhouetted by the bright sky to the east, the rest of the person's body hidden by the intervening mountainside. Nash dropped to a prone position, and sensed Quan do the same. He raised his head slowly, and scanned the sloping rocky terrain to their east where it touched the sky. He saw more movement, the top of a blocky pack bobbing around some rocks before disappearing again.

"Damn!" he muttered. The sniper's group was almost directly across from him, at the same level on the mountain. He had hoped they had gained on the woman, but no such luck. At least they knew where the other group was, and hadn't lost them. Yet. Nash raised his body more and scanned the slopes above him. They would have to veer more to the west, to ensure they weren't seen by the sniper, and climb faster in order to get ahead of her. He saw what looked like it might be a trail. "This way," he told Quan, and pushed to his feet. Scrambling over some loose rock, he found the trail and hurried up it. It looked more like a game trail than a human path, and that was fine with Nash. He didn't want to be running into any enemy soldiers as they scooted up the mountain.

Replete with switchbacks and missing sections, the trail was hard to follow, but did allow them to move more rapidly. The ground was more solid, and while it led them at an angle away from the sniper and her companions, the path allowed them to gain altitude faster than the enemy while staying out of sight. At one point the trail they were following crossed a wider path that angled up to the right, but Nash ignored it. It was clearly a path made by humans, as well as leading right into the sight of the sniper. No, the game trail was fine for now. Nash just wished he could see the area above them more clearly, from a bird's eye view, so he could chose a position that would give him a clear shot at the sniper.

*****

The grease from the limp bacon had so soaked into the thin paper plate that the plate had folded in on itself. Carr sighed and tossed the remaining food onto the ground and shoved the crumpled paper plate into the trash bag hanging from the corner of the track. He wasn't really that hungry anyway, he told himself. Scrambled eggs made from powder, slimy bacon, rock-hard biscuits, and warm orange drink didn't make for a gourmet breakfast. The coffee had been a little better than that Eberhart had made, but not as hot. He watched the now-empty Mermite cans being loaded in the headquarters track, while the CO's driver passed out the mail to representatives from each platoon. Carr hoped he had a letter in the pile from his wife. He turned when Sergeant Samples ambled up, gnawing on one of the biscuits like it was some kind of delicacy.

"How can you eat those?" Carr asked with a grimace.

Samples shrugged. "With my teeth. Good exercise."

Carr scoffed.

"I think you need to talk to Baker," Samples said.

"Baker? Why? What's the matter?"

Samples rubbed his ear. "That ambush last night. I don't know, he's reacting kind of funny."

"How so?"

Samples sighed. "Kind of hyper. Talking more than usual, and kind of fast."

"Well, it was his first firefight," Carr said. "Bound to have affected him some." And, Carr told himself silently, that was undoubtedly Baker's first experience with killing someone. That would give any normal person the heebie-jeebies. If Baker hadn't shown some reaction, then Carr would have really been worried.

"I know," Samples agreed, "but this morning he put on a clean uniform, shaved, and even polished his boots. Nobody polishes their boots out here."

Carr had taken a lot of psychology courses in college, in order to get his degree in sociology, so he knew just enough to be dangerous. It sounded like a Lady Macbeth syndrome: get rid of the evidence of what he had done last night and try to start fresh.

"I'll talk to him," Carr promised. "He'll probably get over it when we start moving again. Meanwhile, let me know if it gets worse."

Eberhart leaned out of the back of the one-three track and yelled for all to hear, "Movin' out in ten. Pack it up."

Everyone started scurrying around, and Carr and Samples had to back out of the way as the men hurried to pull down the RPG screen and put away all their sleeping gear. Samples ran over to the one-one to correct some perceived deficiency, and Carr dodged around Aiello to climb up the side of the track and close his ammo case. He wished Gordon had held a leaders meeting to discuss the day's mission before ordering them to move out, but that was the commander's prerogative. He put on his helmet and picked up his rifle, standing on top of the track to observe the progress of the platoon. Doc Allman poked his head up through the cargo hatch, found his pistol belt lying on one of the cases, and buckled it on.

"Another day, another dollar," Carr remarked to the medic.

"You make that much?" Allman asked enviously. "Wow. Officers got it made."

They both laughed, and then looked up at the sound of helicopters. Carr shaded his eyes and peered to the south, where he made out the shapes of two helicopters headed their way. One was a Chinook, the big banana-shaped two-rotor cargo chopper, and the other the thin firefly-shaped Cobra gunship. He wondered if they were coming to the Alpha Company location, but as he watched he mentally computed their flight route. They were too high to be headed for the mechanized company, and the angle wasn't quite right. Twisting around, he looked at Nui Ba Den and realized the choppers were headed to the peak of the mountain. Probably the morning supply run, Carr surmised, and turned his attention back to getting the platoon ready to move out.

NINETEEN

Sang stopped and looked around, biting his lower lip. Thanh was grateful for the pause in climbing, but concerned that the young man might be lost.

"Well?" Nhu griped at Sang.

"It is here," Sang said dubiously. "Somewhere."

"What is?" Nhu challenged him.

"An old bunker. We do not use it anymore, but it is perfect for you."

Nhu rolled her eyes in exasperation. "We must get into position immediately. The helicopter will be here at any minute."

Sang nodded as he continued to study the area around them. It was mostly barren rock, with just a scattering of bushes and stunted trees. Thanh wasn't surprised that Sang couldn't find the bunker; everything around here looked the same, and the PLA was famous for its ability to camouflage. She slowly lowered herself to one knee and gulped in the air that was noticeably thinner and cooler than down below.

"Ah!" Sang said suddenly. "I think that is . . ." He scrambled away to the east, using his left hand to balance himself on the steep slope and occasionally to hold onto branches or large rocks as smaller stones rattled down, dislodged by his feet. "Yes! Here it is." He stopped and beckoned to Nhu and Thanh. Thanh could see nothing that looked like a bunker, but obediently she stood up and followed Nhu as they carefully made their way across the jumbled scree.

When they reached Sang, he was pointing down at a ragged hole in the ground, almost two meters in diameter and one meter deep. Stones had been piled around the hole, and beside it were some scattered old tree limbs and a crumpled sheet of faded canvas. Thanh was very disappointed by the rudimentary nature of the so-called "bunker."

"This is it?" Nhu asked disdainfully.

Sang shrugged apologetically. "It is old and not used anymore," he explained again. "We can put the canvas up again, and we will be hidden."

"We will be firing into the sky," Nhu shot back, like she was talking to an idiot. "We do not want to be covered by that old dirty canvas."

"It will do," Thanh interjected, slipping her shoulders out of the pack straps and lowering the case to the ground. "As long as there are no snakes in the hole," she added.

"Snakes?" Sang said, his eyes going wide. "Uh, no, there are no snakes here on the mountain." His frightened tone belied his apparent certainty. He stepped back as he looked down into the hole.

"Shut up!" Nhu hissed, and turned to the look out over the plain. Thanh heard it, too: the thrumming beat of helicopters, the sound growing in intensity. Nhu dropped her own pack and began undoing the straps that secured it. "Thanh!" she yelped, "it is time for the launcher."

Thanh eyed the approaching aircraft as she placed the pistol pouch on the ground and began methodically undoing the canvas straps that closed the canvas cover over the metal case. Beside her Nhu was doing the same. She could see that there were two helicopters, a big one and a small one, and they were headed directly toward Thanh. Observing the speed of approach, and mentally going through the steps to assemble and aim the missile launcher, she knew there wasn't enough time.

"Get in the hole," Thanh told the other two, "and pull that canvas over us. If that gunship sees us, we will be attacked."

Nhu looked at the sky and nodded. "Hurry!" she ordered, picking up her case and lowering it into the hole hastily, then turning to help Thanh slide her case in as well. They both jumped in while Sang retrieved the canvas and pulled it over them. Moments later the roar of the helicopters swelled to a deafening cacophony, and their prop wash threatened to blow the canvas away. All three gripped the edges of the canvas and held on until the choppers had passed overhead.

Coughing from the dust that had been stirred up, Thanh peeked out through a hole in the canvas. She couldn't see the big cargo helicopter, but the little gunship was circling the peak of the mountain, flying over them every minute or so.

"It is your fault!" Nhu barked at Sang. "We are too late! Our mission has failed!"

"No," Thanh said simply.

"No?"

"The helicopter will have to leave after the entertainment is over. We can shoot it then."

Nhu's face brightened. "Of course. And that will be better. You told me that the missile works best when fired at the back of a helicopter. Correct?"

"Yes." Thanh sighed. She was still torn about what they were doing. She wanted to complete the mission that Uncle Ho had assigned her, but she didn't want to kill anyone, especially someone who wasn't trying to kill her or anyone else. It was one thing to defend one's self against an attacker, but to kill a civilian was wrong, whether it was the people in Hanoi or an entertainer here.

"The gunship is leaving," Sang announced, lifting up the downhill edge of the canvas to get a better view. Thanh saw that Sang was right; the thin-bodied helicopter was zooming away to the south. Thanh figured that once the big helicopter had landed, the other was no longer needed and went back to refuel or fulfill some other mission.

"It will be back," Nhu warned ominously, "when the big one leaves again."

Sang started to fold back part of the canvas to let fresh air into the crowded hole.

"Leave it," Nhu told him. "We must stay hidden until it is time." She turned to Thanh. "We must get a launcher out and set it up. We must be ready when that helicopter takes off again."

"When will that be?" Sang asked, sitting back to watch Nhu and Thanh remove the canvas covers and unclip the catches on the metal boxes.

"An hour?" Nhu suggested. "Maybe two?"

"Do you need any help with that?" Sang asked, putting his rifle aside and leaning forward to look curiously at the contents of the cases.

"No!" Nhu scolded him. "Do not touch anything!"

Sang shrugged and sat back. "So what is that? A new type of RPG?"

Thanh lifted one of the launch tubes and peeled the protective cloth wrapping. "It is a shoulder-fired ground-to-air guided missile," she explained pedantically. "We use them in the north to shoot down American bombers."

"I have never seen anything like that," Sang marveled.

"It is very new," Thanh replied proudly. "This is the first one to be used here in the South."

"Ho Chi Minh sent her," Nhu added, in a tone that showed she was not impressed. She took the tube from Thanh and held it while Thanh attached the gripstock and battery.

When it was assembled, Thanh took the heavy weapon and inspected it from one end to the other. She left the covers at each end still attached, to keep dust from getting inside. She turned it over in her hands, verifying that it was undamaged by the long journey from the north, and then handed it back to Nhu to be loosely laid on top of Thanh's now-empty case. Nhu picked up the other loaded launcher tube, but Thanh tried to stop her. "We only need one," Thanh protested.

"What if the first one does not work, or you miss?" Nhu said, stripping the protective wrapping off and laying the missile back in the case.

Actually, Thanh realized, that was just what she was hoping. She felt guilty about her desire for the mission to fail, but as the time grew closer, her doubts and concerns were increasing. At least they had only one gripstock, so the second missile could not be fired until that piece had been switched over, and the second battery attached, which would take at least a minute.

"I have to go," she blurted.

"Where?" Nhu demanded. "What are you talking about?"

"I must, uh, you know," Thanh stammered, shooting an embarrassed look at Sang.

Nhu rolled her eyes. "Do it quickly, girl. There are some bushes just down the hill."

"Do you need help?" Sang asked lasciviously while trying to look innocent. Nhu punched him in the shoulder, and Thanh ignored him, although she was disappointed in his remark. She had thought he was a nicer man than that. Thanh stood up and pushed the canvas cover farther back so she could climb out. The morning sun provided welcome warmth to her body, and she could not help but admire the beautiful view of the plains spread out below.

*****

"Shit!" Nash said, not for the first time today. Things were not going as well as he had hoped. He and Quan were squashed together in the narrow opening between two boulders, the only cover they had been able to find on the rough slope of the mountain. The gap was so tight that they had been forced to leave their packs outside, poorly camouflaged with a couple sparse branches from a nearby bush and a sprinkling of loose rock. Quan, being smaller, was crammed awkwardly into the V of the boulders, which left Nash partially exposed on the outside, half kneeling and half standing with sharp rock projections digging into his knees and hip. His left arm rested on rock to support the rifle, making his elbow hurt, and his left palm stung from the scrape he had gotten when he had almost slid down the mountain as they climbed. There was simply no way to get into a comfortable firing position, so this would have to do. He put his eye to the scope and scanned the almost featureless mountainside. Next to him Quan had the binoculars, sweeping back and forth in a wide arc to survey the terrain. Every few seconds Quan would look up from the binoculars and do a 360-degree search to make sure no one was approaching their position.

"I can't see anything," Nash complained.

"They are there," Quan reassured him. "Above bushes."

Nash had reacted quickly when Quan had spotted their prey while they were still climbing, but not quickly enough to see them himself. He had to take Quan's word for it, and while he had learned to trust Quan implicitly, a doubt still lingered in the back of his mind. What if Quan had seen an animal, or some other VC? Was he sure it was the sniper and her two comrades? At the time he had been more concerned about finding a suitable place to set up, but now that they were firmly ensconced in this confining gap, his worries had increased.

When the two choppers appeared overhead, Nash and Quan had pushed deeper into the cleft, worried the gunship would see them and attack, assuming they were enemy soldiers. *That's all we need,* Nash thought, *to be this close to getting the sniper, and then get killed by our own guys.* Nash had heaved a sigh of relief when the Cobra departed, and repositioned to get the best firing angle.

Looking up over the top of the scope, Nash blinked at the bright sun that now was only about twenty degrees above the spot on the mountainside where Quan had said he saw the group. He saw the small cluster of bushes silhouetted against the sky, the ones that Quan had mentioned, and moved his gaze upward, trying to pick anything unusual out of the spare landscape of rocks and gravel. Because of the curve of the mountain, the supposed hiding place of the group was right at the edge of view. Any further away and the spot would be invisible, hidden by the shoulder of rock. A flicker of movement caught Nash's eye. Something grey-brown popped up and fell again. He put his eye to the scope again and tried to find that specific area of rock.

"I saw something," he whispered to Quan.

"What?"

"Not sure. Maybe some cloth. Or maybe an animal."

"Sniper woman," Quan said with certainty.

Nash grunted. He still wasn't convinced that the sniper was there, but at least now he knew that Quan had indeed seen something, and hadn't simply imagined it. But it still could be an animal, he told himself. He didn't know what sort of wildlife existed on Nui Ba Den, but guessed there could be some type of mountain goat or deer. And if there were, the animals would have adapted to their environment by growing coats of grey and brown that camouflaged them. He did a minor adjustment to the scope's focus, and concentrated on the rocks where he had seen the brief movement. He tried wiggling his hips to relieve the strain of the awkward position he was in, but that only dug the rocks into his knees more.

A few minutes passed. Nash raised his head to wipe the sweat off his face with his sleeve. Next to him Quan was studying the area of interest through the binoculars. Nash repositioned his boonie hat and put his head back down to the scope. "Did you see that patrol sneaking up on us from behind?" he asked Quan in a mild voice, smiling to himself.

"Yes," Quan replied. "No sweat, GI."

Nash chuckled. He and Quan were a team, and they got along very well together, despite their vastly different backgrounds. He knew he could depend on the Vietnamese man under any circumstances.

"Yo!" Quan coughed. Nash saw it, too. It was clearly a flap of canvas being thrown back, and then a head appeared. It was a woman, and her hair was very long. She stood up, but she appeared to be in a hole, as only her head and shoulders were visible. Nash put the crosshairs on the woman's spine, and began increasing the pressure on the trigger, but then the woman moved again. She climbed out of the hole to slip and slide down the loose rock toward the bushes. Nash concentrated on keeping the rifle pointed at center mass, but her erratic movement made that difficult. He waited for her to pause so he could get off a good shot. Slowly he realized that this wasn't the sniper; this was the much younger woman, more slender and with longer hair. He eased back on the trigger. If he shot this woman, the sniper would be warned, and he might not get a chance at her.

The young woman went around the bushes and looked over the top of them back toward where she had emerged from the hole. Then in a single motion she pulled down her pants and squatted. Nash looked away, embarrassed.

"Thanh!" Quan blurted.

"What?"

"That is Thanh."

"The Coke girl? Are you sure?"

"Yes."

Nash looked at her face for the first time, and she did look familiar.

"Why is she here?" Nash asked, mostly rhetorically.

Quan didn't answer, probably as puzzled by the girl's presence as Nash. He watched the girl stand back up quickly, pulling her pants up at the same time, but then stop. She made a slow turn and gazed out across the plains to the south. Nash wondered what she was looking for. Her shoulders heaved, as if she had just sighed dramatically. Then her head jerked around as if she had heard something.

"Sniper woman!" Quan whispered.

Nash swung the scope to the left, back to where the hole in the mountain was located, and saw another person's head and shoulders just above the rocks. With broad shoulders and short hair, this was definitely the sniper Nash had seen before. And she looked familiar, for some reason. She was motioning angrily to Thanh, beckoning her to return to the shelter. Nash put the crosshairs on the woman's back as low as the angle permitted and took a deep breath, letting it halfway out as he tightened the muscles in his index finger. Before he could fire, however, she ducked back down inside to make room for Thanh, who had scrambled back up and was ready to jump in. Nash eased off the trigger and exhaled. "Shit," he muttered disgustedly. Another opportunity missed.

*****

At first Sergeant Samples feared that Captain Gordon had gotten lost again. The plan had been for the company to sweep southeast, but just after they crossed the road that led northeast to War Zone C, the company had been halted and then ordered to turn around. As PFC Gunn pulled on the left lateral to swing the track around, Samples jumped down through the cargo hatch so he would be closer to the radio inside. The net was a jumble of commands and questions, with everyone trying to find out what was going on. Finally he heard Gordon's voice cut through the noise and order everyone else to listen up.

"Men, an ARVN company has found a gook ambush on the road from Tay Ninh to Dau Tieng. They are heavily engaged, and we are advancing to support them. When we get back to the road we will head southwest. The march order will be Headquarters, First, Second, and Third. Follow me. Out."

"He didn't really say that," Samples mumbled to himself, shaking his head, amused at the trite slogan Gordon had used. He could just imagine Gordon standing up with one hand raised, emulating the statue at Ft. Benning that supposedly expressed the spirit of the infantry leader. He climbed back out of the cargo hatch and took his seat on the ammo crate, holding on to the 50-cal turret as the track bounced over an embankment and swerved onto the roadway. There was the typical cluster-fuck as the company reassembled in the order Gordon had listed; Headquarters Platoon had been in the middle of the sweep, and now had to move past

Third to take the lead, while Second and First exchanged places to follow.

Samples looked back and saw Lieutenant Carr giving him hand signals, indicating Samples should take the lead of their platoon in the one-one, and the other tracks would follow in numerical order. Samples tapped Jamison on the shoulder and shouted, "Have Gunn slot in behind the last of the Zippos." While Jamison relayed the instructions over the intercom, Samples looked back to make sure the rest of the platoon was falling into line properly. It took several minutes, but finally the company was all in line and roaring down the dirt road at maximum speed, around thirty miles an hour, throwing up huge plumes of dust that quickly coated everything. Samples listened for the sound of distant gunfire, but couldn't hear anything over the roar of diesel engines and the rumble of metal treads.

Inside the 50-cal turret next to Samples, Greenberg was checking the belt of ammo where it fed into the breech of the machine gun. The young soldier pulled an old shaving brush out of his pocket and kept brushing the dust away from the operating mechanism and the black links that connected the brass cartridges of ammo.

"What's that old story about sweeping the sand off the beach?" Samples asked him with a grin.

"Got to do what I can, Sarge," Greenberg answered.

"Atta boy," Samples praised him. All of the men liked the 50-cal, and they constantly argued over whose turn it was to man it, but Greenberg truly loved the weapon. Even when it wasn't his turn, he would help to disassemble and clean the heavy machine gun, and regularly used the special small tool to check the head space and timing. When the platoon went more than a week without making contact, Greenberg would start bugging Samples to allow some "test firing" of the M2. And Samples understood. There was some weird atavistic pleasure in firing the gun, with its pounding thump-thump-thump and the tracers zooming off into the distance. It gave the firer an illusion of omnipotence, of supreme power, that just made one feel good. But Greenberg, unlike some other guys Samples had known, never let the gun take control. He fired in exactly five-round bursts, pausing two seconds between bursts, to ensure the barrel didn't overheat, and grinned like a madman while he did it. It looked like he was going to get the chance today to indulge in his favorite sport.

*****

A high-pitched squeal pierced the air above them, like the call of a hawk on the hunt.

"What was that?" Sang asked, a worried frown on his face.

"A microphone," Thanh explained. "It is called feedback. They are setting up a stage for the entertainment." Thanh had been assigned to help with a political rally in Hanoi once where the same thing had happened, and she felt a little superior over her rural companions. Although they were still at least a couple hundred meters from the peak of the mountain, the sound from up there carried well in the still air.

A few minutes later they heard music, the kind that the American soldiers liked to listen to. It faded in and out, and Thanh could not make out the words or even the melody, but she could imagine the spectacle. At the end of the song she heard shouts, whistles, and applause. The men up there were having a good time. Secretly Thanh wished she was up there with them, enjoying the show, instead of crouching in this hole in the ground under a dirty canvas, holding a deadly weapon in her hands. Thanh had checked everything out again to make doubly sure it was operational. The end covers had been removed, the sight extended, and the electronics verified to be working. All that was left was aiming and firing.

"I should fire it," Nhu stated. She had been arguing for several minutes about the "honor" of shooting down the helicopter.

"You do not know how," Thanh replied.

"You showed me," Nhu countered. "I know as much as you do."

"It is not the same. I have actually shot down an American plane. It is very tricky." Thanh had only damaged the plane, but she exaggerated her success in order to keep Nhu at bay.

"Can we fire it from this hole?" Nhu asked.

"Of course not. The rocket blast out the back is very dangerous. I will have to go out on the mountain to fire it."

"And you will do that?" Nhu asked suspiciously. Nhu had obviously detected Thanh's reluctance to shoot down the helicopter.

"Yes," Thanh asserted, puffing out her chest. "For the Great Teacher, and the Party." She spoke the words expected of her, but deep inside Thanh knew she did not truly believe them. In fact, she did not know for sure what she would do when the time came.

Above them they heard a male voice amplified by tinny loudspeakers, and faint roars of laughter.

"That is Bob Hope," Thanh told the other two authoritatively, although in reality she had no idea who it was. She just felt a need to take charge of the situation, so that neither of the other two would interfere with whatever she eventually decided to do.

"And who is Bo Bo?" Sang asked, mispronouncing the name.

"An important American public figure," Nhu told him. "When we kill him, the Americans will lose heart and leave."

"Why?"

"Because," Nhu said sharply, glaring at Sang to prevent him from asking any more questions. Sang sank back and took on a petulant look, but said nothing more.

Placing the launcher on her shoulder, Thanh stood up and pushed the canvas aside enough to look out. The blue sky was clear of aircraft, and the sounds from the peak were slightly louder, although she could still not distinguish any words. During a brief pause in the noise from above, she thought she heard the sound of a firefight far to the south. She could also see a cloud of dust stirred up by a line of vehicles traveling down a road, but they were too far for her to determine what kind of vehicles they were. American, undoubtedly, but beyond that she had no idea. She pointed the weapon at the moving convoy, just to see what it would look like through the sight, and imagined pulling the trigger. She did not like the feeling.

After a moment she lowered the launcher and settled back in the hole, laying the long tube back on her pack. Above them the laughter continued.

*****

"What the fuck?" Nash breathed, seeing the girl's upper body appear with some sort of device on her shoulder. It looked sort of like an RPG launcher, but with no fat warhead sticking out of the front of it. Why would Thanh have an unloaded RPG launcher, if that was indeed what it was? He reflexively centered the scope's crosshairs on her shoulders and took a deep breath.

"No shoot!" Quan whispered harshly, putting his hand on Nash's arm.

"Why not?"

"She not sniper," Quan said.

Nash acknowledged Quan's logic. He was here to get the sniper, not some Coke girl who was playing with an empty RPG launcher. Although, he thought, that launcher did not look like ones he had seen before; it was sleeker and longer, with a can-shaped device under the front end. And the way she held it suggested it was heavier than an unloaded RPG launcher. Perhaps it was a new version. Nash exhaled and eased his finger off the trigger, just as Thanh ducked back down in the hole.

"What was that thing?" he asked, thinking maybe Quan had seen something like it when he had been a Viet Cong.

"RPG?" Quan guessed.

"Maybe." The appearance of the unusual weapon had started Nash thinking. He had been so concentrated on pursuing the sniper that up until now he hadn't questioned what the sniper was doing up here. And she wasn't carrying her sniper rifle. He mentally ran through the possibilities, and but none seemed to make much sense. And he had finally realized why she looked familiar. She was the sandwich mama-san who always had accompanied Thanh, which meant they had been working together for some time. Probably Thanh worked as a spotter for her, and by posing as a Coke girl and a sandwich mama-san, they had escaped suspicion after the sniper had made a kill. Now, however, their roles had perhaps switched, and Thanh seemed to be in charge. The heavy cases he had seen the sniper and Thanh carrying obviously had held the RPG launcher, or whatever it was, and that seemed to be part of the plan. If he could just figure out what that plan was.

"Why are they here?" he asked out loud.

"Shoot helicopter?" Quan surmised. That was what Nash had been thinking as well. But they had had an opportunity to do that earlier, when the big Chinook had come in, and they had let it go. His thoughts were interrupted by another burst of laughter from somewhere way above them. The Chinook had apparently brought in some sort of USO show to entertain the troops up on the peak, and he had been hearing the music and garbled speech drifting down the mountainside for several minutes. Idly he wondered what sort of show the guys up there were getting, wishing he was there to see it. Then a trick of acoustics, perhaps a shift in the slight breeze, brought an amplified voice more clearly to his ears, and he instantly recognized the unique cadence and tone.

"That's Bob Hope up there!" he blurted happily. "I'd recognize that voice anywhere."

"BFD," Quan said grumpily, using an American phrase he had recently picked up.

"Hey, it is a Big Fucking Deal," Nash admonished him. "He's a big star. I'm surprised he's doing a show up there, though, since it's such a small outpost. I think he did a show in Cu Chi yesterday."

"Maybe sniper woman want to see show, too," Quan joked, but that sparked a serious idea in Nash's brain.

"Or shoot down his helicopter," Nash warned grimly. He looked over at Quan, whose expression had suddenly gotten very serious. Quan nodded.

Nash had heard of gooks trying to shoot down helicopters with RPGs, although rarely successfully. The RPG had a very short range and was unguided, so hitting a moving, high-flying target required a lot of skill and even more luck. The launcher that Thanh had been holding, however, was longer than other RPGs Nash had seen, and with ballistic weapons, a longer barrel meant greater accuracy. Now the various elements began to fall into place.

"They're trying to kill Bob Hope," Nash stated flatly.

"Why?" Quan asked. "He President or something?"

"No, he's a comedian, but he's very famous. If he's killed, it would change public opinion about the war." Nash had once tried to explain the anti-war movement on American college campuses to Quan, but the Vietnamese had not fully grasped the implications. Quan was used to a country where dissent was immediately quashed by the government, by brutal means if necessary. Most South Vietnamese opposed the war in one way or another, but that certainly didn't hinder the continued fighting. Quan could not quite grasp how a shift in the general population's opinion could affect the decisions of the military and government.

Quan shrugged, obviously not understanding, but willing to accept Nash's explanation. "We stop them," he said simply.

"Yes," Nash agreed with determination. "We've got to stop them." He heard more laughter from above, and considered his options down here on the mountainside. Perhaps he and Quan should mount a frontal assault on the three people in the hole. He plotted out such an attack, and knew it would fail. They could not approach the foxhole without making noise, and would be without cover, making them easy targets from within the protection of the bunker. Maybe if they had grenades, and they made some lucky throws, but they didn't. Nash shook his head. Their only chance was the original plan: wait for the gooks to pop up out of their hole, which they would have to do to fire the RPG, and pick them off before they could fire.

TWENTY

A Huey lifted into the air far in front of them, and Lieutenant Carr caught a quick glimpse of the big red cross emblazoned on the nose. The dust from Headquarters Platoon tracks obscured his view of the road ahead, but Carr knew they must be approaching the area where the ARVNs had been in contact. Oddly, though, he heard no gunfire. The tracks ahead of his began to slow down, and Carr could now see another mechanized company in an open field to their left, deployed in a square formation. Some of the other company's tracks had 106mm recoilless rifles mounted on top, and all of the vehicles were remarkably clean and neat, telling Carr that this was the ARVNs. Despite the many complaints American soldiers had about the Army of the Republic of Viet Nam, vehicle maintenance was something those forces prided themselves on.

Up ahead, Captain Gordon's track came to a halt, and the rest of the company closed up behind. The radio below crackled, and Carr heard Gordon's voice. "Platoon leaders, to me."

Carr jumped down and took a moment to brush some of the dust off his uniform. Next he blew dust off his M-16, and began walking toward the front of the column. He wasn't in any hurry, since the other two platoon leaders were farther back and would take more time to arrive. He met Captain Gordon walking back toward him. Carr raised an eyebrow in question, and Gordon just shrugged. Together they crossed the road toward the ARVN laager as Lieutenant Masters and Lieutenant Zee joined them. Gordon's RTO walked a couple meters behind them, ready to relay any commands the commander might have, or report on orders from Higher. Carr and Masters exchanged looks behind Gordon's back, both wondering what was going on here.

A Vietnamese captain waited in front of what was presumably his command track, positioned at the center of the square, and next to him was a sergeant. The captain smoked a cigarette and watched the Americans approach with what looked like impatience, one hand resting on the butt of his holstered pistol. The sergeant next to him held an old WWII-era M3 grease gun hanging from a strap around his neck. Carr had never seen one of those weapons in real life before, just in old movies. Made of stamped steel, the short submachine gun fired .45-caliber rounds at a rapid clip, but Carr had heard it wasn't very accurate, and it wasn't very reliable. Carr wondered if it was left over from the French occupation after the war, or something the Americans had given the ARVNs when handing out war surplus.

Gordon led the small group between two of the tracks facing the road, and Carr glanced up at the men who sat on top, all properly uniformed and holding M2 carbines. The ARVN soldiers stared straight ahead, trying to ignore the Americans, although Carr caught one of them flashing a brief smile at them. For having just come out of a firefight, the unit looked very sharp, and Carr saw only a couple men with bandages. He had been observing the rest of the company so closely that Carr was surprised when they stopped in front of the captain, and he recognized the man. Carr narrowed his eyes at the bantam rooster of man, remembering the way they had clashed a few weeks ago in the Michelin rubber plantation. This Captain Nguyen had been trying to confiscate the cash that Sergeant Jaramillo had captured from the NVA, and Carr had prevented it. Nguyen now glared back at him, obviously recognizing him as well.

"Captain, uh, Nguyen, I'm Captain Gordon." Gordon held out his hand to shake. Gordon had badly mispronounced the man's name. Nguyen reluctantly took his eyes away from Carr, took one last drag before dropping the cigarette, but kept his right hand on his pistol. Gordon let his hand fall to his side. "Do you speak English?"

"Some," Nguyen replied.

"Ah, you requested our support? You had contact with the enemy?"

Nguyen cleared his throat and spat to one side. "Yes. Many enemy. They ambush us."

Gordon gazed around at the formation of tracks. "You had casualties?"

"Yes, many casualties. Choppers take them away to hospital."

"I'm a little confused," Gordon confessed. "I understood you were still in contact and needed reinforcements."

"We break contact," Nguyen told him blandly. "Too many wounded."

"So, uh, where did this happen?" Gordon seemed a little adrift at the situation, which was radically different than he had been led to believe. Carr was not surprised, and wished he could take Gordon aside and explain the facts of life here in Viet Nam. While some South Vietnamese units had earned reputations as fierce warriors, most, especially those led by men like Nguyen, were known for avoiding any contact if possible, and quickly retreating when they did run into any enemy.

Nguyen sniffed, and then pointed vaguely over his left shoulder. "In woods. Many NVA. Bunkers. RPGs."

Gordon pulled a plastic-covered map from his cargo pocket and spread it, turning and refolding it until their current location was centered. Carr crowded in closer so he, too, could see the map. Gordon held it out horizontally between himself and Nguyen.

"We're here," Gordon said, using a finger to point at the map where a road was shown as a red line. "Where is the NVA?"

Nguyen sighed, as if the question was totally unnecessary. He studied the map for a few seconds, and then placed his fingertip on a large loop of green. While most of the area where they were now consisted of open fields and occasional rice paddies, a large section of woods approached the road like a peninsula extending from the greater forest of the Crescent. Where Nguyen was pointing was almost a kilometer away.

"That would be a good place for an ambush," Carr said judiciously.

"Yes," Nguyen said with a false smile. "Big ambush."

"Okay," Gordon said, "what is the plan, then?"

"Plan?" Nguyen asked, apparently puzzled. "You attack."

"Yes, certainly, but how do we coordinate? Which direction will you attack from?"

"Me? We already attack. We have many wounded. My commander say we go home now."

Gordon actually stepped back in surprise, bumping into Masters behind him. "I thought this was a joint operation. You are not going to fight alongside us?"

Nguyen shrugged apologetically. "I have orders. Is your job now."

Carr suppressed a smirk. He was not at all surprised by this turn of events, but he could see that Gordon was completely flummoxed. Gordon just stared at Nguyen, who ignored Gordon and turned away. Nguyen raised his hand and shouted orders in Vietnamese, and all the ARVN APC's began firing up their engines.

Carr tugged at Gordon's sleeve. "Sir? We need to discuss the situation, perhaps over by your track?"

Nguyen climbed up on his track and exchanged his starched and formed boonie hat for the CVC helmet. He spoke into the mike, and the APC began edging forward, forcing the Americans to jump out of the way. Gordon shook his head as if trying to clear it, then turned and led the way back to the road, dodging around the ARVN tracks as they streamed out of their laager and roared away in a column, opposite the direction of the recent battle.

"I don't believe this!" Gordon said when they reached the side of his track.

"Par for the course, sir," Carr told him.

Gordon faced him, a troubled frown on his face. "So what are we supposed to do now? Our mission was to reinforce the ARVNs, but they've taken off."

"Check with Battalion?" Masters suggested.

Gordon seemed to consider it, and then shook his head violently. "No, we have our orders. If there are NVA soldiers in those woods, then we have a duty to attack them. We need to get a body count." Carr winced at this remark. He was tired of hearing about body counts.

"Do you think they're still there, sir?" Lieutenant Zee asked, perhaps hoping they weren't.

"We'll find out," Gordon asserted. He still had his map in his hand, and put it up against the side of the track while the lieutenants crowded around. Pulling a grease pencil from his shirt pocket, he circled the area where Nguyen had said the enemy ambush was. "If it was an ambush planning to hit a convoy," Gordon intoned, "then they would have lined up parallel to the road, here. If we come in from the side, we can roll them up and also block any attempt to escape to the north. What do you think?"

Carr was a little disturbed that Gordon had shown some indecision by asking for their opinion, but he had to admit it was as good a plan as any. Masters apparently agreed.

"That could work, sir," Masters said encouragingly. "Maybe keep the Zippos at the right flank, close to the road, in case the gooks have dug in along there."

"My thoughts exactly. The company will wheel left and attack on line. I'll have the Headquarters tracks fall in behind as a reserve. Any questions?"

"Should we get closer before we swing out?" Carr asked, trying to prod Gordon into making the right choices. If they did the wheel movement now, they would have trouble maintaining a balanced approached due to the scattered groves of trees he could see between their current position and the main wood line.

Gordon nodded. "Yes, I see your point. If we continue down the road, the enemy will think we are walking into their trap, and be surprised when we swing out and attack from their flank. Good idea, Lieutenant Carr."

That wasn't the reason Carr had suggested it, but whatever worked. And maybe Gordon was even right about how the enemy would react.

"All right, men," Gordon said, turning to face them and folding up his map, "let's move out. Good hunting."

*****

There was a long period of applause and whistling on the peak, followed by a short burst of music, and then the noise faded away. "The show must be over," Nhu said. "Get ready."

Earlier, when Thanh had repositioned the assembled launcher on top of the two cases, Sang had eagerly picked it up, running his hands over the long tube and marveling at its intricacies. At Nhu's insistence, he reluctantly handed it to Thanh. She accepted it, but unenthusiastically. As the time drew near, her desire to fire the missile at the big helicopter had totally disappeared. She imagined the craft exploding in flame and crashing to the earth, burning bodies falling from the sky and men screaming in agony. She could not help but shudder. She saw Nhu watching her.

"I should fire it," Nhu stated. "You are not ready."

"No," Thanh said, shaking her head, "I will do it. It is my duty." Even as she said it, however, Thanh knew it was a lie. She couldn't do it, wouldn't do it. She didn't know how, but somehow she would avoid shooting down the helicopter and damning her soul forever. Damning her soul? Where did that come from? She was shocked that the phrase had suddenly come to her, some relic from her childhood, she supposed.

"You are weak!" Nhu sneered at her. "I can see it. Give me the missile." She reached across the hole and snatched at the launcher. Thanh pulled it away from her.

"It is mine!" Thanh yelled at her. "I will be the one." She stood up, pushing the canvas back and poking the launcher out of the hole.

"Helicopter!" Sang warned.

Thanh heard it, too. Approaching quickly from the south was a single gunship, the thin one that looked like a predatory insect. After a moment's hesitation, when she briefly considered climbing out with the launcher and daring the American pilot to shoot her, she sank back down and pulled the canvas back over them. Allowing the helicopter to kill her would be committing suicide, which she knew was wrong. And worse, that might allow Nhu to get the missile launcher and kill the people on the big helicopter. No, this was not the way to prevent the awful event from happening. She just did not know, however, what the right way was.

"Ah," Nhu said approvingly, "now you are ready. But you were right not to shoot down the gunship. We must wait until the big helicopter takes off, for that is our real target. Perhaps after we shoot the big one, then we can reload and shoot down the other." Nhu reached into the Claymore bag Thanh had left on the ground and pulled out the pistol, checking its action and making sure it was loaded.

"Yes," Thanh said weakly, glad that Nhu had misinterpreted her actions. On a professional level, she realized that Nhu's plan was impractical anyway. It took at least twenty seconds to switch the trigger assembly and battery to the other tube, before she could shoulder the weapon and try to acquire the new target. All while they would be out in the open, vulnerable to attack by the gunship's rapid-fire Gatling gun and rockets. Despite having the spare missile, Thanh had always known there would only be time to fire one of them. But she worried about why Nhu now held the pistol.

Overhead Thanh heard the drone of the helicopter fade and return as it circled high above, providing protection for the slow-moving cargo helicopter that was undoubtedly being loaded and readied for takeoff. How could she stop this disaster from occurring? Many ideas flashed through her mind, but none seemed likely for success. She looked at Sang, but the young man was clearly excited, anticipating the great battle that he would be part of. There would be no help there. Her real problem was Nhu: she was ruthless, and Thanh had taught her to fire the missile. She wished she had never instructed the older woman, but back then she had still had the idea that she was on a mission from Ho, and wanted to ensure the success of that mission. Now that she had changed her mind, it was too late to change the past.

*****

"Stay down!" Nash told Quan, pushing him deeper into the cleft between the two boulders. The Cobra was back, circling the mountain, and would soon be directly over them. If the pilot saw them he would assume they were gooks and shoot them out of hand. As far as the pilot knew, there was no one on the mountain slopes other than gooks, and from a moving helicopter at a distance, Nash and Quan would look like any other combatants.

"I have flag," Quan said, squirming beneath Nash. Since Quan had surrendered to the Americans and become a Hoi Chanh scout, he had always carried a small American flag in his pants pocket. That flag had helped them in the Michelin, but Nash doubted it would be of much use here.

"It's too small," he told Quan, talking loudly over the roar of the helicopter that faded in and out. "Waving that flag would be just sending a signal to shoot at us. We'll just have to keep out of sight." Unfortunately, Nash realized, that meant they couldn't watch for the appearance of the sniper, either. Just before the Cobra had arrived, Nash had been watching the camouflaged hole and had seen Thanh briefly appear with the unfamiliar weapon, but before he could take a shot she had dropped back below the rim of the hole. Shooting her would be a problem, he knew. Not only was he hesitant about firing his rifle at a young girl he had actually met once, he knew that Quan had developed some sort of emotional attraction to the girl. He didn't think Quan would interfere if it became necessary to shoot her, but he dreaded the reaction his friend would experience afterward. Nash contemplated shooting just at the weapon, disabling it, but realized his skills were not up to that task. The tube was so narrow, the conditions so turbulent, and his self-doubt so great that the chances were extremely slim. And if he missed, the missile, whatever it was, would fire and possibly cause the greatest political and popular uproar of the war. He had to shoot to kill.

The Cobra zoomed close overhead, and Nash ducked his head, hoping the olive drab of his uniform and boonie had would help him blend into the scenery. He worried about their packs, just outside the gap in the rocks. They had covered them with a few branches from nearby scraggly bushes, but would that be enough? The chopper flew on by, and then the turbine whine increased as the gunship climbed to a higher altitude. Nash peeked up and saw the Cobra spiraling upwards and away from them. As he raised his head further, he heard the sound of jet engines igniting up on the summit. The Chinook was firing up, readying to take off, and the Cobra had moved higher to clear the way. This was the time. Nash lifted himself off of Quan, picked up his rifle, and resumed his position overlooking the enemy bunker. He put his eye to the scope just in time to see the canvas thrown back and two heads emerge.

Thanh scrambled up from the hole, holding the long tubed weapon with both hands, and moved a few steps down the slope, looking up at the peak. Following her was the sniper, and she had a pistol in her hand. She, too, looked up. Nash opened his left eye and in his peripheral vision saw the Chinook clumsily appear overhead, its prop wash stirring up clouds of dust. He kept his right eye pressed to the scope, the cross hairs on Thanh's chest.

"No!" Quan blurted. Nash wasn't sure what Quan meant, but assumed he was opposed to Nash shooting Thanh. He had no choice, however, for Thanh had the weapon, and it looked like she was going to use it. Time seemed to slow down as he took a breath and released part of it, made sure his finger was on the trigger properly, and calculated how he would have to shift his aim immediately after firing in order to take out the sniper as well. Before he could pull the trigger, however, the female sniper snatched the weapon from Thanh with one hand and smacked her in the head with the pistol in her other hand. Thanh fell backward and slid down the rocky slope on her back until her head reached the small clump of bushes. She lay there unmoving.

Nash shifted his aim to the sniper, who was fumbling with the weapon. The man he had seen earlier had popped out of the hole suddenly, an AK-47 in his hand, and the sniper tossed her pistol to him, which he promptly dropped. While he bent to scoop it up, the sniper brought the missile launcher to her shoulder and put her face to the sight. She swayed back and forth as she sought out the Chinook, which was already moving away toward the south, unaware of what was going on below. Nash prepared to fire, but the woman kept jerking around, trying to find more secure footing on the loose stones. Finally she was stable, and held the weapon steady as she did something on the trigger assembly.

Finally he had a good sight picture, and Nash began squeezing the trigger. Three things happened almost simultaneously. Nash felt the rifle buck in his hands, a flash of fire erupted from the back of the tube on the sniper's shoulder, and the Cobra swooshed in below the Chinook. A trail of smoke wound up through the sky and there was a blinding explosion up in the sky. Nash held his sight on the sniper, who sat down heavily and then crumpled over on her side, letting the tube weapon fall onto the side of her head. She wasn't moving, but the man with the AK scuttled over to her and jiggled her shoulder with the hand holding the pistol. When she didn't respond, he looked around wildly, dropped the pistol, and tugged at the launcher. Nash fired again. The man's head jerked back violently, and then he fell forward across the body of the sniper. The back of his head was gone.

Nash looked up from the scope, fearing the worst. He was convinced the missile had struck the Chinook and sent it crashing to the plain far below, but he was surprised to see it still lumbering away in the sky, shrinking as it gained distance. The Cobra, however, was not doing as well. Smoke trailed from the engine compartment, and the pilot was struggling to keep the chopper level as it weaved and slid in the air dangerously close to the mountainside. Nash felt a lump of dread building in his chest, certain the chopper was about the slam into the rocks and explode in a ball of fire, but then aircraft settled down, its rotors spinning at full speed, and its wild antics subdued. Still trailing a small stream of white smoke, the chopper eased away from the mountain and began a slow low flight to the west, probably headed for Tay Ninh.

    Nash let out the breath he hadn't realized he was holding and tried to relax. Instead he was pushed aside by Quan, who climbed over him to get out from between the boulders and began running across the loose scree toward Thanh. He was in such a hurry that he had left his carbine behind. Nash picked up Quan's rifle in his left hand, and with his own in his right he tried to follow. With both hands full, he kept losing his footing, and arrived several seconds after Quan, who was kneeling with Thanh's head in his lap. Nash saw her eyes flutter and heard a groan. Leaving her to Quan, he climbed up to where the bodies lay, feeling them to make sure they were both dead. Laying his and Quan's weapons down on a large nearby rock, he picked up the launcher tube, surprised by how light it was. It was very similar to an RPG launcher in design, but was much longer, nearly four and a half feet. There were markings on it, but in a language Nash was unfamiliar with. The letters looked kind of like the Greek letters college fraternities and sororities used, but Nash could make no sense of them. He set the launcher back down on a rock, away from where Quan and the girl sat.

    While Quan tended to Thanh, Nash looked into the old bunker where the three VC had been hiding. Lying at the bottom of the hole were two dark green aluminum cases lying on top of the canvas covers with straps in which they had been carried. He jumped down in and undid the unfamiliar catches on one of the cases. Inside the case was only some black foam rubber with holes in various shapes cut into it, and a single dark green can-shaped object. The holes were obviously intended to secure the various parts of the launching tube he had just looked at, and the can matched an object attached to the front of the launcher. Closing the lid, he scooted over to the other case. Inside that one was another launching tube, with covers sealing both ends. The launcher was nestled in the same black foam rubber as the other case, with one long depression empty. He picked up the tube and found it was much heavier than the one outside. He guessed it was like the American M-72 LAW anti-tank launcher, in that it came pre-loaded with a missile. But this was not an anti-tank missile, it was an anti-aircraft missile, unlike anything Nash had ever heard of. He put it back in the case and closed the lid.

Nash climbed back out of the hole and half-slid down to Quan and Thanh. The girl was now sitting up, holding on to Quan for support, gently rubbing the side of her head. "How is she?" Nash asked Quan.

"My head hurts," Thanh answered. "What happened?"

"Your friend tried to shoot down a helicopter," Nash said unsympathetically.

"She is not my friend!" Thanh countered angrily.

"Not anymore," Nash agreed. "She's dead."

Thanh looked up the slope and saw the two black-clad bodies. Then she crossed herself, catching Nash completely by surprise. "What about the helicopter?" she asked.

"She missed the Chinook, but damaged the Cobra. It looked like he would make it aback okay, though."

"Thank the Lord," Thanh said, and Nash was again surprised by her piety and sincerity. She reached down inside her shirt and brought out a small gold cross on a chain. She kissed it, mumbled something, and gently let it down, this time outside her blouse. Quan didn't say anything, but he stared at her with such adoration that Nash was worried.

"What is that thing?" Nash asked, pointing to the launcher.

"The Russians call it the Arrow," Thanh told him. "It is a portable, shoulder-fired anti-aircraft guided missile. I was sent here to kill Mr. Bob Hope."

Her frank confession caught Nash off guard. "Why? Who? How did. . .?"

"It does not matter," Thanh said, looking up at him. "You stopped it. I thank you. Now you must arrest me."

Nash gazed into her eyes, and saw the guilt and remorse. This was a situation he had never prepared for. He looked up, and the sky was empty. Both helicopters were gone, but he knew the silence was only temporary. The Cobra pilot would have reported what happened, and there would soon be reprisals. They had to get out of there immediately.

"Quan, go get our stuff. Quick!" With a longing look back at Thanh, Quan rushed off.

Nash looked at Thanh sitting there on the ground, massaging her head, and struggled with conflicting emotions. He didn't trust her; she had been with the sniper, and had brought the guided missile from the north, so her loyalties were pretty obvious. Looking at her, however, Nash saw a young impressionable girl who seemed genuinely contrite and ashamed. His options were limited, though. He couldn't leave her here to be killed by the helicopters that were sure to arrive, nor could he kill her himself in cold blood. There was no viable choice but to take her with them. He would figure out what to do with her later, when they were safely away from the mountain.

"Get the cases," Nash ordered her, grasping her wrist and pulling her to her feet. With no resistance she stumbled over into the bunker while Nash retrieved the launcher. She tossed the smaller case out and let it slide down the rocks until it was stopped by the two dead bodies. She pushed the other one up over the edge of the hole so it could slide down next to the first, then brought out the two canvas covers.

"Put this back in the case," Nash told her, holding the launcher out to her. She nodded and took the launcher, squatting down so she could remove the battery and the trigger assembly. Opening the lid on the smaller case, she pushed the parts into their niches and then latched the case close. Then she opened the long case and pushed the empty tube into its depression next to the other tube before latching that case closed as well. Quan returned just as she started sliding the canvas covers over the metal cases, like she was putting pillow cases on pillows. Quan had the radio and his own pack secured on his back, and carried Nash's pack slung over one shoulder.

"What now?" Quan asked, handing Nash's pack to him. Nash stuck his arms through the shoulder straps and hefted it into place.

"Put that on," Nash instructed Thanh, nodding toward the longer case.

"Yes, sir," she replied obediently, and shrugged into the harness. She stood up with difficulty, the pack towering over her head.

"I'll get the other one," Nash said. He bent down to pick it up by the straps, surprised by just how heavy it was. Those can-shaped things must be heavier than they look, he thought. Sliding his left arm through one of the shoulder straps, he lifted it up and nearly lost his balance on the loose rock below the bunker. "Hand me my rifle." Quan did as he asked, and picked up his own carbine. "Get the pistol and the AK," Nash told Quan. "You'll take point. Get us down the hill as fast as possible. Don't forget about that cave."

Quan nodded, picking up the pistol and jamming it under his pistol belt and then grabbing the AK in his left hand. He skirted around the clump of bushes and headed down the hill as fast as he could over the uneven rocky soil. Nash jerked his head at Thanh to follow Quan, and she did so without hesitation, somehow keeping upright despite the case on her back and her feet clad only in sandals.

Nash found the going difficult, even though he was experienced in hiking the mountains back home. The pack hanging off his left shoulder unbalanced him, and he held his rifle out far to the side as a counterbalance. Going downhill was always harder than going uphill, and his feet kept stepping on rocks that tended to roll out from under him. He felt like he was on the verge of a landslide at every step. When he could divert his attention for a second or two, he would scan the skies for inbound aircraft, but so far they were clear.

In an effort to avoid the cave, Quan was leading them at a slant to the left, which made it a little easier to descend, but would take them longer until they reached the trees and bushes of the lower elevations. Nash stumbled and hopped down the jagged rocky slope, the missile case's canvas cover often bouncing off stones and catching on small bushes. At least the weight of the case was on the uphill side, helping him maintain his balance. Ahead of him Thanh maneuvered with remarkable agility, having no trouble keeping up with Quan and staying upright, and Nash was a little envious.

Within a few minutes they began to encounter larger bushes and stunted trees, and Nash could feel the gradient beginning to ease. They had to get into the forest soon. Nash tried to estimate how long it would take for Army aviation to mount an attack on the side of the mountain, but was too unfamiliar with helicopter operations to make even an educated guess. The damage to the Cobra would almost certainly give those guys a tremendous impetus to retaliate, so Nash decided it would be less than fifteen minutes before the first helicopters would return. He couldn't look at his watch due to the way he was holding the missile case, and his sense of time passing was screwed up by the tension of the moment, but he knew it would be any minute now.

Nash was so focused on placing his feet that he was caught by surprise when they entered the shade of the first few trees. The woods were thin here, but at least there was some concealment, and the ground was more solid and predictable. They weaved through the trees, still heading down, and then he heard the clopping reverberation of helicopter blades. Nash stopped for a moment and looked back up the hill through small gaps in the branches of the trees. He saw brief glimpses of a Cobra and a Huey gunship, and heard the explosions of rockets and the rapid rattle of a minigun. They had gotten away just in time.

Turning back to Quan and Thanh, who had also paused, Nash said, "Keep moving." They had a long way to go yet, and he was still unsure what he would do with Thanh.

*****

Sergeant First Class Samples wasn't entirely comfortable with the way things had been worked out by the officers. The two Zippo flame-thrower tracks had been inserted into his platoon, and he had a healthy concern about what would happen if a Zippo took an RPG round. He could just imagine the giant ball of flame and shrapnel enveloping the tracks on either side of them. The decision had been made, however, and now they were entering the wood line after most of the company had dismounted. Samples had stationed himself on the far right end of the formation, closest to the road, knowing that was the most likely place for the gooks to have set up their ambush. To his left were Sweet and Kirk, and then the one-one track with Greenberg behind the fifty. On the other side of the one-one, he knew, were Sergeant Jamison and Hicks, and then the first of the Zippos. Beyond the Zippo were the one-two, the one-three, the other Zippo, and finally the one-four. The augmented First Platoon would bear the brunt of any contact. Second and Third Platoons stretched out to their left, and Headquarters Platoon trailed the line, with the mechanics, commo guys, and mortarmen spread out between their tracks.

"Awful quiet," Sweet remarked as they pushed through the low bushes that bordered the tree line.

"Think the gooks are still here?" Kirk asked.

Samples didn't answer. He was too busy scanning every tree trunk, bush, and pile of leaves ahead of him for any sign of danger. The shade of the forest was an unwelcome change from the bright sunshine, for it could hide a multitude of dangers. The trees were spaced a ways apart here, giving the tracks plenty of room to maneuver between them rather than try to knock them down. While bushes had formed a thick barrier along the tree line, once past those the forest opened up, with good visibility. To his right Sample could occasionally see part of the highway through the trees, but the thick foliage at the edge of the woods worried him, for who knew what was hidden there. He edged closer to the road, checking out the ground and peering into the bushes, searching for any sign of enemy bunkers or fighting positions. They had gone only thirty or forty meters into the woods when he spotted the first anomaly.

"Hold up!" he barked, raising his left arm in a fist. The command was quickly passed down the line and the company ground to a halt, the tracks' diesels idling, and dismounts dropping to one knee or taking a position behind the larger trees.

"Bunker," Samples said, pointing to his front right.

"Where?" Kirk asked, crouching down and extending his rifle.

"I see it," Sweet said, slowly lowering himself to a prone position. Kirk, looking worried, imitated him.

It looked like a random pile of dead leaves, but Samples could tell it was too neat to be natural. The mound was oblong, and a leafy branch conveniently lay across the north side, opposite the road. He glanced to his left and saw that Greenberg had seen it, too, and had the 50-cal aimed directly at it.

"Sweet. Get me a couple grenades."

Sweet jumped up and ran to the back of the one-one, climbing on the fender to open the wooden ammo crate strapped to the top. He retrieved two of the egg-shaped fragmentation grenades and hustled over to Samples with them.

"Stay here. I'm going to check it out."

"Aaron, wait!" Lieutenant Carr had run up from farther down the line, and stopped just behind the one-one. "Let the Zippo do it."

Samples looked around and judged the difficulty of getting the flame-thrower into position. He shook his head. "This is easier," he said, and handed his rifle to Sweet. "Keep me covered."

With a grenade in each hand, he dodged from tree to tree until he was within a few feet of what he was sure was the back entrance to the bunker. He paused to remove the secondary safety bail from the grenade in his right hand, and slipped his left forefinger through the ring. Theoretically the bunker's firing port faced the road, and the entrance at the rear was the only other opening, so any gook inside would need to show himself to fire at Samples. But there could be other hidden bunkers whose occupants had a clear field of fire toward this one. He studied the bunker, and detected the dark area beneath the branch that was almost certainly the entrance. Taking a deep breath and tensing his muscle, Samples pulled the pin on the grenade and rushed over to the bunker, kicking the branch out of the way as he released the spoon, counting in his head. At the count of two he dropped the grenade into the rectangular hole the branch had covered and then dived away, sprawling on the ground. There was a muffled "whump" and he looked back to see puffs of dirt and leaves erupt from the front and back of the low rectangular mound.

Climbing to his feet, Samples brushed off some leaves and put the other grenade in his cargo pocket. He ambled over to Sweet to take his rifle.

"Reckon there was anybody home?" Sweet asked.

"Not anymore," Samples answered. Lieutenant Carr came up to him, giving him a disapproving look.

"Did you have to do that yourself?" Carr scolded.

Samples shrugged. "I like blowing things up."

Carr rolled his eyes. Together they both looked over at the bunker, where diminishing smoke wafted out of the holes. "If there's one, there's more," Carr said.

"Probably," Samples agreed.

Eberhart jogged up, holding the radio handset out to Carr. "CO wants a report," he said. Carr took the handset and stepped away to make the report, Eberhart trailing behind with the coiled cord stretching between them.

After a minute Carr handed the mike back to Eberhart and yelled out, "Okay, move out." He and the RTO went around behind the one-one to resume their position at the other end of platoon, and the entire company began sweeping forward again.

The next couple hours were stop and start, as other bunkers were discovered. Two were "checked out" with grenades by guys in Second and Third Platoons, but a fourth, found by one-three's Handleman, got a different treatment. While the rest of the company backed away, one of the Zippos came forward and lit up, spewing a stream of fire through the trees that blanketed the bunker. Samples knew that if the bunker had contained any gooks, they would either have been burned to a crisp or suffocated by the lack of oxygen. When the flame thrower cut off, the leaves and bushes near the bunker continued to burn, smoke rising up through the trees. As the fire died down, the order came to continue, with the tracks and dismounts giving the scorched area a wide berth.

"That was fun," Samples remarked to Sweet as they strolled through the forest. "Nothing like a good campfire."

"Yep," Sweet agreed. "But it looks like the gooks are all gone."

"Maybe the ARVNs scared 'em off," Kirk suggested seriously.

Sweet and Samples both chuckled. "Yeah, right," Sweet said sarcastically.

Samples looked at his watch. "It's just about lunch time. They probably left for their siesta." He was about to add another comment when he heard the unmistakable crack of an AK-47. "Hit it!" he yelled, diving for the ground. Above him he heard Greenberg crank the charging handle on the fifty and then a powerful drumbeat of noise as he began firing. His fifty was quickly joined by the thumping explosions of the others, along with the sharper rapping of M-16s. The company had erupted in a mad minute of massive firepower, spraying the woods with bullets. Samples didn't join in, preferring to conserve his ammo for a target he could see. Soon enough the cease fire order was passed, and the firing sputtered to a halt. Samples jumped up and ran to the rear of the one-one, opening the ramp personnel door and sticking his head in so he could hear the radio.

Captain Gordon was trying to find out what had happened, and various other guys were offering their opinions in a mish-mash of radio traffic. Samples saw no reason to add his own interpretation. It was obviously a sniper, and either the deluge of gunfire had killed him, or it hadn't, and if it hadn't, they would be hearing from him again. No sooner had he thought that then there was another shot, and every weapon in the company opened up again. Since he had had his head inside the track, he had no idea where the shot had come from, and doubted if anyone else did either. Then he heard someone in Second Platoon calling for a medic to the two-two track, and knew the sniper was either very good, or very lucky.

"Cease fire, cease fire!" Gordon was screaming on the radio, and the once again the noise subsided. Greenberg dropped down from the 50-cal to snag another box of ammo and saw Samples halfway in through the door.

"What the hell, Sarge?" Greenberg asked, shaking his head.

"Hey," Samples told him, "don't shoot unless you have a target. Just because everyone else is doing it, doesn't mean you have to."

"You sound just like my mom."

"I hope I don't look like her." Samples jerked his head to signal that Greenberg needed to get back behind the fifty.

On the radio Gordon was asking if anyone had seen where the shots came from. Somebody said it was from a tree, and another said there was a hidden bunker out there. As Samples knew, with single shots in the woods, it was hard to pinpoint where they were coming from. Samples shook his head and stepped back from the ramp, checking to see where his men were and what they were doing, leaving the door open. Some had taken shelter behind the tracks, others were prone. PFC Dubois was in a textbook kneeling supported position behind a tree. The problem was that with a sniper, nowhere was really safe unless you knew for certain where the sniper was.

Two more shots rang out, a split second apart, and clearly coming from different directions. One of the bullets clanged as it hit the side of the steel cupola on the one-two track and ricocheted off into the woods behind them.

"There's two of 'em!" Greenberg shouted angrily. "Where the fuck are they?"

"That tree!" Hicks yelled, pointing at the canopy a few yards away. The Zippo TC, who had been reloading the fifty-cal mounted beside the flamethrower nozzle, nodded and ducked down inside. A moment later a tongue of fire reached out and bathed the designated tree in napalm.

"Yeah!" Greenberg cheered with vicious joy, raising a defiant fist, but immediately dropped out of sight, yelping in pain.

Samples climbed in the track to find Greenberg squatting on top of the ammo boxes, his right hand clamped on his left bicep, blood seeping between his fingers.

Samples grabbed the porkchop mike dangling from the radio and press the button. "Medic to one-one!" he yelled into the mike, to be heard over the gunfire that had broken out again. Doc Allman showed up a few seconds later, jumping in and squeezing past Samples to take care of Greenberg. Samples climbed back out and saw Hicks a few feet away, firing around a tree trunk at God only knew what. "Hicks, take the fifty!" Hicks looked over, saw the machine gun was unmanned, and ran to the track, clambering up the side and jumping into the turret. Samples saw a bright silver metal scar appear on the side of the Zippo next to the one-one, and knew they were still taking fire, despite the barrage the company was laying down.

The TC of the Zippo, who was wearing his CVC helmet, looked over at Samples and yelled, "Anybody behind me?" When Samples shook his head, the guy spoke into his mike and the track began backing up. When Samples shot him a questioning look, the guy shrugged apologetically and yelled, "I'm out of juice." As the tall vehicle rolled backward, Samples could now see farther down the line, where the other Zippo was squirting fire into the trees in a semicircular pattern, clearly hoping the flames would be some sort of deterrent. The formation had somewhat devolved into chaos, with guys shooting at anything that looked suspicious, and many running to take shelter inside the tracks.

Samples gritted his teeth in frustration. A couple of snipers were holding down an entire mechanized company, and there seemed to be nothing they could do about it. Samples wished Gordon would come up with some sort of plan. The logical move would be to withdraw and call in an arty strike. He glanced back inside the track to see that Greenberg now had his shirt off, and Doc Allman was wrapping a bandage around his upper arm. "How bad?" he called to Allman.

"He'll live," Allman replied. "Good thing he's right-handed."

Then Samples heard Gordon on the radio, calling all members of the company. "Charge!" he yelled.

"What?" Allman looked up from Greenberg's arm and stared at the radio in disbelief. "Did he just say, 'Charge'?"

Samples couldn't believe it either. That was a command he thought had been relegated to history, when soldiers still rode horses. He stepped back from the open door of the one-one to see the company commander's track roaring forward, wending its way between First and Second Platoons, with Captain Gordon standing up behind the driver's hatch, holding on to the side of the machine gun turret with his right hand and waving his left hand forward. As the track burst out in front of the line, the gunners all stopped firing to avoid hitting their commander, gazing with wonder at the ridiculously brazen move. With no other choice, the rest of the company's tracks moved out as well, forming a shallow V as they struggled to catch up. Samples slammed the personnel door and latched it, running along behind it to do so as the track began rolling.

"Come on!" he yelled at the dismounts, and with varying amounts of confusion they jumped to their feet and tried to keep up, moving closer to the tracks so they could seek shelter if needed. Gordon's track, with its head start, was at least thirty meters in front of the next closest track, with Gordon waving and yelling like a madman. Samples was running now, pacing alongside the one-one feeling like he was in a bad movie, thinking of the Charge of the Light Brigade and what a disaster that had turned out to be. Directly ahead he saw a green pith helmet pop up out of the ground and an AK-47 swing toward Gordon's track, firing at full automatic. Gordon wavered for a second, and then fell backwards into the open cargo hatch. The pith helmet immediately disappeared into the ground.

"Gunn!" Samples yelled at the one-one's driver. Gunn, whose head was just barely out of the hatch and ensconced in the CVC helmet, somehow heard him and looked over. "Run over that son of a bitch!" He pointed at the unseen bunker, the NVA soldier having already ducked back down inside. He didn't know if Gunn had seen the brief appearance of the soldier, so he began firing his M-16 at the spot as he ran, stirring up the leaves if nothing else. Gunn got the message, and steered the APC right toward it, weaving around trees until his treads were right on top, where he stopped.

"Pull forward!" Samples shouted, holding his rifle pointed at the spot where he had seen the gook, now covered by the road wheels and treads of the track. With his left hand he dug out the other grenade from his cargo pocket and thumbed the safety bail off.

The track rolled forward a few feet, revealing the small entrance to the bunker, now half collapsed by the weight of the M-113. Samples fired two shots into the hole, and then brought the grenade over next to his rifle so he could pull the pin with his right thumb without letting go of the rifle. "Fire in the hole!" he yelled, releasing the spoon and holding the grenade for a two count before dropping it into the narrow opening. Diving away, he sprawled on the ground and squeezed his eyes closed, wishing he had both hands free to cover his ears.

The ground bounced against his chest as the grenade exploded, and then there were secondary explosions that deafened him and showered him with dirt and leaves. The bunker had become a small and briefly erupting volcano. RPG rounds, Samples thought, waiting for the detonations to stop. Except for the ringing in his ears, it quickly became very quiet. Samples opened his eyes, hoping he hadn't gone deaf. Raising his head, he saw tracks spread out in a semi-circle through the trees, all stopped with men in between them, warily scanning the forest around them. No one was shooting, and that included the gooks, Samples realized. As he stood up, Carr ran to him.

"Are you okay?" Carr asked anxiously as Eberhart caught up with him.

"As far as I know," Samples answered. "How's the captain?"

Together they looked over at the commander's track, just as another Headquarters track jerked to a halt beside it and dropped its ramp with a thud. Three guys swarmed out and rushed into the other track through the personnel door.

"He's alive," Eberhart informed them, listening to the radio.

"I think you're in charge now," Samples told Carr. Carr looked stunned for a moment, and then drew himself up.

"I guess so." He took a deep breath and looked around like he wasn't sure what to do next.

"There's another sniper out here somewhere," Samples told him.

"Right." Carr grabbed the handset from Eberhart and held it to his mouth. "A Company, spread out and find the other sniper, over."

Samples saw Eberhart wince at the lack of proper radio procedure, but the call had the desired effect. The men began circling the area, probing at the ground with their feet, their rifles held ready.

"Found him!" came a shout from someone. Carr and Samples jogged over in that direction and found one of the Second Platoon guys pointing up in a tree that had been scorched by the Zippo. The limbs were still smoking, and all the leaves were gone, leaving the tree a bare skeleton, like American trees in winter. Halfway up the tree, straddling one of the larger limbs, was the blackened husk of a man, a rifle still clutched in his claw-like hands. Samples looked away, disgusted by the sight, and saw that Carr was turning an odd shade of green.

Lieutenant Masters walked up, glanced up at the body, and dropped his gaze to the ground. "What should we do now, commander?" he asked Carr. With a violent shake of his head, apparently trying to clear it, Carr looked at Masters and Samples for moment; then he nodded.

"I think we're done here," he said.

"Amen," Samples endorsed the notion.

"The CO needs a medevac," Eberhart informed them.

"Let's get everyone back out in that field," Carr said. "They can land the chopper there." Masters ran to get his platoon organized, and Samples grabbed Eberhart to do the same for First Platoon. He watched Carr trudge over to the commander's track, obviously not relishing his new level of authority.

"First platoon, on me!" Samples shouted.

TWENTY-ONE

It was well after sundown when Nash, Quan, and Thanh reached her village, and due to the curfew no one was out and about to see them. They quietly entered her hooch, dumped their loads, closed the shutters, and collapsed. Nash was exhausted, and marveled at Thanh's stamina, for she had kept up with him the entire way back from the mountain. Now, however, she looked as tired as Nash felt. She offered the two young men water, and then she fell onto her low bed, one foot hanging off the edge, and appeared to go to sleep.

"We need to call in a sitrep," Nash said to Quan, who had sat down at a small table, his legs sprawled out from the chair, his head slumped forward. With a sigh he leaned over to where the radio lay on the floor, switched it on, and held the handset out for Nash to take it. Nash stumbled over to the table, slumped down in the other chair, and took the mike. It took him several tries before he reached the Staff Duty NCO in Tay Ninh, and his report was short and vague. Once they had left Nui Ba Den he had called in a more explicit report, but had limited it to the fact that the VC sniper had been killed. He withheld any information about Thanh, the missile launcher, or the planned attack on Bob Hope, rationalizing that the radio was not secure enough to be transmitting such information. His real reason, however, was that he was still deciding on what to do about Thanh.

Around noon, when they had reached level ground and taken a break in a small grove of trees, Thanh had told them her whole story, which Nash had found nothing short of amazing. She had not held back, admitting to her having been a dedicated communist, relating her meeting with Ho Chi Minh and the training on the missile launcher, and describing her trip down the Ho Chi Minh trail. She had told about her assisting the sniper, whose name Nash now found out was Nhu, and her growing disillusion with the war, especially when "Robert" had been killed. All the while she was speaking she had rubbed the cross that dangled from a chain around her neck. When she told them about the ARVN captain named Nguyen, Nash and Quan had exchanged meaningful looks. Quan had questioned her about Nguyen in Vietnamese, and then nodded at Nash. It was the same guy they had had problems with before.

Nash looked over at Thanh, and saw the slow rise and fall of her chest as she slept. He glanced over at Quan, who was also looking at Thanh, but with a less detached expression. Nash needed to sleep, but he knew they had to make plans. He put his elbows on the table and leaned forward. "What do we do with her?" he asked quietly.

Quan shifted his gaze from Thanh to Nash. "Let her go?" he suggested.

"She was sent her by Ho Chi Minh to kill Americans," Nash countered. "She has valuable information. We should turn her in."

"They put her in jail?"

Nash shrugged. "Maybe."

"She sorry. She not kill anyone. She tell us everything." Quan was offering every excuse he could think of.

Nash rubbed the top of his head. His duty was to turn her in, but he tended to agree with Quan. He could just imagine the long interrogations Thanh would go through, and feared that the Americans would eventually hand her over to the South Vietnamese. Who knew what would happen to her then? But what else could they do? What could she do? With no friends or family, how could she survive? Nash rubbed his eyes. He could no longer think straight, he was so tired. He would have to sleep on it, and hopefully in the morning it would all become clear to him. He slithered out of the chair onto the floor, crawled to his pack and laid his head down on it. He shifted his hips once to try and get comfortable, and then he was out.

*****

Lieutenant Carr picked his way between the parked vehicles, tents, and cots, past the stinking shitter, and found his platoon on the berm line. The moon was rising, so it was possible to pick out the individual shapes of the tracks, each with someone behind the fifty-cal pulling guard. Otherwise there was no motion or sound, for those not on guard were taking the opportunity to get some much-needed sleep. Carr was relieved to find that Sergeant Samples was still awake, sitting on one end of his cot drinking a soda. Carr flopped down next to him.

"Why aren't you asleep?" he asked, wishing he himself was so occupied.

Samples barely acknowledged Carr's arrival, taking another sip of soda. "Thinking about today," he finally said. "What a cluster-fuck."

"Captain Raymond's back," Carr said. "He was there when I went to report to the colonel."

"So being queen for a day didn't last long, huh?"

"No, thank God. I've got enough problems with you and the rest of the platoon; I don't need to take on the whole company."

"Yeah," Samples said, and Carr could see his grin, "you're not ready anyway."

"Fuck you, Aaron."

"It'd be the best you ever had, sir."

Carr elbowed him and chuckled.

"How's Gordon?" Samples asked. "Heard anything?"

"The colonel says he was hit twice, once in the shoulder and once in the side, but they think he'll be okay. He'll probably go back to the World."

"Get a Purple Heart, too."

Carr took a breath and exhaled loudly. "More than that, I think. The colonel was talking about maybe giving him a Silver Star." He felt the cot shake as Samples sat up straight with a jerk.

"For getting his ass shot doing something stupid?" Samples' tone was dripping with scorn.

"I know. But the way the colonel sees it, Gordon led a successful assault on the enemy, showing great courage and leadership."

"Shit. Fuck up and move up." Samples spoke a phrase common in the Army, based on all-too-often past experience.

"Well, he's out of our hair, anyway. For all we know, he might be a general someday. Wouldn't that be something?"

"Yeah. But why is that? Why do the assholes get to be generals?"

"The same way assholes get to be E-Sevens," Carr jibed. Samples scowled at him. "And, you know, maybe someday a Sergeant Major."

Samples shook his head. "I think I hear your mother calling you," he said dismissively.

"I think you're right," Carr said, standing up. "Sleep tight, Aaron. Don't let the bed bugs bite."

"They'd be better than those damn red ants," Samples rejoined. Carr walked away, hoping Eberhart had set up his cot for him.

TWENTY-TWO

A small clinking sound brought Nash out of a deep dreamless sleep instantly, and his eyes shot open in a search for the threat. Across the room Thanh was squatting next to a small hibachi-like stove boiling water, and he realized that must have been what he heard. Stretching his muscles, he uncurled and slowly sat up, rubbing the sleep from his eyes as the previous day's events ran through his mind. Today, he knew, he had to decide Thanh's fate, a responsibility he hated. She glanced over at him and smiled.

"Tea?" she asked, holding up the pan of hot water.

Nash nodded, running his tongue around the inside of his gummy mouth. A few feet away Quan slept on the floor, snoring gently. The light coming in around the shuttered windows was grey, so it was either not yet dawn, or it was a cloudy morning. Nash checked his watch; it was five-thirty. He stretched one leg out to nudge Quan's foot with his boot. Quan woke up, looking around wildly for a second before he realized where they were. "You want tea?" Nash asked him.

Quan sat up, rubbing the wrinkles on the side of his face that had been lying on his backpack. He grunted and looked over at Thanh, who was now pouring from the pan into small porcelain cups. He asked her something in Vietnamese, and she shook her head regretfully. Quan stuck his hand inside his backpack and rooted around, then brought out the shiny brown plastic packet from a C-rations box that contained toilet paper and condiments. This one had been previously opened, and Quan pulled out a couple packets of sugar and dry creamer, along with a white plastic spoon.

Meanwhile Thanh handed Nash a cup of the steaming brown liquid, and he took a sip, burning his tongue. When she gave Quan his cup, he quickly added sugar and creamer, stirred it, and then lifted a spoonful up and blew on it before putting it in his mouth like soup. Nash just blew across the top of the cup and waited for it to cool enough to drink without scalding him. Thanh didn't pour herself a cup, putting the pan back on the little stove. Still squatting, she gazed at Nash with a serious look on her face.

"He will be here soon," she announced.

"Who?" Nash was startled by the statement, and all sorts of worrisome possibilities flashed before his eyes.

"Captain Nguyen. I told you he gave us the information about Mr. Hope's helicopter. I did not tell you about the money."

"What money?" Nash was now even more confused.

"We gave him money for the information, but we only gave him half of what he asked. He will come today to collect the other half."

"How much money are we talking about?"

"We gave him five thousand American dollars. Today he will want the other five thousand."

"That son of a bitch!" Nash felt a surge of anger. Nguyen had tried to kill Quan and him in the Michelin and had gotten away with it. Now he was selling out the Americans to the Viet Cong. The man didn't deserve to live.

Quan asked something in Vietnamese, and then rephrased it in English for Nash's sake. "When he come?"

Thanh shrugged. "Today. Probably soon. He is very anxious to get the money."

"I'll bet he is," Nash growled. "But he isn't getting it. I'll kill the little bastard!"

"No!" Thanh protested, her eyes wide. "No more killing, please!"

Nash cleared his throat, but didn't say anything. He wouldn't promise not to kill Nguyen, but he began thinking of other ways to punish the man. "Where is the money?" he asked, changing the subject.

"Out in the garden. I buried it. There is more than five thousand."

Nash and Quan exchanged looks. Both of them had already "acquired" large sums of money from the operation in the Michelin, and didn't really need or want more. Nash was still worried someone would find out about all the thousands he had sent home for himself and their former teammates, and didn't want to try and deal with more illicit cash.

"It belong Thanh," Quan said.

"I do not want it," Thanh said with a shudder. "It is blood money."

"But you will need it," Nash said, making a snap decision about Thanh's future. It had come to him that he believed her story, he believed her abandonment of the communist cause, and he felt very protective of her, like a big brother. He realized that they had to arrange for her to stay in South Viet Nam somehow, but to remain anonymous so that neither the Viet Cong nor the South Vietnamese government could find her. He even thought about arranging for her to emigrate to the United States, but couldn't figure out a way to do that without revealing her identity. "How else will you survive?"

Thanh stood up and went over to her bed, reaching under a blanket to withdraw an old wrinkled copy of the military newspaper, *The Stars and Stripes*. She opened it and folded it back to page five before handing it to Nash. "I will go get the money now," she said, and slipped out the door.

Nash started to tell Quan to follow her, but then shook his head and looked down at the yellowed newspaper. There were two articles on that page, one about a battle in Quang Tri province, and one about some Army engineers expanding an orphanage in Saigon.

Nash assumed she meant him to see the orphanage article, which had a picture of American soldiers with tools in their hands surrounded by small children and a couple Vietnamese nuns. He skimmed the article, wondering what Thanh was thinking. He passed the paper to Quan, who looked at the photo with a puzzled frown. A minute later Thanh came back in, brushing dirt from a bundle wrapped in clear plastic. She gave the packet to Nash and squatted down between him and Quan with an expectant look. Nash peeled back the plastic and withdrew four stacks of one-hundred-dollar bills. He whistled.

Thanh took the newspaper from Quan and held it so Nash could see the article about the orphanage. "What do you think?" she asked.

"I don't know," Nash replied, thumbing the edge of one of the stacks of cash. "You want to give the money to the orphanage?"

"Yes," Thanh said, enthusiastically bobbing her head. "I will help the children."

"Okay," Nash said doubtfully. "But what will you do? After you give them the money?"

"I will be a nun," she assured him confidently.

"A nun?" Nash saw the crestfallen look on Quan's face. Thanh's plans obviously didn't include him. "Can you do that?" While Nash had been raised a Catholic, he wasn't really sure how a woman went about becoming a nun. He had some vague feeling she had to be a virgin.

"Why not?" Thanh challenged him.

"I don't know. Don't you have to apply, or take a test, or something?"

She gave him a patiently dismissive look. "Of course not," she said, but then her face clouded. "I don't think so," she said with less conviction.

Nash thought about it, and came to the conclusion it wasn't a bad idea. "You would change your name," he pointed out, "to something like Sister Mary Peter Paul, so no one would know who you really are. You would be safe, even from people like Captain Nguyen. Maybe that would work."

Thanh regained her smile. "Yes. And I would be helping children, and I would be honoring my mother."

"That, too. And that would be a great use for the money. What do you think, Quan?"

Quan had trouble hiding his disappointment, but he nodded his agreement. "Thanh be good nun. Money good for kids. Okay."

Nash stood up and put the money on the little table, thinking he needed to go outside and take a leak, but then he lifted his head at the sound of an approaching vehicle. He darted to a window and peeked through a crack in the shutter. A jeep was coming straight toward them, with only a driver aboard. Through the sparkling clean windshield Nash could see it was Captain Nguyen. "It's him!" he hissed at Quan while darting over to the other bed, where Quan had dropped the AK-47 and the Makarov pistol. He scooped up the pistol and hoped the safety wasn't on. Quan grabbed up his carbine and rushed to stand beside the right side of the door. Nash went over to the other side of the door and pressed his back against the wall, holding the pistol up across his chest.

Thanh gave Nash a conspiratorial look and snatched up the stacks of money. She stepped to the center of the room, facing the door, with the money displayed prominently in her hands. The door burst open and Nguyen walked in like it was his own home, his eyes immediately drawn to the cash Thanh was holding. His gaze was so focused on the money that he didn't see Nash and Quan behind him as he swaggered across the room, reaching out toward Thanh, who was subtly backing away.

"Don't move!" Nash ordered, putting his pistol to the back of Nguyen's head. Nguyen froze, and Nash could almost feel the wheels turning in the ARVN captain's head. He began very slowly leaning forward, away from the pistol, as he slowly brought his right hand down toward his own pistol, but then Quan appeared in front of him with his carbine pointed at Nguyen's stomach. Quan said something scathing in Vietnamese and Nguyen gradually raised his hands up to the level of his shoulders. Stepping more to Nguyen's right side, and moving the pistol until the barrel pressed against the man's ear, Nash used his left hand to unsnap Nguyen's holster and pull the chrome-plated revolver out, tossing it onto the bed a few feet away.

"Sit!" Nash ordered, pushing Nguyen down onto one of the chairs by the table. Nguyen sneered at him, and Nash had to resist the urge to smash the man across the face with his pistol. "Get the green tape," he told Quan, stepping back just enough to keep Nguyen from being able to leap forward and grab his gun. Knowing just what Nash intended, Quan handed his carbine to Thanh and knelt down to dig through his backpack. Thanh held the carbine at her waist, pointed at Nguyen, and Nash could see in her expression that she was seriously reconsidering her desire to avoid killing. He caught her eye and raised his eyebrow. She took a breath and relaxed a little.

Quan got the roll of dark green duct tape and jumped up, coming over behind Nguyen and roughly jerking his arms down behind the back of the chair. With a ripping sound he pulled away the end of the roll and began winding it around Nguyen's wrists, smacking the man on the back of his head when he tried to pull away. Then he came around and squatted in front of Nguyen to wrap tape around his ankles. Nguyen tried to spit on Quan, but missed. Quan calmly slugged Nguyen in the stomach as he stood back up, making the captain sag forward with a groan.

With Nguyen now secured, Nash moved closer and pulled off the man's shiny helmet liner and tossed it away. He grabbed Nguyen's pomaded hair and jerked his head back to look him in the eye. "You greedy mother-fucker!" he growled at him.

"You take money," Nguyen snapped back at him accusingly. Nash wondered just how much Nguyen really knew, but decided Nguyen was only talking about the bags of cash his team had captured and kept from Nguyen, not the portion they had kept for themselves.

"But you sold out your country," Nash accused.

"No," Nguyen spat, "I only sell out Americans. This not your country."

"Your sergeant killed my friend, and you tried to kill me and Quan."

Nguyen glared at him. "So? You kill my sergeant and men."

Nash saw there was no point arguing with the man. He turned to Quan and Thanh. "What should we do with him?

"Kill him," Quan said without hesitation.

"No," Thanh said, "not like this."

"Then what? We can't arrest him, or make him a POW."

"I don't know," Thanh said helplessly.

Nguyen began yelling something in Vietnamese, and to Nash it sounded like he was calling for help. Nash clamped his hand over the man's mouth, pulling his head back as he struggled to keep Nguyen from biting his hand. Quan quickly pulled a strip of tape from the roll, and Nash slid his hand down to Nguyen's chin to keep his jaw closed while Quan taped the man's mouth shut.

"See if anyone heard that," Nash told Thanh, who handed the carbine back to Quan and ran to the door, which was still open. She looked around outside, then stepped back in and closed the door, shaking her head. Nash looked down at Nguyen's face, and the captain's almond eyes flared with anger. The arrogance of the man was astounding. Even in this situation, Nguyen clearly felt he was the man in charge. Nash wanted to somehow make this man realize what a despicable person he really was. "Do you have scissors?" he asked Thanh. When she looked puzzled, he made a snipping motion with his fingers and repeated the word, "Scissors." Finally understanding, she shook her head.

"First aid," Quan said, and Nash immediately knew what he meant. The first aid kit Nash carried in his back pack included angled scissors for cutting away clothing from a wound and for trimming gauze.

"Watch him!" he told Quan, and went over to kneel down beside his pack, pocketing the pistol as he did so. He found the kit and pulled out the scissors. He went back to Nguyen and with an evil smile worked the scissors right in front of the man's nose. Nash was gratified to see a spark of fear in Nguyen's eyes. Moving around behind Nguyen, Nash slipped the open scissors under the cuff of his shirt sleeve and began snipping the cloth, cutting the sleeve open vertically up to the shoulder, and then across the shoulder to the open neck. Nguyen's eyes were now expressing both fear and confusion. Nash just grinned at him and went back behind to do the other sleeve. Finally he positioned himself back in front of Nguyen and stared into his eyes as he clipped off the buttons of his shirt one by one. The butchered shirt fell away, exposing Nguyen's narrow and hairless chest. Nguyen's eyes gaped and he gasped through his nose when Nash touched his nipples with the cold edge of the scissors. Nash smiled at his captive, saying, "No, not yet."

"Thanh," Nash said, "help me take his boots off." After cutting through the green tape on Nguyen's ankles, Nash stuck the scissors in his shirt pocket and knelt down to unlace the man's spit-shined left boot. Thanh hesitated, and then joined him. When Nguyen tried to kick him, Nash grabbed the man's leg just above the knee and squeezed as hard as he could. Nguyen screamed through his nose and went stiff as the nerve endings sent electrical pulses through his body. In high school Nash and his friends had called that move "The Claw" and used it against each other as a joke. This time, however, the recipient wasn't laughing. Nguyen stopped resisting, and quickly his boots and socks were removed. "Ticklish?" Nash asked, stroking the sole of Nguyen's foot with one finger. Nguyen wiggled in the chair and tried to pull his foot away, but Nash held on with his other hand and continued the mild torture. Finally he stood up.

"That was fun, wasn't it?" he asked. "This will be even more fun." He reached down and unbuckled Nguyen's belt, and then unbuttoned the fly. When he started to pull on the pants, Nguyen tried to stand up, but Quan clubbed him in the back of his head with the butt of his carbine. Nash pulled on the pants, lifting Nguyen's hips off the chair, and jerked the tight-fitting trousers down his legs and off his bare feet, dropping them on the floor. He laughed when he saw Nguyen's tight, bright red underpants. "Ooh, sexy!" he commented, chuckling. "Those will have to go."

Nash lifted the scissors from his pocket and slipped them under the leg of Nguyen's shorts. With the blades that close to his privates, Nguyen went totally still, whimpering. With a few careful cuts Nash split the shorts from cuff to waistband on both legs, then pulled the cloth out from under Nguyen, who clamped his legs together tightly to protect himself.

"What are you going to do?" Thanh asked anxiously, having turned away to avoid seeing the man naked.

"Send him home," Nash answered, "so his troops can see that the emperor has no clothes." From his weeks with Quan, Nash had learned just how modest Vietnamese men were, to the extent they would even bathe with their underwear on. With a man so proud and arrogant as Nguyen, appearing naked in front of his soldiers would be the ultimate embarrassment.

Quan, now realizing what Nash's plan was, grinned and nodded. "You watch him now," Quan told Nash, putting his carbine down on the table. Nash nodded and pulled out the Makarov. Quan asked Thanh a question in Vietnamese, and she pointed to a cabinet over against a wall. He went over and looked through it, coming up with a black bottle and a long thin paintbrush. Squatting down in front of Nguyen, Quan opened the bottle and dipped the brush inside. With great care he began writing on Nguyen's abdomen, and then drew an arrow pointed down at his crotch. He stood up and stepped back to admire his work.

"What does it say?" Nash asked, not recognizing the Vietnamese words.

"It say 'very small dick'," Quan answered proudly. He grabbed Nguyen by the bicep and pulled him to his feet. Nguyen crouched down, keeping his legs together, while Quan spun him around, lifted his arms up, and began writing on the man's back. It was many words, followed by another arrow pointing down between the man's buttocks. Nash didn't bother asking what the words meant.

"Okay," Nash began, as Quan put the brush and bottle on the table. "Quan, is your Honda still in Cu Chi?"

"Yes," Quan answered, "at house of cousin."

"Thanh, you stay here for now. Quan and I will use his jeep to take Nguyen to his soldiers, and then I will take Quan to his motorbike. Quan, can you come back and take Thanh and the money to Saigon?"

Quan nodded.

"So Quan will take you to the convent, and I will take the missile to our intelligence people. Okay?"

Thanh nodded, still not looking at Nguyen.

"Sit down," Nash ordered Nguyen, who was now totally subservient. He sat down with his legs together, and Nash picked up the shredded underpants and laid them across his lap. "Here," he said to Thanh, handing her his pistol. "You can look at him now. Shoot him in the knee if he moves." Thanh took the pistol reluctantly and turned to face Nguyen, looking only at his face. "Hey," Nash said to Thanh, suddenly remembering something, "where's the sniper rifle?"

"The Dragunov?" Thanh replied. "It's under the floor over there."

"I'll get it. Quan, let's start loading up the jeep."

It was mid-afternoon when Nash parked the jeep in front of the PX. He lifted out the two packs containing the metal missile cases and slung one over each shoulder. No one was paying any attention to him, so he began walking to Division headquarters, which was several hundred yards away. It had been a busy day, and it wasn't over yet, but at least the hard part was done.

He and Quan had pulled up just outside the ARVN laager site around ten, and from the road they could see the men were all lounging around, doing minor maintenance on their tracks or just being lazy. Some of them looked out at the jeep stopped on the road, but when they saw Nash and Quan, they lost interest. Nguyen was curled up in the back, staying as low as possible. Nash pulled the man out and sent him walking toward the compound with a kick in the ass. Grinning with malicious pleasure, Nash jumped back in the jeep as Quan gunned the motor and sped away. Now he smiled again as he imagined how Nguyen would have been greeted as he stumbled naked to his men, his hands taped behind him, his mouth sealed, and rude messages painted on his body. The men would probably have been sympathetic and obsequious to his face, but would all have been laughing behind his back. He would never again have the respect of his soldiers, which would make him a failed leader and doom his career.

After driving to his cousin's house, Quan had turned the jeep over to Nash and went into a shed to get his Honda motorbike. He had taken the AK-47 and Makarov to hide in the shed. Nash drove on to the Cu Chi basecamp, and his worries about driving an ARVN jeep in through the gate proved to be unfounded. When he told the gate guards he was with MACV, despite his 25th Division shoulder patch, they had waved him through without question. Back at his barracks, he had dropped off his and Quan's packs and the radio, and hidden the Dragunov under his bedding. He left his XM-21 rifle and Quan's carbine at the arms room, and went to lunch at the mess hall. As he returned to the barracks, he narrowly avoided running into Captain Banning, his CO, who would have undoubtedly insisted on immediately hearing a full report of his actions, something he was not yet ready to do. He ducked out of Banning's sight and jumped in the jeep to take it to the PX.

He carried the two big packs to the small unmarked building that housed the G2 intelligence staff, the door of which was guarded by a soldier who was tilting a metal folding chair back against the wall, his rifle leaning against the wall beside him, while he studied a Playboy magazine. He looked up when Nash approached and put the magazine in his lap as he leaned forward to put all four legs of the chair on the ground. "You got a badge?" he asked Nash with a bored look. Nash had noticed the last time he was here that the G2 guys all had laminated security badges clipped to their pockets.

"No, but I need to see SFC Carotto."

The guard rolled his eyes and stood up, carefully laying the magazine down on the chair, and went up the two steps to the door. He knocked three times, and a few seconds later the door opened a crack. "Some guy wants to see Sergeant Carotto," he announced through the narrow gap, and someone inside replied, "Wait one."

The guard came down from the steps, picked up his magazine, and sat back down to find where he had left off. Nash doubted the man was only reading the articles. Nash set the two packs on the ground and wiggled to get the kinks out of his shoulders. About five minutes later the door opened and Carotto stepped out, carefully closing the door behind him. When he saw Nash his expression lightened and he came down the steps with his hand held out in greeting.

They shook hands, and Nash said, "Is there somewhere we can talk?"

Carotto looked back at the building for a second and said, "Not in there. Let's go to the barracks. What have you got there?" He looked down at the packs curiously.

"That's what I want to talk about," Nash said, bending down to pick them up.

"Want me to take one?" Carotto offered, holding out one hand as he unclipped his security badge and stuck it in his pocket.

"I got it," Nash assured him, waiting for the other man to lead the way.

Although the barracks building looked similar to other such buildings on the outside, inside Nash saw that it had been subdivided into small rooms by wooden partitions. Carotto led him down the narrow hallway and ushered him into the second room on the left. The room was about eight-by-eight, and had a metal bunk, a small field desk and chair, and a grey metal wall locker with rusty edges.

"Welcome to my humble abode," Carotto said with a rueful smile.

Nash set the packs down on the floor, and Carotto pulled the chair out from the desk and offered it to Nash, while he sat down on the neatly made bunk.

"How did your trip to Nui Ba Den go?" Carotto asked politely.

Nash took a breath and blew out air loudly. "It's complicated. I'll tell you some of it, but don't ask a lot of questions, okay?"

"Sounds mysterious," Carotto said.

"No, just complicated. We got the sniper, so that's the end of that. We also got these packs. You need to look inside. That one first." Nash leaned down and opened the long pack, sliding the metal case out and pushing it over to Carotto.

Carotto bent over and looked closer at some faded printing on the dark green case. "That's Russian," he observed.

"Can you read it?" Nash asked.

"No, I don't speak Russian, but I've seen enough stuff to recognize it." He fumbled with the latches on the side, and then lifted the lid. When he let the lid fall back on the floor, he stared at the foam-encased launchers. Meanwhile Nash pulled the other case out and opened it to display the batteries and gripstock.

"Holy shit!" Carotto breathed. "That's an SA-7. Where the fuck did you get this?"

"SA-7? I was told it's called the Arrow."

"Yeah, the Russians call it the Arrow, but its NATO designation is the SA-7. It's something brand new. I've seen drawings of it, but they're highly classified. So where did you get it?"

"That's where it gets complicated. If I tell you where I got it, then you would have to investigate, and somebody would get in trouble. Let's just say I found it on the ground. Like maybe it fell off a truck or something."

Carotto frowned at such a suggestion, but turned his attention to the two tubes in the long case. "Has that one been fired?"

Nash nodded. "But not the other one."

Carotto looked at him, his eyebrows raised, unable to frame his next question.

Nash stared back at him, keeping his expression neutral.

"Wait a minute, you were on Nui Ba Den, weren't you? I heard a Cobra was nearly shot down with an RPG, but I'll bet it wasn't an RPG, was it?"

Nash kept his face a mask.

"Jesus, man, you've got to tell me about it. This is the biggest fuckin' thing I've ever dealt with. I've got to have some sort of story. My bosses will go ape-shit."

"Okay," Nash relented, "but you can't tell anybody it was me. I don't want to be involved at all. I want to keep a low profile."

"Hell, man, you could get a medal for this, get a job with the CIA or something."

"I don't want any medals, and I certainly don't want a job with the CIA. You can get the medal and the job, if you want it. You helped me out before, and now I'm repaying the favor."

"But what will I tell the officers?" Carotto was almost pleading.

"Tell them an anonymous donor left 'em on your doorstep. Tell them some Chieu Hoi turned them in and then got blown up by a rocket attack. I don't care, just don't mention my name."

"The door guard saw you," Carotto said significantly.

"Yeah, but he was too busy thinking about tits and ass in that magazine to pay any attention. He's probably already forgotten me."

"He's short. He DEROSes in two days," Carotto admitted. "He'll be gone before anyone thinks to ask him." DEROS meant Date Estimated to Return from Overseas Service, the day a soldier was to end his tour and leave Viet Nam.

"See? No sweat. And you've got time to come up with a good story. Keep these here for a couple days before you turn them in. By then I'll be long gone, the guard will be gone, and you can make up anything you like. You'll be a big hero, too."

"I don't care about that shit," Carotto denied, but Nash could tell the idea intrigued him.

"Whatever," Nash said. "Just keep me out of it. I've got to go. I have to make up my own story for my bosses." He stood up and headed for the door.

"Sergeant Jaramillo," Carotto called to him. Nash turned around to find Carotto extending his hand. "I thank you, and your country thanks you."

"Bullshit," Nash snorted, but took his hand.

"It's not bullshit," Carotto insisted. "But I'll keep you out of it. I've already forgotten your name. Johnson, wasn't it?"

"Right," Nash said with a smile. "No offense, but I hope I never see you again."

"None taken. Don't mean nothin'. I hope you catch that big silver bird soon."

"Me, too, brother." Nash slipped out the door and heard Carotto lock it from inside. Nash left the G-2 barracks and headed back to his own hooch, far on the other side of the base camp. He idly wondered when someone would notice the abandoned jeep at the PX. Would they trace it back to Captain Nguyen? Would Nguyen accuse Nash of stealing it? He doubted Nguyen would be accusing anybody of anything now, and even if he did, no one would listen to him. He thought about the Dragunov for a second. He wondered if he could figure out a way to send it home. He smiled to himself. He hoped Thanh enjoyed being a nun.

Printed in Great Britain
by Amazon